THE PERFECT LOCATION

Kate lives in Melbourne, Australia with her husband, two children and can be found nursing a laptop, surrounded by magazines and talking on the phone, usually all at once. Kate is an avid follower of fashion, fame and all things pop culture and is an excellent dinner party guest who always brings gossip and champagne.

To find out more about Kate visit www.kateforster.com or find her on twitter @kateforster.

T0312515

KATE FORSTER

The Perfect Location

AVON

AVON

A division of HarperCollins*Publishers*
1 London Bridge Street, London SE1 9GF

www.harpercollins.co.uk

A Paperback Original 2012

A catalogue record for this book is
available from the British Library

ISBN-13: 978-1-84756-308-8

Set in Minion by Palimpsest Book Production Limited,
Falkirk, Stirlingshire

There is not a writer who is published who doesn't owe somebody something at some point in their career. Writing books is collaborative, even though a few writers' egos might argue otherwise.

Without the following people in my life, who knows where I would be and what I would be doing. I want to say thank you to them, it's not nearly enough but it's a start. Yes, I could drop them a bottle of wine and a thank you card but I would prefer to see their names in print for posterity and all that jazz. They put up with me; they deserve something more concrete than a Pinot Grigio and a scrawled note. Trust me, I can be hard work.

*Warning: gushing ahead. Look away if it offends.

To my mother Joan who never censored the books in our house and who has champagne taste and a song for everything.

To Emma and Fiona for being the first readers of everything I write. Thank you for telling me to keep writing. I am here now, because of you both. You are my ideal readers and ideal best girlfriends.

To my agent Tara Wynne at Curtis Brown for taking the call, seeing something in the first draft and taking me on, typos and all. Tara, you are a tigress, a patient teacher and always, extremely fabulous. I am blessed to have you in my corner.

To Domonique for her cheerleading across the pond and never-ending belief in me.

To Claire Bord and Sammia Rafique, thank you for your support, collaboration and sound advice. It has been a dream to work with you both and I am very thankful you took me on.

To Tansy for keeping me up to date with everything and telling me when something is really 'lame'.

To Spike for having such faith in everything I do and not complaining (much) when dinner doesn't always arrive on time.

And to David for understanding I didn't have a choice and wanting me to be happy more than anything else.

For Nicole whose 'deliberately vague'
directions steered me here.

PART ONE

Pre-Production

CHAPTER ONE

Rose Nightingale walked into LAX, hiding behind large Dior sunglasses and ignoring the photographers that lurked at the international terminal, waiting for celebrities to come and go. They took their chance to harangue them, usually when they were holding travel-weary children and pushing a trolley full of luggage. It didn't matter how fabulous you were, travel was travel and it was a bore.

As Rose approached the United Lounge, she was greeted by a flight attendant who ushered her inside a door to the sanctity of the private space.

'Hello, Ms Nightingale. May I have your passport, please?'

Rose handed it over with a smile.

'Can I offer you champagne and a light snack?'

'No, thanks,' said Rose as the attendant led her towards a private seating area.

Rose's phone rang and she answered it as she sat down in a corner of the lounge, ignoring the flickers of recognition from other travellers.

'Slapper,' said Rose, seeing Kelly's name appear on her phone.

'Tosser, you all ready for Italia?' Kelly's thick Northern accent came down the line and Rose smiled at the sound of her oldest friend's voice.

'All sorted, babe. You and Chris there already?'

'Yeah, we got here two days ago. Shit, it's gorgeous, Rosie.

You're gonna flip when you see your villa, I checked it out yesterday, although the housekeeper is like something out of central casting. "Super Nonna", I call her.'

Rose laughed. Kelly always had a way with words that summed up a person or a situation perfectly.

Rose and Kelly were from different parts of England, both geographically and economically but these differences were never remarked upon or noticed even by each other. The only acknowledgements they made to their upbringings were their nicknames referencing people's perceptions of them, Rose being an upper class girl and Kelly being from Yorkshire.

Rose was the daughter of a successful novelist and a television writer. Her intellectual father had been nominated for the Pulitzer twice and her mother created and wrote a popular crime series for television. Rose moved amongst the society crowd at her private day school and her brief relationship with a minor European royal gave her enough social currency to be named the most eligible girl in England by *Tatler* magazine. Appearing on the cover in a dress handmade by Lacroix himself from fresh rose petals, the headline read 'A Rose by any Other Name'. Rose could have then married well and faded away from fame with an occasional photo in the social pages of *Jennifer's Diary*.

But Rose was no wallflower or country wife and she decided on a more precarious road, successfully auditioning for acting school in London. She worked hard at the school to be more than just the beautiful girl, but never overcame the stigma of being close to perfect.

It was the other women on her course who were the worst in their treatment of Rose. Deliberately excluding her from parties and events and even at one point calling a group meeting with her where they each told her what they disliked about her in a round circle as a way of 'helping her fit in more'. Rose despaired, her self-esteem was gone, her confidence shot, and she hated herself and the way she looked.

It was Kelly who saved Rose from losing her mind. Students from The London School of Make-up Artistry were to create the make-up for the third year students' production of William Congreve's *Love for Love*. Rose had the lead role and Kelly, the best student in the course, was given Rose as her subject.

The heavy Restoration make-up required for the play meant Rose was in the chair earlier than the other actors. Even though Kelly liked to call herself psychic, it didn't take much to realize that Rose was ostracized from the rest of the cast. Kelly thought Rose seemed pleasant enough, if not a little quiet.

As the play's short run went on, Kelly realized that Rose was on the outside of the circle, deliberately punished for her beauty and her background. A shared joint at the cast party between Rose and Kelly bonded them. Kelly made an effort to include Rose in her group of interesting and creative friends from the make-up school and Rose was grateful for the company. Kelly's friends were without the affectations of her school friends and without the competitiveness of her acting school peers. They celebrated Rose's beauty and encouraged her to try new looks and styles with her face and even her clothes.

Kelly's belief in new age philosophies was at odds at her country upbringing and it was something that Rose was interested in. She wasn't sure she believed in it, but was always surprised at Kelly's ability to intuit what another person was feeling.

'You are a rose in a field of onion grass,' Kelly said to her best friend after she graduated. 'You need to go to America where they will appreciate you more.'

Rose ended up taking the US by storm and when it was Rose's turn to help Kelly after she had made her mark in Hollywood she did it without a moment's doubt. Rose got Kelly a job as an extra's make-up artist on her next film, and soon Kelly was on her way to becoming the most sought after make-up artist in Hollywood.

Bringing her thoughts back to the present, Rose tuned in to Kelly's voice on the other end of the phone.

'Hey, are Wendy and Bruce coming over to stay?' asked Kelly.

'I don't know. They're being weird about it. I think Mum thinks it all a bit much, you know, Italy and flights for her and Dad. I asked Martin and Fiona and the kids too. I just think it would be nice to spend some time together. It's not like I'm heading back to London anytime soon.'

'I'm going back for Christmas,' said Kelly.

'Really?' said Rose, not noticing the surprised faces looking at her.

'I want to show him Skipton.'

'Well, that should take half a day, what else will you do while you're back in your old stomping ground?' Rose teased.

'Piss off, big city girl,' laughed Kelly. 'We're going to visit my family and then head to London for a few days, you should come back with us,' Kelly asked impulsively, although she already knew the answer.

Rose smiled thinking of her and Kelly in London. Drinking, dancing, more drinking. God, they had had so much fun until Rose moved to Hollywood.

'I don't think so, the English paps are relentless.' Rose claimed it was too much hassle on her family to come back to London with the constant media intrusion. The truth was that Rose had only been back a handful of times in fifteen years and only then for fleeting visits, staying in a suite at The Dorchester.

Shooting *The Italian Dream* would give her the perfect opportunity to bring the Nightingales together in Italy on her own terms. When her agent was negotiating the deal, she had a number of villas to choose from. Rose chose the one with the most bedrooms on offer for her family and their brood.

Lauren, her trusted assistant, had organized a myriad of inflatable toys to be FedExed over, so Rose's nieces and nephews could play in the infinity pool looking over the endless hills of Umbria. She had also sent board games, dolls and books and had a Wii installed in the den, with a large flat screen TV and a huge selection of DVDs.

'No, I can't come back to London, I'm booked up till the middle of next year, so that's why I wanted them to come to see me,' said Rose. 'Hey, I'm really looking forward to working with TG,' she said, in an effort to change the subject quickly.

'TG's really excited to work with you too, he told Chris,' said Kelly.

'He's a great guy, I'm surprised we've never worked together till now,' said Rose.

'TG', as everyone in the industry called him, was Tim Galvin, the hottest young gun director in Hollywood. A teenage skateboarding world champion who became an NYC film graduate, he made his mark directing videos for some of the LA garage band scene. He shot his films quickly, used quick edits and loud soundtracks, he possessed a rare gift: he could create a happy film set. His best friend and Director of Photography was Chris Berman, Kelly's husband.

'He's a good egg,' said Kelly, 'although he's been around a lot since he and Lisa broke up. He's a bit mopey, I need to find him a root.'

'She was a piece of work,' said Rose, mentioning TG's ambitious actress girlfriend. 'He's better off without her. I only

7

met her at your place but she was scary, like a reptile. He seemed sad at the audition, more low-key than usual although maybe he was nervous.'

'Probably. I think he was amazed you agreed to audition but he said the studio wanted to see all the women.'

'Oh God, I don't mind auditioning,' laughed Rose. 'Puts me back in my box, reminds me that the fame is fleeting.'

''Tis true, 'tis true,' said Kelly. 'So, call me when you arrive, yeah? I miss you like crazy, Tosser.'

'Love you too, Slapper. Call me every five minutes,' said Rose, giggling at the use of their old names for each other.

Rose settled down in the chair and opened her script. She already knew her lines but she always liked to do as much work as possible. As she read the scenes between her and her on-screen lover, she wondered who it would be. Her agent Randy said that the role wasn't cast yet but she was so keen to be a part of the film, she signed on without knowing who would take the role opposite her. For a brief moment she panicked it might be Paul but then she dismissed it with a silent laugh. There was no way the universe or TG would be cruel enough to cast her ex-husband, she thought.

Rose stared out the window, watching the planes take off and land. The LA smog was settling in over the city and she hoped it would not affect the flight. She despised lateness and lived by a rigid schedule. Organization gave her a sense of control.

A text message came through on her iPhone from her equally organized assistant, Lauren: *Car service will pick you up on arrival and drive you to the villa. If you get stuck then call Guilia, TG's assistant. I have keyed number into your phone.*

Rose already had this information printed out neatly on her letterhead, tucked away safely in her iris calf leather Smythson travel wallet. But she appreciated Lauren's attention to detail and concern.

Rose poached Lauren from the director, Jerry Hyman, who Rose was shooting a film with after her divorce from Paul. Daily she had watched him berate Lauren and abuse her in front of the crew. His constant comments about her weight, sexual innuendos and the ridiculous demands that she had to fulfil became painful for everyone to watch. Rose saw Lauren losing her self-esteem, wanting to please the obese tyrant and failing at every turn. Towards the end of shooting, she took her lunch tray over to sit with Lauren who was typing on the computer, with five mobile phones in front of her. Each one was labelled neatly in Dymo labels: *Home, Studio, LA, NY, Other.*

Rose put her tray aside and sat down. Lauren looked up, surprise registered on her face. 'Um. Hi,' she said.

'Hi, yourself,' replied Rose sunnily. 'How are things?'

Lauren looked at the screen, 'Fine, fine, Jerry's very busy. I've always got something to do.'

Rose looked at the phones. 'So, let me guess,' she said as she picked up the phones and laid them out in front of her. '*Home* is the wife and kids. *LA* is his agent and the studio. *NY* is his dealer. And *Other* is his whores. How did I do?'

Lauren looked shocked, and then pulled herself together. 'No, no, entirely wrong.' Rose smiled and bit into her apple.

Lauren went back to typing, feeling unnerved by Rose's correct guesses about Jerry's many phones. The stars never talked to her. Granted, Rose seemed nicer than most. Just that morning she had raised her eyebrows comically at Lauren when the director went on one of his tirades at Lauren because his latte was too hot.

Looking at Lauren's eyes twitch and her mouth tighten, Rose

wondered what the notorious director had done to her. She knew his reputation; he liked to dominate women in every way. Rose herself was too much of a class act and too outspoken for his tastes. He liked them young, thankful and ambitious.

Rose pondered a little longer then said casually, 'Anyway, I have a job opening. I really need an assistant. They need to be super organized. I like lists and Apple Macs.' She stared disdainfully at the PC Lauren was working on. 'I only have one mobile phone, so that may be a put-off to any potential applicants. I can offer them their own office, a BMW and I promise to never hit them with a phone. I will not make them do ridiculous jobs; I'm capable of buying my own tampons. I need help with schedules, Christmas and birthday lists, help with some of the charities that I work with. And someone to field the media and my agent.' She smiled at Lauren and walked away. Always leave them wanting more, she thought, as she felt Lauren's eyes on her.

That evening, after speaking to Lauren on set, Rose found Lauren's professional CV and cover letter expressing her interest in the job on hotel stationery, slipped under her hotel room door. Rose smiled when she opened the envelope; she knew Lauren was perfect for her.

The boarding call sounded over the loudspeaker and Rose's mind was brought back to the present. Rose walked to the desk, and handed her passport and boarding pass to the flight attendant. The girl took them with a smile and then passed them back to her. 'Thank you, Ms Nightingale, your flight to Italy is boarding now.'

Rose placed her passport in her bag and headed towards the plane. Italy, here I come, she thought, excited by the idea of living in a new country, even for a short amount of time.

* * *

Rose arrived in Perugia reasonably relaxed, although feeling a little grimy. As predicted by the wonderful Lauren, her car was indeed waiting for her. Surprisingly, there were no paparazzi lurking around and Rose was relieved. I hope this continues, she thought, as she sank into the back seat of the Mercedes.

When she arrived at the villa and got out of the car, the housekeeper stood on the front step, waiting to greet the surrogate grandchildren she assumed were coming from all the toys that had been sent over.

Instead it was just Rose who shook her hand and walked inside the cool foyer. Lucia walked over to the car to check there were no children inside. She shook her head. 'Bizarro,' she mumbled as she followed Rose inside.

Rose was tired but not enough to dull the beauty of her new home for the summer. A restored 200-year-old villa, it was surrounded by green lawns and a grove of olive trees to one side. There was a magnificent outdoor terrace, covered in grapevines and wisteria, giving much-needed shade throughout the day. The pool looked out over the hills and the garden was filled with roses, lemon trees and lavenders.

Inside were six bedrooms, each with its own bathroom. Lauren had sent Rose's luggage by FedEx with all the toys, so Rose didn't have to wait at the airport. Lucia had hung all her clothes in the solid oak wardrobes, marvelling at the tissue paper and the scented sachets from Maryse à Paris. Her Smythson beauty case had been unpacked and all her toiletries had been placed carefully in the bathroom cupboards. The Egyptian cotton sheets with a 250 thread count had been washed and dried in the Umbrian sun by Lucia and placed on the bed.

'Signorina, you want something to eat?' asked Lucia hopefully. She was looking forward to feeding up this skinny girl with her imaginary children.

Rose smiled. 'No, maybe just a cup of tea and a biscuit. I might have a bath and lie down for a while.'

Lucia wandered off, mumbling in Italian to herself. Rose thought she heard her saying something about ghost children and she reminded herself to listen more to the Italian lessons on her iPod. Ghost children, she thought. My Italian is worse than I thought.

Rose walked into the bathroom. It was astonishing, even by Rose's Hollywood standards. The floors were covered with beautiful stone tiles in natural colours and the surrounding walls whitewashed. At the end of the room were three steps that led down into a large sunken tub. Above the tub was a leadlight window that opened wide, letting the warm summer breeze float into the room.

At the foot of the tub was a gorgeous gift basket filled with a selection of products from Santa Maria Novella, a 13th century apothecary, once run by Dominican monks with a note from the film's producers welcoming her and thanking her for taking the role in the film. The handmade basket was overflowing with vanilla bath and shower gels, pomegranate bath salts, lily and rose water, summer candles smelling of the sea and a selection of fragrances including honeysuckle, opoponax, orange blossom, tuberose, and the stunning Angels of Florence perfume – a blend of jasmine, lilac, peach, violet and white musk.

Lying next to the basket of scented items was a tower of towels, all with the Frette crest embroidered on them, an exquisitely folded ivory bathrobe, several quilted spa mitts and a pile of beautifully folded bath sheets in dusk and sandstone.

Tiredness washed over Rose and she sat on the antique armchair in the corner of the room. Lucia knocked at the open door and saw how weary Rose seemed. Clucking in Italian and bustling into the bathroom, she walked over and turned on the water in the bath. Rummaging through the basket of bath and body goodies, Lucia pulled out citrus bath oil and poured a few drops under the running water. She undid the robe and shook out the bath sheets.

'Come, signorina. Time to bathe, very nice for you, quiet. I bring you your tea, yes?'

Rose nodded her acceptance and was actually grateful for someone taking over while she was in her jet-lagged state.

Lucia felt the temperature of the water. 'All ready now, signorina.' She left the bathroom and brought back a tray with a silver teapot with strainer, a bone china cup and saucer, a small matching pitcher of milk and tiny bowl of little sugar cubes, a silver spoon and a selection of Italian biscuits and left Rose alone.

Rose slowly undressed and stepped down into the tub. If this was Italy, then I never want to leave, she thought.

Downstairs in the kitchen, Lucia moaned to her husband, the gardener, about Rose. No children, too skinny, too old, should be married . . . the list went on of Lucia's complaints about Rose. It wouldn't do, said Lucia to herself, deciding then and there she would have to draw Rose's future to her. All the women in the family had the gift and Lucia knew she had no choice but to magic a man and some children into Rose's life. *Pronto!*

CHAPTER TWO

Calypso Gable woke up, fully dressed, in the biggest suite of the Hotel Brufani Palace in Perugia and checked her phone for the time. Nine o'clock in the evening. Damn, she had slept all day, she thought, exhausted from jet-lag.

She wanted to be amongst the action, not stuck in a villa in the country, playing house. Basing herself in the city of Perugia meant she could stroll the streets and explore with almost no one recognizing her. Her TV show had not been shown in Italy and her latest film had yet to be released in Europe. Besides tourists, no one knew who she was and she was looking forward to exploring the city and some of the gorgeous antique shops she had spied on the drive through the city to her hotel.

She was shocked that she had won the role. Rumour was that Jessica Biel, Carey Mulligan, and Scarlett Johansson were up for the role. Calypso only went because her manager told her she needed to be seen by a better class of directors.

Calypso hadn't worked with the director, TG, as he was known, but she did know his ex-girlfriend, Lisa. She had always been on the make, trying to get up the next step of the career ladder, fucking and sucking her way to the top. She had made quite a few films, starring in supporting roles and then starting to get more leading roles. Labelled as the next Indie Queen, she and TG were the star couple of LA and New York.

But Calypso knew it was all bullshit. She had seen girls like her before over the years. Underneath the façade of the intellectual, art house style she displayed was just another actress desperate for the Spielberg epic and the paycheque.

Now the ex was dating a studio head, Calypso had heard. An obese, sweaty man who was notorious for his penchant for sexually deviant activities. His favourite was having his partner bite him during sex, all over, till he was black and blue; he loved it even more when they drew blood, apparently. Calypso shuddered at the thought.

The audition for *The Italian Dream* had been torturous. Calypso was nervous and said 'fuck' throughout the meeting and drank from the Coke can on the table until she realized it wasn't hers but the director's. He hadn't seemed to mind and seemed to be okay as far as directors went. At least he didn't try to hit on her but he looked at her oddly throughout the audition and she wondered of she had something in her teeth.

She knew she gave a shocking read and although she could do the part, she fucked it up and would have put money on Scarlett getting the role. But apparently the director saw something in her that she didn't see in herself, her manager said when she rang with the news.

To celebrate, she had spent a morning at the Miu Miu store in LA, hoping to channel the Italian style she admired so much while trawling *The Sartorialist*. Now she looked at the piles of luggage piled in the corner of the suite and wondered if it was too much. The store on Rodeo Drive had closed for her for two hours while she tried on everything. Calypso now had in her possession bags and boxes of the latest season and even some of the upcoming season that had not yet been copied by Zara. Miu Miu's classic, super cool look wasn't exactly Calypso's style – she preferred something a little more eclectic – but what the hell, she could always accessorize to make it a little more Calypso and a little less Miuccia.

Calypso had left the Miu Miu store in a carbon wool-fringed short jacket over her white American Vintage t-shirt. The jacket dressed up her black J Brand cigarette-style jeans and brought an almost European style to her California look. She had swept back her perfectly lightened blond hair – 'Buttercup', her colourist called it. Calypso's hair was one of her signatures and she returned to the salon every two weeks to have her roots done. A natural redhead, with tight corkscrew curls, she now wore her hair long and straight, courtesy of the Brazilian blow waves she got every six weeks. With a tiny frame and lean muscles courtesy of a combination of yoga, Pilates and a fat-free vegetarian existence, Calypso had a pretty voice and an even prettier face.

As she lay in the hotel bed thinking of the shopping spree, she remembered the paparazzi hounding her in LA outside Miu Miu. Some actors sought that attention, even tipping them off themselves with their whereabouts. But not Calypso. The media's intrusion was a recent problem for her. Now that she was a part of the film circus, she understood that often the film studios started the rumours and hired the photographers to drive the heat and interest for whatever vehicle they were pushing. Calypso wondered who had made the call to them. Her studio, her stylist, or was it one of the store employees? The more she thought about it, Calypso began to suspect who had tipped off the media, and it made sense the longer she considered it.

She remembered the last conversation with Leeza before she left for Italy.

'Hi, Mom.' Calypso had answered her cell phone impatiently; they'd only spoken an hour ago.

'Hi, baby!' Leeza breathed. Always so eager. 'How was shopping?'

'It was great, Mom. But . . . err . . . Mom . . ' Calypso licked her lips nervously. Why was she always nervous when questioning her mother?

'Mom, did you tip off the paps?' Calypso was smart enough to know she wasn't a big enough celebrity yet for her studio to have called in such an overwhelming number of photographers.

'I just made one call. Were there many there?' Leeza had sounded happy – she thought all publicity was good publicity, especially when you were an unknown.

'Mom, it's not good. It's weird. It makes me look desperate and sad. Leave that shit for Miley and Lindsay. Greg will kill me when he finds out. He's being really careful about my exposure right now. You know this already! Jesus!'

'Have you heard from Greg or Mandy?' asked Leeza, ignoring Calypso's frustration.

Calypso's hiring of a new manager, Mandy, had replaced her mother who had held the title since Calypso was six years old and in her first commercial. The decision resulted in a huge fight with Leeza who locked herself in the bathroom for six hours at Calypso's house. She only emerged after Calypso slid a back copy of *Variety*, with an article on Mandy in it, under the door and was finally satisfied that Mandy might be able to do the job.

Now Calypso felt free as she lay in bed. Free from Leeza, the paparazzi and from LA. Stretching, she stepped out of bed, peeled off her Burberry silk shorts and Calvin Klein singlet and walked into the bathroom. Turning on the shower she examined herself in the mirror. Her hair looked amazing, straight and yet with body, thanks to the blow-dry she had just before she left LA. She was due to have another in six weeks but since she was on set for twelve weeks, she wondered if they had them in Italy. She reminded herself to ask Kelly, the head make-up artist on the film, although it may cost a lot here compared to US prices.

Calypso lived on a budget, despite her moderate wealth. It was too easy to overspend and she was mindful of her money, having worked so hard for so long. Besides, Leeza was always in her mind, reminding her never to stray from her budget. It wasn't as though Calypso was tight with money, however, she was just very aware of what it was like not to have any. No one but her and Leeza and her father knew how tough things had been for them when she was trying to make it in Hollywood. All the money her father had earned had gone into nurturing Calypso's talent. Although her father had a job, it was meagre pay and trying to make it in Hollywood was expensive. Dancing lessons, headshots, acting lessons, clothes, and flights for auditions to New York for the attempts to make it on Broadway. Her agents and lawyers both demanded a cut when she did work and it was a struggle at times. Calypso knew her parents had gone without for her. She remembered the nights without electricity; the beans on toast for dinner, or sometimes just the beans. Once she found her father in the yard, nailing the soles of his work shoes back together.

The sense of responsibility Calypso felt to ensure she was successful and to look after her parents was what drove her – and what stopped her from losing her head. Calypso had been offered drugs, sex and all the other temptations during her years growing up but she abstained, thinking of the faith her parents had placed in their only child's talent. Whenever she was interviewed, Calypso painted the picture that she was the typical California girl, growing up in middle-class affluence and wanting for nothing. She claimed she grew up in the house she had actually bought for her parents in Brentwood, whereas in fact she and Leeza and her dad went from place to place until the money ran out. Leeza would check them into rough hotels and trailer parks when the money was really low. Sometimes they skipped paying the bill if they could, just to save a few dollars here and there.

It all changed for a while when Calypso was cast on a variety show, singing and dancing her little heart out until she grew breasts and the show was cancelled. Calypso received the news she had been let go the day before the producer found out the show had been cancelled. She never told anyone, only she and Leeza knew. That day, Leeza sent out a press release saying that Calypso was leaving to explore other opportunities. It was a smart move. She was always seen as the kid who left early and avoided being a part of an axed show. Leeza was considered an excellent manager for knowing when it was time for Calypso to move on.

The next opportunity did not come though until Calypso was nineteen. She did a few bit parts and commercials and this helped the bank balance. She urged her parents to use the money she earned from the show but her father wouldn't hear of it, so they were back to where they were before. Scrounging and living hand to mouth, job to job.

Now she was in Italy, shooting a film with Rose Nightingale and Sapphira De Mont. She could hardly believe it. Rose Nightingale was her hero and Sapphira De Mont was the hottest star in Hollywood. Why the director, TG, had asked for her, she had no idea. She wasn't a huge name yet, and certainly not in film, she had thought when Mandy had rung to her gauge her interest in auditioning for TG.

Against Leeza's advice, she had knocked back the action film that was on offer and had jumped at the chance to act opposite Rose and Sapphira. This was her chance to move into the big league. No more TV, only film and opposite the best actresses in Hollywood. Convincing Leeza was a different story though.

'But, honey, if you take the action movie, think about it. A percentage of the profits, royalties, Comic-Con appearances and your own action figure. You'll be a movie star, honey, big time.'

'Mom, a movie star is different to an actor. Cameron Diaz is a movie star. Meryl Streep is an actor. You can't be both. Well, maybe if you're Reese Witherspoon, but there aren't many others. I want to be an actor.'

'Being a movie star is what we always wanted,' Leeza said, forgetting she had recently been demoted in Calypso's life from manager to mother, as she carefully prepared the salad with no-fat dressing for a family barbeque, protecting her acrylic nails with a new French manicure.

No, Mom, it's what you wanted, thought Calypso.

But she said nothing. Instead she signed on the next day, letting Leeza know her decision via text message. It was time she ran her own life, she thought and now that she was in Italy, she was excited.

Showered and dressed in a towel, she read the room service menu. 'Blah,' she said, putting it down again.

Wandering over to the window, she looked outside. She had meant to go for a run when she got back to the hotel but the tiredness from the jet-lag was still in her system and instead she fell asleep, fully dressed, until sounds from outside drifted up to her window. It was nine o'clock at night, but it seemed most people were only now going out for dinner. What the hell, she thought, I'm going out.

Opening her wardrobe, she chose a pair of black vintage cigarette silk pants and teamed them with a floaty silver Catherine Malandrino camisole and pink Costume Nationale flat sandals. The hills of Perugia would murder her heels; flats were sensible and Calypso was always sensible, particularly when it came to looking after her clothes. Leaving her hair down, she grabbed a vintage beaded clutch and skipped through the door into the bustle outside.

Wandering around the ancient city, the sound of smooth jazz came up a laneway and Calypso followed the music.

She found herself in an elegant thoroughfare filled with laughing students from the university, families with sleeping children in strollers and tourists all mingling together in the warm evening.

The cafés were filled with people who spilled out onto the stone ledges and steps, listening to the jazz. Calypso thought she knew the song from an old album her dad used to play. 'There's a somebody I'm longing to see, I hope that he turns out to be, someone who'll watch over me,' she sang quietly to herself.

An older couple walked out in front of the band and started to dance to the old Gershwin classic and Calypso felt her eyes fill with tears as she saw the tenderness on the man's face.

It was an almost perfect moment except for the gnawing in Calypso's stomach. I haven't eaten in fourteen hours, she counted as she moved towards some bright lights in the side of a stone wall. *Sandri Pasticceria* it read. The window boasted some of the most delicious pastries Calypso had ever seen.

21

Never would she allow herself something so fat-filled in LA but here, without the gaze of the paparazzi and her trainer, Calypso decided to live a little. Stepping inside the crowded shop, she was pushed forward by the crowd until she found herself at a stool at the marble bar.

A red-coated waiter placed a chocolate-filled pastry with glazed berries on top of it in front of her with a cappuccino. 'I didn't order this,' she said to the waiter who had already turned his back. She sat awkwardly, unsure of what to do.

'I would just eat it,' said a voice next to her over the din in the bar.

Calypso turned and was faced with Eros himself. Impossibly handsome, with long, light brown hair loose and curling around his face. Smiling at Calypso, his teeth were the whitest and straightest that Calypso had ever seen, which was quite something, considering she lived in California, the state of orthodontists. '*Ciao, bella*,' he said, his green eyes dancing as he took in her face.

'Hello, gorgeous,' said Calypso, doing her best Barbra Streisand impersonation.

'I know that voice, that's Barbra, *si*?'

Calypso laughed, 'Yes, that's Barbra.'

'*Mangia*,' he said, gesturing.

Calypso paused. It did look divine and saying a little prayer to the God of Cellulite to stay away, she took a bite.

'Oh my God, it's amazing.' She sputtered pastry flakes across the table, not caring to wipe the chocolate cream from her mouth.

The Italian watched her, amused. 'You like?'

'I like,' said Calypso, her mouth full.

'So, what is your name? Barbra?'

'No,' she laughed. 'Calypso,' she smiled shyly.

22

'Beautiful name, the nymph of the sea, *si*? I am Marco. Lord of the planet Mars.'

His bewitching accent and the way he looked so intently at her, as if wanting her approval was endearing. Calypso smiled. She had made her first Italian friend.

CHAPTER THREE

Sapphira De Mont arrived in Italy courtesy of the film studio's Gulfstream. She would have liked to have flown the plane herself but her instructor said she was not yet ready for such a large aircraft, much to Sapphira's disappointment.

She stretched her back like a cat as she unbuckled her seatbelt on the plane. Her skin across her shoulder blades was tight from the new tattoo she had recently added to her thin body as a nod to her newly gained pilot's licence. *Alis volat propri*, it read in a serif script across her back. A Latin phrase, meaning 'She flies with her own wings'.

All her life experiences were illustrated by the tattoos on her body. On her left wrist was a tiny crab – her sun sign; on her right wrist a symbol for Leo, her astrological Moon sign. On one foot was a delicate vine that wound its way around her ankle and on the outside of each ankle was a tiny fairy curtsying. On her back, underneath the new tattoos, was a tattoo of a tree, the one she dreamed of most nights. She had explained it and the tattoo artist had drawn it repeatedly until he got it right.

Sapphira's life had been one of adventure and saying 'yes' to whatever came her way. Italy was like a new affair to her; she wanted to get to know the country, learn the language and understand its moods. Spending six weeks in a foreign country was exhilarating and made Sapphira feel safe.

The private plane had been an indulgence that the studio

was only too happy to agree to when Sapphira's agent requested it to get her to the film's location. She was a big star and had taken a slight pay cut to do the movie – compared to what she had been paid after the last two action hits she had starred in. There was big money to be made with Sapphira's name on the marquee and they knew it. The studio was only too happy to keep their bankroll comfortable. A little gift from them for her having to audition, she thought.

It was her first screen test for four years. Her agent told her she should hold out and they would come round and just give her the part. She ignored him. She ignored most advice. Instead, she arrived smoking a cigarette, and in a coffee coloured silk blouse so transparent it showed the outline of her tattoos and no bra. TG was ready to dismiss her until she did the lines of dialogue more perfectly than the writer could have wished for. She was a chameleon when she acted and he was excited to work with her. He was also smart enough to realize she would bring a new audience to this genre of film.

It was not as though the idea of flying a commercial flight was beneath Sapphira, but she had more reason than most to need the private flight.

Sapphira held her Bottega Veneta black leather tote bag close to her chest feeling the little beads of sweat form on her forehead. The door of the aircraft opened and Sapphira heard the pilot talking to the officials in Italian as he stood at the top of the steps.

'They need to just check your details and do a quick look around,' he said as two Italian airport officials came aboard the plane. Sapphira sat up straight and smiled her million dollar smile. The men were instantly smitten. Handing over her travel documents, Sapphira attempted to greet them in the basic Italian she had learned.

'*Ciao. Grazie per lasciarlo venire al vostro paese bella,*' she said, a little uncertainly.

The Italians looked at each other, pleased that such a big American movie star would bother to try speaking their wonderful language. They gave a cursory glance at her documents. Sapphira smiled again, this time they melted. 'Welcome, Signora De Mont.'

'My mother is Italian. I'm so pleased to be here in her country that she speaks so warmly about,' Sapphira said.

She left out the fact that her mother was now in the best nursing home in LA, all bills paid for by Sapphira. The years of alcohol abuse had caught up with her and most days she didn't even remember she had a daughter.

'That is why you are so beautiful,' said the older man. 'Your father must be Italian also?'

'No,' said Sapphira, almost apologetically. 'He's French.'

And dead, she left out. A minor French aristocrat, dying from a heroin overdose when she was twelve years old and she'd been left with her mother to raise herself.

One of the men held out a small notepad and asked shyly for an autograph. Sapphira signed quickly and posed for a photo with each of them taken on their cell phones. Deciding that such a beautiful star with an Italian mother was absolutely no security risk, they waved her through Customs and soon Sapphira was in the back of her car, and heading towards her new home. Relief flowed through her as the car pulled away from the airport and towards the villa booked for her stay.

The villa, a former 12th century monastery, was not the biggest in the region but it had the most security. Surrounded by large, stone walls with locked gates, security cameras were set to capture every angle of the property and it came with a set of security guards to protect its guests.

Sapphira lit a cigarette and wound down the window. Her driver looked at her in the rear mirror. She seemed tired and unwell, he thought, as he drove through the picturesque countryside. Italy will fix anyone, he thought proudly.

The car pulled up outside a large set of iron gates. There was a scrolled crest on the gates and ivy grew on the walls on either side. With its palm trees and green lawns, the property looked like an oasis, Sapphira thought.

As the gates swung open, the car drove slowly along the gravel drive and soon the villa appeared. A tower rose from the centre of the building, with a cross on the top. Remembering it was once a monastery, Sapphira prayed it was a sign of protection while she was in Italy.

When the car pulled to a stop, a stylish young woman came out of the arched oak doorway. The woman smiled warmly. 'Welcome, Ms De Mont, to Villa Castello Saint Carolina. I hope you enjoy your stay here.'

'Please call me Sapphira,' she said and indicated to the driver to take her cases and bags inside.

'I am Giulia, TG's assistant while he is in Italy. He requested I come and ensure you have everything you need.'

'Thank you, Giulia. I appreciate it,' Sapphira said, wishing she were upstairs in the privacy of a bedroom.

Giulia walked inside and stood in the magnificent foyer. High above them was a ceiling mural of Madonna and the baby Jesus, surrounded by cherubs in the Garden of Eden. It was breathtaking. Sapphira stood with her neck craned back trying to drink in the picture.

Giulia spoke again. 'I have your set of keys and your map of the property as requested. The kitchen has been stocked to your requirements and all your other requests have been fulfilled.'

Sapphira nodded her approval.

'The security are on site at all times and will do their best to not disturb your privacy, but please contact them or myself if you should require anything extra during your stay here. If you give me your phone I will punch my number into it so you can contact me day or night.'

Sapphira dug into her handbag, searching for her phone. Her hand ran over her secret and she felt like she might vomit. Finding her phone, she handed it to Giulia who expertly keyed in her number and name.

'*Bene*,' she said. '*Finito*.' She handed it back.

Sapphira stood waiting. There was an awkward silence. 'Well then, I go,' said Giulia.

'Thank you, Giulia,' Sapphira said, relieved.

'One more thing, you want me to take your bags to your room?' asked Giulia.

'No,' said Sapphira a little shortly. 'I'm fine.'

Giulia looked at her almost skeletal arms and wondered how on earth she would manage the array of cases the driver had left in the foyer up the flight of stairs.

'The staff will come by every morning to make up your room and restock your kitchen once you are on set, as requested. They have all signed the confidentiality papers and these have been faxed to your agent.'

Sapphira nodded and Giulia walked out the door. 'Thanks again,' Sapphira called as Giulia climbed into her red Alfa. Sapphira closed the door behind her.

Giulia sat in the car for a moment, looking for her car keys. Sapphira's appearance troubled her. Her demands, while not extraordinary compared to some stars, still seemed covert and secretive when she had received them from Sapphira's agent. She required no one to look after her in the villa, didn't want a tour of the vast property, only a map to be left for her in Italian. She asked for two cartons of Marlboro Light cigarettes and an espresso maker with the best local coffee blend. Seeing her in person, she seemed edgy and anxious, and clearly could not wait for Giulia to leave. Giulia knew it was more than tiredness; she had seen it in her brother years before when he had come home from living in Rome. She picked up her mobile phone. 'Hello, TG? It's Giulia.'

'Hey, how's our star Sapphira?' he asked as he jumped out of the shower.

'Okay, all settled. She seems fine.' She paused. 'She's a little, how you say, *preoccupato*. Worried. Anxious, you know?'

TG laughed. 'That's Hollywood stars for you, Giulia. They're all a little crazy, although she is supposed to be great on set, so don't worry about it, she's fine. Kelly said so and she's worked with her plenty of times.'

'Okay then, I will not worry. You all okay for tonight?' she asked as she turned on the car engine.

'Fine, it all looks great, Giulia. Thank you, you are a star! *Arrivederci*.'

'*Arrivederci*,' Giulia replied and drove off down the driveway, the huge gates closing behind her.

Sapphira watched Giulia on the phone in her driveway from the upstairs window. 'Go,' she said as she willed her away from her house.

Finally the red car disappeared and the gates closed in the distance. Walking over to the bed, she emptied her bag out onto the crisp white bedspread.

Opening a small Comme des Garçons bag, she took out her instruments and prepared her hit.

Thankfully her tattoos were placed all over her body and so she was always accustomed to covering them up. If she knew she would be showing a lot of flesh then she shot up between her toes. Citing privacy, she always dressed herself and never allowed herself to be partially dressed in front of the costume or make-up crew. Living with her addiction for the last ten years had taught Sapphira a thing or two about secrets and how to hide them. A few of her lovers had been addicts as well, sharing her bed and her smack till she got sick of them. She had tried to get off it, taking OxyContin, which her LA doctor had only been too happy to supply. But there was nothing like pure snow, she thought.

Sapphira was a big enough star not have to go through the medical tests for insurance. Her record on set was flawless, she was a hard worker and big money earner; as far as the studio could see, there was no problem.

Coming to Italy was not a problem on the private jet, once she had been waived through Customs. She had enough to get her through the next eight weeks and then she would have to sort out her next supply. No problem, she thought. Rome is filled with drugs, I'll send someone off to score. Who that might be, she was not sure, but there was always someone to help Sapphira De Mont, she figured.

She took an alcohol swab out of the bag. Getting her spoon, she wiped it down with the swab and placed the chunk on it. Filling the syringe with water, she squirted it onto the spoon and lit the tea light candle she carried in her kit. Melting down the smack, she rubbed her fingers with another swab and then placed a small piece of cloth on the spoon. Rubbing between her toes with the alcohol swab, she drew the shot up into the syringe and looked for a vein. Finding one between her little toe and the one next to it, she put the needle in, withdrawing it slightly to ensure she had it in the vein. Seeing a small prick of blood come out, she injected herself.

The OxyContin worked when she was doing the action movies, as she had to be fit and trained everyday. But the hit from heroin lasted longer and so she was back on it whenever she could get away with it. When she took it she felt like nothing would ever go wrong in her world again. She stopped injecting once, a long time ago but then started again after her hopes and dreams had been shattered. That was too much for anyone to handle, she had justified at the time.

As soon as the needle touched her skin she lay on the bed and felt the relaxation drape over her like a blanket. She breathed in and out, listening to the sound of herself in the silence, thinking about the first time she took heroin.

What was the guy's name? she wondered. They had met at a party for someone whose name they didn't even know, and the attraction between them was instant. The knowledge that Sapphira had with her a bag of coke, twelve joints pre-rolled in her father's Cartier diamond Art Deco cigarette case was also appealing. They blew her bag of coke together in the bathroom, smoked three joints in the spa and then fucked at her apartment.

She tried heroin because she could. There was no thought that she would be hooked, no thought of her father's addiction. She was attached to nothing and addicted to no one but the drug had other ideas. The first time she was sick. The second time she thought she was kissing God. And now all she did was shoot up trying to chase that feeling.

The sex with the guy on smack was beyond anything she had ever felt before. It lasted for hours and Sapphira recalled a continual searching for something elusive, not finding it, yet still being incredibly satisfied.

'Ethan,' she said out loud. 'That was his name. Ethan.'

She felt strong enough to rise up from the bed and finally

31

explore her surroundings. Walking downstairs, she took in the frescos on the wall, depicting magnificent gardens and angelic characters. Grabbing the map and the large set of keys from the hall table, she stood in the foyer and tried to get her bearings. Sapphira loved this part best: being in the mystery, finding her way. Wandering from room to room, map in one hand and lit cigarette in the other she was almost happy.

Where the church had originally sat in the centre of the monastery had been transformed into the most amazing sitting room. The pews were now around the outside of the walls; the vaulted ceiling had angels and demons carved into the ancient stone. While the space was awe-inspiring, however, it was not really to Sapphira's taste. A little too overdone and European, reminding her of her father's house in LA, filled to overflowing with his family's heirlooms.

Looking at the map, she took in the pool, the pool house, the kitchen, the bedrooms and the bathrooms. She noticed a smaller room on the other side of the property; *biblioteca*, it read on the map. Padding barefoot through the villa, Sapphira felt at home. She had an almost chameleon-like ability to feel instantly at ease wherever she was, one of the few benefits that came from her gypsy-like childhood. Touching the silk tapestries that covered the walls, she headed down the hallway and checked the map of the villa. The *biblioteca* should be here, she thought, as she stood in the huge passageway. She could not see a door anywhere. Stopping, she tried to get her bearings. Yes, there was the room there on the map. So where was the freaking door, she wondered, loving the mystery unfolding before her.

Standing in front of the huge tapestry where the door should have been, her eyes squinted at the needlework of knights and maidens in front of a doorway. In the doorway was an angel, holding what seemed to be the Holy Grail and a book. Sapphira stood and looked and then got the message. Knowledge is God.

Pulling back the heavy tapestry, she found the doorway to the room behind the image. The door was heavily carved in Latin, but Sapphira didn't know what any of it meant. She tried the brass handle but the door was locked. She grabbed the set of keys from her pocket and looked for the oldest one. There were three. She tried the first one but it did not turn; the next one didn't work either. Finally, she heard the click of the lock as it opened for the third key.

Filled from ceiling to floor with books of all shapes and sizes, it was the most beautiful room she had ever seen. There was a long sofa, as wide as a double bed, filled with cushions and covered with blankets and quilts. The room was long and had thin tall windows along the top of the walls. Running across the centre was a table, similar to one in a royal dining room, but this had Tiffany lamps on it for the readers who sat at it, poring over whatever tome they were interested in. Wooden ladders on wheels leaned against brass rods that ran around the walls of the room to enable its climbers to visit the highest realms of knowledge. Sapphira looked up at the ceiling, which was covered in a painting of the nine muses dancing under the moonlight. A bit racy for the old monks, she thought, noticing the exposed breasts of some of the dancers.

A small, single-arched doorway seemed almost hidden among the books and wooden panelled walls. Sapphira walked over and discovered an exquisite small bathroom, with a shower and walls of azure mosaic tiles. This is perfect, she thought. I can live in here, surrounded by books and I will have no one looking in on me!

She had found her secret hiding place. Her dream come

true. She used to hide in the tower of her father's house when he had his infamous parties, escaping the noise and the endless parade of people who used her father for drugs. The hidden library made her feel safe. It was comforting to be surrounded by all the knowledge. She wished she had more schooling, even though she knew she was smarter than most actresses around her. She could learn anything if she was shown a few times, she thought defiantly.

Looking at the many books, she was pleased to see some were in English, and she clapped her hands in joy and ran out along the hallway and dragged her bags into the room. Scrabbling through a suitcase, she found her iPod and Bose portable speakers. Plugging them in, Billie Holiday filled the room singing 'Strange Fruit' and Sapphira sang along.

Looking around the library, her eyes searched out the perfect hiding spot. Crawling under the long table with the Comme des Garçons zippered purse, she felt along the underside and sought out the ledge she instinctively knew was there. Placing the purse on it, she clambered out and stood in the centre of the room. She was safe.

PART TWO

Production

Sometimes film sets can be magical places. When everyone comes together with the same goal, and egos stay off the set, great films are made.

TG thought that hosting a dinner at his villa with the female actors in attendance would create a connection between everyone. Giulia, his Italian assistant, had been working for the last two weeks with Italy's premier party planner to create the perfect welcoming event. Lanterns had been strung across the vast courtyard in the centre of the villa. Candles were all around the outside, giving the place a ceremonial feel. There were two long tables running down the centre to seat the sixty guests and armfuls of sunflowers had been placed in tall vases with lengths of grapevine laced between every place setting. The soft orange linens lay on the table with an array of glasses in different sizes and shapes.

Local chefs were to provide a Tuscan feast for the crew. When asking for the dietary requirements of the leading stars, Giulia was relieved to find that there were not too many quirks to cope with. Calypso was a vegetarian, so Giulia ensured that there were delectable pastas that would appeal to her as well as salads and breads. The thought quickly passed through her mind that maybe this American actress was 'carbophobic', but she pushed it away again. Who doesn't love pasta, she mused as she moved the chairs around the tables.

Upstairs, TG was being interviewed on the phone by a *Variety* reporter about *The Italian Dream*.

'Tell me about the film, it seems very different than your other films, more of a chick flick,' said the reporter.

'I don't know about that,' said TG, trying to keep the exasperation from his voice. Why wouldn't Hollywood ever allow you to change, he wondered. 'But, yeah, it is, very different,' said TG. 'It's a story about three women in Italy all at a crisis in their life. Sapphira De Mont plays the role of the woman mourning the loss of her husband and trying to renovate a villa so she can sell it to return to the US. Rose Nightingale's character plays a woman discovering herself after leaving her husband who cheated on her and Calypso Gable is a young backpacker who finds love in Italy. It's an ensemble piece and I'm really excited about working with such great women,' said TG. He was actually terrified of fucking it up but he didn't say such a thing. *Variety* wanted to hear about the biggest film to be released next year, destined to be a critical and commercial success, provided TG could pull it off.

'Your last film had the most expensive car chase ever filmed. How are you going to go from filming such high-impact scenes to filming women talking about their feelings?' laughed the reporter.

TG paused. He asked himself the same thing every night since he had agreed to direct the film. 'Telling the story is what I do. So whether it's a car chase or an interchange between two actors, I do my best to get the story across.'

As the interview finished, TG hung up the phone and ran his hands through his hair and walked over to the large window in the study, staring at the amazing view in front of him. The hills of Umbria rolled out in front of him, the violet skies signalled twilight and TG knew the party was soon to start.

He sent a small wish out as he saw the first star start to twinkle. Please let the shoot go well, he thought and laughed to himself, wondering what the *Variety* reporter would think of him, if he knew he was wishing on a star.

TG walked downstairs and looked at the party Giulia and her party planner had organized. It was a sight to behold: the lanterns and candles were lit, citronella was in the air and, as dusk fell, the courtyard was heavy with atmosphere and romance. The waiters stood by waiting for guests and ready to ply them with Prosecco and wine. The chefs were busy in the huge kitchen, applying the finishing touches to the feast. All they needed now were the guests.

The lower members of the crew arrived first, then the producers and finally the stars. Calypso arrived, always punctual, as taught by Leeza. She glowed in the courtyard like a firefly, stunning in a One Vintage gold lamé dress from the 1920s that had been reworked for her. The beaded appliqué around the low neckline shimmered and a tulle detail around the skirt edged up over one side to reveal just the right amount of thigh. Worn with a pair of patent leather Christian Louboutin black slingbacks and her new evening bag from the Perugia flea market, Calypso shone in the dark. Gratefully accepting a glass of champagne from a waiter, she took a sip to relieve her nerves.

The start of any job, big or small, made her nervous. Self-doubt and worry stayed with her till her director made her comfortable. Working with TG, she hoped, would be easy and he would be helpful. Calypso relied heavily on her director for both moral and directorial support. While she was a good actor, with sound comedic timing reminiscent of a young Ginger Rogers, she lacked the self-confidence and maturity to truly explore the options for the character. The last film she had done had really just required her to say her lines, look gorgeous and do her perfect laugh several times – the laugh which made audiences fall in love with her. This shoot was going to be different; she was really going to have to act, particularly in the scenes with Sapphira and Rose. Christ, she thought, I hope I can cut it.

She felt a little sick. Looking around for a familiar face, she spotted Kelly talking to two men, with their backs to Calypso. She walked over towards them, aware all eyes in the room were on her, except for TG in a navy blue velvet jacket and worn jeans laughing with Kelly. He whispered something in Kelly's ear and she looked over to Calypso and smiled, waving her over.

'Hi, doll, you look divine. God, what a dress! Calypso, this is my husband Chris, who is also the DOP. And I presume you already know TG,' she said warmly, motioning towards the man in the blue jacket.

TG turned and looked at Calypso. Jesus fucking Christ, he thought, she is stunning. When she had walked into the audition back in LA he was instantly attracted to her but he had sworn off actresses and especially ones in his own films.

'Yes, yes, hi again,' he heard himself saying. He remembered Calypso was gorgeous but had no idea how beautiful she really was till he saw her dressed in gold and so luminous. The light of the candles lit the shadows under her cheekbones and made her hazel eyes almost seem yellow in the light. He felt a chill run down his spine.

Calypso smiled and took a sip from her glass and remained silent. When she was nervous she said too much, and right now, she was really, really nervous. Any minute he'll find out I'm an imposter, she thought.

'How's things, Cal?' asked Kelly. 'How're you settling into bella Italia?'

'Great. I slept for nearly eighteen hours, I think, then woke up and went to dinner and ate the most amazing pastry and met a boy.' Calypso stopped, aware she had just run on and then swore in front of her director again, just like in the audition. I must look like a kid to them, she thought as she felt them staring at her.

There was no judgement from her audience though. Chris was thinking: I can't wait to shoot her. She is gorgeous.

Kelly was thinking several things: She met a boy? Already? Well played, Calypso. And then looking at Calypso's slender figure, she thought incredulously, she ate carbs!

TG didn't hear a word Calypso said. He just watched her mouth move and the way the light flickered over her face and shoulders. He felt himself mesmerized and tried to pull himself together.

A boy? he wondered. Man, she was fast. Lucky bastard, he thought. Shit, TG, you just broke up with an actress. You know what they're like! The last thing you need is a distraction. Get your head in the game, boy, he admonished himself. Smiling thinly at Calypso, he turned his back on her and walked towards the bar.

Calypso felt her cheeks flush with shame. He thinks I'm an idiot, a silly little girl, she thought as she watched him walk away.

The inadequacies she felt always came back, leaving her feeling stupid and uneducated. She watched TG as he chatted to someone by the bar. He was probably one of those uptight intellectual New Yorkers, she thought and immediately decided to hate him. Partly because this was her normal reaction to someone when she felt less than them, but also because it protected her. Leeza had drummed into her: 'If they don't like you, then fuck them, you didn't like them first.'

For all the self-help and self-improvement books she had read over the years, when Calypso felt threatened, everything she thought she had learned went out the window and she returned to being Leeza's daughter again, defensive when doubted or questioned.

Kelly watched TG's reaction and Calypso's response to him carefully. Knowing TG as she did, he was clearly attracted to her. Yet this is what he always did, she thought. He runs away, afraid of his feelings, and the woman always has to chase him. Looking at the young girl in front of her, she reached out and touched her arm, her skin soft beneath her hand. 'He's a little wound up, always like this before a shoot. He really is a great guy, you'll see.'

'Whatever, it's cool,' Calypso said to Kelly but inside she was fuming.

Looking around for any other faces she knew, she saw Rose Nightingale had arrived. She hadn't seen her come in but couldn't miss her now. Tall and slender in a peach georgette chiffon, halter-neck Chloé gown, Rose was beautiful. Her shoulders and arms were lily white, and she wore a gold Etruscan cuff on one arm and matching gold hoop earrings, which showed off her long neck.

Her brunette hair was swept up into a ponytail and she had applied her make-up in such a way that it looked as if she had barely any on but her features were perfect. Calypso knew this kind of make-up took over an hour to apply and she was a little star-struck. Rose was an icon and had the power and respect in the industry that Calypso hoped to one day have herself.

Seeing the girl in the gold dress staring at her, Rose made a beeline to her. 'Hello, I'm Rose,' she said with a smile. 'I'm thrilled to be working with you. I saw your film on the plane on the way over. You were great, well done.'

Rose had a way of instantly putting people at ease. After her experience at drama school in London, she worked hard to make women at ease with her. Her warmth and kindness, just when Calypso felt so vulnerable, was exactly what was needed.

'You're very funny, it's so hard to be funny. I can't ever do it. It's easy to cry on set, just think of your dog dying or something and then the waterworks start. But to make people laugh, well, that's hard.'

Rose was so sincere and earnest that Calypso believed her immediately and decided to like her straightaway. Seeing her relax in her presence, Rose touched her arm. 'Let's sit together at dinner, shall we? I want to hear all about you.'

Calypso nodded eagerly. Rose's motherly instinct was exactly what Calypso needed at that moment.

TG walked over and kissed Rose on both cheeks. They had known each other through the industry A-list parties and events and Rose was thrilled to be finally working with him.

'Well, hello there,' he said. 'I see you've met Calypso.'

Calypso glared at him. If Rose noticed any tension she didn't let on, instead she talked about how happy she was to be in Italy and how she hoped her family would come and visit her here.

While she spoke, TG did not look at Calypso once, even though Rose included her in the conversation several times. Calypso was becoming more and more incensed. This guy is an asshole, she thought, wishing she had taken the action film instead.

TG was aware of Calypso next to him though. Her presence was electric and whatever perfume she was wearing was driving him crazy. He knew if he turned to face her he would want to touch her face, her hair, her body. Oh my God, he thought, as Rose kept talking, I'm insane. I'm tragic. What kind of a guy falls for a woman he has just met? This isn't right. It must be the candles and the fact that I haven't had sex for five months.

Gun-shy from his experience with the ambitious starlet, he made a vow he would never date an actress again – until he met Calypso. He glanced at her from the corner of his eye and saw her looking at Rose as she spoke. She seemed tense; maybe she was nervous. Perhaps he should say something to relax her, he thought.

Racking his brain he said the first thing that popped into his head. 'Calypso ate a pastry.' The shock of this sentence ran through his body and he felt himself cringing.

Calypso shot a deathly stare at him. Was he worried she was going to get fat in Italy? Was he making fun of her? I'll have to ring my trainer and get her to send me a DVD tomorrow to do while I'm here, she thought. Fuck, what the hell does that comment mean?

Rose clapped her hands, her gold cuff catching the light. 'Oh God, the food here is wonderful. I plan to get really fat after filming! I want my family to come over and we'll go on a gastronomic tour of the region. What sort of pastry did you have?' she asked.

Calypso's mouth was set in a straight line. 'Berries, chocolate.' she answered through gritted teeth.

TG saw her face set and knew she thought he was a dick. Oh well, at least I won't have to worry about my crush if she hates me, he thought.

Giulia walked over and suggested to TG it was time to sit down for the dinner as the chefs were getting worried their feast would be spoiled.

'Is Sapphira here yet?'

'No, not yet but she's on her way. I rang her driver,' Giulia replied.

'Great, we'll start to get everyone to the table and begin without her.'

'Excuse me,' he said to Rose and Calypso, and walked towards a group of people, gesturing at the table.

Rose and Calypso wandered over, setting down their glasses. Rose pulled out her chair and sat down before the waiter standing behind her had time. Patting the chair next to her, she looked up at Calypso, who was debating whether to run away. 'Come on, sit next to me. This'll be fun.'

Rose's enthusiasm was infectious and Calypso decided things would be all right if she stuck with her for the shoot. The party sat down, and TG stood and tapped his champagne glass with his fork. As he did, Sapphira arrived and the whole table fell silent. She stood in the doorway of the courtyard, wearing a white leather Pucci mini dress, with a huge silver and black eagle on the front looking as if it were about to land on its prey. She wore no jewellery and long black hair hung loosely down her back. Her legs seemed to stretch forever, ending in a pair of Balmain suede calf-high boots, with five silver buckles up each side. Her entrance stunned the room; it was dramatic and powerful, not unlike Sapphira herself.

TG spoke, breaking the moment. 'Well, I was about to make a speech but one of our stars took the words right out of my mouth,' he said, laughing.

The table joined in his laughter and Sapphira smiled at the group, getting the joke. She felt good tonight; she had slept this afternoon and had a gorgeous swim in the pool. She had lain in the sun and was instantly sun kissed. She looked great and she knew it. Looking along the table, she recognized Rose. Everyone knew Rose, but she didn't know

45

the young girl sitting next to her looking anxious. Sapphira didn't watch television or films, preferring books and providing her own entertainment. The industry did not interest her but the craft of acting did, so she tried to read and experience as much as she could so she would have emotions to draw on when she was working.

Rose waved at her and smiled. They had met at a few Women in Hollywood functions and while it was only small talk, they had found each other pleasant. Sapphira didn't have girlfriends. In fact, she didn't have any friends; she only had lovers or ex-lovers.

Friendship was not something she'd had growing up. Her mother hadn't had friends and her father only had people who used him for drugs and parties at his house. The pack she ran with in her teenage years had not stayed together; drug overdoses, rehab and prison time had split the group up and then Sapphira became a star. It was problematic enough trying to maintain a steady sexual relationship, let alone an emotional one.

Walking towards Rose, Sapphira hoped she would be easy to work with and not get too close. People always tried to be her friend but she would have none of it. Besides, she didn't want people to know her secret. Better she spent her time alone. It had worked for her fine, so far.

'Hello there,' said Rose. 'You look amazing! Well done, you. That dress looks as though it was made for you.'

'It was,' said Sapphira, without any arrogance. Designers made her outfits all the time and she chose the ones she could wear, instead of the dress wearing her. She had seen too many celebrities on red carpets overdressed and struggling with their trains and fussing over a lost Harry Winston earring on loan for the night.

'This is Calypso Gable, our other actress. We're the three amigos, I guess,' laughed Rose.

'Hi,' said Sapphira.

'Hello,' answered Calypso, intimidated by Sapphira's sexual presence and beauty.

'Calypso has just made a big impact in her new hit film. Have you seen it?'

'No,' said Sapphira, sitting down. 'I don't watch films or television,' she shrugged unapologetically.

'Not at all?' asked Rose.

'Nope, I prefer to read,' she answered.

'Well, good for you. Although if people didn't watch anything then we would be out of jobs, I suppose,' she said, laughing at her own joke.

The fog of worry began to envelop Calypso again. She was not of this calibre, she thought. Rose, the greatest actress of this generation; Sapphira, an intellectual and sexual powerhouse. And her, little Miss Hollywood. She pulled out her phone and began to text her mother, then took a big swig of the red wine that the waiter had put in front of her.

TG tapped his glass again. 'Thank you, everyone. If I can have a moment . . . Sapphira, is that okay with you?'

The table laughed again and Sapphira nodded majestically towards him, as if allowing him his time in her spotlight.

'This is a big thrill for me, having such a great team to do justice to this wonderful script. For those I've worked with before, thanks for helping me out again. For those I've not yet worked with, I look forward to building a great relationship.'

As he said these last words, he felt his eyes drawn to Calypso. She was looking at her mobile phone, not listening to him at all. Probably texting her boyfriend, he thought. Maybe Kelly was wrong; maybe she is just a spoilt little brat.

He paused. Hearing the silence Calypso looked up at him. He felt a shock run through his body. 'So, thank you. I'm available for any of you night or day. Please let me know if you need anything – and here's to a great shoot.' He raised his glass as did everyone else at the table. 'Salut!' he cried.

'Salut!' the table cried in unison.

'Let's eat!' Rose called out.

The dinner was a great success, the food amazing. Bruschetta, fresh asparagus, seven types of pasta dish, some with the black truffles of the region grated over them, fennel and orange salad, duck breast with cabbage and glazed vegetables, three cheeses from the region. The Umbrian red and white wine flowed all night and they finished with chocolate and crema di fragola, with fresh strawberries on the side.

It was a decadent feast, with Rose the only one allowing herself to try several of the pastas. Calypso, still smarting from TG's comment, stuck to the salad and vegetables and some cheese. Sapphira took some duck and salad but pushed it around the plate. She did eat the chocolate, however, allowing herself to indulge as her body always craved sugar.

None of the male co-stars were on set yet. TG wanted to shoot all the collective scenes with the women first, then he would shoot their individual scenes later.

Rose was working hard to draw more information out of Sapphira, as she seemed a little glazed. Probably just jet-lag, thought Rose.

'How's your villa?' Rose asked. 'Mine's lovely.'

'It's okay. I haven't really looked around much,' Sapphira said vacantly.

'Oh,' said Rose surprised. Once she had awoken from her sleep, exploring the house and the garden was the first thing she did. 'Well, plenty of time for that, I'm sure.'

'How about you, Calypso? How's your villa? The views from mine are amazing.'

'Um, I'm staying in a hotel,' she said, instantly regretting her reply. Now I look like the child in the hotel and not grown-up enough to have a house, she thought. 'I was offered a villa,' she added quickly. 'But I wanted to be in the city.'

'Yeah, I get it,' said Rose. 'That's where Kelly and I were when we were young. Any good shops I should visit?'

'Did you know Kelly before LA?' asked Calypso.

'Yeah, we went to school together, best friends since we were fourteen,' laughed Rose.

'How great, and now you are here together,' marvelled Calypso. She would have done anything for a best friend from school.

'I know, amazing, really,' said Rose, looking fondly at her best friend telling TG off for something.

TG came over and pulled up a chair opposite the women. 'Hello, ladies,' he said, in his smoothest professional lounge voice. 'We're all getting to know each other?'

Calypso and Sapphira were silent, so Rose spoke. 'Yes, it's lovely, we're all becoming fast friends now, I think?' She looked to the other women; Sapphira and Calypso smiled.

'Thank you for this, TG. I'm really excited to explore my character with you,' said Sapphira.

There was an open invitation in her voice and Calypso was startled. Jesus, the eagle on her dress wasn't just for show! She was a hunter and TG was her prey.

TG smiled. 'Sure, I think we'll all do great work on this. Please speak to me about any ideas you may have on the character or the scenes and we can work through it all together.'

Calypso noticed that he didn't seem to take Sapphira up on

49

her offer; instead he kept his professional mask on. Probably didn't want to mix business and pleasure, she thought, although Sapphira was incredible in her beauty and presence.

TG was called by Giulia and Calypso watched him walk away. 'Is he gay?' Sapphira asked.

'No, no, he just broke up with someone in LA, I think,' Rose answered vaguely.

Sapphira watched him walk away. A shame, she thought. Might have been some fun while in Italy. Oh well, there's always my co-star.

Sapphira's ego was large enough not to take TG's snub as insulting. She factored it down to him being broken-hearted – something she could have fixed, but she wasn't going to chase after him. She stood up, smoothed her dress, drained her wine glass and set it on the table.

'Rose, Calypso, I look forward to working with you both. Goodnight.' Then she turned and walked out to her driver and car.

Rose and Calypso sat staring after her. 'Well, that's lovely,' said Rose unconvincingly.

'She's weird,' Calypso replied and Rose couldn't disagree with Calypso's assessment.

Sapphira was certainly more than unusual, thought Rose, but it was more than being eccentric. Rose understood eccentric, she was friends with Kelly after all. No, Sapphira was troubled, Rose was sure of it. Behind the façade of fabulous was fear.

Rose wondered what on earth Sapphira had to fear. The girl had everything.

CHAPTER FIVE

'What do you mean they can't find the time?' Rose barked down the phone to Lauren as Lucia placed a bowl of apples in front of the apricots on the table.

'Well, I tried to tee it up but they're really busy, and it's the wrong time of the year for some of them with school and work,' said Lauren.

'Bloody hell. Now I have this fucking giant villa filled with stuff and no one to use it. No wonder the housekeeper thinks I'm mad. She keeps mumbling "ghost children" at me in Italian and now it makes sense,' said Rose, biting into the crisp fruit.

Lauren laughed, 'That's too funny!'

'Really? You think?' rebutted Rose.

'I know you're sad but your family have lives also, Rose. I know you may think I'm out of line but you can't expect them to drop everything just because you have a villa and a box of Snakes and Ladders.'

'I know that. It's just I never see them. My niece and nephew never see me anymore except in *Hello!* magazine,' said Rose sadly.

'Well, maybe you can head over there before you start shooting the next film and spend some time with your family. I can move a few things and make some more room in your schedule.'

Rose could hear Lauren tapping at the keyboard. 'Maybe, we'll see,' said Rose.

It was irritating that her family never met her halfway when she asked them. They had no understanding of her fame or if they did, they were unaffected by it. In fact, Rose was certain her parents had not even seen her last two films. Rose had offered them premiere tickets but they declined, saying they had promised to babysit for Rose's brother and look after the grandchildren.

Rose had yelled at her mother down the phone from her hotel suite, claiming she didn't care, which her mother gently pushed back onto Rose. 'Rosie,' she had said, 'I had promised Martin I would help him and Fiona months ago. I cannot drop everything just because your face is on the trams. First in, best dressed,' her mother had explained in her usual unemotional way.

Rose had begrudgingly apologized to her mother and later, with her therapist, had acknowledged that her parents' refusal to be spellbound by her job and instead retain equal relationships with their children was to be commended. Sometimes though, Rose felt a little left out, being so far away from England and with no grandchildren for her mother to babysit.

Rose's temper was legendary in her family. If anyone threw a tantrum, they called it 'doing a Rose'. It was something she was able to keep a lid on when she worked, but privately she could rage and rage. It never had any effect on Paul; in fact, it became worse when she was married to him. She would yell and throw things just to be heard but he just ignored her. His cruelty was astounding, something she did not realize he had in him till it was too late. His favourite way to punish her was to ignore her; he would literally cast her out of his life till he decided to forgive her. She never knew when this would be. He would eat at the same table, sleep in the spare room but he would not answer her, not even flinch when at times

52

she slapped him. If he had a message for her, he would leave it with their bewildered Mexican housekeeper. Once, her parents came to visit in the middle of one of these episodes. Whenever they were around he would act as if they didn't have a care in the world. The minute they were out of the room, he started ignoring her again.

Her ex-husband, Paul Ross, had been a teen heartthrob and had become a household name, loved by critics and the public alike. After seeing Rose in a small independent film that she had made when she was first in LA, Paul had pursued Rose relentlessly.

Rose, at twenty-two and fresh out of acting school had been entranced by his fame, good looks and energy. But the more Rose learned about Paul after the ring was on her finger, the more she realized he was unhinged. Taking huge doses of vitamins and prescription and non-prescription drugs, convinced that they would help him stay young. Drinking a bottle of tomato ketchup every day to prevent prostate cancer. His obsession with immortality even went to the extreme of his forging an obsessive relationship with a South American plastic surgeon, whom Rose secretly called Doctor Dorian Gray.

Rose and Paul's sex life was uninspiring but a sexually inexperienced Rose hadn't known any better. They tried for a baby – well, Rose did – but it's hard to make a child when your husband won't even talk to you, let alone have sex with you.

After ten years of marriage, Rose was no closer to having a baby and no closer to fulfilling the talent and potential that she had shown in her first film.

The treatment ate away at Rose's self-esteem. She started to see a therapist and while she told him of her marriage problems she never told the whole truth about the way Paul rejected her.

'You need to talk more, you and Paul. Communication is the answer,' advised the therapist.

Rose nodded and smiled. She had finally communicated her frustration by running into a wall with a small kitchen knife to her chest. Not that anyone besides Paul, her agent and her mother knew this – and her trusted doctors, of course. After intensive therapy and a five-week stay in hospital, Rose slowly revealed the years of Paul's mental torture. She still remembered the look on her doctor's face when he spoke to Rose. 'He's a bully. Anyone who treats another person like this is in pain. They hate themselves and they hate everyone else. He feels better when you feel bad. It gives him power. It's abuse, Rose.'

What he said was the truth, as Rose knew in her heart, but to leave Paul was the biggest decision she would ever have to make. The suicide attempt had actually saved her, as had the film in Europe. Maybe this was why she worked so much. When she worked she was safe and busy and did not have time to think about what her life lacked or the choices she had made.

Had she been serious about wanting to die, Rose often wondered. Was she trying to get Paul to notice her? Or did she just want to feel something, prove she existed? Thankfully, her agent, Randy, had arrived in time to get her help and cover up everything so it didn't end up in the tabloids. But not once did Paul visit her in hospital, not even a card or a phone call.

Lauren's voice pulled Rose out of her dark memories. 'You have dresses from Oscar De La Renta, Zac Posen, Dior, Elie Saab and Chanel for the Cannes Film Festival opening. I can send you images via email or FedEx them over if you like.'

'Send over the images and I'll have a look.'

'Maybe you can wear one of them there. You sure you don't want me to send them over?' asked Lauren, looking at the divine dresses hanging in the office.

'Nah, I've nowhere to wear them. All I do is try not to eat the entire contents of this house,' Rose sulked. 'The housekeeper feeds me every five minutes, I swear. I'm going to be too huge for the dresses anyway. Call Weight Watchers, they just got themselves a new spokesperson.'

Lauren knew this voice. Rose was feeling sorry for herself. 'What about Sapphira or Calypso? What are they doing?' she said, ignoring Rose's self pity.

'Ha!' said Rose. 'You've got to be joking. Sapphira is as odd as a box of frogs and Calypso is so young, it makes me feel old just looking at her. Maybe you can come over and play Snakes and Ladders with me,' Rose laughed. 'I could throw a fit and send a private plane for you, courtesy of the studio and you can come and visit with me.'

Lauren was silent on the phone.

'Lauren, are you there?' asked Rose.

'Yep, sorry, I'm here, just distracted,' came back Lauren's tight voice.

'Did I say something to upset you?' asked Rose, confused.

'No, no. Not at all. I would love to come, of course, but I've lots to do here, you know that,' said Lauren, and the ease between them closed over and Lauren was back as an employee.

Rose shook off her concern and put Lauren's reaction down to her being over-friendly. She had to remember to put up professional boundaries, her therapist said. But boundaries were not Rose's strong point; she barged in and tried to fix everything in everyone's lives. Choosing not to explore Lauren's reaction to her invitation in the name of boundaries, she and Lauren then chatted about the emails Lauren was forwarding her and then she rang off.

Hanging up from Lauren, she walked around the grand salon. She didn't want to watch TV; Italian TV was odd, filled with semi-nude women and dancing – and that was just the nightly news report, she thought. Lucia had left her a delicious looking frittata and salad. She had asked for no more carbs, like pasta. Lucia mumbled to her husband that Rose was 'too thin, needed feeding'.

She walked down to the study and stood looking at the Wii machine. Wondering how it worked she opened the manual and, following the prompts, played around with the buttons until it sprang into life on the screen. What did she want to play? Tennis? Baseball? Basketball? Bowling?

I was always good at tennis, she thought, remembering her days back on the school team. Playing through the demonstration, Rose found it easier than she expected. Next thing she knew, she was playing the machine and laughing and cheering herself on. An hour later, she was in a lather of perspiration and her serving arm was quite sore. Who needs a trainer, she thought as she drank from a bottle of water she grabbed from the large kitchen.

Opening the fridge, she cut herself a large slice of frittata and put some salad on the plate. Wandering into the lounge, she turned on the TV. Flicking through the channels, she saw a film that Paul had made during the time of their divorce. He seemed so beautiful onscreen, untouched by the drama in their personal lives. Paul had dealt with the breakup by dating a new starlet from Romania, tipped to be the new Bond girl. Rose knew she was with Paul's agent, so didn't believe the relationship; the agency manufactured relationships between their stars all the time. For years the rumours about her and Paul's marriage was that it was a business deal. Perhaps it was to Paul but to Rose it was a real marriage and even though she was happy to be free, all the same she grieved for what life might have been like.

The last time Rose and Paul had faced each other was with their lawyers at her lawyer's plush offices to sign the papers and work out a satisfactory financial deal. Paul had been charming to Rose, friendly and caring, claiming he wanted the best for her and mostly for her to be happy. Rose had sat waiting for the change in him to manifest but Paul kept up the act until the lawyers left them for a moment in the large boardroom.

As the door closed behind them, Paul had leaned over the table and hissed, 'You will get nothing, you slut. Nothing, you hear me. I am gonna bury you. That affair with that asshole was the final straw. I always knew you couldn't keep your legs shut.'

Rose sat silently, relieved to see the Paul she knew come back. His act in front of the lawyers was disarming; this Paul she felt she had finally learned to handle.

'Be very careful, Paul,' she said, doing her best Judi Dench impersonation. He was always intimidated by her English accent. 'I happen to know about you and your South American surgeon, or should I say lover. I had my lawyers look into it with a private detective and if I were you, I would stay tuned to *Inside Edition* to see the highlights of the tape I have in my possession.'

Rose took a punt and it worked. He was shocked and his face visibly paled in front of her. This time Rose hissed across the table. 'I want only what I deserve after putting up with ten years of your lies, abuse and bullshit. You're the asshole. You didn't even come and see me in hospital, you prick!' She spat out the words.

Paul sat stunned and Rose felt a tiny bit sorry for him. 'Paul, if you're gay then just come out. You don't need any more money. You are beyond wealthy. You are living a lie and you and I know it. If you care about your doctor then tell him, be with him.'

Paul looked up at her, his eyes filled with tears and Rose finally understood why he was like he was, always trying to push down his sexual urges, trying to control what he couldn't when what he wanted to control was his attraction to men.

'Rose, you know . . .' His voice was soft, real almost, and then the door opened to the boardroom and the lawyers walked back in. Paul straightened his posture. 'Whatever Rose wants, guys. She was a good wife and I'm sorry it didn't work out.'

And with that he grabbed the divorce papers on the desk, signed them with his Visconti pen, stood up, walked around to Rose, kissed her cheek softly and left the room. It was the most tender moment of their marriage that she could remember.

Rose pushed the thoughts away and changed the channel on the TV remote. Satellite had been installed and there were more channels than back in LA. Flicking over, she saw something she recognized. 'Yay!' she squealed and sat down with her dinner on her lap and watched an episode of *The Bill*, alone but content.

In the kitchen, Lucia was less than content with Rose being alone. Apples were a start, she thought, apples would draw a lover to her but it was apple with cinnamon that would bring the man faster to the woman.

Lucia busied herself in the kitchen. *Mele speziate con sultanine*, she thought. Spiced apple with sultanas. No one could resist Lucia's cooking, it was magic, everyone said so. Lucia sang as she worked. If only they knew, she thought.

CHAPTER SIX

There was no rehearsal time for *The Italian Dream*. TG wanted the actors to be ready to film once they came on set. The affable guy who had greeted the women at the dinner party the previous night had disappeared and in his place was a man focused on his task.

'I'm going to try and shoot as much as I can in order for your sake and the DOP. Chris and I have worked out some shots which won't require long set-up times but some may take a while, so please be patient,' said TG as he addressed the women in the make-up trailer, who had already been in hair and make-up for the past two hours, before walking back to the dilapidated villa where the shoot was taking place.

'He seems stressed,' said Calypso to Kelly, worried about the day ahead.

'Nah, he's not stressed, just focused. He's pretty single minded when he wants to be,' said Kelly as she moved about the trailer lining up make-up brushes. 'He's a funny one, all soft on the outside but if anyone fucks with him or people he loves he gets all Tony Soprano on their ass.'

Calypso watched TG as he and Chris stood talking as she walked over for her call in wardrobe.

They were discussing the first scene where Rose and Sapphira's characters arrive at Rose's character's villa looking for a place to stay.

TG walked across to wardrobe, where Calypso was about to be dressed by the costume crew. Her character was a young backpacker who had just finished university, so they had pulled together jeans and cut-off shorts, t-shirts, singlets and sandals, as well as a few pretty dresses and shirts. It was casual and homespun; the kind of clothes Calypso felt the most comfortable in. Walking into the dressing room trailer, TG found her standing in a tiny Calvin Klein pink polka dotted bra and pants. With a full face of make-up and her hair in loose plaits, courtesy of the hair department, she looked like a young Brigitte Bardot. She took TG's breath away, not because she was so incredibly sexy but because she looked so innocent. Her figure was insane, he thought. He could see her tiny waist and pert breasts, her toned legs and gorgeous ass in the mirror behind her.

He felt his cock start to move. Nooooo, he thought, barking at her to cover his embarrassment. 'Hurry up, you ready yet? We're waiting.'

Calypso looked at Helen, the costume head, who shook her head slightly as if to say, I don't know what bug got up his ass.

Calypso slipped on denim shorts and a pink singlet, and sliding into her sandals, she stomped out of the trailer. 'Isn't it kinda hard to be behind when you haven't started shooting yet?' she retorted to TG.

This was going to be a nightmare, she thought as she walked towards the set.

TG wanted to kick himself. He knew he was being an asshole; he was always an asshole when he was nervous. Walking towards the set, he headed towards Calypso, wanting to apologize, but she was deep in conversation with Kelly. No doubt telling her what a prick he was, he thought, as he saw

60

Kelly turn and throw a death stare in his direction. Fuck, now he was going to face the wrath of 'Kali', as she called herself when she got mad.

Rose and Sapphira came on set, perfect in their costume and make-up. He called the women over. 'So, this is where we meet you all. Sapphira, your character is already at the villa. Calypso, you have just turned up, with no idea where you are, lost and looking for help. Rose, you know what you are doing?'

Rose nodded.

'Let's run it a few times and get the feel,' TG said.

While the actors walked through the lines and found their marks, the crew were busy, fixing the lighting and the sound. Props were moving items to work with the actors' marks, and make-up stood by waiting to do touch-ups if needed.

The actors had a natural chemistry and looked like a dream through the camera. TG felt they were ready to shoot. Four takes later and they had it in the can. There'd been a spark as soon as TG yelled 'action' and each of them brought their own specialness to the roles. Calypso was perfect, her flustered comedic timing brought lightness to the sadness of Rose's character who was mourning her husband. And Sapphira brought the right amount of enigmatic pathos to her role, balancing out the others perfectly.

'Fucking excellent!' yelled TG as he watched the playbacks. The crew all clapped, as was the ritual when the first shot was done on the shoot.

The morning went like a dream, all of the actors being pleasant and professional. Rose and Calypso instantly bonded and even Sapphira was seen joking with some of the guys in the crew. The assistant director called 'lunch' and the actors and crew walked over to catering. Every imaginable sort of food was laid out in front of them. American, Italian and even some French. TG grabbed a tray and stood while Kelly helped herself to salad, cheeses and bread. Without looking up at him, she asked, 'Why are you being a dick to Calypso?'

'I didn't think I was,' he said, knowing it was an outright lie.

'Well, you are, and it's stressing her out. She thinks you think she's fat and stupid. What the hell did you say to her?'

'Nothing. Oh you know, I said something and it came out wrong and then every time I see her I say something even more stupid than the last time. It's like I've got Tourette's or something. I'll apologize.'

'You better, 'cause the acting you just saw was bloody good from her and the more relaxed she is the better she performs. I worked with her on the *Bazaar* shoot and when she's chilled she is a dream,' she said, waving the salad tongs at him.

TG put down his tray and walked towards Calypso's trailer. Rose and Sapphira were eating with the crew, but Calypso had headed off for time by herself – never a good sign. This film was only going to work if the crew became like a family and right now he had a problem. He saw her door was open, and as he climbed the step he heard her talking.

'He is so mean to me, Mom. He yells at me and I swear he thinks I'm fat. I said I ate a pastry and then he saw me in costume today and looked at me like I was a freaking elephant.'

She paused. 'Mom, it was one pastry! I know, I know, I'll go for a run. Yes. No, I don't want you to come over. I'm fine. Rose is nice and Kelly is sweet to me. I'll be fine. I'm a big girl now. I just hate him. I hate him all the time!'

Calypso sounded like a small child and TG felt awful. Now was not the right time to see her; he would wait and try to make it up to her on set that afternoon.

The afternoon shooting went better but Calypso didn't speak to TG unless he spoke to her first. Any questions she had about her character she ran by Sapphira and Rose, who were really helpful and ran lines with her off set. Rose was great at helping Calypso dissect the script to find the hidden clues about the character, and Sapphira offered different ways to say the lines, which Calypso found inspiring.

'There is no one way. I think finding the right reaction is a process. There is no immediate right response. You can explore and then if you want to use the original choice, then great, but it's worth finding out,' Sapphira explained as she and Calypso sat in Calypso's trailer talking.

'You're so smart. How do you know all this?' asked Calypso admiringly. Sapphira was not quite as weird as she had first thought. Calypso had broken through Sapphira's defensive attitude with sheer persistence and by the end of the first day Calypso hugged her. 'You're a saint, Sapphira. I would have been lost today without you and Rose.'

'You'll be fine, sweetie. You just gotta believe it,' Sapphira said with a casual wave as she walked to her car.

TG was so busy he didn't have time to speak to Calypso and before he knew it they had wrapped for the day and the crew had packed up.

Kelly and Chris walked over. 'Dinner at yours tonight?' asked Chris.

'Sure, sure, make it a bit later though. I have to go through today's rushes and call LA.'

Kelly glared at him; he was not looking forward to tonight's date. He watched Calypso walk over to her car. She turned and looked at him; he felt sick in his stomach. 'Don't hate me,' he said under his breath. He smiled and waved goodbye at her.

Calypso looked at him blankly, and then slipped in the back seat and the car drove off. On the drive to her hotel, she was confused. Maybe he was one of those uptight directors who was a tyrant on set and a teddy bear off. Too hard, she thought, as the car sped along the dusty roads towards the main highway. He wasn't worth thinking about, she thought. Closing her eyes, she let the day and TG slip from her mind.

CHAPTER SEVEN

Calypso waited in Sapphira's trailer while the set was readied for their scene. Sapphira had asked her to run lines, which Calypso was grateful for, although she thought that Sapphira had the lines down fine. It was Calypso who needed the practice. Marco was taking up most of her time outside of filming and yesterday TG had yelled at her when she flubbed a few lines.

Sapphira had watched with interest. There was no doubt TG had a crush on Calypso but he decided to play the schoolyard card and treat her unfairly, thought Sapphira. He was so conscious of not playing favourites that Calypso was being bullied in a way.

'Don't worry about him,' said Sapphira quietly as the focus puller measured them for the next shot. 'He's just a bit uptight, big pressure on him from the studio, no doubt. But I've worked with worse directors, at least he's not Jerry Hyman, what a cunt.'

'That's terrible word,' she said shocked.

'What, hyman?' asked Sapphira, being deliberately ignorant.

'No, the other one, the C word.'

'The C word, Jesus, you're uptight,' laughed Sapphira and Calypso felt very unsophisticated and young.

65

'TG is so weird around me,' whispered Calypso. 'The other day he saw me in costume in my bra and panties and he yelled at me.'

Sapphira made a face.

'What?' asked Calypso at the sight of Sapphira's face.

'Let's make a deal, you don't say the word panties and I won't say the word cunt. They're both equally offensive in my book,' Sapphira stated.

Calypso laughed. 'What's wrong with panties?'

Sapphira shuddered, 'Horrible word.'

'So is the C word.'

Sapphira sighed, and Calypso changed the subject.

'I shouldn't have done this film, I was offered an action movie for much more money. I wish I'd done it.' Calypso sounded forlorn and Sapphira felt sorry for her.

Sapphira laughed quietly. 'Been there, done that. It's all bullshit, babe, don't get stuck in that genre, so hard to break out of.'

Calypso said nothing as Chris came and checked the measurements of his assistant and then went back behind the camera.

'You know why I think he's being a fuckwit?' asked Sapphira.

'Why?' said Calypso grumpily.

'I think he's got a crush on you,' she said as Kelly walked onto the set to adjust Sapphira's powdered face. 'That's why he yelled at you in your underwear,' she said, emphasizing the last word.

'No way!' Calypso shrieked. 'He hates me. I'm pretty sure he thinks I'm Malibu Barbie. I'm surprised I haven't been replaced yet.'

'He's got a crush on you, he likes you,' Sapphira found herself singing softly in Calypso's ear to try make her laugh.

Kelly laughed conspiratorially with the girls. 'Yeah, I reckon he's got a massive keeny,' she said.

'A keeny?' asked Calypso. 'Gross.'

'A keeny, he's keen on you. A crush,' said Kelly.

'No way. Anyway, I've got Marco,' said Calypso defiantly.

'Marco Schmarco,' Sapphira said.

'You gonna come and do a reading after?' Kelly asked Calypso as she adjusted her hair.

'Yeah, I guess,' said Calypso.

'What reading?' asked Sapphira, feeling left out for the first time in her life.

'Kel's teaching me to read tarot,' said Calypso.

'When you gonna give me a reading?' she asked lazily, as though not caring.

Calypso perked up. 'Really? That's so exciting! You want one from me? I mean, Kelly will be there to interpret as well 'cause I'm just learning,' Calypso said, her words tumbling over each other. 'Is that okay, Kel?'

Kelly smiled. 'Of course.' She watched Sapphira as she stood still, perfect but soulless somehow, as though a piece of her was missing. She would have loved to read her cards and this opportunity, although through the innocent Calypso, was too good to pass up. 'Maybe later we can come to your trailer?'

'Great, don't forget your magic wand and broomstick,' laughed Sapphira as the assistant director called places for shooting.

During the lunch break, Kelly and Calypso descended on Sapphira's trailer with tarot cards in hand. Calypso took her role as tarot reader very seriously and was almost ceremonial about the cards, which were wrapped in a purple Pucci silk scarf.

'Okay, so shuffle and think about what you want to ask and then pull cards till I ask you to stop,' Calypso instructed intently.

'You're not serious about this, are you?' laughed Sapphira as she shuffled the cards like a Vegas croupier.

'We are,' said Calypso, looking to Kelly for agreement.

Kelly laughed. 'Ah, Little Grasshopper takes things very seriously.'

Calypso was looking at Sapphira's hands flying over the cards. 'Okay, so now you just spread them in a line and pull them out.'

Sapphira started to pull the cards as Calypso ordered them into a cross formation in front of her on the round table, Kelly helping her.

Calypso stared at the cards. 'Okay,' she started. 'This formation here is the issues your life is centred around at the moment. Is that right, Kelly?'

'Yep,' said Kelly nodding encouragingly.

'Justice and the Knave of Cups. This is the card of . . .' Calypso took the book she had brought with her and started to leaf through the pages to get to the right section.

Kelly looked at the two cards. The cards of dependence, she thought. Sapphira seemed not to depend on anyone, she imagined.

Calypso found the right page. 'You need to stop smoking, Sapphira,' she said, looking with disgust at her cigarette smouldering in the ashtray. 'Justice is the card of dependence. Whatever you are doing to your body is bad. This card is about coming out of a bad place and trying to find balance in your life, health, mind, body, spirit. I've got some books I could recommend,' she said earnestly.

Sapphira defiantly picked up the cigarette and took a long drag. 'Tell me something I don't know,' she said good-naturedly.

'The card which covers it is the Knave of Cups. Maybe you

are thinking about a baby? Maybe you want to be pregnant?' asked Calypso, confused. Sapphira appeared to be the least nurturing person she knew. Not mean, but not at all motherly.

Calypso looked to Kelly for guidance. Kelly looked at Sapphira. 'The Knave of Cups is a child, a child of psychic means. Perhaps in the spirit world.' Kelly looked at Sapphira's face for any sign of recognition. It remained impassive but Kelly saw the tiniest twitch of her left eye.

Calypso spoke quickly, thinking she was off the track. 'Anyway, this next card is the card of unconscious – the Knave of Swords.'

Sapphira sat, her eyes smiling at Calypso's absolute conviction.

'The card of unconscious suggests you're playing tricks with yourself. Using your sword unwisely. You fly planes, don't you? You should be careful,' she said, her voice filled with concern.

Kelly looked at the card – the Knave of Swords was about safety. Sapphira lived as though she was a cat with nine lives; that was something everybody knew, but Kelly intuitively knew it was more than just planes. She wondered what Sapphira was playing with which threatened her safety.

Still Sapphira said nothing, so Calypso continued. 'The past card is the death card – someone has died who had a huge impact on you. This could be one of your parents, perhaps?' She looked to Sapphira for affirmation but Sapphira was smoking another cigarette and shrugged.

Kelly spoke up. 'The death card does not mean that it's bad, though. This card suggests the person who died has travelled and has transformed. Reincarnated, if you like. When this person died, something else changed in your life. I don't know what that is, only you do, but it influences everything you do now, good and bad.'

Calypso looked at Kelly and then at Sapphira. 'How is she? Crazy, huh? She's so wise!'

Kelly laughed out loud. 'Easy there, grasshopper, don't worship me. I'm as human as the next person.'

Calypso looked at the next card and opened her book again to the correct page. 'This is the card of the future. The Ace of Cups. A baby perhaps!'

She seemed relieved finally to have something good and tangible for Sapphira's future.

Kelly looked at Sapphira's face, which appeared as though a shadow had crossed it.

Calypso looked at Sapphira excitedly. 'Perhaps you'll find a new lover.' Calypso was unsure whether Sapphira was straight so thought it best to remain gender neutral.

'Perhaps,' said Sapphira noncommittally.

Calypso continued, slightly self-important in her role as esoteric messenger. 'The card of work is the Eight of Cups, which indicates a break from work for a while. Yes, Kelly?'

Kelly nodded.

'Perhaps you'll take a break after this film?' offered Calypso.

Sapphira shrugged again, thinking of the projects slated for her for the next two years. 'Maybe.'

Calypso thought she was boring Sapphira, so hurried through the rest of the cards. 'The card of home and family is the Seven of Swords. This card indicates deception and betrayal from an unreliable person in your life. Someone with a careful plan.' Calypso rushed over this card, not sure what it meant, but Kelly looked at it with interest. Whatever Sapphira was about to face she needed some damned good protection.

'The card of how you expect things to turn out is the Hanged Man – this is seeing things from a new perspective. Clearer and changing your mind.'

Kelly interrupted. 'It's also about dreams, dreams of the future which indicate you will be released from what keeps you in suspended time.'

Sapphira sat still, saying nothing.

Calypso looked at the last card. 'This is the card of how things will actually work out. The Queen of Coins. This is you. This is the card of the mother, someone who is generous to others. It also tells of charity and aid to those who cannot help themselves. Using your energy for the greater good.'

Sapphira butted out the cigarette.

'Did it make sense? The reading?' Calypso asked, her eyes wide.

Sapphira looked as though she was about to speak but stopped herself. Finally she smiled. 'Spot on.'

Calypso breathed a sigh of relief. Sapphira seemed unimpressed but Kelly pondered the cards. Whatever was in Sapphira's past, present and future was murky and painful and made her feel uneasy. Calypso was called to the set for a close-up and Kelly and Sapphira sat in the trailer.

'Is there anything you need to talk to me about, Sapphira? I know we're not close but I worry about you sometimes,' said Kelly, kindness radiating out of her.

Sapphira sat debating whether to share her secrets with Kelly and then quickly put her mask back up. 'I'm not sure I get the tarot, no disrespect meant,' she said in a low voice.

'Nah, that's fine,' said Kelly, getting the message that Sapphira was as guarded as she ever was.

'Just know I'm always around, here or in America, if you need me,' said Kelly getting to her feet.

Sapphira grabbed her arm lightly as Kelly went to walk past her and out of the trailer. 'The card about deception . . .'

'The Seven of Swords.'

'Yes, that one. What does it mean exactly?'

Kelly spoke slowly. She knew there was something Sapphira was hiding but she wasn't sure what it was; it was up to Sapphira to explore and confront what the card meant. 'It's a fear card. It can mean there is something you fear, someone or something.'

Kelly placed her hands on Sapphira's thin shoulders. The energy from Kelly's body resonated through Sapphira and she felt herself involuntarily shudder.

'Good to know,' she said laughing as Kelly walked to the trailer door.

'Be safe, okay?' Kelly said as she left the trailer.

Sapphira nodded and smiled. She was trying, God knows she was trying.

CHAPTER EIGHT

'Hey Slapper, you want to come over and play?' asked Rose down the phone.

'Who is this?' asked Kelly.

'Haha, funny,' said Rose. 'Really, entertain me, let's go out.'

'I can't, I feel so sick,' said Kelly. 'In bed, sorry, and then I have to shoot the night scenes with Calypso tonight,' she moaned.

'You're a shit friend,' said Rose.

'I know. I aim to disappoint.'

'You're succeeding,' said Rose sulkily.

'Go out and do something, you loser,' said Kelly.

'I know. I will, later,' lied Rose as she hung up.

Opening the refrigerator, she picked at the leftover spiced apple and cream but it didn't make her feel better. Instead, she felt restless. Slumping into a kitchen chair, she decided to 'take charge', as her therapist said, and head into town to see what entertainment could be found there. Pulling the Frommers Guidebook to Italy from her handbag, put there by Lauren and which had remained unopened so far, she looked up Perugia. Leafing through, she spotted the Galleria Nazionale, the home of the finest collection of Umbrian art in the world. Why not, she thought and rang her driver and asked him to be ready for her in 30 minutes.

Climbing upstairs, she had a shower and dressed in a black linen Phillip Lim sundress and a pair of black and white Chanel ballet flats. Pulling her hair back into a low bun, she applied tinted moisturizer with SPF 20 and sun block on her arms and legs. Running downstairs, she threw on her Fendi sunglasses and her panama hat, grabbed her green Lavin tote bag and jumped in her car.

Driving through the countryside, Rose was enthralled by the timeless quality to the houses, olive groves and vineyards. She waved at an elderly man pushing a wheelbarrow down the road. He tipped his cloth cap at her as she sailed past in the Mercedes.

Pulling up the Corso Vanucci, the car stopped and the driver told Rose she would have to walk the rest of the way on foot, as there were no cars allowed on the old roads and pathways. Entering the Galleria, Rose was soothed by the quietness and the coolness of the building. Taking a map from a sleepy guard, who did not seem to recognize her, she stood and decided what route to take.

As she stood assessing the map, she heard voices in the quiet space and looked up to see a man with three little boys trailing after him. Rose smiled as she watched the smallest one with a blue drink bottle in his hand stop and touch a marble statue in the entranceway. She watched his small hands feeling the cold stone as she looked up at the statue of a woman on her knees. The boy's father and brothers walked away but the small boy stayed at the side of the statue. Rose walked over to him.

'Do you like the feel of the marble?' she asked him in a gentle voice.

'It's cold,' said the boy, looking at her, and Rose felt her heart open at the sight of his little face, so earnest and trusting.

'Yes,' said Rose, reaching out to touch the woman.

'Why is she so sad?' asked the boy.

74

Rose read the description of the statue. 'Assetata,' she said aloud. 'She's thirsty,' she explained.

'She needs a drink,' said the boy, looking at the drink bottle in his hand.

'She does,' said Rose gravely.

'Milo, hurry up.' Rose turned to see the boy's father in the distance of the gallery standing impatiently.

Milo ran towards his father and Rose watched him run, carefully hanging onto his drink. Rose walked in the other direction of the family, wondering where the mother was. Hopefully getting some much needed rest from the challenge of three boys and a grumpy father, she laughed to herself as she wandered the rooms.

In Room Three, the earliest paintings and artifacts were housed, showing the start of 13th century Perugian art. Wandering through the rooms, drinking in the history and creativity was Rose's idea of heaven. Her knowledge of European art was extensive, but not Italian art and certainly not as far back as the 13th century.

Facing Duccio di Buoninsegna's depiction of the *Madonna and Child*, with the six tiny angels watching them from above, Rose wondered if she would ever have a child of her own. She was aware time was running out for her on the fertility front. It didn't matter what medicine did to stop the aging process, the plain fact was that if you wanted to get pregnant naturally then you had to do it when you were young. Facing her fortieth birthday in six months, Rose was keenly aware of her biological clock ticking like a time bomb inside her.

As she turned to walk into the next room, she heard the sound of running feet. Milo ran into the room, his little round face streaming with tears. As he ran towards her, he tripped on his shoelace and went sprawling in front of Rose onto his face, landing at her feet.

'Oh dear, what a big fall! Come on, let's get up.'

The child was sobbing quietly, a sound Rose recognized from her niece and nephew, one that a child makes when they have really hurt themselves.

'Ups a daisy. Come on now.' Rose sat on the wooden bench in the centre of the room and lifted the child onto her lap. 'Come on, let's have a look at you then.'

Assessing the child, she saw he had blood coming out of his mouth. Opening his mouth gently she saw he had bitten his tongue but no teeth seemed to be damaged. Rose waited for his parents to arrive, assuming they would be chasing after him, but the room stayed silent. The child nestled his head into her neck and she heard his breathing slow down and his sobs quietly ease away.

'There you are, getting better? I have just the pill to make you tip-top in no time,' she said, remembering the packet of barley sugar she had in her bag that she had brought to suck on when her plane took off. Taking out a piece she unwrapped it. 'Open wide,' she said and the child obediently did so.

Popping the sweet into his mouth, he put his head back on her chest and sucked contentedly. Looking up at the *Madonna and Child* hanging on the wall in front of her, she sent a little prayer up to the Patron Saint of Mothers to send her own little child to her one day.

'Milo, bloody hell, we have been looking for you everywhere. You're bloody hopeless, I'm very cross with you.' A man came into the room, followed by two older boys, about six and eight.

Hearing his father's voice, Milo started to cry again and clung to Rose.

76

'I just wanted to give her a drink,' he whispered in Rose's ear.

Rose was unsure what he was saying and was about to ask him when the child's father interrupted again.

'You cannot run away from me, do you understand, do you?' the father said, tearing the child away from Rose's body and standing in front of him. Towering over the child, the man's face was flushed. The two other boys looked at the floor.

'Dominic and Jasper have been searching everywhere, as have I. Not good enough, Milo, really! Hopeless, hopeless, and where's your drink bottle? You've lost that also, I see,' said the man.

The small child stood frightened and shaking. 'And now you've bloody wet yourself. Jesus Christ, Milo! Can't you do anything right? When we get home, you will spend the rest of the day in your room. Do you understand me?'

Rising from the bench, Rose stood in front of the man. 'Excuse me . . .' she began.

The man snapped his head around to look at her. 'Yes?' he said, his voice slightly menacing. Rose recognized an English accent and thought she knew him from somewhere but wasn't sure. Was he an actor? A politician? She stopped trying to place him when she looked at the small child's face in front of her.

'It's not his fault he wet himself . . .' Rose smiled at the child who was clearly traumatized.

'Really? Well, if he had listened to me when I said he needed to go to the toilet then he wouldn't be here all wet and embarrassing himself, would he?'

Rose tried again, 'Well, accidents happen, nothing that can't be fixed.'

'Are you going to fix it? No? No. I'll have to fucking fix it, as I always have to fix everything. Always up to me, and what

77

do I get from them? Nothing. Just more fucking jobs to do and nothing in return. Christ! You're all bloody useless.' He directed this to not only the children, but also Rose.

Where her rage came from, Rose wasn't sure. Was it because he had blasphemed in front of the *Madonna and Child*, or was it because she felt so motherly towards this little boy? Or was it that his words reminded her of Paul, yelling at her, telling her she was hopeless and then ignoring her as this man wanted to do to the small child?

'You're a bully. No wonder he ran away from you. I don't blame him. I'd want to run away from you, too. And as for wetting his pants, well . . .' She looked down at Milo and held his hand.

'I would have wet myself too, if you had yelled at me that way, and I'm a lot older than him. You should be ashamed of yourself!' she shouted. 'I'm sure their mother would be shocked if she saw the way you speak to them. I think I should meet her or at least discuss your bullying of these kids or is she just like you also?' Rose challenged.

'Well, good luck, because she's dead!' the man shouted back at her.

Rose saw the middle child start to cry now. She felt awful but this man was too much for anyone to bear. She composed herself and put on her sunglasses. 'Well, I suggest you get some therapy, for you first and then for the children just so they can have some strategies to learn to live with you.'

Bending down, she took Milo's face in her hands. 'Don't worry about anything. Your tongue will heal and you will have an excellent excuse to eat yummy Italian gelato now. Never mind about wetting yourself. I wet myself all the time till I was seven. No shame in it, many clever people wet their pants,' she said confidently and Milo looked up at her, his eyes wide.

Milo smiled shyly and Rose stood up. 'Goodbye, boys,' she directed at the children as she walked out of the room.

The man picked up the little boy and hugging him close, he cried, 'I am so sorry, Milo Schmilo. I'm so sorry. Don't run away again, okay? Daddy promises to be nicer, I just get a bit sad and angry sometimes.'

Milo nodded and put his arms around his neck. 'She smelt nice, Daddy.'

He looked at the door she had just exited through. This was going to be complicated, he thought.

Rose, still shaking, headed down to the bathroom in the entrance of the gallery. Composing herself in front of the mirror, Rose was surprised at the venom in her outburst to the man. She did feel awful mentioning their mother but she justified it to herself when she remembered the trauma on Milo's face.

As she walked out of the bathroom, she glanced at the sculpture where she had first spoken to Milo and saw a flash of blue she hadn't seen before. At the woman's feet was Milo's drink bottle that he had carefully carried before.

Rose felt like crying. Bless him, she thought, the little man had given the thirsty woman his drink. She closed her eyes for a moment to control the tears that threatened and picked up the drink bottle and put it into her bag.

Driving back to her villa, she was shocked at how angry she still felt, but realized she was happy to have not had children with Paul. No doubt that's how he would have spoken to their child if she had let him. She could still feel the warmth of the little boy's body on her lap. 'He smelt nice,' she said to no one in particular and she took the drink bottle out of her bag and placed it in the cupholder of the car. It looked right, she thought, the clash of the cheap plastic against the luxury of the car. God, how she wanted her own child's drink bottle in her life, she thought. More than anything else in the world.

CHAPTER NINE

Calypso was having trouble keeping her co-star's hands off her while filming and she figured if anyone had advice, it would be Sapphira.

Calypso sat on her sofa in the trailer drinking her spirulina shake.

'Hmm, smells like toxic waste to me,' said Sapphira, waving away the drink Calypso offered her.

'He's gross,' said Calypso, sipping her drink, which left a faint green moustache on her top lip. 'I swear he had a hard-on today when we were shooting and I'm pretty sure he wanted me to know it.'

'Got waste?' she asked, in reference to the famous milk ads showing stars with milk on their upper lip. Sapphira had shot one years ago and it still made her laugh when she thought about the shoot, trying to get the paste which supposedly resembled milk onto her lip.

'What?' asked Calypso, confused.

'Your lip, babe. It's green,' said Sapphira, lighting another cigarette with the one she was smoking.

Calypso, embarrassed, rubbed her mouth with the back of her hand. Sapphira was like the cool older sister she never had and spending time with her had made her realize how much she wished she had siblings to deflect Leeza's focus and to share things with.

'Raphael's a fucking asshole,' said Sapphira, frowning. 'I met him at Cannes last year. He was promoting some movie but it was more like he was promoting himself.'

'I know a lot of actors like that,' laughed Calypso.

Sapphira paused. 'Listen, I'm not one for gossip and I hate to be indiscreet, but he is bad news. I'm surprised TG cast him. He's seriously fucked up,' she said as she checked the text message that rang through on her cell phone.

'Now you have to tell me,' said Calypso, her eyes widening. Sapphira shook her head. 'Come on, just give me something so I know what I'm up against.'

Sapphira put down her phone and thought for a moment. 'Just watch him, okay? Don't get caught up in the charm. He's a snake.'

Calypso heeded Sapphira's warning and was careful around Raphael. Whatever Sapphira had intimated was enough for Calypso to be aloof on set and keep him at arm's length, which was no easy feat. He flirted constantly with her. She tried to be pleasant but he was wearing and trying her patience.

The chemistry between them was not evident on the shoot and TG was at a loss to understand why Calypso was being almost rude to Raphael, who seemed to be trying hard to win her over. This shoot was harder than he had thought. Shooting on location, they were at the mercy of the weather, the planes flying overhead and the ants that crawled up the actors' legs and bit them.

That morning on set, Calypso was constantly slapping her legs, as the ants seemed immune to insect repellant. In fact, she thought they preferred it.

TG walked over to her. 'Calypso, you have to stop slapping your legs. All I can see is red hand marks up and down your thighs. It looks like you've been beaten up.'

'I can't help it, it's these fucking ants,' she said, slapping her leg again.

'Okay, let me deal with it.' He called out to the second assistant director. 'Can you find the fucking ants' nest and pour coffee down it, please? Do something about the ants!'

The assistant director, who was Italian, laughed outrageously. 'You not get rid of the ants, TG. Impossible.' He kept laughing like TG had just told the funniest joke in the world.

TG stomped back to his chair. Calypso tried in vain not to slap her leg. Standing with a grimace, TG looked up, and walked back over to her. He looked at her legs, reached down and flicked the soft white skin inside her thigh. 'Ow!' she yelled.

'Maybe you should flick them off instead of slapping, okay?'

'Jesus, ow, okay, that hurt,' she said, rubbing her leg.

'Sorry,' said TG, not really meaning it. He didn't know why he was angry with Calypso. Because she largely ignored him, was rude to Raphael. Always running off set as soon as filming started to be with that Italian he had seen on set occasionally.

He walked back to his chair again. He could still feel her soft skin on his fingertips.

Calypso stood confused. Was he physically abusing her now? What an asshole, she thought.

The day's shoot was tense, to say the least, and Calypso was happy when it was finished. As she walked over to her car, Raphael ran up to her. 'Tonight I come to town, you show me a good time.'

'Ah no, I have plans,' said Calypso wearily. She wished he would return to his villa or Rome, whichever was easier.

'What are your plans? I can come,' he said as though his presence was a gift.

Inwardly Calypso groaned. The last thing she needed was

this guy sharing her car and trying to hit on her all the way back to the hotel. 'Umm . . . I'm seeing my boyfriend.' she started.

'You have a boyfriend? Ah, I want to meet the man who vies for my love,' he said dramatically, jumping in the front next to the driver.

Calypso got in the back, relieved she wouldn't have his roaming hands all over her. Surprisingly, he didn't speak to her at all on the way back, talking in rapid-fire Italian to her driver, and her driver talking just as fast back and gesticulating wildly. Calypso prayed he would keep his hands on the wheel and get her back to Marco alive.

Calypso's relationship with Marco was all the talk of the set. He visited her and brought her flowers, much to TG's chagrin, hanging about and talking to the Italian crew. He and Calypso went out with his friends almost every night and even spent time with his parents on their farm, looking for white truffles in the woods, with no success. What had been successful was the sex they had on the floor of the woods, with Calypso never having felt as free before in the open air, abandoning herself to Marco and the nature all around her. None of the boys back home had been so passionate and intense as him. He was insatiable; he wanted her constantly and made her feel incredible.

After he'd asked her so many questions about America one night as they lay in her hotel bed, she suggested he move there to find out for himself what America was like.

'No, no,' he said as he kissed the tip of her nose. 'I will never leave Italy. This is my home. Perhaps I will visit.'

Inside Calypso was disappointed; she knew he wouldn't want to move there. But in her fantasy, she imagined him being a hotshot LA lawyer, her being a successful actress and

84

presenting the Best Foreign Film nominations at the Oscars and being able to say the Italian nomination flawlessly.

Listening to the hysterical laughter of her co-star and the driver, she wondered what they were laughing so hard at. What could be that funny?

The car pulled up in front of the hotel and the doorman opened the door for Calypso. She saw Marco waiting for her, leaning against the front wall. '*Ciao, bella*,' he said sexily. Calypso felt her insides melting, perhaps she loved him, she thought.

The doorman opened up the front passenger door and Raphael jumped out. Seeing Raphael, Marco was instantly star-stuck. Rushing over and shaking his hand and talking in Italian, he gesticulated and pointed to Calypso.

'I didn't know that Raphael Perini was in this movie. He is my favourite actor. I love him,' he said earnestly to her.

Calypso smiled thinly. Perhaps if he knew what an utter dick Raphael was, then he wouldn't be so in love, she thought.

Raphael, always ready to greet a fan, grabbed Calypso around the shoulders. 'It is decided then, we shall break bread together tonight.'

Calypso frowned. She wanted Marco all to herself, not to share him with this self-lover of the highest order.

That night they all ate together at a local bar. Every ten minutes someone came to the table to say hello or get an autograph from Raphael. He was like a god and the Italians were his worshippers. Marco and Raphael spoke Italian most of the night and occasionally interpreted for Calypso, when they remembered she was there.

Towards the end of the dinner, Marco pulled out his phone, rang two numbers and spoke fast down the phone. Calypso looked at him, questioning him with her eyes. 'I've rung some friends. They will come and meet us and then we will drink, *si*?'

'Not for me. I've gotta shoot tomorrow and we have to be on set at 6.30 am,' she said, looking at Raphael.

'*Si si*, but one drink. Come on, *bella*.'

She looked at Marco. He was not paying any attention to her, just looking at Raphael in adoration. Calypso sighed. 'Well, I'm going back to the hotel. Good night.'

She left the bar, expecting Marco to come after her but deep down knowing he wouldn't. She had been usurped by Raphael and she was pissed off. Heading back down the road to her hotel, Calypso was surprised how she felt. She really liked Marco; in fact, she thought she could even love him. His parents loved her and, let's face it, the sex was incredible. Now he seemed like a fawning loser. Fuck it, she thought as she went up to her hotel room. I'll talk to him tomorrow.

After taking a long bath and drinking a chamomile tea, Calypso hopped into bed. It seems too big without Marco, she thought drowsily, as she dropped off to sleep.

She was woken by a loud knocking at the door. She opened her eyes and looked at the clock next to her bedside – 1.00 am. 'Fuck!' she said as she went to the door. 'Who is it?' she called, not fully awake.

'*Ciao, bella*,' she heard.

Marco! Padding over in the dark, she stubbed her toe on a chair. 'Oww,' she cried, hopping on one foot. Opening the door, her foot throbbing in pain, she hobbled back to the bed and jumped under the covers, lying on her stomach. 'It's late, don't talk to me. I have to be up in three hours,' she said as she started to drop off to sleep again.

She heard him undressing and felt the covers pull back and

86

him start to caress her back. 'Hmm, that's nice, but I'm really tired, baby.'

He continued, rubbing her back and buttocks. She felt her legs spread open involuntarily. He placed his fingers down between her thighs and started to feel her. She was wet and ready. Climbing on top of her, he entered her from behind, slowly thrusting and grinding. 'Mmmmm,' she said sexily.

He pulled her up onto her knees and then leant down and held her breasts, fucking her harder and harder until Calypso felt uncomfortable. He started to slap her ass and pulled back on her hair. 'Yeah, *puttana*, you like it!' he cried.

And then he came. Calypso turned around, shocked. In the darkness, she could just make out that it was not Marco who had just fucked her but Raphael. 'What the fuck are you doing?' she screamed. 'Oh my God!' She started to cry, pulling the bed sheet up around her.

Raphael got up off the bed, the semen dripping from his cock. 'What do you mean? You knew it was me when you opened the door naked.'

'I thought you were Marco,' she said, crying on the bed.

'Well, Marco said you were a great fuck and he was right. He said the American *puttana* will do anything. I like American girls.'

'Get out, get out! I'm calling the police, get out!'

Raphael picked up his clothes. 'You liked it,' he said arrogantly.

'Get out!' she yelled again and threw him out into the hallway naked.

She sat back on the bed, sobbing. She knew she should call the police but she could not deal with the intrusion. Once the press got wind of this in America she would be exposed as a slut and her career ruined. She started to shake, uncontrollably. Who could she ring? Not her mother. Maybe Rose or Kelly?

The thought of being on set with him in the morning made her start to vomit. She rushed to the bathroom but didn't make it, throwing up all over the floor next to the bed. Picking up her phone, she dialled the one number she knew would answer.

'Hello? TG? I need you.'

CHAPTER TEN

Aware she had spent much of her time in Italy by herself, Sapphira was looking forward to meeting her co-star. Jack Reynolds was a big star. He was a renowned bachelor who spent part of the year in LA and part in Italy. Speaking flawless Italian, he was a spokesperson for Brioni suits and Longines watches, and had been voted Sexiest Man of the Year for the past three years. Jack was the male equivalent of Sapphira, according to one of the biggest gossip magazines back in the States. He worked only when he wanted to and chose his projects carefully. The role TG had offered him was perfect – a script which promised to create celluloid history, acting opposite one of the biggest female stars of the time and shooting in his beloved adopted country was an offer Jack could not pass up.

His affairs always made the news and he had dated many beautiful young women from all over the world, always brunettes and never for longer than a year. He never spoke about his love life, instead making witty and occasionally ironic comments about the celebrity fascination and culture. He was due on set that morning. Jack arrived on time and chatted freely with the crew, switching from Italian to English effort-lessly. Sapphira came on to the set, walking like a panther and as if Jack was her prey.

'Hello, I'm Sapphira De Mont. I'm surprised we haven't yet worked together.'

'Jack, it's a pleasure to meet you, Sapphira.' He looked at her bemused, and stuck out his hand for her to shake it.

She leaned over and kissed each cheek while pressing herself against him. He stood, his head cocked to one side, his greying temples glinting in the sun.

'Well, let's get to work,' he said and turned on his heel and walked to TG, where he proceeded to spend the next thirty minutes discussing character and plot.

For all his playboy reputation, Jack was a professional in every sense of the word, and when Sapphira sat in the make-up chair, she wondered about his reaction to her.

'Is Jack dating anyone?' she asked Kelly as she dabbed on her pancake base.

'Nope, just broke up with a Swiss TV presenter. No word from her yet. I thought she may sell her story to *National Enquirer* and the like, but I haven't heard a thing.'

Sapphira's reputation preceded her, and Kelly and Chris had a bet on to see how long before Sapphira and Jack were an item, at least for the remaining duration of the shoot.

Sapphira wondered if perhaps Jack was heartbroken. Not fucking likely, she thought.

Walking into the trailer, Jack kissed Kelly, whom he had worked with before and sat next to Sapphira. She knew she looked good in the chair, make-up flawless and artfully applied. Her hair was long and out. She was wearing a strapless black dress, showing off her tattoos and her tanned skin. She was the kind of woman who knew what she wanted and Jack was in her sights. She smiled at him in the mirror. He smiled back and pulled out a copy of the local newspaper, *La Nazione* and started to read it, much to Sapphira's shock.

The assistant director knocked on the door. 'All ready, Sapphira? TG wants to do your close-up, then Jack's. We'll be ready for you.'

'See you then,' said Jack from the depths of his paper.

Sapphira stood up, unnerved. Heading onto the set, she went through the motions of the close-up, standing patiently while they sorted out the angles and focus measurements for the camera. I'll just have to work harder, she thought, having never yet given up on a challenge. This is what she felt the best at, luring her man in on her long line.

TG came on set soon after with Jack and talked them through their first scene. They were inside the Villa and in the kitchen set. 'Ok, so I need you, Sapphira, to have your bare feet up on the table and Jack, you come in. Sapphira, your eyes are shut for this scene. You are worn out from working on the Villa all day. Jack, you rub her shoulders and then you say the lines. Want to rehearse it first for marks?'

'Nope,' said Jack. 'I think we are good.' He smiled at Sapphira, who responded to him with one of her million-dollar laughs.

'Whatever you want, Jacky boy.'

'Action.' Called TG from off set.

Jack came through the door and saw Sapphira with her feet on the table but instead of walking around behind her he sat down at her feet, saying his lines. He started to give her foot a rub.

Sapphira stayed in character and kept her eyes shut while Jack rubbed her feet. He said his lines and she responded.

'Cut,' yelled TG.

Jack stood up. 'I just felt he would rub her feet since it's the first thing he sees when he walks into the room.'

'Yeah fine, worked well from our angle. Let's do it again for different shots, ok?'

Sapphira was panicking. Had he noticed her feet? She had tried hard to cover the track marks but did he know what they were?

She looked at him. He seemed not to notice anything unusual about her feet. They waited for the camera to move. 'Sorry about my disgusting feet,' she said arching her long foot. 'They are covered in ant bites,' she explained, laughing.

Jack didn't look at her. 'You take care of yourself Sapphira, ok?'

'Of course, I always do, Jacky boy.' She threw her head back again and laughed. This is what she felt the best at, luring her man in on her long line.

When her close-up had been shot, and Jack had come on set for his, she sauntered towards him. 'Why don't we meet tonight, Jack? I can come to your place and we can discuss characters, trade war stories, whatever . . .' The open invitation hung heavily in the air.

'I don't think so. I don't play with the talent.' This was true, Jack always played with talent lower than him on the celebrity radar; he was always the racehorse and his new girlfriend was always the donkey. Of course, this wasn't disrespectful but Jack's ego and celebrity were too big for two stars, and Sapphira would be too huge a star to orbit. The pressure of them pairing up might bring the kind of publicity that opened closet doors and let the skeletons out, and this was the last thing Jack wanted.

'That is the saddest thing I've ever heard. You are breaking my heart, Mr Reynolds.'

'I'm sure it will mend, Ms De Mont,' he said, laughing.

Sapphira felt herself relax. She refused to see not seducing Jack as failure. Instead, she understood his rules. She had her own set of rules she conducted her life by; there was a part of her which respected him.

'Thanks for being honest, I guess.' There was something genuine and honourable about Jack; she felt she could trust him.

'Friends?' asked Jack.

'I guess, I don't really have men as friends.'

'What? Just for breakfast?' Jack laughed at his own joke and Sapphira joined in.

Sapphira was quiet. 'You want to know something?'

'Sure,' said Jack not looking up.

'Today is my birthday. Please don't say anything to anyone. I just wanted you to know.' She stared into the distance, her face expressionless.

'I am assuming then, there won't be a party,' Jack said, picking up on the change in Sapphira's mood. 'Well, have you heard from anyone? Family? Agent, at least? They're always good for a useless gift and a sycophantic card.'

'My father's dead. My mother might as well be, we haven't spoken in about eight years. As for my agent, he will ring tomorrow no doubt, being ignorant of the time delay.'

Staring out at the crew busying themselves, a warm breeze blew over them and took Sapphira's mood with it. 'Doesn't matter, age is just a state of mind anyway.'

'Do you worry about being older?' asked Jack.

'Never. I suppose I think about everything I want to do and I panic, as there's never enough time. There's so much to learn, to see, to experience.'

'Amelia Earhart, look out, huh? Next thing you will need to learn is how to fly and you can see the world at your own leisure.'

'I already know how to fly. I learned at the start of this year.'

'Of course you did, why am I not surprised?' he said as he crossed his legs. 'I tell you what, I'm gonna break my own rule. I will throw you birthday dinner. I'll send my car to pick you up at 6.00 pm. We finish early today, which will give us plenty of time.'

'Six? I thought everyone ate later in Italy.'

'Well, I want to take you somewhere special,' he answered enigmatically. 'A surprise, stay tuned, Amelia.'

Sapphira thought of another night in her library, reading and smoking and then thought of an evening with Jack. 'It's a date!'

'Friends, remember?'

'I remember,' said Sapphira. 'You have nothing to worry about. Your virtue is safe with me, Mr Reynolds.' And she stood up and went to the set for her next close-up.

That evening, she was dressed for sex. She wore a Blumarine leopard print silk strapless dress, with huge Moroccan wooden bangles she had picked up on her last shoot in Marrakesh and a pair of Yves Saint Laurent black suede ankle boots. Her hair was swept back into a bun, high on her head, and she wore minimal make-up and a liberal amount of her customized Lyn Harris perfume, leaving a trail of amber, musk and jasmine.

The helicopter that picked her up in Perugia landed at Nicelli Airport at 7.10 pm and Sapphira was whisked straight into a waiting water limousine and taken through the canals towards Jack. Venice was spectacular. The sun was still up and the canals were busy. The white, navy trimmed leather seats and the mahogany panelled walls and tinted windows gave her complete privacy to watch Venice without any interruption or distraction. It truly was an amazing city, she thought, as they sailed down the Grand Canal.

There was a bottle of French Champagne on the small mahogany table with a note written by Jack – *Happy birthday, Amelia, enjoy the ride.*

Pouring herself a glass, she sat forward on her chair and enjoyed the view. The buildings and people floated past her and Sapphira imagined for a moment she was in a magical land filled with the most wonderful buildings the human mind could create, all floating and rocking their inhabitants to sleep each night.

Soon, they turned off the canal and the boat came to a stop. Sapphira heard the captain speaking Italian and then the door opened. She alighted and was standing on the edge of the canal in front of huge carved wooden doors, which opened. Jack stood with his arms open. 'Happy birthday, kid!'

Sapphira walked into them and kissed him on both cheeks. 'Howdy, Jack. Look at this place.'

The palazzo was impressive. Built in the 15th century, it was one of the largest private residences in Venice. Spread over five floors, the palazzo had a perfect view of the Bridge of Sighs and a roof garden for the summer.

Jack was dressed in white linen pants, a black t-shirt and barefoot. His ease in his own home made him all the more attractive to Sapphira. He led her into the huge sitting room, with its high ceilings and three Murano glass chandeliers. The room was filled with antique and contemporary furniture and art. It was Jack in every way – elegant, stylish and urbane.

'Venetian?' said Jack as he opened up an art deco cabinet to reveal a fully stocked bar with every possible bottle of liquor imaginable.

'I'm assuming that's a drink,' asked Sapphira, as she prowled the room studying its contents.

'Yep. Campari, gin, vermouth, amaretto and a twist of lemon.'

'I thought the Bellini was the Venetian cocktail of choice?' said Sapphira as she stood back from a large Francis Bacon painting.

'The Bellini is the choice of tourists, although it is a lovely drink on a hot night on the roof, but not too often.'

'Are you a snob, Mr Reynolds? Are you not a tourist in this lovely country?' Sapphira flirted with him as she crossed the floor to accept the drink he was bringing to her.

'I may be a tourist to the Italians, but it feels like home to me. I love this place more than America, though I would never say so in an interview. The people, the history, the contradictions are what appeal to me. I like being so close to Europe and I like being out of the craziness of the US. Here, a celebrity is someone on TV or a politician or a model. Some American movie star means nothing to them and I'm just fine with that.'

Sapphira looked at his ease and relaxed demeanour and thought he had never looked more attractive. It was as though he was a drug and she wanted more of it, his contentment and satisfaction with life almost an elixir. Sapphira was hooked.

'Grab your drink and I'll give you a tour,' he said.

Leading the way, he walked Sapphira through each level, with a story to tell about his art and furniture, the parties he had thrown there and the peace he felt when he heard the water at night. Finishing on the roof, Sapphira was entranced by the view and the sounds below of the water city.

'Your life is very agreeable, sir,' she said, sipping her drink. 'You live how you want and you do what you want. I admire you.'

'Let's go back down now and talk shit, then we will eat, yes? Then later we can go out for a twilight tour of the canals. It's amazing, it never stops.'

Sapphira smiled, but she knew she was ready for another hit. 'It sounds wonderful. I might just use your bathroom, if you don't mind.'

'No problem, use the one downstairs I just showed you and then I will meet you back down where you originally came in. If you get lost, just holler and I'll come with a search party.'

Walking with Sapphira down the stairs, he left her at the bathroom and then went down to fix more drinks.

Sapphira entered the bathroom and noticed there was no lock on the door. Fuck, she thought. Opening her bag, she pulled out her works and set up. She had been craving more than usual; this happened sometimes but she was careful, writing down in her little notebook when and what she had taken last.

Checking her book, she fixed up the hit and hitching up her dress, injected herself into her groin. The hit was instant; she felt the rush as she sat on the toilet. Maybe she had taken a little more than last time, she wondered, as she felt her legs heavy. She tried to get up but couldn't stand. I'll wait for a while and then I'll go down, she thought. Sitting on the toilet with her head on her chest, the sleepiness was too much to bear and she gave in.

'Sapphira, Sapphira, you need to walk, you need to walk. Come on, baby.'

She heard the voice in the distance but he seemed so far away. She shook her head; whoever it was speaking was annoying her. Come on. She felt herself moving. How? Did she have wings? Laughing to herself, she heard the voice again. 'It's not funny. Come on, goddammit, walk.'

He walked her around the room, up and down, up and down, until her head began to clear a little and she became more conscious of her surroundings. 'Jack?'

'Who the fuck else would it be?'

'What happened?'

'Well, I'm not sure, you tell me?' The sarcasm was stinging in his voice. 'You never came back down. I went to find you and found you asleep with a fucking needle sticking out of your cunt. Nice, Sapphira, nice. What the fuck were you shooting up in my house for? I mean, what the fuck?'

Jack was angry and Sapphira remembered visiting the bathroom.

'I thought I was only there a little while . . .' Sapphira was standing on her own now. Jack let go of her and crossed the floor to the bar and poured a straight scotch. He drained it in one mouthful then spat at her. 'You're a fucking junkie? How the hell did that happen?'

Sapphira felt ashamed of her addiction for the first time. Having hidden it so well for so long, she had never had to deal with the confrontation and the seedier side of admitting she was actually an addict. Picking up her bag and shoes, she walked towards the door of the palazzo and then she stopped. 'You are so fucking judgmental,' she said furiously. 'You have no idea what it's like to live with this and have to feed it. I started because I hurt from something and now it hurts too much to stop. If I could I would but I don't know how, so don't stand there in your perfect fucking playboy of Venice world and treat me like some pariah. You are so far removed from people with problems you have lost your heart. You are all style and no substance.'

The tears flowed down her cheeks and she felt alone and afraid. She turned on her bare feet and walked out the door. Standing alone on the side of the canal, holding her bag and shoes, it was now dark. She pulled out her phone and checked the time – 9.25 pm! Jesus. Maybe she could get to a hotel and get back to Umbria tomorrow?

Looking up the canal, she wondered if you waved to taxis like you did in New York. Christ! She heard the door open behind her and Jack was standing there.

'Get your skinny ass inside, Amelia, and we will work this

shit out, okay? I was a judgmental son of a bitch and I've ruined your birthday high. Come in and we will talk. *Sì?*'

Taking his hand, she fell into his arms and they hugged tightly. 'I am so sorry,' she whispered into his chest.

'I know,' he said as he rubbed her bare shoulders.

Kissing her on her forehead, he opened the door and led her through.

Across in the building opposite, the lone paparazzo could not believe his luck. He had visited Venice for a wedding and thought he would head past Jack Reynolds' palazzo on a whim in hope he would see him, knowing the chances were slim as Jack was very private. Waiting only fifteen minutes, he saw a lovers' tiff between Sapphira De Mont and Jack Reynolds. These pictures were going to make huge money and be across the world within twelve hours.

Jack and Sapphira walked inside and she slumped on the sofa; she was tired and emotional. 'All right, so first things first. You'll have to stay here tonight and you cannot possibly walk around in a slip of silk and no underwear, it's not decent. Come with me,' he said and took them in the lift to the third floor.

Opening up the first door they came to, Sapphira walked into a bedroom, all white, minimalist and comforting at the same time. The only decoration in the room was a huge Venetian mirror, so old the patina was worn in places. The reflection that stared back at Sapphira was hazy. Or was that her eyes? She wasn't sure and she felt terrible.

Jack crossed the room and opened the first door. 'Bathroom, everything you need will be in there.' He opened the door next to it. 'Clothes, take what you need. When you are done, come down. I've taken your kit, so don't even try, we'll discuss this when you're ready.'

He was strong with her but kind, which Sapphira appreciated. She was not an overly emotional person and responded to common sense and facts more than sentimentality.

Jack left the room and Sapphira looked in the closet. There were Juicy Couture tracksuits in several colours and several sizes. A Stella McCartney black dress. Underwear, socks, a few white Calvin Klein t-shirts and several pairs of Chanel ballet flats in varying sizes.

Sapphira pulled out the black track pants and top and a white t-shirt. Taking a pair of La Perla cotton underpants, she dressed and slipped on some black ankle socks. Weird, she thought, that he would have all of this. Maybe it's from his last girlfriend.

The bathroom was more of a surprise. The cupboard was stocked with an entire range of Kiehl's. The drawers were filled with the entire range of Nars make-up and there were hair straighteners, a blow drier, brushes and hair ties.

Sapphira washed her face and moisturized it. Brushing her hair, she tied it back in a bun and looked at herself. Not quite the image she was hoping to impress Jack with, but what the hell.

Taking the lift downstairs, she entered the lounge where Jack was standing, looking out the window.

Hearing her come in, he turned. His face was emotionless. 'Time to talk, Amelia. Spill. You tell me your dirty little secrets and I'll tell you mine. This way we'll be even. *Si*?'

'I don't know what to say to you. I'm sorry,' she said shamefully, her arms crossed over her chest.

Jack walked across to Sapphira and sat opposite her in the armchair. 'There is nothing you can say which will shock me and nothing you say I will judge. I'm sorry for being so rough on you. The truth is, I had a lover many years ago who struggled with addiction. They fought it on and off for years. They were clean for quite a while but then got the urge and took a shot but took too much, forgot you can't take the amount you used to take when you used regularly. I found them with a needle in their arm and dead in our bed.'

Sapphira was shocked. She knew of people outside her circle who had overdosed but no one close to her. 'I didn't know that, I'm sorry.'

'Well, no one knows. It was the saddest time in my life and now I live for both of us. This is why I live the way I do. Life is too short to waste and when you stick a needle in your arm, you are wasting it. You have so much to offer, Sapphira, more than just the acting. Your talent and celebrity could do great things and perhaps, if you got clean, you could do something amazing. I feel you could, I know you could.'

While he spoke, Sapphira started to cry silently, not even aware the tears were running down her face. Then she started to sob and wail as all the years of pain poured out of her. Jack came and sat, holding her shaking body. 'I know, I know, we can do it together. I can help you, trust me to help you.'

Finally she spoke. 'I started ten years ago, I thought I could control it. I thought it was just to help me sleep. I have these dreams, these terrible dreams and the sleep comes when I take it. I know it's crazy but it's the truth.'

'What are the dreams about?'

'Nothing and everything.'

'I understand,' said Jack sympathetically.

'I want to get off, I want to but I'm so afraid the dreams will come back.'

'I think we are dealing with two different issues here. The

101

addiction and the dreams need to be dealt with differently. I can help you with the heroin. Let's do that first and see what happens with the dreams, okay?'

'I can't get off now, I'm in the middle of a film, Christ!'

Sapphira was becoming angry with Jack and his easy approach to something she had struggled with for the last five years. She stood up and walked to the huge, arched window and looked out over the canal.

'I'm not saying now, but soon. If you stay here and do it, I can ensure privacy and can get you the best help in Europe. You can't do it in the States. Those rehab centres are crawling with staff who leak to the media.'

'What if I do get off, what have I got then? Who am I without this? Everything I do is to get the next hit. I fill my time with things to learn when I feel good but then I go down again. I know what you're saying, I know I could do more with my life but not like this. I'm just so afraid. I feel like the smack is who I am. Does that make sense?' Pacing the room now, she continued, not waiting for his answer. 'I live a lie and I'm tired of it, tired of hiding it and freaking out all the time. When you massaged my feet on set, I was sure you would see the track marks between my toes. It's so hard to cover myself and I look at what I project and what I really am and I hate myself. Do you have any idea what it's like, Jack, do you? You live this free and easy life, Mr Fucking Playboy movie star, and have no idea what it's like to live a lie like this. It wears you down, you can trust no one. Do you hear me? No one. I don't even know if I can trust you. It's just fucked, completely fucked.'

Jack sighed. 'Sapphira, I've more idea about this than you realize. Things are never quite what they seem. I know about living a lie, I know about covering your tracks and making sure people don't get too close. It is a shitty way to live your life. I get it, but you have something you can change. You are fortunate to be able to do this. Some people don't have a choice, doll. Take it and run.'

Jack seemed so sad that Sapphira stopped thinking about herself for a moment and kneeled down beside him on the Persian rug. 'What is it, Jack? What is your lie? I've bared my soul to you.'

'You did more than bare your soul to me, honey, I saw the whole enchilada.'

Sapphira laughed, embarrassed; it felt good to laugh again.

'Tell me, Jack. Come on, you know my dirty little secret, time to spill your guts.'

Jack reached over to the glass coffee table and opened an ebony carved box. 'Cigarette, doll?'

Sapphira took one, and Jack lit it for her and one for himself with the marble lighter on the table. Drawing back the smoke, Sapphira became nervous but wasn't sure why. Jack blew out the smoke, creating a perfect smoke ring in the room. He looked even more elegant with the cigarette. Like Cary Grant or William Holden, she thought, remembering the old movies her mother used to make her watch as a child.

Jack seemed to be contemplating his words, and then he turned to Sapphira, held her beautiful face in his hands, and said simply, 'I'm gay.'

He shrugged his shoulders and laughed a little awkwardly. 'So, the "you show me yours, I'll show you mine" time is over. I think a drink is in order. *Si*?'

CHAPTER ELEVEN

There were two things Rose was having trouble putting to rest in her mind. One was that small child's delicious smell and the other was the man's voice, bawling the child out in front of her.

'Who the hell speaks to a child like that?' asked Rose as Kelly applied her make-up for the day.

'I don't know. I try not to judge.'

'Bullshit, Kelly, you judge all the time.'

'I mean I haven't had kids yet, so you know, I can't say anything about his parenting skills. Maybe he was having a bad day. Head up, please.'

'I don't think you should ever yell at a child like that, ever. Especially when the person is vulnerable and three feet high.'

Kelly stood back to assess her handiwork. 'My mum always yelled at us. But then again there were six of us and my dad and the animals. I don't think I ever heard her *not* yell when I was a kid,' laughed Kelly. 'Maybe he's stressed out about something.'

'Well, he did mention his wife was dead,' said Rose not meeting Kelly's eyes. She had purposely edited this part out when reliving the story to Kelly.

'Okay, big plotline hole, babe. How the hell did that come up? Close your eyes.'

Rose closed her eyes. 'When I asked to speak to his wife and then accused him of child abuse. Yeah, I know, I see the look on your face and my eyes are closed. Not one of my finest moments. I'm now staying out of town to avoid seeing him and his children again. I hope he didn't recognize me. Although he did seem pretty self-involved.'

Rose had not left her villa; she was ashamed of the way she flew off the handle although not sorry to have stuck up for the small boy. If someone had stuck up for me when I was married to Paul, then things may not have gotten so awful, she thought as Kelly finished her face.

Rose walked out towards her trailer. They were shooting in the Piazza Del Comune, in the town of Assisi in the early morning. The piazza had been closed since 3.30 am for the crew to set up and now they were waiting to get the perfect shot of Rose's character alone, praying at dawn. Rose and Kelly had been on set since 4.30 am for hair and make-up.

Crossing the set, TG waved at her to stop. 'Hey, Rose, got a minute?'

'Sure, walk with me to my trailer.'

'So . . . Sam, who I hired for the role opposite you, has fallen off the wagon again.'

'Oh, shit, poor Sam. That's awful, he was trying so hard. Janet will be devastated. I'll call her tonight.'

Sam Lowerstone and Rose had never worked together but Janet, his wife, was British and she and Rose shared an affinity for all things English and found solace in each other's accents and sense of humour.

TG opened her door to her trailer for her. 'Well, I knew last week and was hoping he might be able to get it together. But Janet just called to say he's going to Promises to dry out. So I've had to make a call and hire a new actor. I hope you don't mind me not clearing it with you first but Janet asked me for complete privacy and the producers have been freaking out.'

Rose sat on one of the chairs in the trailer. 'Gosh, TG, I understand. I'm sure you've had a terrible time. I know you would use the best person available. Who did you end up getting at such short notice?'

'He's an English actor actually, but has done quite a bit of West End and done a bit of Broadway this last year, a Pinter play, I think. And he does theatre in London. You probably know him anyway.'

'I doubt it, I haven't been back to London to see theatre for ten years and I didn't see the Pinter play. What's his name?'

'Max Craydon.'

'The name rings a bell. Maybe I've read his name somewhere. Well, I'm sure that if you're happy then I will be, TG. Don't worry, I'm not going to pull any diva-style behaviours on you, although I wish I could sometimes, it might make my fee go up!'

'Your fee is plenty high enough,' laughed TG.

'You know I'm worth it,' said Rose, batting her eyelids dramatically.

TG stood in the doorway of the trailer and laughed even more. 'Sure, sure. Well, I thought you should meet, since it must be weird for him coming onto a set where there was another actor cast. Perhaps a dinner tonight at my villa, or maybe a drink if you're too tired?'

'Lovely. Maybe a drink at 7.00 pm?'

Just after seven o'clock, Rose arrived at TG's villa. TG met her at the door. 'You look great!' he said as Rose smoothed out her dove grey satin Roland Mouret cocktail dress. 'Please come in. Max is already here. He seems a bit nervous, so if you could relax him, I think it would help. You're always good at that stuff.'

TG opened the door to the salon. 'Max, meet Rose. I hope you have a good time together on this shoot. Max is thrilled to be working with you.'

Rose looked up and saw her enemy from the Galleria Nazionale in Perugia. He was tall, with a thick crop of black hair hanging almost to his shoulders, reminiscent of a Victorian poet. He was older, perhaps forty-eight or more and his face was handsome, but looked tired or drawn. He didn't look at all surprised to see Rose who, however, was shocked to the core. Embarrassment and indignation flushed through her body, and then she composed herself quickly.

'Max, how lovely to meet you. Thanks for stepping in so quickly. TG tells me great things about your work,' she said, thinking she had already seen his rage at work.

Max looked at her quizzically, then decided to follow her lead and pretend not to have met her before.

'Thank you so much. It's great to be a part of this. The script is fantastic,' said Max sincerely.

His voice sounded melodious, the voice of a man who had worked on the stage for years. Deep, resonant and strong, quite different from when he yells, she thought, looking at him, unmoved by the charm in his voice.

'What can I get you to drink?' asked TG, unaware of the tension in the room.

'White wine, thank you, TG,' Rose replied as she settled on a red velvet chair.

'Same for me, thanks,' said Max, still standing.

'This is a gorgeous room, TG, I feel quite regal sitting on this chair,' Rose said, looking around the room.

Oval in shape, it had enormous French glass doors, which

opened onto an oval balcony overlooking the perfect gardens of the villa. Painted frescos covered the curved walls leading to a red and white marble fireplace. The room was filled with furniture, creating little conversation corners; the high ceiling stopping it from feeling cluttered.

'I guess so, it's a little too formal for me, although I like the walls,' said TG as he handed her a glass of the local Orvieto.

'I think this room is an addition to the rest of the villa, probably in the 18th century,' Max said. 'I read that the owner, many eons ago, married a French aristocrat and she missed home, so she created her own little Versailles in Italy.'

'How do you know that, man?' asked TG, laughing.

'I trained to be an architect before I fell into acting. I like to read about different buildings and the areas they're situated before I visit a region. I feel like the buildings are telling me their own story of the history and who lived there and why they survived. I must say, I was thrilled to come to Umbria. I've been to other parts of Italy but not here before. The region is incredible.'

Rose remained impassive. What a shame he was such a prick to his kids. He might have been good company, she thought.

'*Pranzo*,' a voice called from the doorway.

Rose turned to see Lucia in the doorway. 'Lucia, what are you doing here?' she asked surprised.

TG laughed, 'Everyone said Lucia does the best traditional cooking so I asked her to do dinner for us.'

Lucia smiled broadly as she looked at the men. The younger one was handsome but too young for Rose. The other one looked fine, thought Lucia. Yes, the spiced apples had done their work.

In the kitchen, she checked the food. Pan fried pork ribs for fertility. Rose needed children, thought Lucia. Rice for wealth and sautéed artichokes with mozzarella for blossoming love.

Dessert was a ricotta and sour cream cherry tart. Sex, giggled Lucia to herself. There was no doubt Rose needed sex.

Rose and Max did the best acting job of their lives as they charmed TG through dinner. He was so amused by their humour and their intelligence he didn't realize that they never actually spoke directly to each other.

When the dinner finally drew to a close, Max and Rose said goodbye to TG and walked out to their cars.

'So, let's cut the bullshit, we both obviously recognize each other and while I thought you were a massive tool at the gallery and you treated your kids appallingly, I am nothing if not a professional,' said Rose. 'So let's just do the shoot and then pretend we never met, okay?' Rose took the keys to her Mercedes from her bag.

Max took a step towards her and Rose felt nervous until he spoke.

'Please give me a chance. There is no way I can explain my terrible and abhorrent behaviour that day. Milo, well, he's young and he doesn't remember his mother at all now. He said she has faded from his eyes. He runs away at any chance he can get. The therapist back home said he is not running from me but trying to run away from the pain inside him. They need a mother, you know. Children need their mother and I'm always getting things wrong – library bags, lunch orders, not signing notices.'

Max wrung his hands as he spoke and Rose was sure she saw tears in his eyes.

'I've tried to do most of it myself. I didn't want the boys to think I was handing them over to a nanny but I'll do something and then cry. This is the biggest role of my career, I can't believe I got it and I thought to bring the boys here would be a new start. New push in my career, a holiday with the kids.'

Rose stood listening and then put her keys in the door of her car and then turned.

'You make the mistake of thinking that I care. I don't even know you but you have a responsibility to get it together for your children. You spoke so badly to them that I would hate to see what happens behind closed doors.'

Max winced at her barb but to his credit said nothing.

'If you aren't coping then get help before you do something or say something that can't be fixed,' she said and sat in the driver's seat.

'I will,' said Max. 'I just don't want this to ruin things on-set.'

'It won't,' said Rose tersely. 'I don't know how much movie experience you've had, but you'll know that the best actors don't let personal prejudices get in the way of their work.'

Max let the comment about his film set experience slide also, he deserved to be told off, he reasoned.

'Well, that's good,' he said, trying not to laugh at the haughty expression on her face.

Rose looked at the smirk on his face and sped off and decided that she hated him, hated Italy and that shooting *The Italian Dream* with Max would be a nightmare.

CHAPTER TWELVE

TG lay in the darkness of his bedroom after Rose and Max had left. Sleep was not coming easily these days. The day's shoot ran through his head. He had to call LA most days and the nine-hour time difference made his schedule hectic. I've got to stop drinking all this coffee, he thought as he tossed and turned.

Being honest with himself, he knew it was Calypso who kept him awake. Not that she had any idea. At the shoot, behind the camera, he watched her intently, citing his directorial duties the reason, his heart saying otherwise.

'You have it so bad, that if I didn't love you so, I would laugh at you,' said Chris as they arrived on set together early one morning.

The sun was coming up over the hills and the air was already heating up. TG hung his head in shame like a schoolboy. 'Did Kelly tell you?' he asked, knowing the sanctity of marriage allowed secrets about best friends to be shared.

'No, man. I see the way you look at her, the way you let her take her time, work through her lines and set up the best shots for her.'

'Fuck, is it that obvious? Do I look like I am favouring her? Are people talking about it?'

'I haven't heard anything. I just notice that you're more careful with her somehow. I think maybe the crew thinks it's because she is younger and obviously a little bit scared of you. I mean, you were an ogre when we first started. Typical TG, "I have a crush" behaviour,' Chris laughed.

'It's so high school,' TG moaned.

'Want me to pass her a note over the craft services table? Here she comes now.'

'Fuck off, my friend, and go do your job,' TG replied, playfully punching Chris on the arm.

Calypso walked past TG and Chris and headed towards a table laden with coffee, fresh fruit and breakfast pastries. All the cast and American crew were slowly becoming addicted to the Italian caffeine, although Sapphira claimed she always drank between eight and ten cups a day. Calypso was drinking more and more coffee, finding it helped her stay awake after the long nights of pleasure with Marco.

TG poured himself a coffee and stood next to Calypso as she served herself some fruit. 'Morning, how are you today?'

'Great,' she smiled.

Things were decidedly less tense between them as the shoot went on. She had relied on TG more and more since the other women had left the set for the time being, until they were needed later. TG had only been too eager to help her when she had tentatively approached him for his advice. Together they bonded a little, talking over her character and the choices she had made as a person compared to the choices of the character.

'You know the feeling, when you realize you can do anything you want. The feeling when you leave school and the world is at your feet? That's how your character feels.'

Calypso looked awkward. 'Not really. I left school when I was twelve. Mom homeschooled me.' Leaving out that Leeza did nothing and Calypso was largely self-taught in everything.

112

TG looked at her, fascinated. She was worldly on set and yet seemed so innocent. Unprepared for life, he thought as he watched her make notes in her script with a pink highlighter pen. TG was shocked at Calypso's upbringing: no high school, no prom or dating, no football games or sleepovers.

'Thanks for the help yesterday. It was so good. I was thinking about you this morning when I was in the shower.'

TG looked startled, then she blushed, remembering Rose and Sapphira teasing her in regards to TG's supposed crush on her. 'You know the work we did, not you, that would be weird. Not that you are weird or ugly, I mean I'm sure people think of you in the shower. Shit. I'm sorry, I must sound learning impaired.' Calypso felt nervous, although she wasn't sure why.

TG laughed and blushed too. She noticed how funny his laugh was, like a little boy's giggle.

'Anyway,' she continued, 'I really feel I'm learning a lot here, with the other girls and you, it's turning out okay. Thanks,' she smiled shyly.

TG felt his heart break into a thousand pieces. 'No problem, I'm happy you're okay. I know we kind of got off on the wrong foot. I was a bit stressed but that's no excuse. I need to work on that stuff, try to be less angry and a little more empathetic.' TG rubbed the dirt on the ground with his shoe.

Calypso touched his arm. 'I've a few books you could read. They're back in LA but maybe when we get back, you can come over and I can lend them to you. There are some really good exercises you can do. I can help you.'

TG felt his heart mend instantly and although he had never been into the whole self-help thing, he realized Calypso's offer was genuine. Mindful that she was sensitive, he smiled. 'Thanks, Calypso, I would like that. It's a date!'

113

As she walked away towards make-up with coffee in hand, Chris sidled up to him. 'You sure you don't want me to drop a note in her lap while she's in make-up?'

TG stared after her. 'Man, you never stop, do you?' he laughed.

'Nope, never. I am the Caped Cupid!'

TG smiled as he stared at the ceiling, remembering. Sleep avoided him as he tossed and turned. 'Fuck,' he said into the darkness. He turned his pillow over and thumped it. Count sheep, come on, he thought as his face hit the cool pillow. Then his phone rang. Who the fuck . . . He was thinking it was LA. Picking up his BlackBerry, he saw the Hotel Brufani number come up on the screen.

'Hello?'

'Hello? TG? I need you.' Calypso's voice sobbed down the phone.

'Okay, I'm coming to see you.' He jumped out of bed. 'What's happened? What's wrong?' he asked as he was pulling on his jeans and t-shirt.

Calypso cried down the phone. He couldn't understand her, she was talking and crying but all he could make out was 'Marco' and 'Raphael' and 'ciao' and then more weeping.

Slipping on his Converse sneakers with no socks, he ran downstairs and out to his car.

'I'm in the car. I will be there soon, I promise.'

'Don't hang up,' he heard her cry down the phone. 'Stay with me.' Her voice was frightened and pained; he felt himself breathe in sharply. He felt her anguish as he sped down the road, not caring what speed he was at in the Mercedes. 'I will keep talking to you, you don't have to answer. I will tell you twenty facts about TG and when I get to the last one, I will be outside your hotel room, I promise.'

'Okay,' he heard a tiny voice say down the line.
'All right, let's go . . .

1. My middle name is Ernest. I like to think I live up to it.
2. I like to eat in bed.
3. My favourite flower is a frangipani.
4. I want to retire to Bali and surf and have my kids visit me whenever they want.
5. I want kids.
6. I hate cats.
7. I hate people who love cats and have cat fridge magnets.
8. I didn't bring enough clothes to Italy and I have to go shopping here and I am scared I will end up with a leather jacket and a shiny Guido shirt.
9. I don't believe in God, but I believe in The Force.
10. My best friends are Kelly and Chris.
11. I would prefer to be called Tim, but everyone calls me TG.
12. My secret favourite film is *Truly, Madly, Deeply* but I always say *Citizen Kane* in interviews. I've never seen *Citizen Kane.*
13. I've got three sisters who try to marry me off to their girlfriends.
14. My last girlfriend broke up with me to go out with someone who would be better for her career.
15. I want a dog and I want to call it Luna.
16. I wish I wrote the Harry Potter books.
17. I wish I had made *Star Wars.*
18. I play pinball every night before I go to bed when I'm in LA. I have a Kiss machine. Ace Freely's tongue comes out when you get a free ball.'

By this time TG was at the hotel, parking at the front door. He threw the keys to the doorman, who was half asleep and ran inside and jumped in the lift.

19. I like LA more than New York, although I never say this in interviews.
20. When I like a girl, I treat her bad, so she won't know and then can't reject me. Every girlfriend I've ever had, they've had to chase me.

He knocked on the door. 'I'm outside your door, Calypso.'

Calypso had not said a word while he spoke; he didn't even know if she was listening, but while he talked he heard her breathing calm down.

The door opened a tiny crack. Her swollen eyes peered out the door. She was wrapped in a bed sheet and upon seeing him, she started to sob.

He walked in and took her in his arms in a bear hug. 'It will be okay, whatever has happened. I promise. I will help you fix it. Okay?'

He pulled her away and stood with his hands on her shoulders and looked into her eyes. 'Okay,' she said wanly.

Glancing around the room, he saw the bed was messed. There was what looked to be vomit next to it. Maybe she was drunk, he thought, but he could not smell alcohol and she seemed genuinely distressed.

Leading her to the bed, he tried to get her to sit down, but she screamed and stood up. 'Not the bed,' she cried.

Jesus, he thought, what has happened in here?

'Okay, it's okay, let's sit here.'

He led her over to the sofa on the other side of the suite. After getting her to sit down, he went over to the wardrobe

116

and found an extra blanket on the top shelf. Wrapping it around her to try to stop the shaking, he realized it was not cold she was shaking from, it was fear and shock. He went and put the kettle on in the small kitchen area and waited till it boiled, watching her. She was pale and dazed, her hair was a mess, more than just standard bed hair. Bringing her a cup of black tea with four sugars, he placed it in front of her and waited to see if she would speak first. She was silent.

Unsure of what to do, he thought about his mother. What did she do when they were hurt or upset? Maybe a bath, he remembered from his own childhood. He walked into the bathroom and turned on the taps. Opening the gift basket on the bench, which presumably the producers had sent to her filled with bottles and lotions, he took a few and poured a little of each under the running tap. The fragrant water steamed up the bathroom and he walked out to where Calypso was still sitting, not having moved. He tried to get her to stand, but she seemed too weak. Lifting her gently, he carried her to the bathroom. Kicking off one of his sneakers, he tested the water with his foot, while holding her frail, shaking body.

Leaving her wrapped in the sheet, he lowered her gently into the comforting water. Sighing, Calypso closed her eyes.

Ensuring she was settled, TG walked back and fetched the tea from the table near the sofa. Leaning down next to the bath, he whispered, 'You need to drink a tiny bit, sweetie, just to help your body. The sugar will help the shock. Just a sip.'

He held the now warm tea to her lips and she drank a little.

Slipping her head under the water, she was entirely submerged. Having been under there for almost a full minute, just as TG was beginning to look in to ensure she wasn't drowning herself, she emerged again, a giant, violent wave splashing water across the floor.

'I can't stay in this hotel any more,' she said quietly. 'But I can't stay by myself.'

'Well, you can stay with me if you want. The villa has too many rooms and an Italian woman who is either trying to feed me or marry me; I'm still not sure. Come home with me tonight and I will send for your things tomorrow.'

Calypso was silent. Her head was beginning to clear and she thought about her options. Perhaps she could stay with TG? That would be okay for a little while. She would be safe, but should she tell him about Raphael? If she spoke up now then she would ruin the picture, and then there was her reputation to consider. Hollywood was an unforgiving town and she didn't want to bring her own reputation down. She didn't want to say it, for then it would be real.

'Thank you. I'll stay with you.'

'Do you want to talk about what happened?' asked TG gently.

'Not yet,' she answered, shaking.

Going to her wardrobe, he pulled out a pair of sweat pants, a t-shirt, underwear, a bra and a pair of sandals. When he walked back into the bathroom, Calypso had got out of the bath and was now wrapped in a towel. She took the clothes from him and TG walked out, closing the door.

Looking at the vomit, he thought it best to clean it up. Whatever had happened in here, he knew the last thing Calypso would want was some maid selling secrets about her wild drunken night in her hotel room. Opening the mini-bar, he found a bottle of soda water. He took the bed sheet Calypso had wrapped herself in and cleaned up the vomit as best he could.

Opening the door, Calypso found him on his hands and knees, scrubbing the floor. 'Thank you so much,' she said, her eyes tearing up again.

'No problem. Grab what you need now and I will get the rest tomorrow, okay?'

Calypso took her handbag, papers and jewellery from the safe and walked outside into the hallway of the hotel. TG stuffed the dirty sheet into a laundry bag and they walked down to his car together.

They drove back to his villa in silence. Not an awkward silence but the quietness of those who have just been through a battle and come out alive. Arriving at the villa, TG finally spoke. 'There's a whole wing you can have if you want, then you never need to see me and can be happy and safe at the same time.'

Turning in her seat to look at him, she grabbed his arm, sounding terrified, her voice cracking. 'I can't be by myself, I just can't,' she said, shaking her head like a small child. 'Can I stay closer to you?'

Her intensity was shocking and for a moment TG was unsure of the right answer. 'Sure. I will give you the room next door, okay? There's a door which interconnects between the rooms so if you need me, just knock, okay?'

'Thank you. Please don't tell anyone about what happened to me,' Calypso said as he stopped the car.

'Of course not,' he answered, not reminding her that he still didn't know what had happened to her.

Walking inside, Calypso felt exhausted. TG noticed her skin turning grey. 'All right, off to bed,' he said bossily and bustled her upstairs to the room.

The room was large, with an 18th century four-poster bed with a canopy against one wall. The bed linen was white and gauze curtains were tied to each post. The ceiling of the canopy was embroidered with gold stars. There was a chaise longue covered in white and a dressing table with a white gauze

119

underskirt. A huge tapestry of Diana the Huntress hung on one wall and on the other was a painting of one of the villa owner's ancestors. There was a bathroom off the bedroom with a bath big enough for four people. A small door connected the bedroom and the one next door.

Pulling off her sandals, she pulled back the covers and got into bed. TG moved to leave the room, then Calypso pressed the heels of her hands into her eyes and spoke slowly. TG stood still, waiting.

'I was kind of seeing this guy from Perugia. It was good, I thought. We went out to dinner and stuff and then sometimes he would stay at the hotel with me.' She did not move her hands from her face, as if afraid to look at him, because then she would lose her courage.

'Well, we went out to dinner with Raphael from the film last night. They drank a lot, and I left early 'cause we had shooting today. But Raphael and Marco went out. I went to bed and was woken up at 3.00 am by knocking. I let him in, thinking it was Marco. It was dark and I was half asleep. Anyway, he started to touch me and then he had sex with me, but he was rough and it hurt and he pulled my hair, he called me names. When I turned around it was Raphael. It was awful and I'm so ashamed. I shouldn't have let him in. And I didn't go to the police because people will say I'm just a cheap "puttana", which is what Marco said I was to Raphael. This will ruin the film and my career and my mother would kill me but I don't know how I'll film next week. I just want to go back to my life before Italy.'

Calypso took her hands away from her face. The tears ran down her cheeks and TG rushed to her side. He pulled her to his chest and let her cry. 'Oh God, Calypso. What a fucking asshole.

120

'You didn't do anything to deserve this and you made an innocent mistake. Of course I understand, no one needs to know. No one needs to know anything. This is between you and me and I'll fix this. Don't worry about filming. I'll sort it out.'

'Really?' Calypso asked, her voice resonating against his chest.

'Really.'

She pulled away and with her face almost touching his she said, 'Do you think I'm a slut?'

TG shook his head. 'No, you're not a slut. You are a person who someone took advantage of and I will deal with it. Do you trust me?'

She nodded and rubbed her eyes. 'I feel like a fucking loser. Like some stupid little girl. I imagine him and Marco talking about me, planning this somehow.'

TG felt anger welling inside him but he pushed it down; there would be time to deal with that. Instead he stayed present with Calypso.

'Do you need to see a doctor?'

'No, I don't think so. I hope he hasn't got any fucking diseases or anything. Christ, what an asshole.' Sharing the pain with TG had relieved the burden somewhat and surprisingly she felt a tiny bit better. 'Thank you for being my friend, TG. We're friends, aren't we?'

'Of course, we're great friends! You're going to give me self-help lessons when we return to LA, remember?'

Calypso laughed. 'Yes, well, not a lot of good any of it has done me.'

TG held her hands and raised them to his mouth, kissing them. 'You are amazing and I'm happy we're friends. What you have been through is terrible and I wish it had never happened to you.'

She smiled and closed her eyes. 'I'm tired now. So much crying. It's driving me insane, I swear.'

TG moved towards the door.

'Can you leave the door open?' she asked.

'The one to the hallway?' he asked, confused.

'The one to your room,' she said.

Walking through the room, he stood, his hand on the interconnecting door handle. 'Good night, Calypso,' he said quietly.

'Good night, Tim,' he heard in the darkness and his heart skipped a beat.

TG sat in the darkness, the anger like a torrent running through him.

He wanted to kill Raphael, not just for Calypso but for himself. Ridding the world of men like him was no great loss. TG imagined himself punching Raphael over and over until he was in a bloodied mess. He had never felt such anger in his life. He needed to get control. He needed someone to help, but who did he know in Italy that could bring down Raphael and protect Calypso?

There was only one person who had the contacts and the ability to remain discreet in Italy. He picked up his phone in the dark and dialled.

CHAPTER THIRTEEN

Jack's phone rang as he and Sapphira were sitting in silence. The shock of his confession was a lot for her to take in after the events of the past few hours.

'Hello,' said Jack, answering his phone. 'Hey, TG, what's happening?'

Sapphira looked up at him. Why was TG ringing?

Jack walked to a chair and sat down. 'Yes, that's fine. Come on over, it's a party. Sapphira is here. Yes. It's her birthday, we're having a little celebration.'

She raised her eyebrows at his comment. Not quite, she thought.

Jack continued speaking. 'No problem. Come here and I'll send my boat to pick you up.' He hung up the phone.

Sapphira panicked. 'Why's he coming here? Does he know about me? Did you ring him and tell him before?' Perhaps TG knew and was coming to confront her like those awful rehab shows she had heard about where the family has an intervention.

'Not everything is about you, darling,' said Jack as he sipped his drink. 'He said he needed my help and I was the only one who might know what to do. Poor guy sounded desperate. I don't know what it's about. If you don't want to stay and find out then I suggest you head upstairs and try to sleep for a while.'

But Sapphira was still nervous about TG coming to see Jack. Had he found out about her and Jack's night? Was Jack lying to her? Why would he lie when he shared with her the biggest secret of his life? The questions spun around in her mind. Sapphira had been stunned by Jack's admission and his composure while telling her. Jack Reynolds gay? She could hardly believe it and yet so much of it made sense. Not that she was surprised in hindsight. Jack had not showed the slightest interest in her sexually, which was unusual for a single man. Not that Sapphira was egotistic about it; it was just how it was for her.

Looking around his palazzo she saw nothing that inferred he was gay. No large Mapplethorpe photographs or zebra skin rugs, which she saw in some of her gay associates' houses. Instead Jack surrounded himself with the best of everything. His suits, wine, surroundings, even the city he chose to live in were of the highest quality.

'But you are so not gay,' said Sapphira incredulously. 'Not even a hint of fag,' she said as she drew back on her cigarette.

'I am a man who sleeps with other men. As far as the whole "fag" thing goes, as you so delicately put it, I see no reason to act like a woman and give up who I am and what I like. It's a sexual preference but not who I am. Being gay doesn't define me, never has.'

'Jesus, Jack, I don't know what to say. You have kinda blown my predilection for smack outta the water, you know?' she said, shaking her head.

'Well, I don't know about that. Pretty funny though, looking at you and me, the smack addict and the fag. What a field day the *National Enquirer* would have with this!'

Sapphira drained her glass of wine. 'More please,' she

124

demanded and Jack refilled her glass. 'So what's with the girl-friends I hear of? How do you manage that and how the hell has it never come out?'

'Well, they agree to see me at social events, we go out and get snapped by the paps and then I help them in their career and give them some starting money. They're mostly nice girls. I enjoy their company. Unlike some men, gay and straight, I like women's company. I love women, actually.'

'Does anyone know? How do you keep it secret?'

'Some people know, close friends, but not too many. The person I spoke of who died from the overdose was my long-term partner. He was a lawyer, we were together for ten years. I worked with him to try to get him off the gear for good but . . .' Jack paused, clearly moved by remembering him. 'Well, you know how the tale ends and I don't want it happening to you.'

Sapphira was touched and held his hand tightly. 'Thank you for caring, Jack, I'm touched by your honesty and your concern. I don't know what I'm going to do but when I do you will be the first person I call, okay?'

Jack smiled at her. 'Okay, kiddo, you call me when you need me.'

'Shit,' she said, lighting another cigarette nervously. 'What the fuck does he want? He must know about me.'

'Get over yourself, girlfriend. Why do you think this is about you?' laughed Jack as he tidied the room.

'Because it usually is,' answered Sapphira darkly.

Calypso's reading of her tarot cards had unnerved her more than she had let on. The references to her self-destructive habits, the psychic child and death had unnerved her – not that she had let sweet Calypso know. The reading gnawed at her, coming back when her mind wandered. Now she wondered if the card, which heralded betrayal, was about Jack. Had he told TG and he was coming for a 'carefrontation' to try to get her into rehab?

TG arrived in Venice via a chartered helicopter. He still had no answers on how to deal with Raphael but was confident that Jack would be able to help him, although he wasn't sure why. Jack had a confidence TG admired, a refinement and cavalier attitude TG wished he could bottle for himself. He felt like a schoolboy around Calypso, shy and silly. Fuck, he had even tried to dance like Will Smith around her; only close friends from college had seen him dance like that and only after he had been drinking. Thankfully Calypso had not noticed his awkwardness or stumbling attempts to comfort her.

He sailed down the canal on the boat. He had to sort this out tonight and get back to Calypso. Arriving in darkness at Jack's palazzo, TG didn't notice the incredible sights of Venice or the splendour of Jack's home; he only had Calypso on his mind.

Jack opened the door. 'Hello, director, what brings you to my fair city on this lovely night? Venice is just picking up now. Perhaps we could go out for a drink and take in the sights and sounds?'

'I need to talk to you, Jack. I've got a serious problem and you're the only one I know here who knows how to work the system.'

Jack nodded. 'I've been working the system since I was born, kid, come in.'

'Hi,' he said absently to Sapphira who was standing in the centre of the room.

'Hi, TG, do you want me to stay or leave?' she asked nervously.

126

'Stay, if you don't mind, maybe you can help me, I don't know.'

Sapphira noticed how stressed and anxious he was.

'Okay, so shoot,' said Jack, nursing a glass of red wine.

TG looked at them both. 'Something has happened to Calypso. I can't tell you the details, but needless to say it's shocking and I've got to get Raphael off the set as soon as possible without bringing the producers into it in any way. I cannot have them know of this. Can I trust you guys? Can you keep a secret?'

Sapphira and Jack looked at each other and then back to TG. 'Absolutely,' they answered in unison.

TG told them bare details, ensuring Calypso's reputation was not scarred in any way. TG had no doubts in his mind she was telling the truth. As he spoke, he looked at the floor, remembering what she had said and choosing his words carefully. Sapphira and Jack listened in silence. When TG finished, he looked at them. 'So, what do I do?' he asked with his hands upturned.

Sapphira stood and poured more wine for herself and a glass for TG. She was sure he would need a drink after telling the story; hell, she knew she needed one. TG accepted the glass without acknowledging Sapphira, absorbed in his thoughts. 'I just want to get him the fuck away from the set and her.'

'Sure, I understand, he's a little prick. I know of his reputation from a few Italian actor friends. Not the first time this sort of thing has happened but he's a big star here and no one ever presses charges,' Jack said.

'Poor Calypso, what piece of work.'

Sapphira was enraged. Calypso was a sweet, unassuming girl, who had been taken advantage of in the worst of ways. Sapphira didn't have to think too hard about what TG had alluded to. It was clear Raphael had attacked or, in the extreme, raped Calypso.

'Jesus, how does a person live with themselves?' asked Sapphira.

'Quite well, I think, looking at Raphael. He can have any woman he wants, clearly; whether she wants him is not considered. He roams Europe and gets treated like royalty when he arrives home. He's still mama's boy, going home for pasta each Sunday when he's in Rome,' Jack said, his legs crossed elegantly.

'So, what are my options?' TG asked, sipping the wine but not tasting it.

Sapphira made as though to speak and then paused.

'Out with it,' Jack said, seeing her face. 'What do you know?'

'Okay, well, I will deny this if it gets out, but I heard from a friend that Raphael got very rough with a few of the call girls he liked to use. One of them was found unconscious with several of her back teeth pulled after she had been booked with him,' said Sapphira matter-of-factly, but lighting another cigarette even though the last one was still burning in the ashtray in front of her.

'For fuck's sake!' exclaimed TG. 'What's with the teeth thing?'

'Apparently makes for a better blowjob,' said Sapphira.

TG's skin crawled, thinking of what could have happened to Calypso.

'Why didn't she press charges?' he asked.

Jack looked at Sapphira. 'Who is going to believe a Euro whore versus a Euro star?'

'Exactly,' said Sapphira. 'Yeah, well, he had to leave town pretty quick, once her pimp found out. He's a big Russian oligarch who runs girls on the side for fun. You know, strictly Class A girls, available for private parties and weekends, etcetera.'

'Jesus, why didn't I know this?' TG questioned himself.

'No one knows,' said Sapphira.

'How do you know?' asked TG, almost violently.

'I just do,' she said, her voice low and certain.

It had been the Russian pimp who had got Sapphira her fix while she was in Cannes; it had cost her three times as much but it was worth it for the convenience and privacy. She was with him in his suite at the Hotel Du Cap when the girl was carried through the door and laid on the bed by two of the pimp's burly Russian bodyguards. Unsure of what to do and knowing she needed to get her drugs, she had waited in the corner of the hotel suite, watching as the men spoke rapid fire Russian to each other but not actually tending to the girl who was beginning to wake.

It was Sapphira who spoke up. 'She needs to see a doctor straightaway,' she said as she went and sat on the edge of the bed. Holding the girl's hand, she saw fear and recognition in her eyes and Sapphira smiled gently. 'It will be okay, it will be okay,' she whispered and the girl started to sob violently.

Sapphira waited until the doctor arrived, paid handsomely to shut his mouth and get her into a private hospital. Finally when the girl had been taken from the suite, Sapphira pocketed the drugs that the clearly shaken pimp had given her. 'Listen, I know you are a businessman and I'm not judging what you do . . .' she began.

The Russian looked at her, his eyes steely.

She continued, feeling braver with her stash in her pocket. 'She is damaged now and I suggest you never send her to work again but she is your responsibility. Make sure she is okay, financially and mentally. Don't let her go through this alone. Okay?'

The man sat on the hotel chair, rubbing his eyes tiredly. 'I know, I know. I have daughters. It's too much,' he said in his heavy accent.

'Just promise me she will be okay,' she pleaded, thinking of the swollen side of the girl's face where Raphael had ripped the teeth from her mouth. She didn't even want to think what he had used on the poor woman to get the teeth out.

'I will promise,' he said seriously, and Sapphira knew the girl would be taken care of.

Sapphira never breathed a word of the scandal; it wasn't her style. But she was not surprised when he heard Raphael had left Cannes for a Rome hospital, claiming he had been in a car accident that had left him with four broken ribs, a ruptured spleen and three back teeth missing.

Jack and TG pondered Sapphira's story. Although it was almost fantastical, they knew it was true. Jack rubbed his head in thought. 'You have two options in Italy: death or scandal. Take your pick, TG, which do you want?'

'As much as I would like death, it seems a little extreme,' said TG wryly.

'I'm not so sure about that,' said Sapphira.

'Well then, scandal it is,' said Jack. 'We can't create a scandal around sex, Italy is run on sex. Look at Berlusconi and his machinations as the head of the country. Our only option is drugs. Italy has a very hardline stand against drugs, part political, part religious. Don't forget, it's still quite a conservative country in some ways.'

TG looked at him. 'I don't think he's a drug user. I think sex is his drug.'

Sapphira narrowed her eyes in thought. 'I've an idea. I'm just putting it out there, if it's too harsh then let me know.'

'I don't think anything is too harsh for him. He has done this to Calypso and from what Jack said, this isn't the first

130

time and won't be the last. He is a predator and he needs to be stopped and taught a lesson,' said TG adamantly.

'Well, it's not pleasant but I think it will do the least harm and I know just how to do it.'

Jack laughed, breaking the seriousness of the mood in the room. 'My little dark angel, how easily you hatch these evil plans.'

Sapphira looked at him with cold eyes. 'I've no qualms about doing this, for Calypso, for the film, for you, TG,' she said looking at him. 'Men like Raphael are bastards and I don't feel any guilt whatsoever. To bring this to the attention of authorities in this country, where he is a "god", as you said, Jack, would mean his protection and Calypso's undoing. Her reputation would be ruined and this news would follow her for the rest of her career.'

Jack and TG looked at each other and then Jack spoke. 'All right then, Lady Macbeth, what's going on in that serpent's mind of yours?'

'I need to know when he is next leaving the country. TG, surely you can find that out with his shooting schedule?'

'I do know what his movements are as I will have to postpone his shots with Calypso because of her state of mind. I will get back to you.'

Sapphira spoke carefully. 'What I will do, only Jack will know about. I want to keep you out of the details, TG. The only thing I ask is you give me an alibi if I need it, okay?'

TG nodded. Sapphira possessed a control and lack of emotion that he found more than a little frightening; she was fearless and powerful in this state.

Jack nodded his agreement to her statement.

'But what about Calypso's scenes, who will be her co-star? Who can step in at the last minute? I've already had to recast a part. The studio is going to freak out when I tell them I had to recast again.'

Jack leaned back in his chair. 'No, you will need them to tell you to recast and extend the shoot. But what I can do is ask around my friends in film here and find out who the next up-and-coming stars are and get them lined up for you. I will keep it on the quiet. Don't worry, I'm owed a few favours.'

TG put down his glass and stood up. 'I owe you so much, both of you. What can I offer you? How can I repay you?'

Sapphira shook her head. 'No need, it all balances out. I'm happy to help, I love being here, more than you know, TG.'

She said this so earnestly that TG thought perhaps Jack was behind her sudden emotion. Perhaps they were together, he thought, looking at Sapphira in her sweat pants and no make-up. They certainly had a connection and an ease with each other. TG shook the thoughts from his head and returned to his problem at hand. 'Okay, Sapphira, I will send you Raphael's schedule tonight once I get back to the villa. Jack, I will email you the casting notes for the role. Okay?'

'Okay then, let the games begin,' said Jack.

CHAPTER FOURTEEN

It was the first day of shooting with Max and things weren't going so well. Max and Rose were polite, professional. Rose had to admit he had an easy charm about him while they ran their lines but she said nothing to him other than work-related topics.

Max didn't try to persuade Rose that she should be more pleasant to him. His mind was occupied by trying not to seem like an amateur on set. *The Italian Dream* was the largest set he had been on and he was still amazed that he, of all the actors across the world, would be chosen for the job.

He thought that Rose had recommended him but according to TG, it was Kelly who put a good word in for him after seeing him in an English television series he had made for the BBC.

Max watched as TG spoke to Chris, the DOP, in a hushed but angry voice. Rose glanced up from her script at them. TG wasn't his usual cheerful self, thought Rose but knew to keep quiet when things weren't going right on set.

'What's going on?' Max asked her.

'No idea,' she said and went back to her reading. There were hold-ups all the time on film sets; she was used to it but Max looked nervous. What if they thought he wasn't up for the job, he wondered. They had only filmed one scene, he reasoned, they can't tell after one scene.

TG walked over to the actors. 'There's a problem with some

of the equipment and Chris and his guys are going to have someone come in and have a look at it. So we may not start again for a few hours but be on standby, okay?'

Max nodded and Rose stood up and smiled at TG, then walked towards her trailer, away from Max.

Max rolled his eyes just a little at her behaviour and then went to wait for the boys who were coming on set for lunch with him in the hands of their capable Italian nanny.

Rose didn't come out of her trailer for lunch even though he hoped she would. Today the boys were behaving so well, polite, funny, cute. If only Rose could have seen him then, he thought, flushing with shame at the memory of how he spoke to Milo.

He looked around and saw Milo had left the table but the nanny was gone as well, so he assumed she had taken him to the bathroom.

Milo, however was with neither the nanny nor in the bathroom. He was fascinated by the little houses on wheels that his dad had called a trailer. He liked the idea of a house on wheels that could go anywhere. If he had one he would take his whole family to visit his mother, he thought. He looked at them in a row and thought the largest one would fit him, his dad and brothers easily enough.

Climbing the stairs one by one, his small hand reached out and opened the door. It was neat inside, with a sofa, a table and chairs. Taking in the room, his eyes opened wide. His drink bottle! How did that get there? Before he could ask, Rose walked in from behind a closed door.

'Oh my goodness,' she said, laughing. 'Hello.'

'You have my drink bottle,' he said accusingly. 'I left that for the thirsty lady.'

'I know, she told me. She was so grateful, she said to say thank you,' said Rose, and she handed it over to Milo.

Milo took it from her. His eyes filled with suspicion. 'My dad cried after you left.'

'That's not good,' said Rose, feeling a little bit guilty.

'Dad never yells at me except when I run away,' said Milo settling down on the sofa uninvited.

Rose sat next to him.

'Is that often? Do you run away much?' asked Rose.

'Only to try and see my mummy, but Dad says I have to stay here 'cause he said he would die if he lost me as well,' Milo said very seriously and Rose looked down at her lap.

There was a knock at the door and Max put his head around to see Rose and Milo sitting amiably together.

'Schmilo, you have to stop running away,' he said calmly.

Rose looked at him and saw he wasn't angry, he looked tired and she felt bad again for being such a bitch to him that time.

'I wasn't running away, I came to get my drink bottle,' said Milo, holding out the bottle as evidence.

Rose laughed at Max's confusion. 'A long story,' she said, reluctant to bring up the day at the Galleria in the face of peace.

'Well, don't trouble Rose,' said Max to Milo, 'She's very important, you know,' he said with a slight edge to his voice and Rose laughed.

'Okay, let's call a truce. I think we've both got off on the wrong foot,' she said, gesturing for Max to come inside the trailer.

Max came in and smiled. 'I was a prick,' he said. 'I deserved your anger.'

Milo gasped at his father's language but Max ignored him.

Rose nodded. 'Yes, you were quite the prick but I was a bitch and it was none of my business. I need to apologize for trying to demean you about the film set stuff.'

Max laughed. 'Okay, friends?' he asked and Rose put out her hand and Max shook it firmly.

Max brought Jasper and Dominic to Rose so she could say hello and they spent half an hour talking and laughing together. Rose saw that Max was an attentive father, his sons adored him and that he was patient and kind. Milo spent the time on Rose's lap which she loved and was sorry when their nanny came to take them back to their villa.

But Max stayed in Rose's trailer after the boys left and talked.

While she was not entirely comfortable with his reaction to Milo at the Galleria, she learned of his path over the last eighteen months and his grief and heartache over losing his wife Alice to breast cancer. It had been a long battle, which she had fought valiantly, he said, but one that eventually claimed her life. Max had stayed at home and nursed her with her mother and sister until the end. She died at home, in Max's arms, with the boys having said their goodbyes. Rose was moved by his compassion and focus on the children's lives, trying to ensure they were stable, but time had caught up with him. The help was not as forthcoming as people continued their lives. His parents and Alice's mother helped as much as they could but Alice's father had Alzheimer's disease and she was now overwhelmed with that task.

Max was now trying to do enough work to keep the house afloat and the boys' schedules normal. It was obvious there was more going on in the background but Rose didn't want to pry, instead lending a sympathetic ear and deciding to make his time in Italy on set as pleasant as possible.

The day's shooting went on with ease, much to TG's surprise, as the equipment was restored to working order and he saw that Rose and Max had warmed up to each other. As she was leaving the set at the end of the day, she turned to Max. 'How about you and the boys come over tomorrow? It's Saturday and we can swim and have lunch. I've so many things the boys can play with as I thought my own family would have come over but they've not been able to manage it yet. It's a shame to let all those fun things sit and gather dust.'

'That sounds lovely. I know Milo would like to see you. I must ask what perfume you wear? He keeps talking about how nice you smelled that day when I turned into the giant ogre father figure.'

Rose looked at him sharply. 'That's an odd thing for a little boy to notice,' she said, not mentioning she had remembered the sweet smell of the little child.

'It's a Jo Malone fragrance. Orange blossom.'

'Well, it smells very nice, he has an excellent nose,' he said, laughing.

Rose blushed, and embarrassed at her flaming face, rushed to her car and away from Max's stare.

The next day she awoke to one of those glorious Italian summer mornings where the heat was already starting, the cicadas were singing and the slight haze on the hills in the distance foretold of swimming and lying around. Rose was up early, requesting a summer lunch from Lucia for the boys and getting all the toys and water pistols out for them to play with.

The pool was sparkling and Rose placed cushions on the hammocks and cane lounge under the wisteria and grapevine shelter. She was excited to have company. Max seemed pleasant and she desperately wanted to see Milo again; his little face burned in her mind. Eating a light breakfast of peaches and homemade yoghurt, Rose planned the lunch with Lucia.

'They are boys, so I assume they eat a lot.'

'*Si si*, I know,' Lucia said, pleased to have the tall man and his children over.

'I know what we will eat, do not worry about it, okay? I will cook for your boys.'

'Well, they're not exactly my boys, just friends.'

'Perhaps they can be your boys,' laughed Lucia as she started to bang pots and pans around the large kitchen.

'We will eat outside, is that all right, Lucia?'

'Of course, *si*. Perfect.' It was clear Lucia wanted Rose out of her domain. This is what she felt she was born to do – feed and nurture – and she wanted no help or advice.

Rose ran upstairs and showered, washing herself with the gorgeous Santa Maria Novella products and washing her hair twice. Drying herself on the soft Frette bath sheets, she pondered her wardrobe. She didn't want to look too much like a movie star but she wanted to look nice. For whom, she wondered. Max? The boys? Opening the wardrobe, she looked at the clothes on their satin hangers. Everything was too stuffy, she decided. All too prim and proper. She didn't want to look like she was having a garden party.

She pulled out a Vera Wang red and grey silk tunic from her resort collection, a Camilla Franks white caftan, and a pair of white linen Calvin Klein pants, a black silk singlet and a chocolate beaded Michael Kors silk dress.

Looking at them on the bed, she liked none of them. Pulling out her suitcase from under the bed, she found what she was looking for. 'Help,' she said under her breath. 'What do you wear for four males?'

Pulling on her black Melissa Odabash bikini, she pulled out a Diane Von Furstenberg charcoal jersey tunic dress tied at the waist. Dressing it up with silver hoop earrings and Jimmy Choo silver flat sandals, she thought she looked the best she could expect. Not too dressed but still casual and elegant.

Wearing tinted moisturizer, some blush and waterproof

mascara, she put on some pink lip shimmer from Stila and sprayed herself liberally with her Jo Malone perfume which Milo had admired. Tying her hair back in a low ponytail, she ran downstairs again to wait.

Why was she so nervous and excited? I need to see more people, if this is my reaction to company, she thought, I'm not nearly socialized enough. In fact, Rose rarely entertained anymore. Since her divorce from Paul, she spent most of her spare time on her own, except for a few casual lunches with friends or for business. Going out to industry functions was work not pleasure and Rose had forgotten the fun in preparing and planning for guests.

Rose and Max had planned for a mid-morning arrival and lunch, then home in the afternoon so Milo could have his sleep. At 10.30 am Rose heard the security buzzer on the gates and ran to press them in. The car came down the driveway, stopped and the boys tumbled out of the back seat. 'Stop it, you're hurting me,' said Jasper to Dominic, the eldest boy. 'No, you have to do the red river up the arm and then you get the tingles. Come on, don't be a girl,' said Dominic.

Jasper pulled away and ran to Rose and hid behind her. 'Rose is home free barley. Can't get me if I'm holding onto her. Suffer!' crowed Jasper.

Rose laughed, confused. Dominic snarled at him. Milo stood by the car door and smiled shyly.

'That's enough, boys. Rose already thinks we're savages. Please let's show her we're actually quite nice. I've already apologized to her for my bad mood when we first saw her, so let's keep up the show, okay, lads?'

He ruffled Dominic's hair and Dominic scuffed the gravel drive with his foot. 'Say hello to Rose.'

'Hello, Rose,' said the boys in a singsong voice.

'Hello, boys,' she answered at the same time.

They laughed.

'Come in, come in. I hope you brought your bathers. There's a pool and lots of fun things to do. I've got a Wii and books and colouring things. You name it, I think I have it.'

'Why?' asked Jasper as they entered the cool of the villa.

'Why do I have all that stuff? Well, I think my niece and nephews are coming to visit, so I bought all this gear for them. I'm sure they won't mind you testing it all out for them.'

As they walked through the foyer and into the large open living room that looked out over the pool, the boys saw the blue water filled with floating mattresses and toys. Pulling off their t-shirts and leaving on their board shorts, they made as if to run towards the pool.

'Hang on, hold up,' said Max in a stern voice. 'Sunscreen first please.'

Pulling out a giant pump pack of SPF 30, he started to cream the older boys. 'Do you mind creaming Milo for me, Rose? All over, please?'

'Of course, I can't wait to get my hands on that perfect physique,' she laughed.

Bending down, she helped him take off his red t-shirt. His little body was so cute, with his rounded belly and soft skin. She pumped some sun cream in her hand and lathered him all over. He squirmed under her touch.

'You're tickling me!' he said indignantly.

'Oh no, I'm not. You'll know when I tickle you, just be prepared,' she said, winking at him.

He scrunched his face up to her as she applied cream to his cheeks. Rubbing it into his skin she could see Max's features in him but he must have Alice's colouring, she thought, looking at his blond hair.

'All done,' she said as she stood up. Milo stood in front of her waiting. 'Did I forget somewhere?' she asked.

He crooked his little finger and beckoned her back to his level. As she knelt down in front of him, he smiled shyly. 'Can I smell you?'

He wrapped his little arms around her neck and sniffed deeply into her neck. She held him close, his greasy body pressing against her. He was warm and smelt delicious, like she remembered, but with the smell of sun cream lingering. 'That's nice,' he said as he pulled away. 'Bye.' And he ran to the pool.

Max looked embarrassed. 'I'm sorry, he has this thing about smells. When Alice died, he took her perfume bottles and keeps them next to his bed. Smells them every night. The counsellor says when he doesn't need them anymore then he'll stop and get rid of them himself. I don't think he can remember anything else about her besides her smell.'

Rose looked at the boys jumping in and out of the pool, Milo playing on the steps, trying to get into an inflatable boat. 'They say smell is stored in a different part of our brains and it lasts longer and can activate emotions more than any other sense.'

'Perhaps. I smell the perfumes sometimes when he's at kinder.'

'I understand.' Picking up a tray holding a pitcher of lemonade and glasses, Rose walked towards the door. 'Let's go and watch them. They're so funny.'

'Let me carry that,' said Max and he took the heavy tray from her and walked outside into the sun. 'Where would you like it?'

'In the shade, I think,' said Rose, pointing to the wisteria-covered shelter.

'Can you come in, Dad?' called Dominic from the deep end of the pool.

'Maybe later, Dom,' he said, sitting in the cane chair.

Rose saw the disappointment on Dom's face as he duck-dived under the water.

Standing up, she pulled off her dress and looked at Max. 'Last one in's a rotten egg!' she called and ran to the side of the pool.

Max looked at her dancing on the edge of the pool in her black bikini, her white skin glowing, her body perfectly proportioned; she was utterly gorgeous. She had the body of a twenty-five year old and an expression on her face like a devilish twelve year old.

Pulling off his polo shirt, he kicked off his sandals and ran to the other side of the pool. They stood and stared at each other from opposite sides. Max was not overly worked out like the men in LA. He had muscle definition but was slim, with grey hair on his chest – another thing men in Hollywood had renounced years before. He looked like a man should look, thought Rose, and then caught herself. Oh God, he thinks I'm perving on him. I'm the creepy lady chasing after the grieving widower. Rose, you lech, she admonished herself.

Max saw Rose blush and stopped himself from running his eyes over her body. Lean, lithe and with perfect rounded breasts, almost large by Hollywood standards, real of course, he noticed, then he told himself off. Don't look at her like that; you've already shown her what a bad temper you have, don't show her now what your sex drive is like.

Max had not been with anyone since Alice's death; he just couldn't bring himself to sleep with anyone. He was still in the same home, the same bed and it would seem like he was betraying Alice if he brought anyone into their home, let alone bed.

Max looked into Rose's eyes. 'Ready, on the count of three. One, two . . .' And then he heard Rose jump in.

'You cheater,' he called as she emerged from under the water.

'You snooze, you lose,' she said, quoting her agent, Randy.

Max jumped in and swam towards her. She swam away screaming and the kids all started to yell with delight.

Rose jumped out. 'Max, can you put some sunscreen on me? I'm gonna burn I'm sure.'

Max got out and dried his hands on the towels laid out on the sun lounges. Christ, what a cliché, he thought, as Rose turned her back to him. She undid her bikini top and held it to her as he rubbed her toned shoulders. Her skin was soft but the muscles in her back defined and strong. Her body felt supple under his hands. He rubbed her lower back above her bikini. Christ, he thought, as he felt his cock move. No, Max, no. Think of something else. 'All done,' he said as he turned away from Rose. 'Can you do me now?' he asked, facing the other way towards the house to hide his erection.

Rose put sun cream on her hands and started to rub his back. He had nice skin and a lovely back, she thought, as she rubbed him all over. He also has gentle hands, she thought, thinking of them on her shoulders. She tried to keep her thoughts neutral as she imagined them touching her breasts and felt an aching in her groin. This is so immature, she scolded herself. You need to have sex, Rose, but not with a grieving man. Sex and socialization, she thought to herself. 'Finished,' she said casually.

She ran back and jumped in the pool so he would not see the lust in her eyes. Max pretended to look for something in the bag he brought with him until his erection subsided.

Lucia, still watching from the kitchen window, cackled to herself as she poured extra Tia Maria over the freshly picked strawberries.

143

They spent the morning in the pool, playing games, duck-diving for silver coins which Rose threw in the water. Milo hung onto Rose's back and she swam around the pool as his chariot, doing as he commanded. Soon Lucia called them in for lunch. She had outdone herself. A slow-cooked leg of lamb with rosemary and garlic, a fresh salad with three kinds of vine-ripened tomatoes, basil and buffalo mozzarella, stuffed zucchini flowers with ricotta and anchovies, and French fries for the boys. Lemonade and local wines were aplenty. Lucia had indeed outdone herself and she knew it, now the magic would have to take hold.

Rose clapped her hands in glee. 'I'm getting so fat here, I love the food. TG will have to get my part rewritten as Gilbert Grape's mother, I think, if I keep eating like this,' she said, slipping her dress over her head.

Max looked at her ribs sticking out as she raised her arms as the dress went over her head. 'Yes, I can see you are, in fact, quite hideous. I mentioned it to him, actually, after we met. I said, that woman has an awful temper and is too large for widescreen. What are you going to do about it?' Max joked.

Milo, who Rose was wrapping up in a towel and lifting onto a chair, looked cross. 'No, Daddy, you told me you thought Rose was lubberly when I said I loved her. You said she was the prettiest lady in the world, except for Mummy.' He grabbed a French fry from in front of him and stuffed it into his mouth. Rose looked embarrassed and pretended not to hear.

'All right then, Max, do you want to carve, while I serve the extras?'

Max, pleased to have a task, busied himself with the carving knife and fork.

'Right, boys, a bit of everything?' asked Rose.

144

Max answered for them. 'Dom and Jasp eat everything. Milo eats nothing except chips.'

Rose looked at him. How did he survive, she wondered. 'Well, Milo, today is your lucky day, because I've the best food in Italy. Lucia, who is my friend, made this for me and I will share it with you on one condition.'

Milo looked at her suspiciously. 'What?'

'You try a bit of everything and I will let you sit in my special secret spot. Not even the boys will get a turn.' She looked at the older boys and winked at them. 'Okay?'

Milo nodded excitedly. Rose cut up the tender lamb into little pieces and popped it into his open mouth. He chewed and chewed and then swallowed. He opened his mouth again. 'More lamb?' she asked. He nodded.

Slowly Rose fed him a little of everything, including the zucchini flower, much to Max's amazement. Rose continued the lunch conversation as though Milo ate at every meal and asked the boys questions about their friends, games and thoughts on Italian television. The boys were delightful company and Max felt himself relaxing around them and laughing with Rose at their funny and insightful answers.

Lucia cleared away the dishes and brought out dessert with much ceremony – *una coppetta di fragole e crema* for Rose and Max and a trio of *gelati* for the boys.

'Can I see your secret place now?' asked Milo.

'Yes, absolutely, let's go. You boys stay here and don't follow.'

Rose took Milo by the hand and Max watched them walk away. There was an ease she had with them all that made him instantly relaxed. Except for the brief encounter they had by the pool. He remembered his erection and became embarrassed again. What a fool I am, he thought. Anyway, why would some big Hollywood star be interested in a small time actor from

England? She was married to a big movie star. I've got tickets on myself, he thought, as he topped up Rose's and his own glass with wine.

Rose and Milo walked around the side of the house to a small grotto carved out under the stone. It looked out over the fields and hills and in the space was a day bed, big enough for two people. You could sit up and read or lie down and doze. Rose had placed a light cotton rug on it and filled it with feather pillows. It was the perfect hiding spot and kept cool, even in the midday heat. 'This is where I sleep sometimes, where I hide away from people,' she whispered to him.

Milo ran in with delight. 'Can I lie down?' he asked, already kicking off his sandals.

'Of course,' she said and covered him with the blanket.

'You can go now,' he commanded.

'Okay, I'll come and check on you in five minutes.'

Rose walked back to Max, chuckling at Milo's insistence he be left alone. 'He has asked me to depart, as I've done, but I will check on him in five minutes,' she announced as she sat back down.

'You're too good with him, you're like Bloody Mary Poppins,' exclaimed Max.

'Well, it's not like he's hard to love, is he?' asked Rose, then added playfully, 'Don't answer that!'

Max laughed. 'Well, boys, we should pack up. I should get Milo back for his sleep.'

'That's a shame, I've loved having you here.'

Rose was genuinely disappointed. The time had gone too fast and now she would be alone for the afternoon. Walking back around to Milo, she snuck up to spy on him in his hiding spot. He was asleep. The morning's activities had knocked the wind out of him and he seemed so deeply asleep, she thought his eyes must have closed as soon as his head hit the cushion.

She crept away back to Max. 'He's fast asleep, come and look, he's so sweet.'

They walked quietly to the side of the house and watched him. 'It seems a shame to move him,' whispered Rose.

Max nodded. 'Well, you might be stuck with us for a little while longer. He normally sleeps for an hour or so.'

Rose playfully punched him on the arm. 'Oh no, what a drag,' she said.

He grabbed her round the waist, as if to throw her to the ground. Lifting her up, he was strong and Rose felt butterflies in her stomach. Placing her down on the ground, he looked as though he was about to say something but stopped himself and walked ahead back to the boys.

Rose set Dominic and Jasper up with her Wii machine and she and Max sat in the cool of the lounge, close to sleeping Milo. 'More of Lucia's dessert?' asked Rose as she licked the cream off her fingers as she cleared the plates.

Max watched her mouth and began to have immoral thoughts again, he noticed. He resolved to have sex when he returned to London; there was that woman at the ticket booth at the last theatre he played at who seemed quite keen on him.

'No, thanks, I'm full. Lucia's food is amazing.'

They sat in comfortable silence.

'You don't come back to London much,' he said.

'No, I know. I'm a bad Londoner.' She laughed.

'Why don't you?' he asked. 'Are we too provincial for you now?' he teased.

Rose blushed. In some ways he was right, London seemed so foreign to her now. 'No, it's not like that. I work a lot and

147

the British film industry isn't as big as the US. I don't get offered much there anyway.'

'We couldn't afford you,' laughed Max.

'Probably not,' said Rose truthfully.

'You could do a play, the theatre scene's alive and kicking,' said Max.

'I haven't done a play since I was at school, I don't think I'd be any good.'

'I doubt that,' said Max. 'You just have to be brave enough to step into the light. No cameras to hide behind. It's a very real experience.'

Rose sat in thought. Theatre intrigued her but travelling back to London didn't appeal at all.

Lucia placed coffee and chocolates and strawberries in front of them, the final offering, she thought of it.

Max placed a strawberry to his mouth and sucked the end of it, imagining Rose's nipple in his mouth. It was the most sensual thing Rose had seen a man do in a long time and she shifted in her chair.

'Rose,' said Max, uncertain how to say what was on his mind.

'Yes, Max,' said Rose. The air was thick with expectation.

'Do you . . .' His words remained unfinished when Dominic and Jasper came into the room fighting over who won the Wii game.

'Ah, I think the party's over,' said Max, the moment broken.

Rose sighed. Did she imagine it or was Max about to make a move? But the real question was, what would she have done, she wondered.

CHAPTER FIFTEEN

TG stayed overnight at Jack's villa and returned to Perugia the next morning. He emailed the details of Raphael's schedule to Sapphira and Jack as promised.

Checking on Calypso, he saw she was asleep, her face peaceful and her hair curling around her face.

TG walked into his room to shower. Coming out of the bathroom, wet with a towel around his waist, he saw Calypso sitting on his bed in a t-shirt and shorts. She looked drawn and worried.

'Hi,' he said, wondering when the butterflies would stop.

'Hi,' she said softly.

'How are you?' he asked concerned.

'Terrible. Sick,' she said and started to cry.

TG stood panicked and then rushed into the bathroom and came back with a glass of water and a tablet.

'What's this?' she asked suspiciously.

'A Valium, I use them when I fly, otherwise I'm a basket case. Takes the edge off,' he said.

Calypso washed it down with a quick drink and TG took the water from her and turned and stood in front of Calypso in his towel and felt embarrassed and very turned on. Aware she had been through the most horrific experience of her life he turned away from her.

Calypso watched him. His body was tanned and strong, the body of a surfer. He had light blond hairs on his chest.

149

'What's that?' she asked, seeing the tattoo on his back.

TG stood surprised; he had forgotten about the tattoo. 'It's a mermaid,' he answered quietly.

'Wow, she's beautiful,' answered Calypso. 'Come closer so I can see.'

Can I kiss you, thought TG but he said nothing, just moved a little so she could see it as she knelt on the bed and ran her finger lightly over the mermaid.

The tattoo was tiny, a little black and green mermaid, swimming with bubbles around her.

'Why do you have a mermaid?' asked Calypso as she ran her fingertips over the drawing.

TG shivered at her touch. 'I have dreams about them, ever since I was a kid. I don't know why. Maybe the movie *Splash* influenced me.' He laughed, trying to cover up his reaction to her touch.

'My name means mermaid or sea nymph, did you know that?' asked Calypso.

'No, I didn't,' lied TG. Of course he knew, he used to call his tattoo Calypso, till he met the real one.

The dream had occurred on and off since he was ten. Always he was drowning and a mermaid would come and pluck him from the sea floor and swim him to shore. Only his mother and Kelly knew of the dream and what it meant to him. Now he realized he was drowning when he was with Calypso. Only she could save him and he wondered if they would ever get to shore.

Calypso was surprised at her reaction to touching TG. She was attracted to him even in the midst of her trauma, she recognized how kind and sweet he was. When she had touched him, she felt him shiver and it had made her stomach flip. She wasn't sure if he was caring for her for the film's sake or because

150

he had feelings for her. Calypso was confused. She had just been through the worst experience of her life, so how could she have feelings for TG? Maybe it was just a little crush. She was projecting onto him what she wanted to feel.

Calypso clambered off the bed.

'How are you?' he asked, still not dressed.

'I'm angry,' she said.

'You should be, he's a fucking asshole,' said TG passionately.

'No, I'm angry at myself,' said Calypso.

'Why? You didn't do anything wrong,' said TG.

'No, I am angry at myself,' repeated Calypso sadly. 'For letting myself be taken in so easily by Marco, by Raphael, by the whole thing. I was an idiot.'

'I disagree,' said TG softly, wanting to pull her to him but knowing he couldn't.

Weeks of tension between them dissipated and Calypso smiled at him.

'I'm so grateful,' she started. 'How can I thank you, Tim?'

He shook his head. 'No, none of that. We're friends, okay, and that's what friends do.'

Calypso nodded, her eyes filling with tears again.

'Okay, I'm gonna get dressed and then make us something to eat,' he said cheerfully. 'I'm not the greatest cook but I can do toast and pancakes. I can also always call the housekeeper if you want something more than that.'

'No, I'm not hungry.'

'I know you're not, but you have to eat. Otherwise you'll get run down and feel even worse.'

'Okay,' she said, overwhelmed by his caring voice.

TG stood still in the towel. 'Okay, scoot and gimme some privacy,' he said and Calypso blushed.

Calypso walked from the room, tears filling her eyes. Most

of all she felt angry for not seeing that the right one for her was there in front of her all along.

Calypso stood outside the door, her forehead leaning on the wood. The Valium was kicking in and she was feeling calmer and braver.

'Kelly said you had a crush on me,' she said through the partition.

Silence greeted her from the bedroom.

What the fuck had Kelly said to her, thought TG.

TG opened the door. 'Sorry, I didn't hear you, what did you say?'

'I said that Kelly thinks you have a crush on me.' She dared him to be truthful. 'Is that why you're helping me?'

'Kelly thinks I have a crush on anyone single and female that I speak to longer than her,' said TG laughing.

Calypso waited in silence.

'I'm helping you because it's my job to help you, and to keep the film on schedule and because we're friends. Now come downstairs and I'll make you something to eat.'

Calypso watched him as he spoke. Perhaps Kelly and Sapphira were wrong. He just wanted her to be well again to finish the film. Disappointment flooded her and she bowed her head.

'Makes sense. Actually, I'm feeling a bit trippy from the Valium. I might lie down,' she said and turned and walked into her room and shut herself in.

It was TG's turn to put his head against the closed door.

Fuck, he thought. Fuck, fuck, fuck, as he banged his head lightly against it.

He had lost his moment and he wondered how a man who could direct action films could be so inept at taking action in his own life.

CHAPTER SIXTEEN

Sapphira was dressed for seduction: her long legs encased in a pair of Pucci python leather skintight pants, a pair of perilously high Louboutin red suede ankle boots, a white silk racerback singlet and a crab pendant with rubies in its pincers on a long platinum chain swinging between her breasts, bra-less, beneath her singlet. Entering the hotel lobby, she was oblivious to the stares directed her way; she had a job to do and she was going to play her role.

There was no doubt in Sapphira's mind that Raphael was guilty of raping Calypso. She didn't need the details from TG to imagine what he had done to the girl. He was guilty of being a misogynistic pig and guilty of preying on women. For her, it was not a matter of being right or wrong, it was a matter of principle – and Sapphira liked principle. Her code of conduct was based on equality and not doing harm to others, where possible. Although she had slept with married men and caused consternation and division among families, this was not Sapphira's problem as far as she was concerned. If the men got too close she pushed them away and chose to always stand on her own two feet.

Growing up in Hollywood, she knew it was still a man's world; in fact, it was not just Hollywood which was run by men, the whole world seemed like that, no matter what Oprah said on her show each week. As she drove over to the hotel, she had thought about Calypso's options as a young, beautiful actress from Hollywood. She didn't have a chance in hell to get out of this unscathed, and this made Sapphira's blood boil. Raphael would cry consensual sex and Calypso would have to testify in court, her name and career dragged through the mud. The studios were careful of their actors, and Calypso was a rising star who did not have the runs on the board to get out of a scandal like this. Everyone knew it, even her. Not going to the police was smart, agreed Sapphira, but letting Raphael get away with this was not an option. They had discussed it after TG left Jack's villa.

'You sure you want to do this?' asked Jack as he walked her to her bedroom upstairs.

'Yep, I haven't a worry in the world. Whatever happens to him after this is not my problem, but at least I know girls like Calypso will be safe from him in the future,' said Sapphira defiantly.

'Vigilante De Mont,' laughed Jack. 'What a night. I swear I haven't had this much action in years. I'm getting too old for this shit!' he said, doing a Danny Glover impersonation.

'I'm sorry about the whole thing earlier,' said Sapphira as she opened the bedroom door.

Jack stood and looked at her seriously. 'I know you have to get to the point of wanting to get off it, but when the time comes, I hope you will consider my offer. I will do anything I can to help you, Sapphira, and I know your life will be better than you can imagine off heroin. I hope you realize that one day soon.'

Sapphira hugged him close. 'Jack, you are a true friend. I think you are my only friend. I don't want to fuck this up.'

'You won't, babe. We have a good thing going,' he said, kissing her forehead. 'Off to bed now, okay?' And he smacked her butt.

'Anything?' she asked, jokingly.

He cocked his head to one side as if listening to himself. 'Nope, still gay.' He shrugged his shoulders and Sapphira laughed.

Lying in bed, she thought about Jack. It was incredible he had managed to maintain his secret from a world which was obsessed with his every move and relationship. That was a true actor, she thought as she closed her eyes.

Sleeping fitfully, she woke late and padded downstairs to find Jack, as refined as ever, in a blue silk dressing gown with white trim. Sitting in the kitchen, he was being served breakfast by his housekeeper – fresh fruits, bread and coffee. Sapphira took the coffee he held out to her, gratefully.

'How did you sleep?' asked Jack as he leafed through his morning paper.

'Not so great, weird dreams and thoughts about last night. All a bit too much, even for me,' she said ruefully.

Jack closed the paper. 'Let's get dressed and then I will fly you back to Perugia and we'll put our plan into action. But first, your clothes. You look like an off-duty Pussycat Doll. The paps have already caught on to our little "affair", according to my publicist, the photos are all over the web of us together last night, and while I'm not so worried about them associating me with you, I am concerned I could be photographed with you looking like that,' he said, pointing up and down at her sweat pants and singlet.

Sapphira threw a grape at him. 'Fuck off.'

'I've taken the liberty of ringing my friend, Chiara, who manages Gucci in Venice and she has had a few things sent over for you to choose from. They're in my bedroom if you want to go and pick something that looks suitable for the lover of the sexiest man in the world.' He said the last sentence in a deep voice like Barry White.

Sapphira rolled her eyes as she exited the kitchen to find an outfit. On Jack's bed were boxes and dress bags and at least ten shoeboxes. Sapphira opened them to find pants and dresses, tops in gorgeous silks and accessories. Jewellery, watches, sunglasses and hats. If Sapphira were into fashion, then this would have been like Christmas, but instead she found herself overwhelmed. 'Jack?' she called down the stairs.

'Coming,' he cried and ran up to her. 'Fashion crisis?'

'I'm not so good at this. What the hell will I put on? I always wear the same thing, which is fine for me but this is too much,' she said, waving her hand over the bounty on the bed.

'Okay, well, I always think about the role I want to play when I dress up. Am I going for urbane man about town or casual playboy?'

'Is there a difference?' asked Sapphira sarcastically.

'Oh, honey, I have so much to teach you,' he said, pursing his lips.

'Okay, I take it back. How on earth did I ever think you were straight? You are gayer than a Mexican tablecloth,' she said, holding out her arms to her sides. 'All right, Henry Higgins, I am your Eliza. Dress me!'

Jack looked over the clothes and pulled out several pieces and then stood back and looked at her. He then went back and scrabbled through the bags till he found what he was searching for.

'Put your hair in a ponytail. Low and to the side,' he commanded. 'Minimal make-up but red lips please. You will find a Nars lipstick in the drawer in your bathroom called Red Lizard, which will do fine,' he said imperiously.

'I don't even want to ask how you know that,' said Sapphira as she walked to her bedroom on the other side of the hall. When she emerged, Jack had the clothes laid out on the bed.

'All right, get your gear off,' he ordered.

Sapphira paused.

'It's okay, sex kitten, what you got cooking I ain't eating,' Jack said, taking the labels off them.

Sapphira quickly undressed and stood naked in front of him. 'Very nice,' he said, appraising her. 'Although a little heroin chic. Some weight would serve you well at some stage.'

Sapphira narrowed her eyes at him. 'Careful there, tiger.'

Ignoring her, he pulled out a garment. 'All right, step into this.'

He held out some pant legs for her. Pulling them up around her, she saw it was a jersey jumpsuit, with a singlet top and the thinnest spaghetti straps Sapphira had ever seen. 'How does this stay up?' she asked.

'It's a boob tube top, the straps are for show,' Jack said, straightening them out.

The jersey clung to her frame and lengthened her legs even further than they already were. The black showed off her skin and tattoos, giving her the air of a rock chick on holiday. Jack pulled out a scarf, brown and black with the Gucci pattern printed subtly across it and with a dark purple edging. Laying it flat, he folded it in a long bandage style and wrapped it around her head, tying it underneath. He pulled open the shoebox on the pillow and held a purple patent leather sandal with a single gold zip on the side. 'Put these on,' he said.

Standing back from Sapphira, he smiled. 'Nearly done, my little Galatea.' Taking a magenta leather bag from the bed, he handed it to her. 'Done,' he said, stepping back to survey his handiwork.

Sapphira looked in the mirror. 'I don't look like myself, but

I look okay, I guess,' she said, unimpressed by the image reflected back at her.

'You look amazing. I'm not a big fan of wearing all the same designer, it's a little Japanese or Russian for my taste but you gotta work with what you got. Gimme a moment and I will change and we'll head off. I've called the helicopter for midday.'

Sapphira packed her few things from the night before and put them into her new Gucci bag. Finding her toothbrush she laughed and then cleaned her teeth, careful to not destroy her lipstick. Hearing Jack call for her, she went downstairs to find him in a complementary ensemble: black pants and a black t-shirt. While simple, the clothes hung on his frame perfectly. Standing next to each other, they looked like the quintessential Hollywood couple. As Sapphira went to open the door, Jack stopped her. 'Wait,' he said, and pulled a pair of tortoiseshell, large-framed sunglasses from his pocket and put them on her face. 'Now we are ready.'

Placing a pair of aviators on his chiselled face, he picked up his bags. 'I'm going to stay at yours for a while. That okay?'

Sapphira shrugged. 'I guess so, although I'm quite boring, so don't expect much fun.'

'Lucky I packed my own fun!' said Jack as he handed his bags to the captain of the boat at the door.

As they walked into the sunshine, towards the water limousine to take them to the helicopter, Sapphira heard the cameras around them. The clicking and whirring and the calls of their names from the paparazzi startled her a little. She climbed into the boat with Jack holding her hand. As she navigated the gangplank in her new shoes, she smiled her thanks to him and they settled into the privacy underneath the deck.

The photos were shown around the world. Sapphira's look, as styled by Jack, was copied by every fashion outlet and Gucci sold out of all the pieces she was wearing in three days. A new Hollywood power couple was in town.

Now Sapphira was dressed to seduce, again, styled by Jack. They had laughed all morning going through her clothes at his running commentary on her style. 'I'm surprised you're not gay either. You have this whole lesbian chic thing going on.'

'I've been with women, but I wouldn't call myself gay or straight, for that matter. I'm not into labels, unlike you,' she said playfully.

Jack had chosen her outfit but even Sapphira thought she looked good. She had not entertained the thought for a moment that Raphael would deny her. He was an easy target – too easy for Sapphira, and one she would not normally bother with, but today was not about her.

The lift opened and she found the number of the penthouse suite TG had said he was staying in. Knowing he was about to fly to America to meet his new US agents, she had to work fast. She knocked at the door. Raphael opened it and his mouth dropped.

'Hello,' said Sapphira sexily, inside laughing to herself.

'*Ciao, bella*,' said Raphael back at her. He knew who she was, he had seen her films and was disappointed when he was cast that they would not have any scenes together. 'Come in,' he said, gesturing her inside.

Sapphira walked in and stood in the centre of the room. 'I just wanted to say "hi". I'm a big fan and was so sad we weren't having any scenes together.'

Raphael couldn't believe his luck. 'I was thinking the same thing. We are together in our minds,' he said, laughing. He eyed her breasts and legs hungrily, imagining he could fuck her then boast about it to his friends.

Sapphira saw the way he looked her over. The man was disgusting, she thought, as she put her hands on her hips.

'So I was thinking, maybe we could, you know, hang out,' she said casually.

Raphael looked at her then at the clock next to his bed. His car service was coming in five minutes to take him to the airport – not enough time for a fuck but maybe she could blow him and they could save the best till he got back. He walked towards her and stood in front of her, almost menacingly. 'Maybe we can hang out a little now? *Sí?*'

He bent over her and kissed her hard on the mouth, his fat tongue rolling around her teeth. Stopping herself from pulling away, Sapphira responded, kissing him harder and then biting his tongue.

'Ow, what the fuck?' he held his tongue, tasting blood in his mouth.

'Sorry, baby,' purred Sapphira, trying not to laugh, thinking about what Jack would say. 'I like to bite sometimes when I get horny.'

Raphael decided to not push on the blowjob he was hoping for, since she liked to bite. Instead he grabbed at her breasts and pinched the nipples making them erect. Sapphira tried not to jump. That fucking hurt, she thought. What had he done to Calypso if this was what he was like with her?

'I have to go to America now but I'll be back in three days. Maybe we can hang out, as you say, then.' He was still playing with her breasts, his hands rough on the outside of her singlet.

She smiled and put her hand into her pocket then she put her arms around his waist. Slipping both hands into the pockets of his tight jeans, she squeezed his ass, hard, and she felt his cock harden against her hip.

'I would love that. Call me when you come back, okay? We can hang out and fuck, hopefully.'

Raphael looked at her; she was his kind of woman. 'I am going to fuck you so hard you will cry,' he said arrogantly.

Like you did Calypso, no doubt, she thought angrily, but instead she sucked his bottom lip, and then bit it hard. 'You never know, I might make you cry, *bello*,' she said as she walked out of the room. '*Ciao*,' she said, as she left him blotting his lip with toilet paper.

Returning to the villa, she found Jack waiting at the front door. 'Well?' he asked expectantly.

'Done,' she said and walked inside. 'I have to take these shoes off, they're killing my feet.'

Taking off her shoes, she walked into the lounge room and sat on a chair. 'First I've got to make the phone call, then we wait. *Si*?' she said coquettishly to Jack.

'What was he like? I can only imagine from what I've heard,' asked Jack as Sapphira rubbed her feet.

'Want me to do that? I've done it before,' he said, reminding her of the day on set not long ago when she was afraid of him seeing track marks between her toes.

'I was so sure you noticed the track marks on my feet.'

'I didn't but I picked up something weird about you. I wasn't sure what. You seemed so edgy and worried,' said Jack as he rubbed her feet.

Sapphira looked at his hands. 'Well, now you know, and I know about you, and only you and I know about that disgusting pig, Raphael. He was awful, rough, leering and so filled with testosterone I wanted to throw up. I hate men like him.'

'Well, let's hope he gets what he deserves,' said Jack.

'All right, I'm going to make my call.'

Sapphira left the room and Jack walked around the sitting

161

room in her villa. It was as though she didn't live there. No personal items were out at all. Nothing was touched. The magazines were straight on the table, the sofa cushions all carefully plumped by her housekeeper, he supposed. What room did she sleep in, he wondered.

He had slept in the master bedroom. When he asked where she slept she had evaded the question. He had woken early to look for her but couldn't find her anywhere in the house. She was an enigma wrapped up in a riddle, he decided.

Sapphira returned. 'Done,' she said. 'We have to shoot tomorrow and you have one week to find a replacement actor. Any news?'

'Yes, I have a few options for TG and I've emailed him from my BlackBerry. Once this all comes out, we'll have to move fast and quietly to keep it all hushed up. Enough of that, though, we just have to wait and see what happens. What shall we do today?'

'Babe, you can do what you like but I'm going to read. Feel free to use anything or go anywhere. Okay?'

'Where will I find you?' asked Jack, wondering where she was planning on reading.

'I will find you,' she said as she closed the door behind her.

Jack gave a little laugh. The girl sure knew how to make an exit.

CHAPTER SEVENTEEN

'Jesus, have you heard?' Rose asked Kelly as she arrived on set on the Thursday morning.

'Yep,' she said, setting her brushes in order. Kelly liked order, especially on mornings like this.

'I can't believe it. I'm always shocked when I hear about a scandal. I suppose I like to think the best of people,' said Rose as she settled in the chair in front of her.

'Really? I never do. You hear the strangest things in this chair. Nothing shocks me anymore,' said Kelly laughing.

When the scandal broke overnight and Raphael had been charged with drug possession entering LAX, the studio had been on the phone right away, insisting TG fire him and recast and re-shoot the scenes with Calypso.

'But drugs? A dirty bag of heroin in his pocket! What a fool. He probably thought he was a big enough star to get them through, but LAX is a nightmare now. All that checking and scanning. Poor TG, what a mess. What's he going to do?' she asked.

'I don't know. I'm staying away until I'm asked otherwise.'

'Wise move, lady,' said Rose and she closed her eyes for Kelly to work her magic.

Rose walked onto the set looking for Max. He hadn't been in make-up when she was there and she was looking forward to seeing him. Heading into town the day before, she had bought some Perugian chocolates in the shapes of different animals. When she saw them in the shop, she thought of the boys immediately.

'Is Max around?' she asked Chris as he walked by her while she waited for the shot to be set up.

'I think he's in his trailer,' said Chris, waving in that general direction.

Rose went to her trailer and took the bag of gifts to Max's trailer. Knocking on the door, she waited for him to answer. 'What?' she heard Max yell from inside.

'It's Rose.'

The door opened and Max stood in the door, expressionless.

'Um, hi. I saw these in town and I thought of you,' stammered Rose nervously.

Max seemed nervous, too. 'Thanks, you didn't need to do that,' he said, taking the bag from her.

'I wanted to. It's just some chocolate, everyone likes chocolate. I put labels on them so you know which one is for which boy. I got Milo the cutest chocolate teddy bear and Jasper . . .'

Max interrupted her. 'Listen, Rose, that's very kind of you, thanks. I will make sure the boys send a note but I've a few calls to make if you don't mind.'

As he shut the door in Rose's face, she was shocked. He was unfriendly; it was the Max she had first met without the yelling. What had happened to create such animosity, she wondered.

The mood on set was tense. Max was terse and unresponsive to Rose unless they were acting. It was a tough day and as Rose walked to her trailer at the end of the day, she felt herself wanting to cry. Max was being totally unreasonable and Rose didn't know why she cared so much. She had worked with other bad tempered and rude actors before but Max was more than just another actor to her.

Max was in his trailer preparing to go home for the day, when he saw the bag of chocolates Rose had given him. Opening it, he saw a teddy bear for Milo, a toolset for Jasper and a motorbike for Dominic. She knew them perfectly, he thought, as he put them back in the bag.

Max felt awful. He had tossed and turned all night thinking of Rose and feeling guilty about Alice. His solution was to punish Rose and now he felt like a prick. He was a prick, he decided.

'Fuck,' he said, as he realized Rose had left for the day. What should I do, he wondered as he drove home. Make some big gesture or would that be weird?

Entering his villa, Milo came to greet him, after spending a day with his brothers and their Italian nanny. 'We went on a bear hunt in the woods,' said Milo, climbing up his father's leg.

Max picked him up and walked out to see his sons, who were playing in the back garden.

'Boys,' he called. They ran over to him. 'Rose bought something for you all and asked me to give them to you.' Handing out the chocolates, the boys ripped off the wrappings and started to stuff their faces.

Max watched them tenderly. It's so simple for them, he thought. Why do adults make things so confusing? Then he stopped. 'Boys, can I ask your advice?' The two elder boys looked at each other, confused. Their father never asked them their advice.

Max went on. 'I've made a mistake and I was a bit rude, actually a lot rude, to someone and I think I was wrong. What would you do?'

165

Jasper piped up. 'Say sorry.'

Dominic interjected. 'No! Give them a present.'

Milo looked his father in the eye, his mouth covered in chocolate. 'Kiss them.'

Max smiled at them. 'How did I get such smart men?' he asked. 'Do you mind looking after the boys for a bit?' he asked the nanny. 'I have to see someone.'

As Max drove back up the driveway, Dominic turned to the nanny. 'It's about Rose. Dad's a loser around her though,' he scoffed, as he stuffed more chocolate into his face.

Max parked and nearly lost his nerve. What the hell was he doing there? Summoning up his courage, he walked to Rose's door and rang the bell. Lucia answered. '*Buongiorno*, Signor Max, I will let Rose know you are here,' she said conspiratorially, as she led Max into the sitting room.

Max waited nervously and then Rose came into the room. Her hair was wet from the shower and she was wearing a white cotton dress and no shoes. She looked like an angel! Warily, she stood in front of him. 'Hello,' she said.

'Hello. I believe I have to apologize to you. I'm very sorry for being such a shit today. I've not been myself and I'm afraid you keep seeing the worst in me.'

Rose waited. She had nothing to say and Max seemed to have a lot on his mind. 'You see, the thing is, well fuck, I will be honest with you. Excuse my language.'

Rose shrugged her shoulders, not caring about his use of profanities.

'I'm being a schoolboy. I've had feelings for you since our dinner and I feel like I'm betraying Alice. I'm sorry, it's not your business or your fault. You are just being you, which is lovely, by the way. I've no right to act like I did today and I

166

hope you will forgive me.' He wrung his hands and then put them in and out of his pants pockets, unsure of what to do with them.

Rose sat down, shocked at his candour and slightly exhilarated at the same time. So she hadn't imagined it, she thought. He did have feelings for her.

Max continued, 'I've not had feelings for anyone since Alice died and it's too much almost. I never thought I would think about anyone again and then I met you. I feel guilty in some ways, yet when I'm with you, I feel at peace again. It's bloody awful. I promise to not let this get in the way of making the film in any way. I've been a dickhead, I know that. My feelings are not your responsibility but I want to thank you all the same.'

'For what?' Rose asked quietly.

'For bringing me back to life. Even if these feelings aren't reciprocated, it does feel good.'

Rose smiled. 'Oh Max, you're an idiot. I was being nice when I bought the chocolates, not asking for your hand in marriage.'

'I know, I am an idiot, aren't I?' he said as he paced on the rug. Bending down in front of her, he took her hand. 'I'm not socialized enough, the nuances pass me by.'

Rose held his hands tight and then leaned forward and kissed him on the mouth. Chaste, but lingering. Max pulled away and looked her in the eyes. 'Is that the kiss of friends?'

'Yes, I feel sorry for you.' Her eyes twinkled as she spoke.

Max was serious. 'Rose, I've got three children and I haven't been with anyone since Alice. I thought I was done.'

'Oh Max, again, I'm not proposing marriage. I'm talking sex,' said Rose, laughing.

'God, I'm hopeless. Christ.' He hung his head in shame.

'Come on then, sympathy sex, nothing better,' said Rose and

pulled him towards her. She was surprised how much she wanted him, it was lust and laughter mixed together.

Max fell back on top of her and Rose embraced him. Their kisses were so tantalizing, Rose wondered if she actually wanted him to stop. This was almost enough, she thought, and then she felt his hands holding her breasts. He unzipped her dress at the back and pulled the cotton off her shoulders; her wet hair brushed against his cheek. Her dress pulled down to her waist, he touched her wondrous breasts and Rose sat, being worshipped and explored. She undid his buttons and pulled off his shirt, kissing his chest and running her hands over his back. 'I have wanted to do this since the day beside the pool,' she murmured, her voice thick with lust.

'You have no idea what you did to me that day, what I wanted to do to you,' he said huskily.

Rose laughed and wriggled out of her dress; underneath she was wearing just a pair of silk underpants. 'Then show me now,' she said, lying back on the rug.

Max undressed and lay next to her. They began to explore each other's bodies, slowly and rhythmically, the touch electric when their skin came together. Max entered her and she sighed in ecstasy. It had been so long since either of them had been with anyone and Max and her fitted perfectly. Wrapping her legs around him, they moved together until Rose came quickly and then Max came after. She held him close inside her, until he rolled off and she rested her head on his chest.

Max kissed her and held her close. 'I asked the boys what I should do to apologize and they said I should say sorry, kiss you and give you a present. I've done the first two but not the last one I am afraid.'

Rose nestled her head into his chest. 'Yes, you did. I haven't had an orgasm in a long time. That's the best present a woman can ask for.'

'Well then,' said Max, 'I can give you one of those as often as you like, my lovely Rose.'

'Sexellent!' she said, and lifted her head and kissed him passionately.

Max responded and rolled on top of her again. 'I haven't been able to do this since I was a teenager, but I think I'm ready to give you another present.'

Rose felt his erection against her and lazily opened her legs for him. 'Come on then, you sad sack,' she teased, as he entered her again.

Leaving Rose's villa that night, Max returned to his boys, who were about to be tucked into bed by the nanny. 'How did you go, Dad?' asked Dominic as Max came to say goodnight.

'Very well, thanks, Dom. All is sorted. You were right and all is forgiven.'

'Say hi to Rose for me,' said Dominic cheekily as he pulled the covers up around him.

Max was startled. Kids are smarter than we realize, he thought as he turned off the light.

Rose and Max slipped into intimacy easily. Both were longing for connection again and their joy at being with each other and the boys was infectious. Max and the boys spent most of their time at Rose's villa, almost moving in. The boys delighted in her company and Rose was able to fall in love with them as fast as she was falling for Max. Their energy was obvious on set and TG found their connection transferred into the scenes they filmed together.

On their days off they spent time with the boys, exploring

the countryside or lazing by the pool. Lucia revelled in them being a family, cooking and minding the boys when Max and Rose went out alone at night for dinner.

It was everything Rose wanted and she didn't want it to end, saying as much to Max at dinner in town one night. 'Perhaps we can stay here forever?'

'I'm not so sure that would work, lovely Rose,' said Max as he ate his pasta.

Rose moved the silk shawl around her shoulder; she was aware time was slipping by and soon the filming would end. 'So, it's a fling? A summer romance?' she asked, overcome with sadness.

'I don't know, Rose. We need to work out a lot of things. We lead very different lives. I'm just a jobbing actor in London, and this is the biggest film I've ever done. The kids are at school. I don't know what we will do, Rose, but let's enjoy it and see what happens. If Alice's death taught me anything, it's just to enjoy the moments and not plan too far ahead.'

Rose looked into her wine. She had waited for a man like Max for a long time and yet she had a different life to him in LA. There was no way she could give it all up for something she didn't know had a secure future.

It was just a summer romance she reminded herself. Just for Italy and not for forever.

CHAPTER EIGHTEEN

TG was desperate. He wanted to see Calypso smile again and he would do anything to make this a reality. He wanted to tell her he loved her and would slay any dragon to fix it all, to hold her close and stroke her hair and touch her face.

TG had moved the schedule as much as possible to accommodate her but they were due to shoot again next week and the producers would not let her have any more time, threatening to fire and sue her simultaneously. TG's insistence that her condition was serious and private and he had it all under control was the only lifeline Calypso had – not that she knew any of this.

The shock wore off after the night Raphael came into her room and then shame took its place. Calypso ran the night over in her head repeatedly and she still blamed herself. If she hadn't opened the door, if she had put a robe on, if she had taken more pride in herself. The reasons she was at fault were endless; it drove her into a deeper depression.

TG's support was infinite. When she cried in her sleep, he checked on her, left the door open between their rooms. He had the entire season of *Fresh Prince of Bel Air* flown over to make her laugh, after she mentioned she had a crush on Will Smith as a kid. He brought her tea and coffee and cakes and treats from the set. She left them mostly untouched, but sometimes she poured the tea or coffee down the bathroom sink, to make him think she had drunk it, just to see him happy.

When the shame threatened to engulf her one night, she picked up her phone and rang home, desperate for familiar voices. Her father answered. '*Ciao*, Caterpillar. How you doing?'

Her father's gentle voice down the line made her cry and she sobbed into the phone.

'What is it, darling?' asked Bob again. 'Come on, Caterpillar, you can tell me.'

Calypso knew she could never tell her father what had happened to her, he would be devastated; he couldn't even protect her from Leeza growing up. He had tried to step in whenever Leeza was on one of her managerial rampages, but years of her belittling him had made him a broken man and Bob had tried to stay out of the show business world as much as he could. He was proud of Calypso and her rising fame had brought him a level of comfort he could never bring to the family.

His voice saying her name repeatedly brought Calypso out of her sobbing and she tried to get it together. 'It's nothing, Dad, just a bit homesick, that's all.'

'You sure, Caterpillar?' His voice was uncertain. Calypso rarely came to him with emotion. In fact, he hadn't seen her cry since she was fourteen, when she'd had to go to an audition with a bad flu.

Calypso heard her mother walking towards the phone. 'Who is it, Bob? Calypso?'

Leeza grabbed the phone from Bob and her voice came down the line. 'What's wrong, honey? You okay? That director being an asshole again? Want me to come and give him a mouthful?'

Calypso calmed as soon as she heard her mother's voice. However pushy Leeza was, she was a fierce lioness when it came to Calypso.

172

'No, Mom, it's okay, he's nice actually. I'm just a bit home-sick, that's all.'

'Well, honey, you made the choice to go there and make this movie, you could have done the other film here, so I guess you gotta enjoy it. Any cute boys around who can ease the homesickness?' Leeza laughed at her own joke.

Calypso sat and thought about Marco and realized she didn't care for him anymore. The only face she saw in her mind was TG's. 'No, no. I'm just working a lot, you know.'

'How's the director? He's cute, I saw him on *E Online*. Had a horrible break-up with that girl. Poor thing, I felt sad for him. Ted Casablanca said he had wanted to marry her but she ran off with the fat guy from Paramount. She's a piece of work and so skinny, like a sack full of antlers.'

Calypso thought of TG constantly trying to get her to eat, tempting her with pancakes and pasta. Getting in fresh fruits and sweet Italian pastries from town and leaving her little notes to encourage her to eat and take care of herself when he was shooting.

'Hey, Mom, I gotta go. I just wanted to hear your voice, okay? I love you.'

'Okay, baby. Do good on the film,' Leeza said as she hung up.

Calypso wondered why her mother could never say 'I love you' to her. Do good on the audition or the film was the most encouragement she ever received from Leeza, although her father was far more forthcoming with his affection to her. Bob had sent her a few emails since she had been in Italy with links to items on eBay she might like or photos of the latest piece of furniture he had done up. Her father was more technology savvy than Leeza and she liked the fact Leeza had one less mode of communication with which to hassle her.

Thinking about TG after she hung up from Leeza, she wondered about the girlfriend. It must have been heartbreaking for him to want a life and the girl to only want a career. TG deserved more, even Calypso knew that. There was a small town innocence about him which appealed to Calypso. TG had integrity and was kind to everyone he met, interested and present in conversations.

Even through the haze of her anguish since her rape by Raphael, she was beginning to see in TG a reliability and strength which she did not know existed inside her. Perhaps Sapphira and Rose's teasing about him having a crush on her had been right. She found him looking at her sometimes in a way which made her stomach flip. And when they were sitting outside on the terrace on the large swing seat, she unconsciously placed her feet on his lap, and he rubbed them gently as they lay, swinging in the dusk, him drinking a beer and her a mineral water. At that moment she could not think of another place she would rather be.

Sometimes, when she was up to it, they sat downstairs and watched old *Fresh Prince* episodes together. TG would get up and attempt to dance like Will Smith and she would laugh. 'Stop it, you are so bad,' she would say as he tried to moonwalk.

'What? Girl? You are crazy. I am a fly mutha and I have moves you ain't seen yet!'

They would laugh and then Calypso would remember and she would stop herself from feeling good. TG saw the sudden changes in her but instinctively knew not to push her. Kelly had advised him not to when he asked her one evening when she had come for dinner without Chris.

'You need to just wait and show her you are there for her, not in a creepy predatory way but you want her to be well.

174

Whatever has happened to her is obviously awful and I think your friendship is all she has at the moment. Tread lightly, my friend.'

Of course, she was right. TG knew this was no time to make his intentions or feelings known; in some way they had taken a back seat to wanting her to become herself again. TG made a pact with 'The Force' that he would be prepared to give her up, should that help her.

It was Sunday morning when she heard a knock at her bedroom door. 'Come in,' she said as TG entered.

'Come on, lady. Time to leave the cave. I have planned us a date,' he said and Calypso looked up at him, her eyes wide with surprise.

A date, she wondered, happy for the first time in a while until she saw his face. He was red and shook his head. 'Well, not a date, an outing,' he said quickly.

Calypso felt her disappointment rise; of course he wouldn't want to be with her. She was damaged goods, she thought bitterly.

TG could have kicked himself. Why did he use the word date? The last thing she needed was some guy assuming he would want a date with her. She needed to heal, he remembered Kelly saying.

'Where are we going?' she asked softly.

'A surprise. Be ready in ten minutes.'

'Ten minutes?' she exclaimed.

'Yep, dress casual,' he said as he sauntered out of the room.

Heading out in the sunshine, Calypso was more excited than TG had ever seen her. Pointing out sights and reading the map TG had given her, pointing the direction where they were headed. Playing her iPod on his car stereo, she serenaded him with her collection of bizarre 80s tracks, of which he knew most. 'I love Martha and the Muffins,' she said, yelling over the sound of the car, singing to 'Echo Beach'.

'Why do you even know this stuff, this is so not your era of music!' he yelled.

'I don't know. I just like it, some things you can't explain,' she yelled back.

How right you are, thought TG. They drove through Perugia and continued onwards. TG then drove into a small town.

'Where are we?' asked Calypso, looking around.

'Todi,' answered TG, looking at the map. 'Yep, this is where we need to be.' He drove a little further into town and then parked the car.

'All right, let's get going,' he commanded, and Calypso jumped out of the car, ready. It felt good to be out, she thought and she was grateful they were away from Perugia and Marco.

They walked up the stone road, people greeting them amiably as they passed by. It was a busy morning. Turning the corner, Calypso gasped. They were at a huge antique market, stalls lined the square and there was furniture and bric-a-brac everywhere.

Calypso squealed. 'Oh my God! I love flea markets. Thank you,' she said and spontaneously hugged TG. He hugged her back and she kissed his cheek. 'I don't have any cash though, we will have to go to the bank,' she said, looking around.

'No need, I've got plenty and you can pay me back later,' he said.

She darted off into the crowd, calling his name to follow her. They walked the length of the market and TG became as enthusiastic as she was, bargaining, comparing and arguing about their purchases. Returning to the car, Calypso had bought a white lace beaded dress from the 1920s, a black crocodile clutch purse, a long strand of jet beads and matching earrings, and a vase in the shape of deer, which TG secretly wished he had bought but teased her about it all the same. 'Is Bambi all wrapped up safely?' he asked.

'She's fine, how's your Michelin Man?'

TG had bought a Michelin Man lamp that glowed when lit. He had also bought a straw pork pie hat, and an old Super 8 camera with its original case. Putting the items in the trunk, TG announced it was time for lunch.

'Lunch?' exclaimed Calypso. 'I'm still stuffed from your pancakes at breakfast. I'll be your Michelin Woman soon. Maybe he needs a wife.'

TG laughed. 'You are gorgeous and you know it. Come on, Mrs Michelin, let's fatten you up.'

Calypso laughed and blushed. God, she had it bad for him, she knew it now.

They walked in silence while Calypso thought. TG noticed her quietness but decided not to push her. She would talk when she was ready, as Kelly had said. They wandered through the medieval town, TG marvelling at the intact city. Stopping on the main road outside a picturesque café, TG asked, 'How does here look?'

Breaking her thoughts about TG, Calypso looked up. 'It looks fine,' she smiled.

They entered and found a table at the back.

'Isn't it funny we're here now, after the way we started meeting at the audition, me stealing your Coke, being a dickhead to you at the party. God, I'm so ashamed,' she said, looking down.

TG smiled. 'Yeah, what was that at the party?' he asked.

'I thought you were ignoring me that night because I said I ate a pastry and I thought you were thinking I'd get fat and ruin the film.'

177

Calypso held her hand to her mouth in shock and to stop herself speaking.

'What? You're crazy! No, I was weird that night. I was nervous and stressed about the film and all that crap,' he said, thinking to himself, and I was overwhelmed by you.

'Oh God, I was such a little shit to you, because I thought you hated me.' Calypso looked down at the table ashamed of her behaviour.

'No, I was just as bad. I was being a dick. I'm so sorry.' He looked ashamed also. They both looked up and laughed at each other.

'Well, I owe you so much and I just want to say thank you. I can try to get through the scene with Raphael if you need me to,' said Calypso bravely.

TG looked at her face and was certain he loved her. 'No, I've had that taken care of. Let's not think about the film today. I've got a day off and right now this is perfect.'

He looked at her for a long time and Calypso felt her stomach flip again.

Looking down intently at the menu, TG saw her face flush. Oh no, I've said too much, he thought. Shit!

'What do you want to drink? Wine? Water? What do you like on the menu?'

TG was nervous; it felt like a date to him and he was trying to keep it together.

Calypso put down her menu. 'I've no idea. I can't read Italian. I just say 'no meat' to the waitress and I get a vegetarian dish. That's the extent of my language skills.'

TG laughed and it became easy between them again. The waitress came to take their order. Soon they were eating their way through a gorgeous antipasto and drinking white wine from the region. It was perfect, thought Calypso. They talked about everything, Calypso's childhood in the industry, TG's childhood in the Midwest. They shared stories and gossip and argued about the merits of music from the 80s versus the 90s.

Looking around, Calypso was surprised. 'They're setting up for dinner. Come on, we've been here for three hours,' she said.

Paying the bill, they wandered back to the car. 'I'm sleepy,' said Calypso. 'It's the wine, I think.' She leaned her head on TG's arm as they walked. He tensed up and Calypso pulled away. 'Sorry,' she said, and they walked in silence to the car.

Driving home, Calypso fell asleep and TG was lost in thought. Why had he pulled away? Was he reading that she had feelings for him? Was he hoping this and projecting? He banged the steering wheel in frustration and Calypso woke up. 'What's wrong?' she asked, rubbing her eyes.

'Nothing,' he said. 'Just a hole in the road.'

Arriving back at the villa, they were quiet. There was a sense of something in the air that TG could not understand. Calypso walked ahead with her purchases from the market. 'I'm going to put these upstairs,' she said.

'Okay, want anything to eat?'

'Not a thing, I'm stuffed,' she laughed. 'I want to get changed, I'm a bit dusty.'

'Okay, I'm going to check my messages. I'll be in the lounge.'

TG rang his phone message service. One message from Jack and one from Sapphira, sounding almost as though she was enjoying her role in the espionage. Their mission was complete, they said.

Calypso walked into the room. She stood in the doorway, wearing her white lace dress from the market.

'What do you think?' she asked.

The dress hung on her as if it were made for her. With thin straps, the beaded silk clung to her shape and showed off her skin. Her neck was long and her hair upswept in a messy bun, with small tendrils escaping.

'You look like an angel,' he answered, his heart in his throat. TG walked over to her. 'You are the loveliest thing I've ever seen.'

He stood above her, her head reaching his chin. She was tiny and he felt like he wanted to put her in his pocket to protect her.

She looked up at him. 'Thank you,' she said softly.

Then TG leaned down and kissed her. He couldn't help it, he was filled with desire and had wanted to kiss her since the first night they met at the party at his villa. She stood and accepted his kiss without moving.

'Sorry,' he said and pulled away.

Calypso reached up and pressed her lips back onto his, her thin arms winding around his neck. The tension of the day gave way to passion and they were breathless, almost as if they were trying to consume each other. TG could not believe it; he stopped her and held her face. 'Are you sure?' he asked anxiously.

She answered by pulling her dress above her head. Underneath she was naked and TG gasped with longing. Taking his hand, she led him upstairs to her bedroom. Lying him down on the bed, she undressed him slowly, stopping to kiss him occasionally. As she leaned over him to pull the t-shirt over his head, her breasts swung above his mouth. He greedily sucked her nipples and buried his face between them.

Lifting her up by her hips, he sat her on his face and he inhaled her scent, licking and kissing her until she squirmed with desire. She pulled away and went back to her task at hand. She undid his jeans and pulled them off, his cock hard underneath his black underwear. He reached down and pulled off his socks and they sat on the bed facing each other. She smiled at him with a slow, sexy smile.

'I've wanted you since you danced *Fresh Prince* style for me,' she said cheekily.

TG laughed and rolled her onto her back. He caressed her slowly and she responded to his touch, arching her back and pushing her pelvis towards him. Entering her slowly, he watched her face to ensure she was okay. She eagerly met his gentle motions with grasping hands on his buttocks, pushing him further into her. He flipped her over and she straddled him, her hair falling about her face. TG thought he was in a dream as she rode him. He held her breasts as she rocked back and forth, grinding herself into him. He felt her tighten as they moved and he knew she was about to climax. She looked down into his eyes and held them as she came. So moved was TG by the sight of her pleasure, by all he had wanted for so long, he climaxed with her.

She fell onto the bed, breathing heavily. 'So, you do have a crush on me?' she teased.

'Oh baby, I passed crush a long time ago,' he answered softly, and they lay in silence, holding hands until they fell asleep.

CHAPTER NINETEEN

Sapphira and Jack were cohabiting nicely at her villa. They stayed out of each other's way and he said no more about her addiction. She was continuing to shoot up but she was more careful and mindful of what Jack had been through in Venice with her. Sapphira thought more and more about a life without addiction but still she was afraid of living without the drugs. Jack, to his credit never said a word but made sure she was eating properly, so in some ways Sapphira was healthier than she had been before she met Jack.

He had followed her to her lair one night without her knowledge and while he did not disturb her peace, he was happy he knew where she was at least. But Sapphira was finding herself spending less time in the library, seeking out Jack for conversation and company. They were like an old married couple and he brought her peace, which she was grateful for.

Shooting the final scenes together had been bittersweet, for Sapphira knew he would return to Venice and she would leave for the US alone again.

'You can stay longer if you want,' she said as they left the set together one evening.

'I may stay for a little longer, just to make sure you're all right.'

'I can look after myself, thanks. I just thought, if you don't have anything to return to straightaway,' she answered him crossly.

Jack laughed at her. 'Face it, babe, you are under the spell of Mr Reynolds and there ain't nothing you can do about it.'

Sapphira hopped in the Mercedes on the driver's side. She had given up the driver and she and Jack drove themselves to work each day. 'You're an arrogant son of a bitch, but I love you anyway.'

'I love you too, baby,' he said and kissed her on the cheek as she started the engine.

Arriving at her villa, she knew she needed to shoot up again. It had been four hours and her body was telling her to fulfil her job.

'I'll just be a moment,' she called out, making her way to the library.

Jack dumped his bag in the foyer and walked into the lounge room. 'Fuck,' he yelled. Sapphira came running in and cried out. On the wall was a giant image of a dead foetus, with the words *murderer* written underneath it in red paint.

'What the fuck?' said Jack as he hustled a screaming Sapphira from the room.

He pressed the intercom for security and two men came from the back of the villa. 'How the fuck did that happen?' said Jack, pointing to the room.

The guards entered the room and swore in Italian. One of them crossed himself. Jack reached for his mobile phone from his pants pocket, dialling TG's number. He yelled into the phone. 'I need you here now at Sapphira's. Now!'

Taking Sapphira upstairs, he laid her on the bed. She was beside herself with anguish. He heard the guards on the phone to the police, and within twenty minutes he heard TG's car arrive.

'I want twenty-four hour security on her. Okay?' barked TG at the guards. 'Where are the cameras? I wanna see the tapes.'

The guards took TG to the security room. The tapes of the

front door and the sitting room were missing. Whoever had done this had been into the security room and taken the tapes when Jack had called security to the lounge.

TG felt sick. What the hell was going on?

He ran upstairs to see Jack and Sapphira, who was sobbing and shaking uncontrollably. 'She needs a doctor,' said TG anxiously.

'I'll sort it out, you go and talk to the police,' said Jack forcefully.

Sapphira was hysterical. Running downstairs, Jack made his way to the library and saw she had pulled her kit out on the table; she must have been about to shoot up when he called her. Grabbing it and its contents off the table, he hid it under his t-shirt and ran upstairs again.

Locking the door to the bedroom, he set up the works and expertly melted the heroin and drew it back into the needle. Holding her arm, he found a vein and shot her up.

The relief was instant and Sapphira closed her eyes. She started to speak slowly. Jack listened, holding her hand as she spoke as though it were only yesterday.

'I met a guy. He taught me how to use the needle. I got pregnant. I wanted to keep it but the doctor said it wasn't able to survive once born. I blamed myself. I was high when she was conceived. That's why she wasn't right.'

Sapphira's voice caught in her throat.

'It was the hardest thing I have ever had to do and now I try to push myself, to feel something close to that pain but there is nothing like losing a child. Even if you are pregnant for a moment, you are a mother forever,' she said, tears running down her perfect face.

'Oh, sweetie . . .' said Jack, unsure how to console her.

'And when I came home from the hospital, someone had

184

sent me a little coffin with a baby doll inside covered in blood.'

'Oh, fuck,' said Jack, and he sat on the bed with her until she became sleepy. 'Who'd do such a fucking awful thing?'

'I don't know, I don't know, Jacky.' She cried in his arms falling asleep.

As Sapphira went to sleep with Jack stroking her arm, she realized she forgot to tell him about the dream she had after finding the coffin. This was a dream she had regularly since then. She dreamed of her baby that night. Sitting under the tree, the image of which was tattooed on her back, looking across the plains of some unknown foreign land, the baby spoke to her,

'Come and find me. I will wait for you.'

Leaving her to sleep, Jack went downstairs and found TG talking to the police. 'They want to talk to her.'

'They can't. She's taken a sedative. Tomorrow,' said Jack in a tone of voice no one was prepared to argue with.

TG looked at Jack. 'She can't stay here. She'll have to stay with me till the end of the shoot. There are always people around and it's busy.'

'I'll ask her,' said Jack, knowing it would not be acceptable to Sapphira. 'I'm here for a while longer, so we'll see what she wants, okay?'

TG and Tom left to go back and discuss security on set and at her home. The police took photos and fingerprints, which was useless. Jack sat in the kitchen waiting for Sapphira to rouse herself. When she finally came downstairs, it was 1.00 am. The house was silent and she poured herself some juice from the fridge.

'Thank you,' she said, sitting down at the table. 'I am a handful, which you may have worked out. Trouble seems to follow me.'

Jack smiled kindly. 'What an ordeal you've been through. Does this person harass you often?' Concern flooded his face.

'Maybe. Whoever they are used to send me presents but it got weirder and weirder. I've had private detectives looking into it, the police in the US were no help, although they tried. They just seem to know where I am and what I'm doing all the time. It's more than just a crazy fan, you know?'

Jack nodded. He understood crazy fans; he had a few crazed fans himself. But this was more sinister and so personal. It unnerved him, he thought, imagining what it did to Sapphira.

'Well, I will stay here for the rest of the filming and there will be extra guards and they are putting in more cameras, if it helps at all.'

'It does,' she answered thoughtfully. 'How did you know how to shoot up?' she asked.

'I had to do it a few times for Armondo, my lover I told you about, when he was too sick to do it himself,' he said, not looking at her.

'I've asked too much of you.' She started to cry.

'No, not at all. I'm your friend and I want to help you.'

She wiped her eyes and looked at him across the table. She held out her hands and Jack took them. 'I will come to Venice with you after this is over. It is time. I cannot live in a haze hoping it will go away. I need to control my destiny.'

Jack kissed her hands. 'It will be better, I promise.'

'I hope so,' she said, scared to the core of what her future might bring.

'I know so,' he replied.

CHAPTER TWENTY

'So, I will see you soon. I will come over, and you can come and see me. Okay?' she said to Milo.

'I hope you have a good flight with them, they're excited to be going home,' she said lightly.

Max pulled her into his arms. 'Thank you, Rose,' he said, holding her tight.

'Call me sometime,' she said softly. They had agreed it was just a fling, nothing more.

'Of course,' responded Max. He walked around to the car door.

Lucia ran out of the house and pressed a canvas bag into his hands. 'Limoncello, I made it myself,' she said proudly. Max smiled and gave the older woman a warm hug.

As he was about to get in the car he stopped and looked at Rose and said in his best Irish accent, 'T'was nice to know you, Rosie.'

And with that he got in the car, started the engine and drove away.

Rose was despondent when they left. Her family not visiting her had been eased by Max and the boys' presence in her life. More than that, she felt a connection with them all unlike anything she had known before. The laughter and busyness of the boys helped her and Max navigate each other after so long of not being in a relationship. The informality the children brought to the house pushed her and Max into instant intimacy. Milo would come into bed with them some nights, much to Max's horror and Rose's delight. She did art projects with Jasper and timed Dominic swimming laps in the pool, to try and beat his last time. While she was careful to not push herself into the role of their mother, she found herself slipping into the role naturally.

Max was astounded at her ability with the children. 'You are so good at this. I thought you would have kids of your own,' he said as they cleaned up the boys' toys from the back garden after the boys were settled watching a DVD.

'No, I wanted children when I was married to Paul but it never happened.' Rose had not spoken of her marriage before. Max was quiet and let her talk. 'I'm not sure he wanted children but I did, desperately. That was the saddest thing when we divorced. I want children but want to share the experience with someone. I don't want to be a single mother. I want to share the moments and laughter and celebrate my child with a partner. You know?'

Max smiled. 'Yes, that's what I miss most about Alice, sharing the moments. When she first died, I would find myself looking at the boys doing something and I would turn to share it with her. It's hard, to have a partner go and be alone with the moment.'

Rose picked up a giant water gun off the ground. 'What a pair we are. Morose and his side kick, Melancholy.' Laughing at herself, she squirted the gun at Max, who received a face full of water. As he ran towards her, she ran backwards and fell into the pool. Max jumped in after her. 'Are you okay?' he asked, trying to catch his breath.

'I'm fine.' She laughed hysterically and swam to the edge of the pool. Standing up, her wet t-shirt clung to her breasts and

Max looked at her intensely. 'You need to have a shower, I think.'

'I think I just had a bath,' she laughingly replied.

'Upstairs and into your bathroom, please. I will be there in one minute to check on you.'

Max sounded very serious and commanding. Rose looked at his twinkling eyes and ran up to the bathroom. Turning on the taps in her giant bath, she filled it with Gardenia bloom bath oil she had brought with her from home. The fragrance filled the air and the steam rose off the water. Standing in her wet clothes, she waited for Max. He charged into the bathroom. 'I told you to take off your clothes, didn't I?' he asked, his eyes narrowing at her.

Rose stood defiantly. The ache of anticipation was starting to overwhelm her. 'Well, I will have to take you in hand, young lady.' Walking over to her, he pulled her wet t-shirt off. He walked around her, looking at her in her black bikini top. 'You are out of control, Rose Nightingale,' he said in an upper crust British accent. 'You are unclean and rude in every way.'

He walked around to her front and undid the button and zip on her shorts. Pulling them down, she stepped out of them, standing in her bikini bottoms.

'Did I say you could step out of them?' he continued.

She shook her head, trying not to laugh.

Walking around her again, as if inspecting her, he undid the straps of her bikini top. 'I don't like these on a woman. They should be covered from head to toe if possible.'

The top fell down over her stomach. He undid the back clasp and the top fell to the ground.

Rose felt her nipples become erect and her skin was beginning to rise in goosebumps, not from cold but from desire.

189

She reached around to grab his cock but he stepped back from her. 'Right, that's what you want, is it? Well, let me tell you, Ms Nightingale, you will get what you deserve but only when I give the order, okay?'

He said this in her ear very quietly but firmly. Rose's knees were weak from lust and she was trying not to laugh. He undid the side of her bikini bottoms with both hands and they fell.

Walking back to her front he pointed at the bath. 'Get in, please,' he commanded.

Rose did as he asked and stood in the bath. 'Sit down and start washing yourself.' Rose picked up the washer and rubbed it over her arms and breasts, looking at him.

'Well, I can see you have no idea how to wash yourself. I will just have to do that, I suppose.'

Stripping off his wet things, he got into the bath, his erection standing to attention in front of him. Rose sat waiting. He took the flannel and poured a liberal dose of oil onto it and started to rub her body. He washed her all over, using the hand-held tap to wash her hair. Rubbing her breasts – they were slippery and full in his hands – he looked her in the eyes. 'Kiss me,' he commanded.

Rose kissed him passionately, Never had she been this turned on before. He rubbed her nipples between his fingers. 'Fuck me,' he ordered and Rose climbed onto his lap and felt him slip into her. Their bodies, oiled and warm came together in perfect harmony. She thrust herself against him. 'Harder, Ms Nightingale, I want to know you mean it,' he whispered in her ear. Rose rode him as hard as she could, her breasts bouncing against his chest, her warm flesh enveloping his cock. 'Very good, very good, you are becoming cleaner by the minute,' said Max, his voice breaking.

'Oh, shut up,' said Rose, and together they climaxed.

Lying back in his arms, she laughed about his role. 'What was that exactly?' she asked.

'What do you mean? The accent?' he said.

'Yes, *Dad's Army* or Mrs Slocombe from *Are You Being Served*?'

Max laughed uproariously. 'You are a very naughty little girl, Ms Nightingale,' he said and slid under the water.

Remembering Max now made Rose want to cry. Why was her life so complicated, she wondered. All she ever wanted was to do some acting and have some children. Now she had a glittering career and no life. Max's arrival had made her realize how truly lonely she was.

CHAPTER TWENTY-ONE

It was the last day on set.

Sapphira had sent everyone on the set a rare bottle of vodka with their names engraved on it. Rose had sent a huge basket of Tuscan food items to the crew that she had hand picked with Lucia and Calypso had handwritten everyone cards with personal details about how they helped her and how important they were. Of all the gifts, Calypso's was the most sincere. She had taken the time to know her crew and had touched on each of their skills to make them feel important in the process of making the film.

Rose and Sapphira worked well together on set, both consummate professionals. Sapphira had learned so much from Rose through the filming, about text and language and objectives.

'You have to have an idea of what your objective is for the scene but also what your super objective is as the character,' said Rose to Sapphira at lunchtime as they ate. Well, as Rose ate and Sapphira drank coffee. 'You know, what the big goal is in her life.'

Sapphira nodded. She finally understood, she knew what the super objective was for her own life for the first time and she had Jack to support her.

Sapphira had changed over time and Rose found her warmer and less distant. Rose had heard about the intrusion into her home and was concerned for her. 'Are you sure you're okay? You're welcome at my place if you want,' said Rose, hopeful for the company.

'Thanks, but Jack is with me still. He stayed on and then I'm going to stay with him in Venice for a while.'

Rose was surprised but didn't let herself show it. Sapphira and Jack together seemed right and wrong at the same time, she thought. Jack had always dated below himself on the celebrity scale and Sapphira was his equal, perhaps even further up than him.

'That's good,' she said, meaning it. 'Jack is one of the nicest men I know.'

Sapphira smiled. 'I believe you could be right.'

Heading into make-up for a scene change, Sapphira saw Calypso already in the chair. 'Hi,' she said as she sat down.

She was pleased Calypso was clearly doing so well and her affair with TG was obviously healing all sorts of wounds. Calypso responded. 'Oh my God! I so need to talk to you.'

Sapphira was nervous. Did she know about Raphael? 'What about?' she asked on alert.

'Well, I had a dream about you.'

'Really?' asked Sapphira, intrigued.

'Yes, I dreamed you were an angel and you came and told me everything would be all right. You said you could take care of things for me. How weird is that? And then the next day everything started falling into place for me. Funny, huh? Maybe you have hidden wings that we mere mortals cannot see.'

Sapphira laughed. 'You've busted me,' she said and pulled down her shirt to show Calypso the pair of angel wings tattooed on her back.

'I love it!' clapped Calypso. 'TG has one of a mermaid he got before he even met me. How weird is that, Kelly?'

Kelly listened as she did her work on both women, with her assistant standing by, helping when required.

'Hmmm . . . maybe, but not super weird,' said Kelly absently.

Sapphira looked at Kelly. Nothing fazed that woman, she thought. She was like the Buddha incarnate.

'I'm so happy that I'm annoying myself. For real, I'm making myself sick being around me,' said Calypso seriously.

Kelly and Sapphira laughed at her joy.

'Told you so,' said Sapphira.

Kelly hoped it wasn't short-lived. TG and Calypso belonged together; she was sure of it. Not that she was going to say anything. If she had learned anything, it was to shut your trap until asked otherwise, Buddha or no Buddha.

On the last night of filming, there was a cast and crew party, with everyone in attendance apart from Max who had flown to London to get the boys back to school. Calypso had thrown herself into the party planning with Giulia, turning the courtyard into another room in the villa. Bringing most of the furniture outside, the walls were draped in red velvet and ivy. The candles were spread about the space, creating a gothic feel. The rococo and Louis IV furniture was arranged conversationally and there were paintings hung on the walls, and huge bowls of fruits, looking like still lifes. Birdcages, with religious candles hung, strung across the open roof of the courtyard. The wait staff were all dressed in black, with red velvet masks and the theme on the invitation read 'gothic masquerade'.

Sapphira arrived with Jack, wearing a black silk, full-length dress with long sleeves and a high neck. The back of the dress was cut down to her buttocks, showing off the angel wing tattoos on her back. She wore her hair long and straight, with heavy eye make-up and red lips. Jack wore a straightjacket and a Hannibal Lecter mask. 'Come on, Morticia,' he said as he hustled her out the door.

'Fuck you, Hannibal,' she said cheerfully.

Since she had made her decision to go to Venice with him and try to kick her habit, she and Jack were closer than ever. 'Such a shame you're gay,' she said as he got into the car.

'Well, for you maybe, but I'm fine with it,' he quipped.

'I'm sure you are,' she laughed.

'There are plenty more straight fish in the sea, doll. Stick around, you never know who might hang themselves off your line,' Jack said as he drove out the gates, the security guards waving at them.

'I'm not looking for anyone,' said Sapphira as she peered into the darkness from the car.

'Well, that's the best way to be. Don't look and they will come and bite your line,' said Jack, speeding through the winding roads towards TG's villa.

'No, really, I don't care at all. I know women say that, but I mean it. I've never had a significant relationship and I've yet to meet a man who can keep up with me or who I could share my secrets with. Till you,' she added.

'So the father of your baby?' asked Jack. 'Where is he now?'

'I have no idea. I rang him when I found out and left him a message but he never called me back. Probably got shit scared and ran away. I've never heard from him again,' she said without emotion. 'She would be seven now. I wonder what my life would have been like with her. No drugs, no films maybe? I don't know.'

Jack pulled into the driveway. 'No looking back, okay? You're here now, we are here together and I am going to get drunk.'

Pulling on his mask and costume, he jumped out of the car and opened the door. Sapphira slipped her hand through his arm, tied back in the costumed straightjacket, and they walked into the party.

Rose came to the party by herself, dressed as Ophelia from Hamlet. 'She suits my mood,' she explained to Kelly, who was dressed as a gypsy. 'I feel like I'm going mad since Max left. It's crazy, how can someone get under your skin so quickly? Maybe I'm in love with the boys too much. I keep thinking about them, my thoughts going around in circles.'

Kelly touched her arm, which was wildly waving a glass of white wine around. 'Why don't you go and see him, see if it still works in the real world and not in the heady heat of Italy?'

'Nah, it was just a fling. A summer romance,' she said dramatically.

'You sure? Maybe you just need to think about what you want, what you really, really want. I would tell you to meditate on it but then you might throw wine at me.'

Rose laughed. 'Too fucking right I would.' She held her wine glass up to Kelly in a mock throw.

Calypso came towards them dressed as a mermaid, with shells strung in her hair and a divine jewelled bra top, courtesy of the costume department, and a skintight shot silk skirt in sea green with white organza around the bottom, kicking out when she walked, like the foam on the ocean waves.

Barefoot and brown from the sun, TG thought she had never looked more gorgeous. He was dressed as Johnny Rotten, much to Calypso's amusement.

The party went on well into the morning, and with the arrival of Sapphira's promised case of vodka, the guests danced till 4.00 am, when TG kicked them out.

'We did very well, I think. If things in LA don't work for us, then party planning could be the next career option,' TG said as he wiped off the make-up Calypso had applied.

'It was great, huh? Everyone had a good time. How funny was Chris dancing to the Britney medley! He's hilarious.'

TG laughed. 'I think we should have more parties when we get back to LA.'

'Your place or mine?' she asked as she brushed her teeth.

'Let's wait and see,' he answered, as they fell into bed.

Calypso was awoken at 6.00 am by her phone vibrating on the bedside table. Answering it, she heard Greg, her agent in LA. 'Hey, Greg. Do you know what time it is here? We had the party last night. I've gotta go to sleep. Can this wait?'

'No, Calypso, I have to talk to you. There's a problem here and I need you to know before it gets out. If it gets out,' he added.

'What? What's happened?' Calypso sat up in bed, waking TG, who sat up next to her.

'Well, it's kind of hard to say,' said Greg nervously on the phone. Shit, he had not been primed for breaking this kind of news, he thought.

'What, Greg? For fuck's sake, I am freaking out here, just tell me.'

'When can you get back?' he asked.

'Tomorrow, I can leave tomorrow. What is it? I will freak out all the way back on the plane. Just tell me.'

'You remember the director, Jerry Hyman, you did that film with him when you were a kid?'

'Yeah, I remember. What about him?'

'He's been arrested for rape. He's been taping women during sex, some of them unconscious after accepting a drink laced with some "roofies" apparently. Some of them were consensual though.'

'So, why do I care about him? I never spent any time with him, I just was cast and went on set. I remember he was an asshole, but that's all. There won't be a tape of me, I'm sure of that. Don't worry, Greg,' she said as TG rubbed her back.

'It's not you, Calypso. A package turned up this morning in my office. It's a DVD . . . of your mother and Jerry.'

'Was she unconscious?' said Calypso, her heart in her throat.

'No. Wide awake, I'm afraid, and giving head to Jerry. It's grainy but looks like her. In the package there's a note saying unless you pay two million dollars then they're going to release it to all media outlets.'

'Fuck!' said Calypso.

The Italian dream was over.

PART THREE

Post-Production

CHAPTER TWENTY-TWO

Sapphira arrived in Venice two days after filming stopped. She sent her agent and manager an email, saying she was unwell and would not be returning to LA anytime soon. She cancelled all meetings, leaving her representatives to get her out of the next film she was scheduled to do. Sure, there would be a shit storm but she was committed to kick her habit and, for the first time in her life, she had support.

Jack's friendship was the most important relationship she had ever experienced and she was not going to let him down, she promised herself. He had been on the phone constantly since she had spoken to him about trying to detox. Speaking Italian and English, she had tried not to listen to his one-sided conversations. She didn't want to know what he had planned; if she did, then she was afraid she would lose her courage.

Flying into Venice, Sapphira had been warned by Jack's assistant that the press would be there. Photos of them were hot property now; any opportunity was seized by the relentless pariahs and their cameras. Jack's plans were intricate, including hiring doppelgängers of them both and paying them handsomely, with ironclad confidentiality agreements to leave his villa the next day in the daylight and fly to Spain, Switzerland and France for several days and then lose the paps, hopefully, sending them on a wild goose chase.

Sapphira knew none of this. She had been trying to cut

down over the last few days and was starting to feel sick from her self-administered detox. Jack had set her up on the top floor, which was self-contained. Bedroom, bathroom and sitting room. Included was a plasma screen, satellite dish, phone, computer, massage table and a small kitchenette.

'This is where I keep my mistresses,' he said as he showed her around.

'Very nice, you never need to leave,' she said, sitting on the bed.

'Eventually they do, when the time is right, but don't you worry about a thing, you will stay here as long as you need, okay?' He sat next to her and put his strong arm around her thin shoulders.

Sapphira rested her head against his arm. 'I feel sick, I just want this over with.'

'Well, we start tomorrow. I will be there every step of the way and I've employed some of the best doctors to help you.'

Sapphira started to cry. 'Why are you doing this? Why are you so fucking nice to me? You hardly know me, Jack.'

Jack bit his lip, his own eyes welling with tears. 'Because I love you. You are amazing and you don't even know it yet. You are brave and beautiful and one day you will see what you can do with this. I know it, and you know what else?' Sapphira shook her head. 'I will always be known as Sapphira De Mont's ex-lover and that's good for business,' he laughed, wiping his eyes.

Jack's assistant came into the room. It was Giulia from the film set. 'Hello, Sapphira,' she said.

'Hi, Giulia, I didn't know you worked for Jack.'

Sapphira was taken aback. She had spoken to Giulia often on set and she seemed capable and helpful to TG, staying in the background and not being overly friendly with the actors, which some assistants tended to do, hoping to trade up to a bigger star.

'*Si*, Jack lent me to TG for the film, as he needed someone he could trust and who spoke Italian,' said Giulia, holding a black folder.

Sapphira looked at Jack, her eyes asking if Giulia could be trusted with what she was about to go through.

Jack answered her openly. 'Giulia is my assistant and my dearest friend, and in many ways, she is my sister. Giulia is Armondo's sister. She is my lifeline and together we laugh and cry and she helps me stay organized. Giulia knew you were an addict; she picked it up right away and told me, but I figured it was just an occasional thing. I didn't realize how bad it was until the night here.'

Sapphira looked down at her feet. Giulia spoke up. 'Jack and I have organized everything and I believe this will be the right thing for you. I hope you get to live your life. I am sad that this was not in existence when Armondo was trying to get off the drugs.'

Sapphira looked up at her and saw kindness in Giulia's face. 'Thank you, Giulia, I am very sorry about Armondo. Jack loved him very much, it sounds like.'

Giulia smiled. 'I love Jack and we are friends, *è il mio fratello*. He is my brother,' she translated for Sapphira.

After she left the room, Sapphira lay on the bed. 'Crazy stuff, huh? I never knew.'

'I never told you, but it doesn't matter anyway. She is amazing. Her family is a very old established Venetian family, ancestors of the third Doge of Venice or something. Her brother's addiction and homosexuality was hidden by them carefully, but they are kind to me and they love that Giulia works with me. I trust them implicitly.'

Sapphira was feeling sick again. She rolled over on the bed.

'Hang on, honey, it will all be over in a few days and then the real healing begins,' said Jack, rubbing her back.

Sapphira just wanted it to be over.

The next day, Jack and Sapphira's doppelgängers arrived through the back entrance, which was covered by an awning and impossible for the paparazzi to get a good shot of.

They were dressed according to Jack and Giulia's instructions, in the clothes which had been sent to them via FedEx. They walked into the villa, nervous. This was the craziest gig they had ever done, but for US$500,000 each, a trip across Europe and free clothes and accoutrements, they knew it was too good to pass over.

Jack walked down and met them in the sitting room where they waited with Giulia and Jack's lawyer. 'Hey, you look just like me,' laughed Jack, breaking the ice. The faux Jack laughed also. Shaking his hand, he kissed the faux Sapphira on each cheek. She even had the same tattoos painted onto her body, courtesy of transfers she'd had made for her appearances in the US. 'Nice work,' said Jack as he turned her around to look at them under her silk singlet. 'Weird.'

Sapphira entered the room. She felt violently ill but was prepared to put on a brave face. This was part of the deal. She walked over and held Jack's hand. 'Thank you so much,' she said gracefully, smiling brilliantly. The doppelgängers were awestruck and stood excited before them.

'So, I suppose my lawyer and assistant have explained this gig? Sapphira and I are in love and we want time alone here but the media are going crazy. No speaking to the media, keep your heads down as much as possible. You will head off for ten days and then disappear, leading them away from here. Yes?'

'Yes,' they answered in unison, still amazed at their mission.

'I would be so grateful if you stuck to the contract I believe you have signed. No mention of this ever or we will sue you for your firstborn children and body parts.' Jack laughed but his eyes threatened the actors.

Nodding their consent and agreement, the actors were afraid of Jack and Sapphira whose mere presence was powerful.

Jack and Sapphira said goodbye and the faux pair got ready for their debut to the media. Giulia opened the door and the bodyguards hired outside held the media back as the pair walked down into the waiting boat to take them to the airport. The noise came through the open door into the sitting room, where Jack and Sapphira waited. 'Jesus, poor bastards,' said Jack as the door shut.

Sapphira went upstairs to lie down again. She had been taking less and less heroin and today was her worst day, timed to be almost clean for her treatment.

Jack came upstairs. 'Everything will start in about an hour, okay?'

Sapphira nodded, scared.

'Give me your kit, sweetie. Just in case,' said Jack softly.

Sapphira pointed to the drawer beside the bed. Jack took the bag and leaned down and kissed her on the forehead. 'Hang in there, kiddo.'

Within the hour, there was a Swiss doctor and nurse in her room, with an IV set up and confidentiality agreements signed. The doctor was not surprised to see Sapphira in the room. When Jack's lawyer had contacted him about needing to help someone famous, he was indifferent. An addict was an addict and he had treated many famous and powerful people this way, in the privacy of their own homes.

He explained to Sapphira that he was going to sedate her and do a rapid detox, using a combination of drugs, as well as keeping her hydrated and infusing her body with the multivitamins and amino acids her body would be lacking. After that, he would put her on tablets for a period to stop the cravings and then she could have an implant which would last anywhere between nine months to a year, depending on her progress.

Sapphira was silent, it seemed too much to take in and she just wanted to stop feeling sick and sleep for a long time. Changing into pyjamas, Sapphira lay on the bed and let the nurse insert the IV into her arm. Sapphira was ready.

Five days later she awoke. She felt like shit, but a manageable kind of shit. Not so sick, just groggy and a little spaced out. Jack was sitting by her, the nurse in the room, writing in a chart. 'Hey there, sleepy,' whispered Jack.

'Hey,' said Sapphira tiredly.

'What day is it?'

'Friday.'

The nurse came and bustled Jack out of the room. 'Time to go, enough, she is awake. Now we have work to do.'

Sapphira was kept in the room for another five days. It was not easy and at times she fantasized about jumping out the window and into the canal to swim to try and score but slowly she began to walk and eat. Her body's cravings stopped and the doctor prescribed medications to counteract the worst of the symptoms. Jack had organized daily massages, which helped relax her, as did the acupuncture and Chinese herbs, which tasted foul but Sapphira had promised to try them and she did.

After fourteen days upstairs, Sapphira was allowed down to sit with Jack in the kitchen. He was doing the crossword. 'Five letter name for hell.'

206

'Jacky,' she replied and sat down carefully.

'Very funny. Hades,' he answered himself and wrote it down.

'What's news, pussycat?' he asked, putting down the paper.

'Um, I am allowed to walk around now. Big day for me.'

'I can see that and Nurse Ingrid hasn't got you on her leash, so things must be improving.'

'Yes, I'm apparently doing quite well, although I can't keep anything inside me yet, so food is out of the question.'

Jack made a face. 'Poor love. How long will that last?'

'Not long, it's getting better I think. I'm going to have a massage in a moment. I just wanted to say thank you.'

'No problem.'

'I will pay you back, I promise, when I get things sorted.'

'Don't you even try, lady. I will just donate it to my charity anyway.'

'You have a charity?' Sapphira mocked him. 'What? Free fashion advice to badly dressed women?'

'Indeed I do, any self-respecting philanthropist has one.' Jack ignored her barbs.

'Who do you help?' asked Sapphira, interested.

'Drug addicts and their families,' answered Jack, going back to his paper. 'You have to find something which means something to you, otherwise it's all bullshit and you don't get anything done and fuck knows there's too much to be fixed in this world.'

Sapphira walked upstairs wondering what she cared about. Well, not much really, besides shooting up and occasionally doing something challenging like learning to fly a plane or jumping from bridges in New Zealand. The past two weeks had been the most challenging of her life and she realized everything she had done till now was to serve her own ego. 'Hedonism' her counsellor called it in the first session they had over the phone yesterday. Always looking for the next hit, in life, through drugs, through sex. Sapphira was shocked and she realized she hated her life and where it had gone. She had never really liked it, her life was being wasted and she realized it. Her doctor had put her on anti-depressants; self-realization sometimes came with a price and this kind of reaction was common in recovering addicts, he had said. The solution was to try to find a new focus, he advised her, something outside herself. The only problem was, Sapphira had no idea what the world looked like outside heroin.

CHAPTER TWENTY-THREE

Rose returned to LA to find Lauren in shock. The director Jerry Hyman had been arrested and the police had contacted her, telling her they had video of her being raped on the plane. Rose was shocked but not surprised about Jerry's behaviour; she just wanted Lauren to be okay. Calling her on her cell phone after she received the message, Rose had her driver go straight to Lauren's apartment.

Lauren was there with her mother, who had flown in to stay with her. Rose hugged her close. 'I'm so sorry, I'm so, so sorry,' she repeated in a soothing voice.

Lauren cried in her arms. 'I knew it, I knew it when I got off the plane but I couldn't think straight and now I know why and then he was so awful on set. Thank God you took me away, Rose, thank God,' she cried.

Lauren told Rose the story of what had happened years before. Remembering it made her break down several times as she recalled the moments before and afterwards. On the flight over he had been charming to Lauren, plying her with French champagne and delicate little hors d'oeuvres that she had never tasted before. Lauren remembered feeling lightheaded and asking to lie down. When she awoke as they landed, she was on the bed. She remembered lying down but nothing afterwards, and she felt odd, hung-over and slightly sick. She went to the bathroom and went to the toilet. When she wiped herself, she was sticky, like she had just had sex. Her pubis bone was aching as though she had knocked it somehow. Lauren walked out of the plane's bathroom and saw the director talking on the phone.

She waited for him to finish his call. He signalled to her he was going to be some time. She waited longer. He kept her waiting for twenty minutes while he spoke on the phone. When he hung up, she said, 'Did something happen when I went and lay down?'

He looked at her closely, his eyes narrowed. 'No, honey, you went to sleep from all the champagne and I made a few business calls. Check my phone if you want.' He held out his phone to her.

She shook her head. 'Okay, I just feel a little weird.'

'That's flying in a private plane for you, babe, you feel everything real close.'

'I made the choice,' she finally said, 'to choose my job and my reputation over what was right. I could have helped other people.'

Rose held her close for a long time. 'You did what you felt was best at the time, darling. There is no point going over it again and again. You have to move forward otherwise you are truly the victim.'

Rose held her hand as Lauren's mother handed her tissues. 'What's next, Lauren, what do we do now? What can I do to help?'

'I have to find a lawyer, I think, but I don't have one.' Lauren started to cry again. Lauren's mother left the room, clearly distressed at her daughter's situation.

'Use mine, they're the best. All bills will be taken care of by me and this will be sorted in no time. What else?'

Rose was amazing in a crisis. She took charge in a way that

210

never felt like she was being bossy, just calm and in control. Lauren was quiet. 'Come on, what else do you need right now at this moment?'

Rose could tell Lauren was hiding something. She sensed it and it reminded her of herself a long time ago. 'Tell me please, Lauren, I want to help you.'

Lauren put her head in her hands. 'I want to die. I want to die of shame from the police seeing the video. I want to die. People will see what he did to me. I saw it, I had to identify myself. I am a ragdoll. He was awful and I look like I'm dead while he rapes me. I want to die,' Lauren wept.

Rose felt sick for her. Her eyes filled with tears. 'Oh, Lauren, he should die, not you. I know who you need to talk to. I want you to talk to my doctor, okay?'

'I don't want medication,' she answered passionately.

'No, a therapist. Did me the world of good a long time ago when I was unwell. I wanted to die also once but I'm glad I didn't,' she said, thinking of Max.

'Really?' asked Lauren, disbelievingly.

'Really,' said Rose.

'What happened? If you don't mind me asking you? I just don't know if I can ever live a normal life again after this. I keep seeing myself in the video.'

Rose held her hands and looked into her eyes. 'We all have great battles in our lives, Lauren. This is yours and it's a terrible one. My battle was a horrible marriage and psychosis from depression. I ran into a wall with a knife to my chest. It was terrible for me, and for my housekeeper who found me. I survived, got divorced and started again. Everyday, I start again. Some days are easier than others but I get up and that is what therapy has helped me to do. I think this will help you have control over this situation, not the situation control you.'

Lauren nodded fiercely. 'That's how I feel, like my life has been taken away from me.'

Rose searched her phone to call her doctor. Lauren touched her arm softly. 'I'm glad you're here, Rose. I'm glad you survived and are in my life. Thank you.'

The tears that had threatened to fall when Lauren told her story to Rose now ran down Rose's cheeks. 'Lauren, it is an honour to help and to be your friend.'

Rose dialled the number of her therapist; the time had come to pay it forward.

Rose's life in LA was tumultuous since the arrest of Jerry Hyman. Lauren had taken an extended leave of absence. Rose had asked her to consider resigning until she knew what her future held, but Lauren insisted she just wanted some time and would be back as soon as she was able.

Rose hadn't heard from Max, although he was constantly on her mind. She missed the sex and the company. She missed the sounds of the boys playing outside, yelling and demanding her attention.

Rose retreated back into herself in LA. Avoiding events, she sat at home most nights.

After returning from a rare night out at Kelly and Chris's house for dinner, she was overwhelmed with missing Italy. Moving about the kitchen she opened the liquor cabinet to see the limoncello that Lucia had given her before she left. Opening it, she sniffed it and reeled backwards. It was a strong potion and Rose poured herself a little over some ice and sat on the deck sipping the sweet but tart drink.

This is becoming ridiculous, she thought as she drained the glass, I'm going to see Max. She wondered if the limoncello had influenced her judgement but didn't care. Logging onto her computer, she efficiently organized her own first class flight to London the next day including a car and driver, but decided against accommodation. She could stay with Max, she thought, imagining them all back together again.

Leaving the next morning, Rose was excited and nervous. She never did things like this; she was controlled and a planner. She had written a list of pros and cons about Max but gave up after the only con was him being in Britain. It was not as though she thought he was perfect; it's just that she didn't know him enough to list them. They had spent an idyllic time in Italy, seeing the best of each other, with real life not interrupting them. Now it was complicated and Rose wondered how much she would have to give up to get what she wanted.

On the flight over, she sat in first class, with a nerve-steadying Tanqueray and tonic. She knew his address from having sent parcels over to the boys of movie paraphernalia from the studio. What was she going to say? Would she ring the doorbell and wait, or call him from her hotel?

Rose played over the scenarios in her mind. 'Listen to your heart,' she heard Kelly's voice in her head. Rose sat still in her seat and closed her eyes. She tried to listen to her heart but heard nothing but the quiet hum of the plane. Shit, she thought to herself, not even my heart has anything to say.

At Heathrow, it was chaos from the waiting paparazzi. Even though Rose had security to get her through the airport, she knew she had to go to Max straightaway. Her arrival would be in the papers the next day and she wanted to see him before he found out she was in London.

Getting into the car the hotel had sent, she instructed the driver to take her to Max's address. Pulling up in Primrose Hill outside a white Victorian terrace, badly in need of painting with a red front door, Rose told the driver to unpack her luggage onto the kerb beside her.

Steeling herself, Rose walked up the path and rang the doorbell. She waited for a while, then she heard Max's voice. 'Coming,' he yelled and then he opened the door.

Surprise registered on his face. 'Rose!'

'Yes. Hello,' she said shyly.

'Hello, wow, what a surprise. You didn't tell me you were coming.' Max had a tea towel over his shoulder and was wearing jeans and t-shirt with a stain on the front. His hair was messy and he looked tired. Rose had never found him more attractive.

They stood in the doorway. Max looked down at the luggage next to her and then back up to her, confusion in his eyes.

'Can I come in?' asked Rose, puzzled by his reaction. Was he pleased to see her or not? 'Yes, yes, of course,' he said. 'Excuse the mess, the boys are back at school and I'm trying to clean up and wash everything after breakfast. Chaos reigns, as you can see.'

Rose looked around the living room they were standing in. There were pairs of shoes and tennis rackets on the floor. Half-drunk glasses of milk and a cereal bowl on the coffee table. Unread papers and a pile of letters sat on the stairs in the hallway. There were clothes draped on the backs of chairs and the room smelt stuffy. It was the bachelor pad of all bachelor pads, Rose decided.

It could have been a nice room, probably once was when Alice was alive, thought Rose. There was a lovely fireplace and the furniture was comfortable: a large couch she recognized from the Conran shop, a few old pieces, maybe family heirlooms. Silver frames with pictures of the boys and Alice and Max from years ago.

214

Rose stood in the room and tried not to look around too much, as much as she was desperate to look at the picture of Alice more closely. Instead she heard herself lying to Max. 'I had to come over for work, a last minute thing. I tried to ring you but the line was busy. I thought I would pop by and say hello.'

'I'm glad you did, although I wish I had known, then I wouldn't have had so much mess around me. Cup of tea?'

'Lovely, yes please.'

Rose followed him to the kitchen where she was sure a bomb had gone off and she had to stifle herself from saying something. Max turned to look at her. 'I know, I know what you're thinking and you're right.'

Putting on the kettle, he sat down at the kitchen bench, gesturing Rose to sit next to him. 'I am terribly embarrassed. I suppose this is why I didn't want you to come over. My life is, well, bedlam to say the least. I'm not the most domesticated of beasts and I've had to learn since Alice died. The cleaning lady left me, said it was too much and I guess it is. I just have never been able to get a handle on it. My priority is to get the boys fed and dressed in clean clothes each day and hopefully fit in some work when I can. Italy was the first trip we had had as a family without Alice and it was lovely, for all of us.' He took Rose's hand. 'I really like you, Rose, in fact, there's a distinct possibility I love you, but this is my life and I have to sort it out. I cannot and will not ask you to make any sacrifices to be with me until I get on top of things. It's not fair on anyone, least of all you.'

There was a pause, while Rose thought of what to say. She waited and then heard herself speak. 'I love you, Max, I'm sure of that. I know you have things to sort out. I'm not trying to butt in but I've waited my whole life to be with you and I know you are the right one for me. No matter how long it takes, I will wait till you are ready for me, and if you are never ready or should decide you don't want to be with me, then I will accept that. I am happy I've known you and your boys even for a little while.'

Rose sat still. This was what Kelly meant about speaking from her heart. She had listened to Kelly's advice and every word she spoke was true. Max smiled at her, with tears in his eyes. Rose looked around at the overflowing sink, the dead flowers on the table, the fridge door filled with out of date school notices and spoke again from her heart. 'Fuck, what a mess though, huh?'

Then they laughed till they cried.

'Done,' said Rose as she put the last cup away in the cupboard. A natural organizer, Rose had taken to Max's house with enterprise and with his blessing they had cleaned up most of it before the boys were due to be picked up. Rose had taken off her pink Theory shirt and had slipped on one of Max's old but clean t-shirts. Tying back her hair with a band she found at the bottom of her bag, she and Max talked as they worked. Rose dusted and aired the house. Max swept, mopped and vacuumed, and they did the dishes together.

Rose looked at the bathroom and closed her eyes, then threw half a bottle of toilet cleaner into the bowl. 'That's your domain, my dear,' she said as she led him by the hand. 'Give it a good clean and then wipe down the seat with this,' she said, handing him some cleaning wipes and a toilet brush.

Max laughed. 'Jesus, we've gone straight into domesticity, haven't we?'

'Perhaps, although I refuse to clean your toilet.'

While Max was in the bathroom, Rose went downstairs and

looked into the lounge room. The picture of Alice beckoned her. Picking up the silver frame, she saw a young woman, with a small boy on her lap, maybe Dominic, she thought. Blond hair, a pretty face, smiling into the camera. She looked happy, thought Rose.

'That's Alice with Dominic,' said Max from the doorway.

'I thought so. She looks happy. Dominic is very sweet,' said Rose, putting it down again.

'She was, we were,' said Max simply.

Rose turned to look at him, waiting for him to speak. She knew he was thinking of the right way to say it. 'Rose, you are the only person I have been with since Alice died. I haven't slept with another person. In some way, as you can tell by the state of my house, I've been on hold. Stuck back when she died. Then I met you and after a disastrous first encounter, we connected. Then I came back here and it all felt like a dream, Italy and you. I care about you, Rose, so much, but I am not quite ready to let Alice go. You see, she has been coming to me in my dreams. I know you may think I'm silly or mad but she does and she is trying to tell me something.' He started to cry, weeping openly and Rose felt her heart break. 'I don't think she wants me to be with you yet. Maybe someday, but not yet. I'm sorry, Rose. I am so, so very sorry.'

Rose walked over and held him close. 'I understand. When you are ready and when Alice is ready, come and find me.'

And she picked up her bag and walked out of the clean house, leaving Max sitting on the stairs, his head on his knees.

'I'll send someone for my bags,' she said with more ease than she felt and turned from him.

Rose walked towards the tube station in a daze. Having lived in London growing up, she knew where she was going and she bought a token with the small amount of pounds she always kept in her travel wallet and got the train. Sitting on the tube, she didn't feel people looking at her, trying to see if it was Rose Nightingale; her dirty t-shirt and messy hair gave her some level of protection. Rose got off at South Kensington and walked a few blocks. She walked up to the door and rang the bell. She heard footsteps coming and the door opened.

'Mummy?' Rose said, and then burst into tears.

CHAPTER TWENTY-FOUR

The news about Leeza's video of her blowjob had shaken Calypso to the core and she had jumped out of bed as soon as Greg had rung to tell her. Her head was reeling from too much vodka and not enough sleep. 'I have to fly back to LA now,' she said as she started to pull on clothes.

'What happened?' asked TG, concerned and getting up to get dressed also.

'Something's happened in LA and I've got to go back now,' she said.

'What? What's happened?' asked TG as he followed her to the bathroom, where she started to throw her cosmetics into a bag.

'I've got to deal with something. I'll call you when it's over,' Calypso said, not looking at him.

'Christ, Calypso, tell me. There are no secrets, I want to help you.'

'You can't,' she said, walking to the wardrobe and pulling out her clothes.

'I can, let me try at least. Jesus,' he yelled.

'I'll have to leave some things here and send for them when I get back,' she said, not listening to him.

He stopped her walking past him and held her by her shoulders. 'What has happened? Tell me so I can help you, goddammit.'

'There is nothing you can help me with, all right? I have to

219

sort this out. It's private and terrible and if I need you I will let you know. I'm not a child, so stop treating me like one.' She was angry now.

'Then stop acting like a fucking child. We are in a relationship. You tell the other person when shit happens, you share it, Calypso. Do you think that Raphael got kicked off the film by accident? No, I did that. I helped you so you would be okay. I can make things happen.'

'You did what?' said Calypso, incredulous.

'I took care of it. I can help with this, I know I can.'

'Jesus fucking Christ!' said Calypso as she ran down the stairs with her things. 'I never asked you to plant drugs on him. I always thought that was weird. The guy can never work in the US again. What the hell were you thinking?'

'I was thinking of you. Anyway, I didn't know that was going to happen. I just asked some people for help and that's what happened. Don't be sorry for the guy; he raped you, for fuck's sake!'

They were screaming at each other now.

'I didn't ask for that and I won't live with it either. I had no idea that's what you did.'

'You have no idea about anything, Calypso. You live in some idealistic world. Things happen and we have to take care of them and yes, sometimes that means doing the wrong thing to make something right. Don't stand there and judge me, I did what I did for you, not anyone else, not the film, for you! Do you know why?'

Calypso didn't answer him; she was stuffing her passport into her handbag.

'I did it because I love you, that's why. And that's why I want to help you now.' He spoke softly, pleading with her to understand.

Calypso stood by the front door, holding her bags. 'I never asked you to go to those lengths. I never asked you to love me. I've got to deal with this myself. Just as I should have dealt with Raphael by myself. Goodbye, TG.' And she closed the door and walked out of TG's life.

Trying to get on a flight to LA was a nightmare. On the plane, Calypso relived the memory that she had tried to convince herself wasn't real for the last twelve years. She remembered she was sick. That her head was pounding and her nose streaming and that she had felt like crying. She remembered pleading to Leeza. 'I just want to go home. I feel terrible. We shouldn't have come, Mom. I don't think I can do it.'

'Don't be ridiculous, Calypso,' her mother was brusque. 'Dr Footlights always gets any good actor through. Out, out! Come on. Time to show them what you've got.'

Leeza had walked around to the passenger's side of the old orange Chevy. The paint on the door was peeling and Calypso remembered it made a terrible creaking sound as she opened it. Calypso rested her head against the cold glass of the plane and closed her eyes. It seemed like yesterday, and she allowed the memory to flood back to her.

Leeza had made her stand up straight by poking her long fingernail into her back.

'You look fine. A little pale, but that just adds to your beauty, honey. Let's go.'

Walking briskly in her high-heeled silver sandals, she pushed open the door to the office in front of them. The receptionist looked over Leeza's mother. Clad in pale blue Gloria Vanderbilt jeans, a tight white t-shirt, with large breasts, bottle-red hair blow-waved like Marilu Henner, she was the stereotypical Hollywood mother.

Looking at the child, she was surprised to see she did not fit the bill of most child actors who came in for castings. Small, extraordinarily pretty, pale, and quiet, she showed none of the standard Hollywood potential child star precociousness. Usually they started performing as soon as they opened the door, just in case the receptionist became a 'somebody' one day.

'Hello, this is Calypso Gable.' Leeza made a waving movement with her hands towards her daughter. 'I'm her manager, Leeza. We're here for the Baked Goodness commercial audition.'

'Please sit and wait till her name is called,' barked the receptionist.

Calypso sat, and let out a little cough.

'Don't cough,' hissed Leeza. 'It's revolting.'

Calypso rolled her eyes. How can you not cough? It's impossible. Closing her eyes, she prayed for bed or death. The cold had not seemed serious two days ago but now it was a full-blown flu and a double dose of Tylenol hadn't helped. Her mother had dragged her out of bed that morning by her feet, literally.

She felt too hot in what Leeza had made her wear. A red-plaid woollen skirt, a long-sleeved white blouse with a lace collar, white woollen tights, a red knitted jumper with snowflakes all over it, and black patent leather Mary-Janes. Jesus, she looked like a reject out of a Target Christmas catalogue, she had thought. Never mind it was going to be 96 degrees that day. The commercial was for a baking brand for Christmas goods, so Leeza had gone all out on the perfect little 'white bread' Christmas costume.

Calypso was fourteen years old and about to play a ten-year-old for the audition. Being tiny of stature had served her well when she was younger, but as she matured the roles dried up, the phone stopped ringing and soon she was out on the hustle again, with Leeza at the helm, pushing and cajoling Calypso within an inch of her life.

'Calypso Gable?' She heard her name called.

Standing up, Leeza followed her. 'I'm sorry, ma'am, only the talent in the auditions,' the casting director cut her off.

Leeza stood outside the door trying to listen. When Calypso emerged weeping a few minutes later and ran out to the car, Leeza followed, her stilettos clicking on the concrete of the car park. 'What happened?' she cried.

'He told me to fuck off and I shouldn't have come because I'm sick,' said Calypso, struggling to open the car door.

Leeza fumed. 'Who the hell speaks to my baby like this? You're the best and he needs to know it. It's not right for someone to abuse my baby like that!'

Leeza opened the car door for Calypso. 'I'm going to tell him what I think about this. You wait here.'

She stalked back across the car park, tossing her hair in defiance. Inside the office, the receptionist was not sitting at her desk. Stomping down the hallway, Leeza passed empty, dusty offices. A temporary place for casting agents to use for auditions. At the back of the building, she saw a man sitting at a desk. He was on the phone, laughing. She stood in the doorway.

'Are you the director who just told my daughter to fuck off?' she demanded.

'Hang on, buddy, I will have to call you back.' He hung up the phone.

'Are you the mother who sent a clearly sick child to an audition?' he answered her back as rudely as she had spoken to him, as he stroked his unkempt beard. With a knee-length black leather jacket and thinning hair pulled back into a pony-tail, Leeza thought he looked more like a bounty hunter than a director.

Leeza stood her ground. 'She is the best actress you will see. If you had any smarts you would see past her limitations today and recognize her true talent.'

The silence was thick with tension. They faced each other off. Finally, Leeza spoke again. More softly this time. 'She really needs this job.'

A pause.

'Oh hell, I need this job.'

The truth was out.

He looked at her closely, pleading, making it clear she would do what it took to pull him over the line. Well, she is hot, in a kind of porn-star way, he thought. Big hair, big earrings, big tits, although they looked real, which was surprising. He was a nobody TV commercial director who hoped to make his own feature film from a script he had been writing since he was twenty. The only thing was, he was thirty-five, and so far the height of his career was this commercial.

Leeza tossed her red hair and walked over to him, placing her hand on his crotch. 'You saw her on a bad day. She is very talented and very good at what she does, as am I.' Her long orange nails scraped gently over his penis. He looked at her, eyebrows raised.

'That's right, you enjoy yourself,' she whispered in his ear. 'I would like to suck you though, if you will let me.'

Why not, he thought. He nodded.

'Yeah. Yeah,' he said, quickly and breathlessly.

'Well, I would but I need to know my baby is going to be your girl for these commercials?'

'Okay, okay,' he whispered, feeling like he was about to

224

explode from her hand rubbing up and down on his swelling shaft.

'Well, you need to make a call, honey. You need to call her agent and tell him she has the job, okay?'

He nodded as she shut the office door, went down on her knees, unzipped his pants and placed his swollen cock in her mouth. Waiting patiently while he pulled his phone out, his cock was hard in her mouth but she just let it lie there till he had done his part of the deal. She dialled the number, keeping his penis in her mouth, then handed it over once she heard it ring.

When the receptionist answered, he asked for Calypso's agent.

'Hi, you sent Calypso Gable for the audition with me today?'

Every time he spoke Leeza sucked, when he paused she stopped again.

'Yeah, I'm good, man.' He let out a moan. 'I'm fine, man. I was just stretching, it's been a long morning.'

'Anyway, Calypso has the gig. I'll get production to send over the contract tomorrow. No problem, man, my pleasure, seems like a talented kid.'

As he hung up, Leeza sucked with an intensity he had not expected from an older woman. He felt himself being sucked into Leeza's vortex and he didn't give a shit; he was about to come and all was good in the world. Finally he burst into Leeza's mouth and she expertly swallowed with no fuss. Standing up and wiping down the knees of her jeans, she walked over to her handbag, rummaged around, popped a mint into her mouth and reapplied her coral lipstick.

'Thanks,' she said, dusting herself off from what was in her mind clearly a simple business negotiation.

'No problem,' he replied with a sigh, zipping himself up and trying to catch his breath.

Leeza left his office, hearing him call out a meek, 'Thank you' after her. Sometimes that's what it took and Calypso would never know. It wasn't cheating on her husband, she never even considered it as that; it was just what she had to do. She would rather suck the cocks of Hollywood than have her baby do it. There was no need for any of that now, was there?

Calypso got out of the car. Her head was throbbing, she was sweating profusely and she was crying. She had followed Leeza into the office to make sure she didn't embarrass her in any way. Her mother was crazy sometimes and Calypso often felt like the adult. Walking inside, she saw the receptionist coming back to the desk.

'Um, hi, my mom has to speak to the director. Can you tell me where he is?'

'Down the hall, last office on the right.'

Calypso walked down the hall. There was no one around, and she heard laughing from somewhere in the building. Last office on the right, the girl said. She opened the door slightly to peep in and saw her mother on her knees with the director's penis in her mouth. His eyes were closed and his face was red. Calypso shut the door quickly.

Running down the hallway, she blurted to the receptionist, 'Don't tell my mom I was here, I was supposed to stay in the car.'

'Okay, whatever,' said the girl, not interested in the slightest.

Calypso pretended to be asleep when her mom got in the car, and when she went home she slept for sixteen hours straight. Waking up, she imagined she had dreamed what she had seen, although her father, Bob, had found her crying outside the trailer the next day. She couldn't tell him why, just

226

cried in his arms, then straightened her small frame and never spoke about it again. If she didn't talk about it then it wasn't real, she told herself.

By the end of the day, she convinced herself the fever had made her hallucinate and she had seen nothing. Although she was not surprised when her agent rang to say she had the contract for the Baked Goodness commercials. 'See honey, I told you they would see your talent. Even half dead, you still outshine them all!'

Calypso had smiled weakly at her mother, happy at least the commercial would ease the constant arguments about money between her parents. But the image of Leeza on her knees, real or imagined, stayed with her as her profile grew and the work became more frequent, and she was never quite sure whether she had a career based on her talent for acting or Leeza's talent for blowjobs.

As the plane taxied onto the tarmac at LA, Calypso was tired from lack of sleep and from the memories that haunted her but she wanted to get the situation sorted. There was no time to waste. She knew that the blackmailer would move swiftly if she didn't contact him. She rang Greg from the airport. 'I'm here, yes, I'll come straightaway.'

Leaving LAX in a cab and going to her agent's office, she thought about Leeza. So she hadn't imagined her blowing the director years ago when she had the flu, she thought as she watched LA go past her window. Her mother had been formidable and Calypso had never stood up to her. But now Calypso was going to have to sort it out. Two million dollars was money she did not have. She could find it if she had to but then this person, whoever was blackmailing her, would keep coming back for more, possibly selling it to the media for even more money.

Calypso was beside herself. Her concern was not for her career but for Leeza and her father. What would this do to them?

As she pulled up outside the building, Calypso paid the driver and signed an autograph. She was back in town and this was one problem she had to fix herself. Greg came and led her by the arm to the boardroom. Sitting at the large round table was the head of the agency and Mandy, her manager. 'This is a fucking nightmare,' started Greg. 'I cannot tell you what harm this will do to your career. In fact, I doubt you will even have a career if this gets out.'

Calypso sat down and poured herself water from the jug on the table, her hands shaking. 'I want to see it,' she said strongly.

'No, you don't,' said Greg.

'Yes, I do. I have to know,' she insisted.

Greg looked at the head of the agency, Julius Gelfman, who had been in the industry for forty years. He had said nothing, just watched her and Greg. Julius had seen it all, many times. Nothing fazed him, this was just another problem they had to smooth over.

Julius nodded. Greg flicked a switch on the remote control on the table and the screen at the head of the room flickered to life.

There was an office on screen, and Jerry Hyman sat at his desk. A woman walked in, her back to the camera. She talked to him for a while, but there was no sound. Then he undid his pants and the woman walked over and got on her knees and sucked his cock. Calypso did not move a muscle while she watched. The woman then got up and said something else, the man laughed and as she turned, Calypso confirmed to herself it was her mother. She knew, from the way she walked, the way

228

she tossed her red hair and the jumper she was wearing. It was Calypso's favourite jumper growing up that year. A blue one, with two dancing bears appliquéd on the front. Calypso also knew it was her mother from the way she gave head to Jerry. It was just like she had seen Leeza, years ago after the audition.

'Turn it off,' said Calypso.

Julius spoke quietly but firmly. 'What do you want us to do, Calypso?'

'Does my mother know?'

'No,' answered Greg. 'Not yet.'

'I've a few strategies I can run by you if you want. Ways to deflect the media if this comes out,' said Mandy, leafing through long pages of notes in front of her.

'No more secrets, no more strategies. I want you to call the police,' she said firmly.

Greg called the police who then called the FBI. Calypso left Julius to brief them with the details. She had to see Leeza.

Leaving the meeting with her agent and a copy of the tape, she realized nearly four hours had passed since she touched down in LA. She checked her phone and saw she had six missed calls from TG and three from Leeza. Greg dropped her home. Getting out of the car, he opened the door for her and brought her bags to the door.

'You okay?'

'No, but I will be. Thanks for being so great about this. It's so fucking awful, I don't know what to say.'

Greg smiled at her; she was a good kid and talented also. 'Calypso, I know what you're thinking but I want you to know this much. You are where you are in your career because you are talented, not because of your mom, okay?'

Calypso smiled. 'Thanks, Greg,' she said, but she didn't believe him.

229

Her house welcomed her and she relaxed slightly being among her familiar things. The light breeze coming in over the pool blew the cobwebs away from too little sleep and her overactive mind seemed to be turning in circles.

Calypso lived in West Hollywood in a renovated house that had once been a pool-house for a former mansion, long since pulled down. Built in the 1930s, it was light and airy, with polished floorboards and white shutters. Nice and private, it had a large wall and gates that kept the fans and the paparazzi outside – most of the time. A hot-pink bougainvillea grew up over the side of the house and a huge frangipani tree swept gracefully over the kidney-shaped swimming pool in the back-yard. Somehow the pool house survived during the great destruction of Hollywood's architectural history during the 1980s and Calypso had lovingly decorated it in her own inimitable style.

Bohemia meets the Jetsons, is how she described it when asked by visitors. French chandeliers hung over a modern Danish dining table and the walls were painted in bright Indian pinks and turquoise. Framed movie posters of some of Calypso's favourite films were hung on the walls next to convex mirrors and Calypso's collection of framed antique fans.

Calypso liked quirky and crazy, something she was finding it harder and harder to be since her star was on the rise. Hollywood is a processed city. Everything you say, wear and eat is watched, supervised and analysed. To show your real self is rare and frightening to the studios. Calypso wondered what the studio would think of her house if they saw it in all its glory. It certainly wasn't interior decorated within an inch of its life, to be ready for the pages of an *In Style* magazine shoot.

Calypso used to frequent the flea markets in Hollywood when she had the time. Nothing made her happier than lugging home a new find and restoring it to her own taste. Chairs, dressing tables, even clothes all found a place in Calypso's heart and home. Now she settled for eBay, having her treasures delivered to her parents' house, or her manager's office. The thrill of the find was all part of the attraction for Calypso.

Taking a shower, she emerged to find two more messages from TG. She didn't listen to them; she had to deal with her mother first. He could come later, she thought.

Picking up her phone she dialled Leeza's cell phone. 'Hi, Mom, I need you to come over to my house now, without Dad, okay?'

And not giving her mother time to speak, she hung up on her.

Leeza was over within thirty minutes. Letting herself in with her own key, she came into the living room where Calypso sat waiting.

'Baby, what's wrong, what's the emergency? You okay?'

'Sit down, Mom,' said Calypso.

Leeza ignored her and walked into the kitchen. 'You want a juice, some tea? What can I get you? Did you eat in Italy? You look thin.'

'Mom, sit down now.'

Leeza came back from the kitchen, her eyebrows furrowed. 'Okay, okay. What's the problem?'

She sat on the chair opposite Calypso who turned on the TV with the remote in her hand.

'Am I going to see what you did in Italy, baby?' asked Leeza, sitting forward.

Calypso was quiet and let the tape speak for her. She watched her mother's face, not wanting to look at the screen again.

'That's Jerry Hyman, what a mess he is in,' she said. 'I'll tell you all about it.'

'Just watch, Mom.'

Then Leeza came on the screen and Calypso saw her recognize herself. She saw her sit back in her chair. 'Turn it off,' she said quietly.

'No, Mom. I had to watch it today, I think you should sit through the director's cut.'

Leeza started to cry. 'Turn it off, Calypso, goddammit!'

Calypso stood up, calm. 'No, I won't turn it off, Leeza, just like I could never fucking turn you off. "Try harder, Calypso, don't eat that, Calypso, you have to work more, Calypso, we need this, Calypso". You are such a tyrant and you sucked other people's cocks to get me to where I am. How do you think I feel about that fact, Leeza?'

'I did it for you, baby,' said Leeza, crying. 'It was so hard in those days. Do you remember? You worked so hard and your dad and I went without so much. And look at you now. It's everything you ever wanted.'

'It's everything *you* ever wanted, Mom. What you wanted was this career for yourself, you never asked me. My life was predestined before I could even talk,' Calypso snapped back. 'And now I've got to sort this out. Do you know what I have to do? Pay some asshole two million dollars or he is going to release this to the media. No head job's gonna get you out of this one, I'm afraid.' Calypso's voice was pitiless.

Leeza was stunned at the revelation. What had she done? Who else knew? The questions ran through her mind.

'Oh God,' she said and leaned over her knees as though she was about to faint.

'Get out of my house, Leeza, get out of my house and out of my life. Do you understand? I never want to see you again for as long as I live.'

Calypso walked to the front door and opened it, waiting for Leeza to leave.

'No, Calypso, no, please, I am sorry, I really am. I don't know why I did it, please don't hate me.'

'I don't hate you, I just want you to get your own life, your own dreams. You've lived through me long enough. It's too much responsibility to make you happy. God knows, I can't do it for myself,' said Calypso sadly. 'Just go, okay. I will let you know what happens. I will get Greg to call you. Give me my house key.' She held out her hand and Leeza dropped the key into the waiting hand with a little cry.

Leeza stood, wobbly in her white high heels, clumsily trying to hug her, the tears and snot running down her face, make-up streaked. Once she had been the ringmaster of Calypso's life, now she was just a sad clown, Calypso thought as she gently pushed her mother away.

'Go,' she said, and Leeza walked out the door.

Calypso walked back into her sitting room, noticing that TG had called her again. Not yet, she thought. She had a feeling he would be there for her forever and she had to get her own life in order before she let someone else into it. Pulling off her clothes as she walked to the back garden, Calypso stood naked at the edge of the water and dove in. Water always helped her think, she thought, as she sank to the bottom of the pool.

CHAPTER TWENTY-FIVE

Three weeks had passed and Sapphira was doing well detoxing, better than she had expected. With Jack's insistence she had managed to eat a little more and her stomach had settled down. The daily massages had released her body of the tension and helped soothe her restless legs. The acupuncture was helping her sleep and she had not yet had one of the awful nightmares, even after the terrible intrusion in Italy. The police were no further forward in their investigations, warning that her stalker would be following her to where he thought she was.

'Lucky there is your likeness out in the world,' said Jack as he leafed through a magazine, showing photos of their doppelgängers, shot from a long lens at a ski resort in Switzerland from a few weeks before.

'But they've finished their gig now,' said Sapphira. She had been worried about the girl, hoping the stalker didn't try to contact her or attack her, but thankfully she had been safe.

'Well, he doesn't know we're here, so you're safe till they find him,' said Jack as he walked over to the window, looking out. All of Jack's windows had reflective tinting so he could see out but the public and media couldn't pry into his life.

'I feel like I'm wasting your time. Surely you could be doing other things rather than minding me?' said Sapphira as she tidied the kitchen for something to do.

'When you bore me, I'll kick you out. Meanwhile I'm happy

you're doing so well. So shut up with the needy whining and let's play some Scrabble.'

'Scrabble?' asked Sapphira.

'Yes, I am the king and you shall be shocked and awed. Get ready,' said Jack, walking towards the huge Louis XIV sideboard in the sitting room, opening the door and pulling out a well-loved box of the game.

'Get ready, Mr Reynolds. I've got words you ain't even used yet,' said Sapphira as she clicked her fingers in front of her face.

So Jack and Sapphira settled into a routine. Her chosen therapy in the morning, lunch, a rest, then an afternoon of games. Boggle, Scrabble, Monopoly, even Operation. Jack had every single board game imaginable. He was crazy about them and incredibly competitive. 'Splenetic is not a word,' he yelled.

'Yes, it is,' defied Sapphira. 'In fact, you are being it now. Jack Reynolds is a splenetic man.'

'I'm looking it up,' he said, reaching for his computer.

'You know the rules, if the word is in the dictionary then you lose a turn,' she said, leaning back in her chair.

Jack's cell phone rang. 'Saved by the bell,' he said, answering the phone.

Sapphira laughed and went to the kitchen to give him some privacy. Making herself and Jack a coffee, she thought about her life in Italy. It was surreal and safe. The idea of heading back to LA anytime soon scared her immensely. LA was easy to score drugs, the group of 'friends' there were mostly addicts of some kind. Heroin, sex, cocaine. Sapphira knew she wasn't ready to go back but she wondered how long she could stay with Jack. She knew he had put his life on hold for her and while she was grateful, she was unsure of where to go next.

Her therapist had told her to wait till she had the implant inserted, which stopped the cravings for heroin and nullified the hit if she did shoot up. The physical cravings were gone but the mental desire for the drug was still in her system and until it left her, she was afraid of the outside world.

Jack came into the kitchen. 'Hey, that was a friend of mine from LA. Alex Wright. Do you know him?'

Sapphira shook her head. 'I know of him, seen him at awards and such but I've never actually met him,' she said, vaguely remembering a tall, blond-haired man.

'Well, he's broken up with his girlfriend. All very ugly and in the media, apparently. He wants to come and visit me, get away for a while. I said I would ask you first. I don't want you to feel overwhelmed, but he is my closest friend, I guess. Great guy. I've known him for years. He knew Armondo, was amazing when he died. Stayed with me for weeks. I didn't say anything about you, just said you were taking a break here. If you aren't cool with it then I will let him know. I'll just say I have stuff on.'

Sapphira shrugged. 'I don't care either way, not that I am much company. I will just do my own thing. It's fine.'

'Thanks, Sapphira, it means a lot to him. Might be nice to have some other company anyway. You must be getting sick of me.'

'Never,' she said as she walked past him, chucking him under the chin with her hand and heading to her floor.

It was true Sapphira didn't care either way about Alex staying at Jack's palazzo. Sapphira thought about nothing or anyone else but herself. She was constantly checking in with herself to see how she was feeling, craving, wanting. It was sending her more into herself and Jack was hopeful the arrival of Alex might help her integrate herself slowly into the world a little more.

236

Alex arrived the next day on a private plane, coming straight to Jack's palazzo, and entering through the back entrance away from the odd paparazzo who was hanging around outside hoping for a sighting of them, although it was unconfirmed they were still in Italy.

Sapphira heard Alex and Jack greet each other warmly, with much laughter from downstairs. She stayed in her room, giving them time to catch up, a little afraid of meeting someone new in her fragile state. Sapphira was not a vain woman but she knew she looked unwell. The weight had fallen off her since her detox and she had not seen sunlight properly for a few weeks. She was pale, with black shadows under her eyes. Her hair long and unkempt, she knew she needed sunlight, a haircut and to eat more. The tiredness overwhelmed her at times, and she wanted to sleep at the oddest hours of the day. Sometimes even after she had only been awake for two hours. It took enormous effort to do the smallest tasks, and Sapphira, who had always fired on all cylinders, even while on heroin, felt as though her body was trying to recharge at a deep cellular level. For the first time she listened to it. If she was tired she slept. She craved odd things, like fruit and vegetables. She wanted to stretch, her muscles feeling unfamiliar and weak. Jack had organized a private yoga teacher, who came most mornings to gently coax her body into flexibility again and Sapphira felt her body responding, waking some mornings sore from the exercise but not from the cravings.

'Saph,' she heard Jack call through the intercom. 'Come and meet Alex.'

Sapphira walked downstairs, instead of using the lift. She was trying to get stronger and the stairs, although just a few flights, took an effort to manage. Walking into the living room, she held onto the doorframe for a moment, while the dizziness stopped. Jack came over and grabbed her arm and led her to the nearest chair.

'You okay, babe?' he asked, concerned. 'Sapphira has had a terrible case of Epstein-Barr Syndrome,' he said to Alex who was standing, looking with concern at Sapphira. 'She picked it up in Perugia, so I brought her back here. She lives alone in LA and doesn't have anyone else to look after her. Can't really heal in a hotel room, so Nurse Jack is doing his thing,' he said cheerfully.

Sapphira felt her head clear and she smiled at Jack gratefully. 'I'm fine now. Sorry about the dramatic introduction,' she said, and stood to walk over to shake Alex's hand.

Looking up, she saw the most beautiful man she had ever seen. Tall, handsome, around thirty-six, she guessed, he was the perfect specimen of what a Hollywood movie star was supposed to look like. Blue eyes, tanned skin, great body, she noticed underneath his white v-necked t-shirt and jeans. Wholesome, and yet with a distinct air of sex about him. Sapphira felt herself assessing him and then stopped herself. No time or energy for anything but healing, she reminded herself as she accepted his extended hand.

'Hi, you okay? My sister had Epstein-Barr when she was at college. My mom had to take care of her for three months. She still gets tired easily. You should try Vitamin B shots, they helped her a lot,' he said sincerely.

Sapphira smiled. 'Thanks. I'll look into it.' And she sank into the sofa opposite him. Jack and Alex sat down.

'I'm surprised you two don't know each other,' said Jack easily. 'I thought you'd move in the same circles in LA.'

'I don't really move in any circles, I guess. I try to stay out of all the hoopla. LA is a crazy town that steals your soul if you let it.'

238

Sapphira laughed. 'I know what you mean, I grew up there. I think I lost my soul a long time ago.'

Alex looked at her dark eyes and her jutting collarbones underneath her singlet top. She was unwell, clearly, but it was more than Epstein-Barr, he was sure. His sister had never looked like Sapphira; she just slept a lot.

'I doubt it, if you are friends with Jacky then you must have something in you that resembles a soul. He's the greatest man I know,' said Alex warmly.

Sapphira looked at Jack, who was reddening, 'Enough, please. I already have an ego the size of Russia. You're both great friends and I hope you will become friends with each other also. Nothing would make me happier, other than a night with a sexy Italian man who can keep a secret,' he laughed.

Sapphira and Alex laughed and then tiredness washed over her. 'I might head off for a sleep, leave you two to talk shit,' she said as she started to leave the room.

'Oh, there'll be plenty of that,' said Alex. He stood as she left the room, watching her thin frame clad in black leggings start to climb the stairs. Epstein-Barr, my ass, he thought.

Sapphira had her small dinner in her room that night and stayed on her floor for the next few days, while her therapists came and went. She had no idea what Alex and Jack were doing but she heard them coming and going. Jack buzzed her on the intercom but she said she was fine and would come down when she was ready. In truth, Sapphira was feeling a little better; each day brought a new challenge but also a new awareness.

Finally Jack insisted she come out of her solitude and join him and Alex on the roof for a traditional Italian Sunday lunch. Sapphira was torn between wanting to stay in her cocoon and knowing she needed to join the world. 'Just for a little while,' she said.

239

'Well, can you please wear something other than those fucking leggings?' laughed Jack.

Sapphira screamed with laughter. 'Always the style guru, Mr Reynolds. I don't think either you or Alex really give a shit what I wear.'

'Well, I do, so look nice, lady,' instructed Jack.

Jack had seen the way Alex had looked at Sapphira, and her reaction to his beauty. He was beautiful and uncomplicated in ways that Sapphira was an intricate web of secrets and mystery. When Alex had rung, trying to find a safe harbour from his relationship breakup back in the States, Jack saw the opportunity for Sapphira and Alex to meet. He knew it was too soon for a relationship for either of them, but they had to know there were other people in the world. And what the hell, he thought, a little matchmaking was always fun.

Sapphira had looked through her things. Everything seemed too slutty or hard. Clothes for a person she no longer was. Not that she was hankering for Liberty prints but she wanted clothes that caressed her, not defined her. Remembering the bags of Gucci from when she stayed with Jack previously, she buzzed him. 'Do you have any of that Gucci from last time or did it go back?'

'It's in my wardrobe. I'll bring it up.'

'I'm not even going to ask why it's in your wardrobe,' she replied, laughing.

The bags arrived with Jack, who was dressed in linen, his standard Venetian wear. The air was getting cooler as they were heading into autumn and Sapphira's clothes were all for the Italian summer. Jack pulled out a pair of black pants and a lace shirt. 'Too girly?'

Sapphira picked up the shirt. The lace was soft, not scratchy. It was silk, a fine pattern, not overdone like the lace that

240

Sapphira had always stayed away from, but a small delicate weave that did not overtake the wearer. The black gabardine pants were simple to offset the lace shirt. 'I don't know, Jack,' she said, holding the shirt against her. 'It seems too much.'

'Try it on with the black singlet underneath which you seem to love so much.'

Sapphira pulled off the t-shirt she was wearing and put the black singlet on with the shirt over the top. Jack looked at her and then went to her wardrobe. 'Wear it with this,' he said. And threw her dark denim Joes Jeans at her.

Slipping into them, she realized how much weight she had lost. They hung around her waist and were a little baggy in the back. 'Wear the shirt out,' Jack instructed, as he left the room. 'With black flats,' he called from down the stairs.

Sapphira did as he said. Who was she to argue with Jack? And besides, it felt good to be wearing something more than the stretchy clothes she had been wearing for the past few weeks.

Plaiting her hair and applying a small amount of make-up to disguise the shadows on her face and add some colour to her pallor, she headed upstairs to the roof garden. The light was lovely and Jack had had his staff set up a table for the three of them. Alex was up there, waiting for her and Jack. He turned when he heard her come into the space and smiled. 'Hello, you look lovely,' he said sincerely.

Sapphira gave him a friendly smile. 'Thanks, I'm feeling better lately.'

'Good, I'm glad. Jack's been worried about you. He really loves you.'

'I love him,' she said simply. 'He saved my life, I think.'

Alex didn't push her any further.

Sapphira took a cigarette from the open packet on the table. 'Do you mind?' she asked.

'Not at all, they're mine,' he said, taking one himself.

'Sorry, I thought they were Jack's,' she said. 'I should give up.'

'Well, we all should, but what the hell. There are worse things you can do,' he said as he lit her cigarette, cupping his strong brown hand around hers, as she sheltered the flame from the light breeze, and then lit his own.

At the touch of his hands, Sapphira felt a small shiver through her body. It had been a long while since she had touched a man's body in any way other than friendship, she thought, looking at the muscular shape of Alex's legs underneath his jeans.

'So, how long are you staying here?' she asked Alex, blowing smoke into the air.

'Till the dust settles back home. I broke up with someone, it's a fucking circus back there. I have no idea why my love life is so interesting. It isn't,' he said vehemently.

'What happened? If you don't mind me asking,' she said, pushing her Gucci sunglasses that were on her head onto her nose.

'Nothing, we went out for a long time. I wanted to get married, and she didn't, simple. Then one day I got sick of asking. Told her I was leaving and now she's playing the sad girl victim and I'm left looking like a heel.' He rubbed the side of his jaw thoughtfully.

'It shouldn't be that hard, I thought after a while. If we were meant to be together then we would be, but things kept separating us – work, travel, our friends. I like seeing the world, experiencing things. She liked routine, gym, acting classes and parties. I don't know. We were just in different places throughout our relationship.'

Sapphira nodded, understanding a little.

'What about you? You seeing anyone?' he asked casually, butting out his cigarette.

242

'No, no one. I don't really do relationships,' she said.

'How come?'

'I like my freedom, I like waking up and thinking, what do I want to do today? If I want to work, then I do. No ties, no real home. The world is my home. I like seeing things, learning things. Staying at Jack's has been the longest I've stayed anywhere in a very long time, besides for work.'

'So where do you base yourself? Where are all your worldly possessions?' he asked, fascinated by her nomadic life.

'I have a house in LA, because I have to. I had to buy something, my manager forced me to. I have some books and clothes there but not much else,' she said, thinking she never stayed there because her stalker always knew where she was and started to send her gifts again. Travelling the world continually meant she was harder to find.

Alex assessed her; she was calm today, quiet but fascinating. She was unlike any woman he had ever met in LA; she seemed not to care about the trappings his last girlfriend had worried about. Needing to be seen, always telling her PR person where she was going with Alex, so they could be photographed together. It drove him mad, he couldn't even go for a ride on his motorbike now without the paps following him dangerously, almost wanting him to have an accident, so they could get the shot and the bounty from selling the photo.

'So, what happens after this?' he asked. 'When you get better?'

'I don't know. I've pulled out of film for a year. I'm trying to change my life in some ways and I want to do something more. The only trouble is, I don't know what that is yet,' she said ruefully, putting out the cigarette and sipping her wine.

'You'll know when it comes, stay open to it,' said Alex, smiling kindly as Jack came out onto the roof.

'Thanks,' said Sapphira, looking at his straight white teeth,

243

the type that had never had braces but were a dentist's dream.

'How we getting along, kids?' asked Jack as he poured himself a wine. 'Playing nice on the roof?'

'For sure, man. Just talking shit, as you would say,' Alex said, nodding to Sapphira.

She laughed and Jack sat down.

'Sapphira was talking about wanting to do something after she leaves here but not knowing what it is yet.'

'Well, there's no need to do anything just yet, pussy cat,' said Jack, serving himself antipasto the housekeeper had placed on the table. 'You know you can stay here as long as you like.'

'I know, but sooner or later I have to get a life,' she said, nibbling on an olive.

'You have a life, a good one. You just need to find your purpose. Everyone has a purpose, you know.'

'What's yours?' asked Sapphira with a little smile. 'Besides beautiful boys and luxury goods.'

'I am shocked you think that's all my life is,' said Jack with mock indignation. 'I will have you know I donated over five million dollars to charity last year and attended several important symposiums on the various causes I'm interested in.'

'Really?' she asked, surprised.

'Yeah, he did,' answered Alex for Jack. 'We've done a bit together, actually.'

Sapphira sat back thoughtfully. 'Saint Jack.'

'No, I never tell the media what I'm doing. I've no need for the publicity. I just like to bring people's attention to what is happening in the world. People have more power than they realize to change things.'

Alex laughed. 'Remember when we did that gig in New York and you asked the Buddhist monk where he got the Tod's

244

loafers and he answered they were Richard Gere's hand-me-downs. I thought you were going to get asthma you laughed so hard.'

Jack laughed. 'Very funny night. Very funny.'

'How do you know what to give a shit about? There is so much going on in the world,' said Sapphira.

Alex served himself some bread and broke it, thinking. 'I think you have to look back on your life and see if there is a particular incident or moment that resonates with you. For me, I like the idea of education for everyone. I went to a great school and a great college. I was in a safe place at home to learn. I had a great childhood. I think every child deserves that. So I work with an education foundation that gives out school supplies to kids who need them, write cheques for college tuition for families who are struggling. I like it and it feels good. I get letters from kids who are doing what would have been impossible without the fundraising that I do. You have to do something with the celebrity you have, otherwise you become consumed with yourself. I lead a privileged life, I know that, so I figure I should share some of it while it lasts.'

Sapphira listened. The way he spoke so openly and passionately about his cause was inspiring. What the hell did she have to show for her life so far besides some films, money and track marks?

'I want to do something,' she said.

'Good for you, honey,' said Jack, looking at her shift in emotion from behind his Prada sunglasses. 'I think you will do something . . . amazing,' he added.

She smiled and picked up a piece of crusty bread. 'I'm starving,' she said and Jack smiled from behind his shades.

The next morning Sapphira was up early. She had done her yoga, had her acupuncture and was feeling the best she had in ages. She had spent a few hours on the internet looking at causes and charities across the world. She was looking for something in particular, but could not narrow the choices down. She rang Giulia, who was down in Jack's office.

'Giulia, can I come and see you for a moment? I need some help with something.'

Going downstairs, she was carrying a stack of printouts and had a pencil stuck behind her ear, her hair up in a messy bun on her head. Alex came out of the kitchen. 'Hey there,' he said. 'Hey, yourself,' she shot back at him as she walked past.

'Where you off to?' he enquired.

'Getting some help from Giulia with something. What are you up to?'

'Jacky and I are heading off for a "man trip" today. He wants to go and do some sightseeing. Man time!' he said, flexing the muscles in his arms.

Sapphira laughed, noticing how toned he was. 'Well, look after Jacky for me.'

'Always,' he shot after her as she headed into Jack's office.

Giulia was at the desk, working on the computer. 'Hello, Sapphira, how are you?' she asked, looking up.

Giulia's efficiency and chicness always made Sapphira feel a little bit dowdy, particularly since she had been in Jack's house. Giulia had the effortless ability of Italian women to wear her clothes and not have them wear her. Today she was in a caramel cashmere sweater tunic with black tights and the most gorgeous long black flat-heeled boots Sapphira had ever seen. Her short hair was tucked behind her ears and she wore gold hoops and a single gold bangle.

Sapphira became aware of her jeans and Jack's sweatshirt she was wearing, her feet in socks and her long dirty hair messily put up on top of her unmade-up face.

'Yeah, I'm good, thanks for everything you've organized. I really like yoga now. I might continue it forever. It's quite addictive,' she said.

'Well, that's a good addiction to have,' laughed Giulia kindly.

'Yes, although the Chinese teas I can do without. No chance of getting hooked on them,' said Sapphira, screwing up her nose.

'Anyway,' she continued self-consciously, 'I'm trying to find some information and I'm a little unsure if I'm on the right track. Do you have time to help me? It's fine if you don't, though. I know you're busy.'

'Of course. What do you need?'

'I want to help a charity but I don't know where to start and what to choose. It's a little disconcerting with how much crap there is in the world,' she said, sighing heavily.

'Okay, well, I do this with Jack all the time and I head up his foundation here in Italy. So, I know all the ins and outs and how to go about it. What are the causes you're interested in?'

Sapphira paused. She had spent all night thinking about what resonated with her, as Alex had advised, going over the significant moments in her life. 'I want to help women in Third World countries whose babies are unwell or deformed in some way. Or maybe the mothers are unwell after the birth and cannot access the types of healthcare and choices we have in Western countries.'

Giulia took down notes as Sapphira spoke. 'Do you want to just give money or do you want to get involved a little more? I'm sure with your level of profile that you could be as involved as much or as little as you want.'

'I don't know. I don't even know if they would want me to be a part of it. I mean, I don't have children, so it might seem a little weird,' she said worriedly.

'That doesn't matter. We can work out a press release explaining your passion for women to receive decent healthcare. Come at it from a woman's angle,' said Giulia, not prying into the reasons for Sapphira's choice.

'Yes, that's great,' said Sapphira excitedly. 'The problem is I can't find who the right group is, there are so many issues and causes.'

'Leave it with me. I will find a few I think are what you are looking for and then you can tell me if I am on the right path or not. *Si?*'

'*Si*,' said Sapphira, noticing Giulia's shining hair as it fell over her smooth forehead. 'One more thing, Giulia.'

'Yes?' said Giulia, looking up expectantly.

'I need a haircut. Can you recommend a good hairdresser here in Venice?'

Giulia smiled widely; this was her domain and she was exactly the right person to ask. '*Assolutamente*,' she said and picked up the phone.

Sapphira sat in the chair in her bedroom that afternoon. Stefano had instructed wet hair to Giulia, since she would not be going to his salon on the Grand Canal. Sapphira had had her hair trimmed over the years but it was long and annoying now. It didn't feel like her hairstyle anymore.

Stefano was Giulia's hairdresser, Jack's hairdresser too, and some of the most notable women in Italy flew to get their hair cut and styled by him. He came into the room, speaking Italian to Giulia who walked behind him. Small, wiry and completely fabulous, he clapped his hands when he saw Sapphira. Speaking rapid Italian to her, Giulia interjected, 'His English is not very good, so he only wants to speak Italian, as he wants to concentrate on your hair,' she explained.

Stefano kept speaking over the top of Giulia.

'He says he has wanted to cut your hair for many years and has a style in mind. Is this okay?' she asked, worried Sapphira would want just the ends of her long hair trimmed.

Sapphira nodded. 'Okay, I trust him. I don't like it this long anymore. It just hangs. I need a cut but which I can still pull back. Something with shape,' she told Giulia.

Giulia translated this back to Stefano who looked very serious. Undoing the bag he brought with him, he put a cape around Sapphira with a flourish. As he combed out her hair, Sapphira sat still. He lifted and separated the hair, cutting bits and smoothing it out again. He combed it over her face and then chopped over her nose, talking to her the whole time in Italian. She didn't answer him as her translator Giulia had left the room. Just smiling nervously, she hoped she was giving him the right reactions.

Stefano stood back. He pulled out a large hairdryer and plugged it into the power point beside them. Taking out a bottle of liquid, he put a small bit into his hands and then rubbed it through her hair. Turning on the dryer, he then blew her hair from every direction, motioning her to tip forward in her chair to put her head over her knees so her hair fell forward. Then he pulled her back again, as though she was made of clay and took a large round brush and blew it again, winding the hair about the brush under the hot air.

Finally he was done. He stood in front of her surveying his work. '*Stupendo!*' he exclaimed. 'Giulia, Giulia,' he called.

Giulia walked into the room. 'Ahhh,' she said smiling.

Sapphira stood and shook the hair from her lap. Looking down at the ground she saw a large amount of her hair and became nervous. Stefano undid the cape and she walked over to the mirror in the bathroom. Stefano had cut her hair into a long layer style. It sat just below her collarbones and feathered gently around her face, softening her features. There was a slight fringe that swept over one eye and showed off her large eyes. Her chin seemed less pointed and the feathers on the side of her hair fell gently, accentuating her cheekbones. She looked younger but more stylish. It was the hair of a woman, no longer a girl.

'I love it,' she said. 'It's perfect.'

Stefano knew enough English to understand her pleasure. '*Bella*,' he said and packed up his things.

Kissing her on both cheeks, he said something again in Italian, very seriously to Sapphira. Giulia translated. 'He says he is pleased to cut your hair. This is the hair of a woman in control of her life but who knows how to have fun. You will find great things with this hairstyle. He will cut it for you again anytime.'

Sapphira tried not to laugh, Stefano loved his job a little too much, she thought, but turning back to the mirror, she noticed she did feel different, more in charge than she had felt in a very long time.

CHAPTER TWENTY-SIX

Rose fell into her mother's arms at her childhood home. 'Rosie, what are you doing here?' she asked, concerned. 'What's happened, darling?'

Being pulled into the warm and comfortable home, Rose felt peaceful again. Wiping her eyes, she calmed down and spoke. 'Oh Mum, I've made a complete fuck up of things and I don't know what to do.'

'First a cup of tea and then a chat. Your father's out at the library and so I've got you all to myself,' her mother said, briskly.

For Rose it felt as if time had stopped. Since his retirement her father would go to the London Library in the city each morning and read the papers from around the world. It didn't matter that Rose's brother had set him up with a computer and explained the miracle of Google; Rose's father was a creature of habit and he claimed being surrounded by papers and books helped him think but Rose thought it was to escape her mother sometimes.

Rose had not been home in a long time. She visited London but it was always fleeting, for a film publicity tour or for the BAFTA Awards. And she always stayed at The Dorchester, preferring the luxury of a suite and the comfort of being able to do what she wanted.

She owned a stunning apartment in London but never stayed

there and refused to rent it out for privacy reasons but the paparazzi stalked it relentlessly, so she had let it sit, unused and unfurnished.

Wendy switched on the kettle and set about getting the mugs and spoons. She placed some ginger and orange biscuits on a plate and put them in front of Rose. Pouring her tea into the old blue and white Spode cups Rose loved so much, she sat at the worn pine table. Rose put her feet on the rail that sat below the table and warmed her hands on the cup.

'I should have told you I was coming,' she said apologetically.

'Rosie, you are a grown woman, nearly forty, as I remember. You don't need to tell me your whereabouts all the time.'

'I know, I just feel awful showing up in tears and all that,' Rose said, embarrassed.

'Never mind that. Now, what's going on? Tell all, no details left out, please.'

So for the next two hours and several cups of tea, Rose told Wendy everything. About Max and Italy, the boys, the distant phone calls and the house cleaning, and then about Alice and the dreams Max was having. Wendy sat and asked a few questions but not many, she just let Rose speak. When Rose was finished, she considered her words carefully.

'Rosie, when you married Paul, I didn't think it would last. Don't look shocked, no one thought it would go as long as it did. The only person that man loved was himself. You were the reason that marriage survived for ten years but you can't love enough for two, Rose, remember where that landed you.'

'I know,' said Rose sadly.

'Rosie, ever since you were a little girl you have loved with your heart and soul. You want people to be happy so much, you will give up yourself to be able to give this to them.'

252

Rose was silent. She and her mother had not talked properly since she left for the US after her debut film premiered to great accolades. Even after Rose had tried to kill herself, she avoided any deep conversations with her parents; having to deal with her own grief was task enough without having to talk to her parents about what her life had been like while married to the controlling Paul. Rose had avoided any conversations with anyone, except her therapist in LA.

Now, she sat at the kitchen table where she had done her homework as a child, a thirty-nine-year-old woman weeping to her mother about a man. It felt good to be home.

Wendy continued, 'If this man loves his wife and his children so much, then he is a good man. I'm happy, you deserve a good man.'

'But he won't be with me because of his wife, even though she's dead,' cried Rose loudly.

'What I mean is, he puts other people's feelings before his own,' Wendy said. 'His children and the idea of what he thinks his wife wants from beyond the grave. Which is total rubbish, of course. All women want their partners to go on without them; women understand the cycle of life. If you ask me, he is just racked with guilt. He was probably in a quite comfortable rut with his grief and then you came along and shattered his illusion about what his life was going to look like for the rest of his life.'

'I'm so stupid. I thought I could come over here and clean up his life, kiss his wounds and we would live happily ever after. I think I've been in films for too long. There are no happy endings,' said Rose dramatically.

'Oh Rose, knock off the melodramatics. I'm not saying you haven't been through the wringer, but give the man time to get over what he's lost before he starts looking into a very different future. Coming back from Italy would have been a shock for the poor bloke, back to life again, without you, without his wife.' Wendy looked thoughtful.

Wendy got up to look in the fridge. 'Your father will be back soon. You staying for dinner?'

'Of course,' said Rose.

'It's just a fry-up. I'm afraid I've left it too late to prepare anything.'

'Sounds lovely, Mum,' said Rose, stretching. 'Mum?'

'Yes, love,' said her mother's bottom, sticking out of the fridge.

'Can I stay here for a while?'

'At home?' asked Wendy, turning around surprised.

'Yes, if you don't mind.'

'Of course, Rosie,' said Wendy, cracking eggs into a bowl and hiding the tears in her eyes.

Rose stayed with her parents for ten days. Sleeping in her old room, in the single bed, under the cotton sheets of her youth, she felt comforted again. Max did not try to contact her at all and she did not call him. Instead she revelled in being with her family again, seeing her nieces and nephews, laughing with her father in front of terrible British soaps at night.

She went walking with her mother each morning around Hyde Park and shopping at Brown's and Liberty's and some of the newer stores.

The Christmas decorations were starting to come out and Rose was nostalgic for a white Christmas again after years of sunny Christmases spent in LA with friends. 'I wish I could come back for Christmas but I have to shoot in New York. I don't get any time off really besides Christmas Day and Boxing Day,' she said to her mother when she went to see her off at the airport.

'Don't worry, your father and I are going to Spain on Boxing Day anyway. We've had a lovely time with you this week, Rose.'

'I have too, Mum. It's been good, just what I needed. I'm sorry I've been so wrapped up in myself. I love you and Dad. Thank you.' Rose paused. 'I think I'm going to come back to London for a while when I finish filming and decorate my apartment.'

'Will you come back for Max or for yourself?' asked Wendy wisely.

'For me, Mum. I have a home here, I just forgot for a while. I really love you, Mum.'

'Now don't get all LA on me,' said Wendy, wrinkling her nose.

'Too late, Mum, too late.' And she grabbed her mother and gave her a big hug, much to Wendy's joy and embarrassment.

Rose flew straight from London to New York to start the shoot on the next film. Walking on set for rehearsals, she was over-joyed to see Kelly. 'Kel, I didn't know you were on this?'

'I wasn't, but Liz, who was on it, broke her arm skiing last week in Aspen, so here I am. I thought I would surprise you.'

'I'm so pleased, I missed you!'

'I missed you also, Tosser. Chris is on the shoot also, so I figured I should do this one. Might be the last time we all work together for a while.'

'Why?' asked Rose, frowning.

'Because I'm twelve weeks pregnant. Found out when we got back from Italy. That's why I was sick there, so I hope you don't mind me throwing up every morning while I do your face,' said Kelly as they walked towards the make-up trailer.

'Oh Kelly, I am so happy for you,' exclaimed Rose, throwing her arms around her. 'How wonderful, I want to hear all about it.'

255

Rose was truly happy for Kelly, without any of the old angst she used to feel when she heard people were pregnant in the past. The time with her own family had made her realize what she had in her life, and even if she never had a family of her own, she would always be welcome in their lives.

'How's Max?' asked Kelly as they settled in the chairs inside.

'I don't know. We haven't spoken for a while.' Rose picked up a hairbrush and started to brush her hair.

Kelly looked closely at her. 'What happened?'

'Oh, you are going to love this one. Apparently his dead wife keeps coming to him in his dreams, trying to tell him something. He thinks she doesn't want him to be with me or some crap. I tell you, he was a different man in London to Italy, Kelly. I'm not even sure I like him. He was a bit wet, pathetic and self-righteous. And I bloody cleaned his house like some little scullery maid. Germaine Greer would have had my tits for breakfast. I am a disgrace to feminists. Not any more though. I'm here in New York, the best place for a single woman to be. I plan on having a ball here and forgetting about him,' said Rose, her nose in the air in defiance.

'Fair enough,' said Kelly, disappearing into the small bathroom and then emerging a few seconds later. 'Sorry, thought I was going to be sick.'

Rose looked at her sorrowfully. 'Oh Kel, it's a massive fuck up and who the hell am I kidding? I love him and my heart broke in his house the day when he cried about his wife and those dreams. He cried!'

'Listen, Rose, I'm going to say something you may scoff at but if you feel this deeply then I think you might want to consider it.' Kelly sat very close to Rose, her face almost touching hers.

'You are in the home of magic. New York is the most magical

256

city in the world. Why do you think so many movies are made about this place? Things happen here and the people this city attracts are people who believe in the impossible. I know a woman who speaks to the dead. Maybe you should meet with her and have it out with Alice?'

Rose looked at Kelly incredulously. 'Are you serious? We did that whole psychic bullshit when we were younger, but you still believe that stuff?'

'I never stopped. I have too many experiences to tell me otherwise. This woman is the real deal,' said Kelly, eating a peppermint.

'Why haven't I heard of her on the psychic channel or whatever? Shouldn't she have her own TV show and a book deal now?' asked Rose mockingly.

'That's how you know she's real. She doesn't need any of that crap,' said Kelly.

'So, she speaks to the dead?' Rose asked, her eyebrows raised.

'Yeah, she's a medium. Super expensive, but the good ones usually are,' Kelly said matter-of-factly.

'She's the haute couture of spooky, is she? Gosh, Kelly, I don't know. I've never been into all that woo-woo stuff, it was you who liked that years ago,' Rose said, her face screwed up.

'Woo-woo or boo-hoo. You choose.'

Kelly stood up to get ready for the day; the other actors were due on set any minute.

Rose stood up and took off her jacket. 'I'll go,' she said decidedly, 'but you have to come with me.'

'I wouldn't miss it for the world,' Kelly said with a wink. 'Dead people love me.'

Kelly organized the appointment with the medium for the following Tuesday evening. Rose met Kelly at the apartment block on the Upper West Side. She was surprised, thinking she would be in Brooklyn somewhere in a five-storey walkup, with a man asleep in the stairwell. Instead there was a doorman and plush lobby.

'Are you sure this is it?' whispered Rose as they stood in the brass and wood panelled elevator.

'I told you she was expensive, honey,' laughed Kelly as they stopped on the eighth floor. 'Of course she's on the eighth floor,' said Kelly to herself as they walked down the quiet, carpeted hallway.

Standing outside the door marked 108, Kelly noticed a small fish doorknocker. She knocked and the door opened. A tiny glamorous blond woman of no particular age stood in front of them. She could have been forty or ninety years old.

'Hello,' she greeted them warmly.

'Hi, I'm Kelly and this is Rose. I spoke to you last week.'

'Of course, I'm all set up. Which one is going first?'

The tiny sparrow of a woman led them into an exquisite room with yellow Chinese silk hangings of butterflies on the walls, off-white plush carpet that sank when you stepped on it, and a gorgeous collection of blue and white vases on a Chinese apothecary table. In the room were two pale yellow silk couches and a small Chinese table with dragons for legs sitting in the centre of the room.

She gestured for them to sit down. 'I'm Marion,' she said. 'I'm glad you have come. I am already getting messages for both of you. So many angels surround you.'

Rose nodded politely.

Marion bustled about the room. She took one single white candle and placed it in a silver dragon candlestick in the middle of the small table and lit it.

'So, which one will go first?' she asked with a smile as she

258

sat on the opposite couch. She looked like a grandmother, not a communicator with the dead, thought Rose.

'I'm not having a turn, just Rose,' said Kelly.

'Oh, that's a shame, I have people trying to speak to you,' said Marion.

'Really? Who?' asked Kelly, intrigued.

'I have your little boy, the one in your womb. He says to tell you he wants to be called Otis. That's his name.'

Kelly sat up and Rose felt her skin prickle. Kelly was twelve weeks pregnant but not showing, and no one knew but a select few.

Kelly laughed. 'Of course he does. Otis Redding was my dad's favourite singer. Tell him, Otis it is.' Turning to Rose, she laughed, clearly delighted. 'Chris is gonna freak!'

Rose was nervous. How did Marion know that? She felt a bit sick.

Marion looked at her for a long time. 'Rose,' she said.

'Yes,' said Rose tentatively.

Marion smiled. 'I've many people who want to speak to you. Grandparents, someone from school who has passed over, but you don't want to speak to them, do you? You are trying to call someone, someone you don't know.'

Marion closed her eyes. Rose sat still.

'They are coming from across the seas, over the oceans,' she smiled. 'On angels' wings.'

Marion remained still with her eyes closed, smiling at something, someone. 'Why do you want to speak to her, she wants to know?'

Rose was shocked. 'Who is it, who are you talking about?' she asked, her voice breaking.

Marion opened her eyes and looked at Rose. 'I have Alice, and she said she has something to tell you.'

Rose felt tears roll down her cheeks, she lowered her head and saw tears fall onto her lap.

Marion continued. 'Alice is here, she wants to tell you she thinks you are an angel. Don't give up. She has been trying to talk, but they won't listen to her.'

Marion spoke as though she was in a trance, her voice at times taking on a British accent, but Rose was too moved to be scared. Whatever doubts she had had about Marion disappeared at that moment.

Marion put her head back on the couch. 'Three boys. A man. Italy . . . a sink filled with dishes. So much food.' Marion laughed. 'Food for a feast. A white witch.'

Her face darkened. 'I have all these images flashing before me. She is showing me so many things. Perfume. There's a knife in you, Rose. A stabbing pain.'

Rose gasped, her face turning white. Not even Kelly knew about her half-hearted suicide attempt years ago.

Marion ignored her, continuing with her channel from beyond. 'Alice is trying to bring you something, something precious to her. It doesn't feel bad. Do you know what it is?' Marion opened one eye and looked at her piercingly.

Rose nodded. 'He doesn't want me,' she cried.

Marion closed her eyes again and mumbled under her breath, as though she was having a conversation with Alice. This went on for some time and then she spoke again. 'Alice is angry.'

'With me?' asked Rose fearfully.

'No, with him. He won't let her in when she goes to him. He ignores her. Makes up what he wants to hear,' Marion laughed.

Rose was openly weeping. Kelly sat quietly. The energy in the room was thick with emotion. Marion spoke again under her breath to Alice and then smiled with her eyes closed. Finally she opened her eyes, tears pouring down her cheeks. She smiled at Rose. 'Why are you crying?' asked Rose. 'What did she say?'

'I always cry when they return. The love is amazing and I always get to feel it. It's an honour,' said Marion, as though this was an everyday occurrence.

Kelly looked at Rose's ashen face. 'Well, it seems Max has women pissed at him even from beyond the grave.'

Rose sat in shock but Marion smiled at Rose as though she knew a big secret.

Rose didn't ask, she had had enough of secrets. It was time to live the life she was destined, with or without a man.

CHAPTER TWENTY-SEVEN

The FBI were a humourless lot, Calypso thought as she sat in their offices on Wilshire Boulevard. Sitting with Julius, the agency head, Mandy, Greg and her lawyer and four FBI agents, in various shades of grey, Calypso felt like she was in a bad B-grade movie.

Calypso had dressed for the sombre meeting in black Miu Miu pants and a tight black Chloe leather jacket, done up, with red Marc Jacobs suede high heeled boots. Calypso had channelled Sapphira in choosing her outfit. Tough, uncompromising, and in control. She looked the part on the outside. If only her stomach would unknot itself, she thought as she sat in the briefing room.

'We are going to need you to meet this person who sent the package, Calypso, since it is addressed to you,' said the agent, standing at the table where Calypso and her team sat.

'We will need security, we don't know what kind of nut we're dealing with here,' said her lawyer, Martin.

'Of course, I recommend you meet somewhere public, gives them less chance of doing the unthinkable,' said another agent, more senior than the last.

Calypso felt her stomach flip again. The female agent looked at her sympathetically. 'If it helps, I don't think he's after you. I think he just wants the money.'

Calypso smiled at her wanly. This was one role she never

prepared for. Then she thought about what the world would say, even TG, if they knew what Leeza had done, no doubt countless times before. She sat up straight in her chair. 'Just talk me through it,' she said, shaking back her newly straightened hair.

The plan was made for Calypso to confront the blackmailer the next day and two hours later Calypso left via the underground entrance with Julius and Martin in a car with tinted windows and driven by a young FBI agent towards Calypso's home.

'If this situation wasn't so completely fucked, this moment would be cool but as it stands, this is what I call a cunt of a day,' said Calypso absentmindedly, as she looked at the traffic flashing by them on the road.

Julius roared with laughter. 'Atta girl, Calypso. What doesn't kill you makes you smarter.'

Calypso started to laugh, as did Martin and Mandy. It felt good; it had been weeks since she laughed, since she left TG. She wished Sapphira was here to see her now.

Calypso had avoided TG's calls, texts and emails. As far as she knew, he was still in Europe, going into postproduction on the film. They had planned that she would sail with him along the Amalfi Coast after the shoot but then the call came about Leeza and everything changed. The admission from TG about Raphael had sent her reeling; it was just like Leeza – doing the unthinkable for her perceived benefit. She had never asked either of them for this kind of investment. Perhaps she had used TG the way she had used Leeza, for protection, and saw each of them as saviours. Her mom had always taken care of every problem when Calypso was a kid and then she had handed the baton to TG.

263

The time away from TG had forced Calypso to assess many things in her life. Leeza, her relationships, what she wanted and what she needed. For the first time, she had no one in front of her, protecting her and fighting her battles. It felt oddly exhilarating, as though she could do and be anything. The only trouble was she didn't know what that was.

When Kelly called her to see how she was doing back in LA, Calypso was frank with her. 'Listen, Kel, if TG has asked you to ring then tell him I'm fine, okay?' she said shortly.

'He hasn't, I promise you,' Kelly said honestly. TG had been over the night before for dinner, pumping Kelly and Chris for information on Calypso.

'Has she called you? Have you heard from her?' he had asked. He had skipped the planned trip to the Amalfi Coast and had flown back into LA soon after Calypso.

'No, I haven't,' said Kelly.

TG pulled the label off his beer as he sat on the deck of Kelly's house. The frangipani tree dropped flowers into the pool in the breeze and TG thought how much he wished Calypso was with him in the balmy air.

'I've called her constantly,' he moaned to Kelly.

'Let her be for a while. I get the feeling she's trying to deal with something big in her life right now and it has nothing to do with you,' Kelly advised as she put a large salad down on the table.

'Why won't she let me help her?' TG asked.

'Because, you lovely fool, she wants to do this by herself. I think Calypso has had everything organized for her since . . . well, forever, and now she's trying to stand on her own two feet,' Kelly explained as she sat down opposite him.

'But she let me help her in Italy.' Just saying the word Italy

264

stabbed his heart and he remembered the easiness between them, something he thought he would never have again.

'If she gets through this challenge, whatever it is, by herself, then she will be the person she wants to be moving ahead in her life. Let her go, TG,' Kelly said, gently but firmly.

'Free, free, set them free,' Chris sang the Sting song to accentuate Kelly's point.

'Fuck off,' said TG good-naturedly. Inside, he knew what Kelly was saying was true. Calypso needed to do what she was doing; he just wished he could be there to catch her if she fell.

TG drained his beer. 'Can you ask your woo-woo gods what's going to happen between Calypso and me?' He laughed but his eyes were serious.

'Oh, so now you want the woo-woo?' Kelly said with a glint in her eye.

'Well, you know, I'm grasping at metaphysical straws here,' TG answered, embarrassed.

'As a matter of fact, I do know what's going to happen but I'm not going to tell you 'cause you're a fair weather seeker,' said Kelly, crossing her arms.

Chris walked over to the table, setting down the veggie burgers. He sat down next to TG. 'Buddy, she has been in that woo-woo room of hers, chanting your name, chanting Calypso's name, and then there was white smoke pouring from the chimney. I think the signs are good.'

TG looked at him hopefully and saw he was teasing and punched him lightly on the arm.

Kelly became serious. 'Dude, you need to let her know you're there for her but also let her know that she has the freedom to explore what she needs and fight her own battles. Okay?'

TG nodded, listening. 'Okay, I can do that.'

Kelly took his hands from across the table. 'Then the rest is up to her. Free will and all that bullshit.'

TG felt his heart sink again. What if she didn't choose him? He didn't know if he could stand the waiting but deep down he knew he had no choice.

Calypso, however, was all action. TG was far from her mind as she reviewed her life and her future. Leeza's video had thrown doubt into her mind about her career and her talents. What if she had only got where she had through Leeza's seduction and dealings behind the scenes? What would her life be like if she was in charge, she wondered. Calling a business meeting at her house between her manager and her agent, Calypso had a few ideas about where she wanted to head in her life and none of them included her mother or TG. This time it was about her and it felt right.

'I need to know what's happening in my career,' she said to Greg and Mandy, who had come to her home for the meeting at her request. Mandy Freed had left a big agency to start her own talent management firm, taking with her a major male movie star and his equally famous wife. Calypso had approached her in the toilets at The Ivy and the deal was done over a shared love of Nars lip-gloss in Chihuahua. Calypso liked Mandy's candour and her willingness to listen to Calypso's ideas about her own career – not that she had many of them yet.

'Leeza is obviously no longer in my life in any form and I want to know what my options are. Where do you see me going? I want you to be real with me. I know I'm no Meryl Streep and I'm not going to be cute forever.' She made a face. 'So what are my options?'

Mandy and Greg glanced at each other. This kind of candour

was unheard of and Calypso's frankness was unnerving to the two seasoned professionals who were used to managing their clients' egos.

Greg cleared his throat and started. Sitting on a vintage Wegner chair covered in pink paisley, he looked and felt ridiculous. 'Listen, Calypso, I know this thing with your mom has thrown you but I want you to know, as I said before, you are a talented girl who has gotten where you are through talent and hard work. You can be anything you want. Oscars, even.'

'Bullshit, Greg. Do NOT feed my ego. I don't need it. I asked you for your opinion about my career going forward. There is no looking back for me. Come on, Mandy. What do you think?'

Mandy raised her eyebrows. Having come to work for Calypso when Leeza bowed out of the picture, Mandy had been waiting for this moment for the past year. The time had come to have the honest conversation that not every actor wants to hear.

'I think you are very talented. I think you are very lovely to look at and a good person. I think with good directors, you do great work. When you get an average director you fall into mimicry of other actors. Everyone wants to be an actor. A serious actor. But what about the movie stars? Why can't we have them any more? You put on thirty pounds or play a retarded person and then you're a great actor? Winning Oscars? Fuck, Eddie Murphy should have one for all his movies then,' laughed Mandy, clearly on a roll.

Calypso sat down on the overstuffed blue linen couch and picked up a pink silk pillow and held it to her chest. Mandy was mesmerizing; her passion and humour was what Calypso had hoped for when she asked her to take over managing her career.

'Calypso, you could be a great movie star. You could pull the occasional one out of the bag that shows people you have talent, real acting chops, but there will always be someone coming up the path, trying to get the serious roles. Let them have it. What the fuck is wrong with being a movie star, I ask you?'

Calypso was thinking. Greg was wiping his brow with his hand. He was clearly nervous. Calypso was a good client. When he had come here today, he was expecting to be fired. He didn't know why he was worried, but instead she wanted advice about her career. Usually the actors told him what they wanted. This is what he had trained for, he had always wanted to help the talent in the way he knew best and this was his chance.

'Greg, what do you think?' asked Calypso.

'I think Mandy is right, to be honest. I can get you anywhere you want but some things are harder than others. I suppose the question is, what do you want from your career? If you say to me, I want to win a Tony, then I will find you the play and then the rest is up to you. That's the hard stuff. If you want an Oscar nomination, then I can do that also, but you gotta bring in the performance. What do you want, Calypso?'

Calypso looked at them both. 'I'm tired. I'm tired of working. I don't even think I like it that much. I did it because of Leeza. I don't know anything else apart from this and right now I can't think of anything worse. I don't want an Oscar, I don't. I know everyone says that, but I truly don't. I want a life but one that affords me this and helps my father. I am a realist at best and I know I'm not the greatest actor in the world. I want to make one or two films a year and pay my bills and explore my options till I actually know what I want to do with my life.'

Calypso picked at her chipped pink nail polish. 'What do you think?' she asked tentatively.

'I think you are a smart girl,' said Mandy. 'I know what you need to do, I already have a few scripts I think would be perfect. We can make this work.'

Calypso nodded listening.

'It's about image,' said Mandy firmly. 'We need to make you the eternal IT girl but without the bullshit that I see from all those horrible girls from the endless reality shows the networks churn out. We need class and accessibility at the same time. You seeing anyone at the moment?'

Calypso paused. 'No, no one,' she said as she bit into a fingernail.

'Good, that's terrific,' said Mandy, writing on her notebook.

Fucking marvellous, thought Calypso bitterly as she looked out at the pool.

'I think I would like to produce,' Calypso said, trialling her idea on Greg and Mandy. Their relationship was strictly business and she knew she could count on them for an honest opinion. 'I would like to create my own work. Movies I want to see. Fun films that take you away from the crap of your own reality and sweep you into another world. I don't get to see or make enough of those types of films.'

'Fucking great!' said Greg, excitement filling his voice.

'I love it,' Mandy agreed. 'The young, smart movie star who is in charge of her career and her life,' she said, almost to herself.

'We can get a script and we can get a studio to put your name on the producers' credits. They will be happy to have you and then off you go,' said Greg, leaning forward.

Calypso looked at him, her face aghast. 'No, Greg, I really

want to produce and to do that I'm going to have to learn. I don't want some empty image. I want to walk my talk and I want to do the hard yards.'

Greg looked at her surprised. So many of his clients eventually became Creative Consultants on their successful TV series and then moved to Executive Producer roles to get more cut of the profits and prestige. But real actor-producers were rare.

'It's a hard gig,' he said seriously.

'I know I can do it,' she answered him, poised and serious.

Greg had no reservations. What Calypso had been through recently had changed her and she was no longer a girl. Sitting before him was a new woman – and perhaps Hollywood's latest power player.

Once Calypso had informed her management team about her new career direction she mentally looked at the next challenge on her list, which was to deal with the blackmailer. Meeting with the FBI, they worked out a plan for her to meet the blackmailer in a hillside bungalow at the Chateau Marmont, with the FBI in the bedroom, recording and ready to pounce. It was a surreal situation to Calypso and she had to remind herself she was not in a movie anymore; this was her life and she had to deal with it. To add to her stress levels, Leeza rang everyday, leaving messages as if nothing had happened between them. No mention of the tape or the two million dollars, thought Calypso angrily.

On the morning of the meeting, Calypso arrived at the hotel, dressed for her confrontation in her most comfortable Lee jeans, a Paul and Joe orange cotton shirt and a vintage straw bag with a woven parrot on the front which had always made her feel joyful. Today she needed all the help she could get in the joy department, she thought as she walked up to the lobby desk to claim her key.

'Hello, may I help you?' asked the handsome man at the desk, not looking up.

'Hello, I'm Calypso Gable, I have a bungalow booked.'

She pushed her white Ray-Ban Wayfarers onto her head and smiled prettily.

'Hello, Miss Gable, of course. I will get your room key right away.' He jumped into action, recognizing Calypso and wondering how he could get her his headshot and bio.

Calypso waited and then he was back. 'I'll get a porter to bring your bags,' he said, looking around her.

'No need, thanks anyway,' she said as she signed herself in.

'Do you want me to show you where your room is situated?' he fawned as she walked away.

Calypso waved her hand dismissively.

'Bitch,' he said under his breath.

Walking through the tropical, lush gardens, Calypso thought she was going to throw up but kept walking. Stay calm, she told herself as she climbed the steps to the bungalow. Walking inside, the FBI was already there.

'Hello, Calypso,' said the female agent. 'I've got to wire you up, so if you can come into the bathroom, I will get you all set.'

Calypso put down her bag on the chair and followed the agent into the bathroom. The living room was normal but the curtains were drawn. Walking through the bedroom, she saw the three other agents, one of them testing a recording device.

The agent shut the bathroom door. 'So, I will need to tape this to you, the tape may pull a little. I'm pleased you wore something that isn't too tight. It's not bulky but anything tight shows the wires.'

'Won't he know we're recording him?' asked Calypso as she undid her shirt and held out her arms.

271

'Maybe, maybe not. They probably don't think you would have gone to the authorities.' She pulled at Calypso's bra, pinning and stretching the wires up, which were taped to her toned stomach.

'All done, feel okay?' she asked.

'Is that it?' asked Calypso, panicky. 'Now what do I do?'

'You wait,' said the agent, raising her eyebrows at her.

Calypso waited for forty minutes, then there was a call to her room.

'Hello, Miss Gable. I've a guest here for you. They said you were expecting them. Shall I send them to your bungalow or would you like some lunch by the pool? I can organize a table,' he said solicitously.

'My bungalow is great, thank you.'

Calypso hung up the phone and thought she was going to hyperventilate. She banged on the door of the bedroom. 'I can't do it, I can't. They will know,' she hissed through the door.

'Just pretend you're acting,' hissed back the female agent through the crack in the door.

Calypso turned away from the bedroom and opened the curtains of the room. Nervous, she sat on the chair, and then stood again. Take a moment, she thought. Breathing slowly, she composed herself.

There was a knock at the door and she walked to open it. In front of her stood an obese eighteen-year-old boy, or perhaps older, wearing a Sailor Moon t-shirt and a smile. His braces were multicoloured and on one foot he wore a green Converse and on the other was a pink one.

'Hello,' said Calypso, smiling. It was a fan; he must have seen her come in and worked out which room she was in. Or tipped a staff member for the information. This was bad timing, she thought. 'I'm actually meeting someone here in a minute, I'm sorry. Perhaps an autograph?' she said kindly.

'Calypso Gable,' the teenager laughed with a high-pitched giggle and covered his mouth. 'I love you.'

'Thanks,' said Calypso. 'But I really am waiting for someone, so I hope you understand.'

'It's me,' he said, laughing again, running his fat fingers through his blond-tipped hair.

'I'm sorry, have we met?' said Calypso, looking up the path behind him.

'Not yet, but it's me. I wrote you the letter. You emailed me, silly.' He laughed hysterically and slapped his legs which were swathed in pale blue denim.

Calypso took a step back in shock. Her idea of the black-mailer was not this fat, unusual man/child in front of her.

'Okay, well you better come in then,' Calypso said, feeling a lot more confident than she had before the knock at the door.

'Sit down,' she ordered, scrambling for what to do next. 'I'm sorry, I don't even know your name,' she said, changing her tone again into a more cajoling one.

'Jason,' he said, looking up at her with worship in his eyes.

'I'm about to order some lunch, Jason. How about I get us something and then we can talk, okay?'

Jason smiled eagerly at her and nodded. Calypso walked over to the phone and dialled room service. 'Hello, it's Calypso Gable in Bungalow 7. I would like to order a green salad, and . . . a burger and fries?' She looked at Jason. He nodded again. 'Yes, a burger and fries and a Diet Coke and a Coke.'

Smiling at him warmly, she walked back to him and sat down opposite. 'So, Jason, tell me about yourself. Why do you need two million dollars?'

'Well, I've got a website. I write about celebrities everyday. People send me things – videos, photos and that's how I got the tape of your mom. I needed to make some money. I thought you would be happy to take it off me. No one really cares about your mom, but they do about you. You know?'

Calypso was shocked at his naïve yet cunning plan. 'Jason, what you're doing isn't right, you do know that, don't you?'

'But you have money, you're rich. I know, I see the life you all lead. I want to have it too. Why shouldn't I?' He was hostile now.

Calypso was careful. Jason was innocent in some ways yet unstable, clearly feeding on the lives of the famous, desperate to be a part of their world, yet hating them for having what he didn't have.

'I get it, Jason. I get it. We have it all, huh? You deserve some of it also, yes?'

Jason nodded again, mollified by Calypso's apparent understanding.

'How do you want this to work, Jason? Two million dollars is a lot of money to get my hands on, you know that?'

Jason smiled, sweetly. 'I know, but you have to give me the money or I will put the tape up on my website. Either way, I will make money from it.' He laughed and didn't seem so sweet after all, Calypso thought.

Calypso picked up her bag from the chair next to her. 'I will write you a cheque now for $500,000 and then I will pay you three more instalments over the next three weeks. It's the best I can do. I need all copies of the tapes and a signed statement you will never release this footage in any form on any platform.'

There was a knock at the door again and Calypso realized it would be room service. Opening the door, she waved the waiter in, who set up the food. As she thought, the food was too tempting to Jason. Eating at the Chateau Marmont with Calypso Gable was a dream come true for him. The circumstances were irrelevant; he didn't seem to show any concern at all other than licking his lips at the burger.

Calypso took a sheaf of papers and a pen from her straw bag and placed them in front of Jason on the small coffee table. Picking up the bowl of fries she placed them down beside him. Taking a fry from the bowl, she popped it in her mouth.

'If you can just sign these, I can give you your cheque. Then we can eat. Cool?' she said brightly.

The smell of the salty fried food was too much for Jason. Taking the pen, he nodded eagerly. 'Cool,' he said.

Calypso placed the documents in front of him. He signed all and then put a fry into his mouth. 'Yum,' he said, like a small child.

He was intriguing and repelling at the same time, she thought. He spent too much time looking into celebrities' lives, and now he needed to be a part of them, to belong. And the only way he thought he could make that happen was if he had the money to buy his entry card.

Calypso wrote him a cheque for $500,000 and handed it over. 'So, here is your money,' she said loudly.

'Thanks,' said Jason, folding it up and putting it in his back pocket.

Then the bedroom door opened and the female and young male agent came into the living room. 'You are under arrest for grand larceny.'

Jason looked up at Calypso, his eyes filled with tears. 'You hate me,' he cried.

'I don't know you, Jason,' said Calypso sadly, and walked

away into the safety of the bedroom. One of the other agents was on the phone and the man sitting at the recording equipment smiled at her wryly. 'Hell of a job, huh?'

'I thought he would be older, scarier, not this sad teenager internet dork. It's awful,' said Calypso genuinely.

'You never can tell, I guess,' said the man, packing up the equipment. 'I'm going to need the device,' he said, pointing to Calypso's body.

'Sure, I'll just go and take it off.'

Calypso went to the bathroom and pulled off the tape that held the wires close to her skin. It hurt and for a second she enjoyed the feeling of pain; it made her feel real in an unreal situation.

By the time she walked out of the bathroom, Jason had already left with the two male agents for questioning. The female agent was waiting for her. 'If it makes you feel any better, you weren't the only celebrity he was blackmailing. He had tapes and letters of several high profile people we knew of. We thought it might have been him when this came to our attention but you were the only one willing to sting him. There are a few people who owe you a lot.'

'You mean I was the only one stupid enough to do this?' said Calypso incredulously.

'No, the only one brave enough,' the agent replied.

'But it will still go to court, though. It could all come out then,' Calypso said, worried.

'No, it won't get to court. He'll do a plea bargain. He will do time for this, so whatever is the least amount of time is what his lawyer will push for. Grand larceny in the state of California is a big deal, particularly with people in the spotlight. He's looking at between seven and fifteen years, I think,' said the agent as she walked Calypso into the sitting room.

'But he's delusional, he needs help, not jail. He's a baby,' said Calypso, concerned for the large child.

'He's thirty-two,' said the agent, raising one eyebrow. 'He just acts like he's a kid to claim diminished responsibility.'

'Jesus Christ!' Calypso exclaimed, sitting on the couch.

The agent sat down and ate a fry. 'He has previous convictions for identity fraud, so don't feel too bad. He is a unit, hopefully he will go to minimum security and get the help needed as you said.'

'But now I feel bad, I feel like I should have tried to help him instead of setting him up,' she said remorsefully.

'Sometimes you have to do what you need to do to help everyone. The picture is bigger than just you, if you excuse my pun.' The agent laughed to herself. 'What you did today was extraordinary. You're clever, and the food was a brilliant touch. You knew he would go for it and getting him to sign those documents . . . I'll need those, by the way. Full admission of guilt. No way he's going to show anyone now. We have agents at his property now, taking everything for safekeeping.'

'I feel so bad.' Calypso slumped down. 'I feel like I've sent someone to their execution.'

The agent got up. 'Calypso, what you did today was protect yourself, your mother and many other people. He would have kept doing this for years to come. You did the right thing for the future, even if it feels like the wrong thing now. Don't judge yourself too harshly, you did good. You did it because you want to protect your mom, right?'

Calypso sat in the bungalow for a long time after the agents had left with Jason. Had she done it to protect her mother, as the agent had said? Or was it to protect herself?

A wave of sadness came over her and she felt the tears prick her eyes. Trying to push them down, she pulled out her phone and looked up a number and dialled it.

'Hey Kel, it's Calypso.'

'Hey there. How you doing?' asked Kelly.

'Shit,' said Calypso and started to weep down the phone.

'Come over, okay? Come now and we can talk. Can you get here? Want me to come and get you? Are you at home?'

'No, I'm at Chateau Marmont. I can get there, I think. Text me your address?'

Calypso began to feel calm hearing Kelly's voice. She needed a different perspective on this situation that was tinged with her own guilt. When she arrived at Kelly's, she checked her face in the mirror of her car. I look older, she thought, noticing small lines around her eyes that she was sure weren't there before Italy.

Kelly opened the front door as soon as she heard Calypso's car and walked out and held the girl in her arms. Inside, Calypso sat nursing a mug of chamomile tea and poured her heart out. Kelly listened for almost an hour, saying very little apart from murmurs of support or sympathy. Finally, as Calypso reached the end of her tawdry tale, she wiped her eyes again with the last of the tissues Kelly had handed her when she arrived and raised her eyebrow. 'So what do you think?'

Kelly paused. 'I think this is a fucking romance of the year.'

'What do you mean?' asked Calypso. Her head was thumping and she felt so tired.

'Love makes us do weird things. Your mum, although she did something you and I would find hard to do, loved you in her own imperfect way. She did what she did because she loved you. And underneath all the anger, you did what you did today

278

at the hotel to protect her and your father because you love them.'

'You don't think Leeza just did it because she wanted me to be famous?'

'No, I think she wanted you to be famous, so you could do what she couldn't in her own life. Yet clearly, the boundaries aren't strong between you. She wanted to give you what she knew she would never have. To some people, being famous seems like the answer.'

Calypso laughed cynically.

'I'm not condoning what she did but I think she did it out of desperation, ambition but mostly love.'

'What about me today with the FBI? I don't know why I did it, to protect myself or to protect my parents?'

'Probably both, but that's okay. You have to have some self-respect. What that Jason dude did was wrong and there'll be many people happy to see him off the web for a long time.'

The subject of TG hung over the two women and finally Calypso spoke. 'Did you know what TG did to Raphael?'

'I don't know all the details but Raphael is a nasty piece of work. TG wasn't just protecting you but also the film, other women. It wasn't just about you.'

Calypso felt ashamed. She knew she had been self-involved and self-important when she had judged TG so harshly. 'TG did what he did out of love, didn't he?'

'Yeah, babe.'

'I've been horrible to him but I don't know whether I want to be back with him again after all that's happened. I feel different. I don't think I'm that naïve girl in Italy anymore.'

'Well, you can only tell him the truth,' said Kelly.

'I don't know if I want to tell him about Leeza.'

'Just go with it and do what your heart tells you. You'll know when you see him.'

Calypso pulled out her phone and dialled his number. 'Hi, it's me. We need to talk.'

CHAPTER TWENTY-EIGHT

Never underestimate the power of a good haircut for a woman's ego, thought Sapphira as she dried her hair in front of the bathroom mirror. Jack had insisted on dinner for the three of them at Al Covo in Venice, as he was leaving for London the next day for a few nights to fulfil a publicity tour for a film he had made the year before.

'I'm not sure we should be seen out,' said Sapphira. 'It will be bedlam if the media know we're here together,' she said as she attempted to dunk her pastry into her third coffee for the morning.

Sapphira's appetite had increased and she was slowly putting on weight. It suited her; her face had filled out, her skin was clear and her eyes bright. Jack had been in raptures at her new haircut and Alex had winked at her and said, 'Sexy' as she walked past him on the stairs. Sapphira felt herself blush. It had been a long time since a man had made her blush.

'If we go out, if any paps see us then there will be a nice article about our threesome in Venice,' said Jack from his morning paper. 'We are going out, Sapphira. I'm afraid you are becoming agoraphobic and I haven't the resources to help you with that one,' he laughed.

Sapphira threw a soggy bit of pastry at him. 'You're a shit, Jack Reynolds.'

'I know. I do what I can. Be downstairs at 8.30 pm. Dress to impress.'

As Sapphira finished her hair and make-up, she looked at the clothes in her wardrobe. She decided on a L'Wren Scott, high-waisted leather skirt and a black Dolce and Gabbana high-necked silk poet's blouse in a neo-classical print and ribbons on the sleeves. Giulia had brought it over for her with a cache of other designer clothes she had ordered on Sapphira's behalf. Some of them Sapphira would never have considered wearing before, but now she felt different. Softer and gentler somehow.

Pulling on black fishnets and high patent leather Christian Louboutin platform heels, she clipped in gold hoops, sprayed herself with Bulgari Black perfume, grabbed her black leather clutch bag and took the lift downstairs.

Alex was waiting by the door. Handsome in a black suit and white shirt, open-necked, showing his chest just a little. 'Hello,' he said, looking her up and down. 'You look amazing, as always.'

'Thanks,' she said, flustered by the way he looked at her. 'Too much?' she asked, playing with the ribbons on the sleeves.

'Enough,' he answered and bent down to kiss her cheek, breathing in her perfume.

Sapphira felt her knees weaken a little. 'That's good to know,' she said huskily.

'Hello, young lovers,' said Jack as he came in, attempting to insert his silver cufflinks into his pale pink shirt. 'A little help here?' And he extended each arm to his guests with a cufflink in each hand.

Sapphira and Alex laughed and did as he asked. 'You should not live alone, Jack, you are hopeless,' said Alex, patting down his cuff.

They headed out into the crisp night air. Venice's lights reflected like jewels in the water of the canals. As they sailed towards the restaurant, Sapphira felt excited to be out. She squeezed Jack's hand. 'You are a doll for bringing me out,' she whispered.

Jack smiled at her lovingly. 'You look wonderful, Sapphira. I am more proud of you than I've ever been of myself. You did it. You are doing it! You deserve the best in life,' he said, looking at Alex, who was staring out the window at the traffic on the water.

'Don't get any ideas, cupid. I'm not nearly ready to have any sort of relationship. My doctor says I have to know myself first without the sex before I can start any sort of relationship,' she said quietly.

'Yes, yes. Well, when you do get in touch with yourself, then I would consider it. He is a good man,' he muttered. 'And he likes women,' he added cheekily.

Sapphira sat back in her chair and looked at the people walking by alongside the canals. Couples holding hands, posing for photos. It seemed so foreign to Sapphira, mundane and frightening. What she wanted did not exist, she thought. Someone she could be herself with, not be tied down to, no posing for photographs, ever. She looked at what were clearly honeymooners laughing and hugging as they tried to get onto an overpriced gondola ride.

Arriving at the restaurant, Alex jumped off the boat first and held Sapphira's hand as she disembarked. His touch made her jump and she hated Jack for putting the thoughts into her head. Not that she hadn't entertained them herself but it was too complicated for her current frame of mind, she'd decided. She had tried to avoid Alex at Jack's palazzo as much as possible, without much success. He seemed to always be around, coming into the kitchen when she did, reading quietly while she worked on the laptop in the living room, asking after her health everyday, making her a cup of coffee just when she was thinking of getting up to get one herself. Unused to the attention or care, Sapphira found herself snapping at him sometimes, which he took with good grace, laughing off her moods and guessing she was a Scorpio, because 'she liked secrets' so much.

'Come on,' said Jack as they walked towards the restaurant. 'Everything here is incredible.'

Walking into the restaurant, Sapphira felt all the eyes of the diners turn to them. It felt odd after weeks of being away from the public. Sapphira became nervous. Alex looped his little finger through hers. 'Not gonna leave you, pinky promise.'

Sapphira looked up at him and smiled shyly. 'I haven't heard that since I was a kid.'

'My sisters used to do it when we were kids,' he said laughing, and Sapphira instantly relaxed.

Jack was talking to the owner of the restaurant; they were laughing and slapping each other's back. He led them to a table at the back.

Jack ordered for them; the food and the wine kept coming. Jack ordered mineral water for Sapphira but she decided to drink anyway. 'Easy on the moonshine, Amelia,' he said softly.

'Come on, it's one drink, Jacky,' Alex said, filling up her glass again.

Jack looked at her and raised his eyebrows. The doctor had told him Sapphira was not to drink while she was in recovery. It was a slippery slope and anything could replace the heroin – alcohol, sugar even.

Sapphira ignored Jack's admonishment and Jack, not wanting to cause a scene, let it go. But Sapphira could tell he was pissed with her, which made her anxious and she drank more. Her system was so delicate from what her body had been through, she became drunk quite quickly. Alex seemed funnier than she remembered, she thought, as he regaled them with hilarious stories of his childhood and being a waiter in LA before he got his break.

'You guys are such good friends,' she said wistfully, her cheeks flushed from the wine.

'Friends are important,' said Alex. 'Who are your close buddies?'

'I don't have any,' she said simply. 'Never was in one place long enough.'

'Liar,' said Jack. 'We're friends.'

'I suppose we are although I've taken a lot from you in the past few weeks,' she said sorrowfully. 'Not a very balanced friendship.'

'You, my dear, are a sad drunk. There is nothing worse. Weeping into her wine, bemoaning her lack of friends or lovers. Get over yourself. If you want friends then you have to make them. You make an effort and be interested in people and then they come.' Jack laughed at himself.

Alex watched the interchange with interest.

Sapphira bristled. 'I'm not a sad drunk!'

'Yes, you are,' teased Jack. 'There are three kinds of drunks – a sad drunk, a happy one and an angry drunk. Get happy, you are here with the best looking and most entertaining men on the planet.'

Sapphira laughed at his ego. 'No, there is a fourth kind of drunk. An egotistical one, which is what you are.'

'Game, set, match – to Sapphira,' said Alex.

The ride back to the palazzo in the boat was filled with Jack singing Italian songs at the top of his voice and waving at people as they sailed past. Sapphira and Alex kept their heads down, doubling over in laughter.

'He is crazy,' said Sapphira.

285

'Not crazy, just happy,' said Alex, smiling at Jack as he waved his suit jacket at a bunch of Japanese tourists.

She wasn't sure if it was the wine, the romance of Venice or Jack's infectious mood, but Sapphira was filled with an intense joy she had never felt before. 'Alex, I want to kiss you,' she said, her words slurring a little.

'Well, when in Venice, do what you heart tells you,' he answered sexily.

Sapphira leaned forward and kissed him passionately. Then she leaned out of the boat and threw up.

Jack carried her upstairs. The wine, the Chinese herbs she was taking and the medication made for a bad combination and she passed out on the bed, fully clothed. Jack came downstairs to where Alex was drinking a large glass of water.

'Poor kid, she's gonna feel like hell tomorrow. She can't drink. At all,' he said pointedly to Alex.

Alex took another sip and looked at Jack. 'What's she got, Jack? It isn't Epstein-Barr, I know that much.'

'Sorry, confidential code of friendship, you know that.'

'Come on, man. She looked like hell on earth when I arrived, then avoids me and then tonight kissed me. I want to know. I like her, I think about her all the time. I follow her around. I'm like a creepy schoolboy. Can I help her at least?'

'Listen, Alex. Sapphira is complicated. I'm not saying don't go there but she has some shit to work out and I think a relationship – hell, even a fling – could set her back to where she was, which, by the way, was not a good place. I won't tell you her story, it's not mine to tell. If she wants to talk to you then she will. Just give her some space. Okay?'

Alex looked miffed at Jack's explanation. 'But . . .' he started.

'No buts. This is bigger than you, Alex. It's real and she needs support, not to be fucked with. She needs to be careful when it comes to her health. When I told her not to drink tonight there was a reason, okay? You have to take my word on this one.'

Alex drained his glass and walked out of the kitchen. 'Point taken,' he said as he went to his bedroom. As he walked up the stairs he paused outside Sapphira's door and then kept walking.

Jack left for London early the next morning and Sapphira went downstairs for a much-needed coffee mid-morning. Alex was sitting at the table, reading a script.

'Hey,' he said.

'Hey,' said Sapphira and poured herself some coffee.

'How you feeling today?'

'I feel like shit actually, but thanks for asking,' she said tiredly.

'Ah well, try and punch through and then have something greasy at about three this afternoon,' he said expertly.

At the thought of food, Sapphira's stomach turned. 'I don't think I can eat anything ever again.'

'Famous last words. Stick around, kid, and we'll be on the grease express later today,' said Alex as he left the kitchen.

Sapphira put her head on the table. Perhaps she could sleep here, she thought. Closing her eyes, Alex's face came into her mind. The memory of last night's kiss flew back into her memory and she sat up straight. 'Fuck.' She lay her head back on the wood.

Sapphira slunk back to her room, had a bath and then slept for a few hours. Waking up, she found she was hungry. Ravenous, in fact. As she was looking in the kitchen for something to eat, Alex walked in. 'The three o'clock munchies?' he asked.

Sapphira made a face. 'Listen, I'm sorry about last night. I kissed you, I think.'

'Indeed you did,' he answered casually as he walked to the fridge and stood next to her, peering in at its contents.

'I'm really embarrassed. I'm so sorry,' she said, avoiding his face.

'No need. It was quite nice. Anytime.' Sapphira couldn't breathe. Was it shame or lust? She wasn't sure what she felt anymore. Alex's nearness made her stomach flip and she walked away and sat down at the table.

'So, what do you want? Eggs, bacon? BLT?'

Sapphira looked up at him. 'That sounds good.'

'Done.'

Ten minutes later he had two delicious looking BLTs and a coffee in front of them. They ate in silence.

Sapphira finished first. 'That was good,' she said with her mouth full of the last of the sandwich.

'I'm glad you enjoyed it. Cigarette?' Alex asked as he pulled the packet from his shirt pocket.

Sapphira took one and they smoked in silence again. Sapphira didn't know what to say to him and Alex didn't seem to mind the quiet. Stubbing out the cigarette, she stood. 'Thanks, that was nice,' she said and left the room.

Alex watched her leave, his face impassive. 'No problem,' he said to himself.

Sapphira sat in her room. The energy in the kitchen between her and Alex was too much for her. Thank God she hadn't thrown up on him, she thought, remembering leaning over the edge of the boat and Alex holding onto her hair.

At seven o'clock she decided to brace herself and see if Alex was around, test the waters and see if they could be in the same room together without her going weak at the knees. Walking down to the living room, she found him alone there, watching television. 'What are ya watching?' she asked.

'One of your movies,' he answered, his eyes staying on the screen.

'Oh no, that's so bad. Please turn it off,' she said, throwing her head back and closing her eyes.

'No, I'm enjoying it. You're about to climb the mountain and find the treasure, I think.'

'Come on, Alex. Please.'

'No way, it's good. You speak Italian well, by the way.'

'What?'

Sapphira perched on the edge of the sofa. The film was dubbed in Italian and Sapphira was fascinated by the words coming out of her mouth on screen. 'I look good speaking Italian.'

Alex laughed. 'It's pretty good, actually. You tear up the screen.'

'Thanks . . . I think,' said Sapphira.

She sat back and looked at herself on the television. It was one of her early films; she had been taking heroin for two years when she made it, going on OxyContin during the shoot. She remembered a hellish time, feeling like shit and having to push her body to do the physical stunts required for the role. It seemed like another person on the screen and another time.

Alex looked over at her. 'I'll turn it off if you tell me how it ends.'

'Okay, well, I get the treasure, the angry sultan comes and tries to steal it off me and we fight. Then I get away by hanging off a helicopter, as you do, and then I give the treasure to the country that it was stolen from and return to my lover's arms to live happily ever after.'

'As I thought,' said Alex gravely.

'Well, it ain't Lars von Trier, that's for sure,' laughed Sapphira. 'I never watch my films, I hate seeing myself on screen. I'm always finding ways to do the line better or change the character. Drives me mad, so I don't look now.'

Alex nodded in agreement. 'I know, I never look back either. No reason. Always look forward, I say.'

He clicked through the channels, stopping on each one until Sapphira said 'next'. He stopped on a channel that showed an African mother and her baby at a refugee camp somewhere. 'Stop,' said Sapphira. There was something about the look on the mother's face that Sapphira recognized. Anguish.

Alex got up. 'Coffee?' he asked.

She nodded, engrossed in the documentary.

Alex walked back in and handed her the coffee. She accepted it silently and drank it as she watched. As it ended, she turned to Alex. 'It's so sad. These women in Ethiopia who had prolonged labours or problems get terrible injuries and they are sent away from their villages and their communities. There is this Australian doctor who operates on them. Most of them can be healed. She's lived there for fifty years, and she's eighty-five years old and still does the surgeries. Amazing,' said Sapphira, moved by both the work of the doctor and her patients.

Alex watched her so enthralled in the plight of these people so far removed from her life.

'I know what I've got to do now.' She turned to Alex, her eyes bright. 'I'm going to Africa.'

Sapphira was filled with enthusiasm. 'I really want to help them, I don't know why, it just spoke to me. People should not be punished because they are hurt, it's pure ignorance,' she said passionately.

'That's great, Sapphira, really exciting for you. Let me know if I can help in any way.'

'That's great, Alex, thanks. I'm so excited to do this, I hope I can help them.'

'Are you kidding? They will be thrilled to have you on board. I don't think women's health problems post-birth in East Africa get a lot of attention. Not really a sexy charity, as they say.'

'Who cares about sexy?' asked Sapphira. 'Sexy is bullshit. I've spent my whole life being told I was sexy. Sexy gets you nowhere, trust me,' she said.

'Hey, hey, I didn't say you were sexy. I was talking in broad generic terms.'

'Sorry.' Sapphira played with her cup, moving it around the table.

'Not that you aren't sexy, you are. I mean you're beautiful. You're . . . shit,' said Alex, floundering.

'I'm shit?' she asked, amusement in her eyes.

'No, no, you're not sexy, you're not shit.' Alex was struggling.

'That's the nicest thing anyone has said to me in a long time,' Sapphira laughed.

Alex stood up. 'I have to make a few calls,' he said and left the room abruptly.

Sapphira giggled to herself. Flirting with Alex was fun, harmless and fun. She wandered upstairs to her suite, pausing outside the door. She wondered whether she should go up and flirt more with Alex but decided against it. Opening the door to her room, she reached for the light switch. It didn't turn on. The globe must be broken, she thought, as she clicked it on and off. Walking toward the bedside table, to turn on the lamp, she felt something cover her mouth and her arms pinned behind her back. And then she passed out.

CHAPTER TWENTY-NINE

Kelly knew not to speak as she and Rose left the medium's apartment. Instead, she led her to the nearest wine bar, sat Rose by the fire, ordered a mineral water for herself and a double vodka tonic for Rose.

Rose shivered in her Valentino winter coat. Kelly handed her the drink. 'Come on, babe. Drink up, calm the nerves.'

Rose sipped but remained silent, staring into the fire. Then finally she spoke. 'She could have known about Max and found out about Alice. She might have read about us in a magazine. Done her research.'

Kelly smiled. 'Maybe, but I didn't tell her it was you who wanted the session. I just said I would be coming.'

Rose went to say something but then stopped herself as a young girl came over with menu and a pen.

'Hi,' she said shyly.

Rose took the menu and signed it absentmindedly, smiling at the girl quickly and then turning back to Kelly.

'But how did she know?' Rose asked again.

'I don't know, babe, that's what she does, she's good at it. Rumour has it she holds recitals with Elvis, Michael Jackson and Kurt Cobain at least twice a year.'

Rose looked at Kelly, shocked. 'Really?'

'No,' said Kelly. 'I just wanted you to snap out of it.'

Rose laughed. 'I'm just shocked – shocked and spooked and

believing and scornful all at the same time. It's not that I'm a sceptic, I read my horoscope most days, but this is just out of this world, Kelly. Even you have to admit that.'

'I do think it is out of this world and that's where the information comes from. Wherever Alice is now is out of this world, so yes, I agree with you,' said Kelly calmly.

'I want to cry and I want to forget about it. I want to ring Max and tell him and I want to forget this night ever happened.' Rose looked at Kelly. 'I don't know what I want.'

'That's okay. Maybe that's the lesson. You've spent so much time working and waiting and yearning and you've not taken the time to just be in your own life. Enjoy it for a while. If Max comes back to you, then great, if not then learn to find the moments that make you content, even happy.'

'I've spent the last ten years alone, Kelly. I want something more. I want to stand by someone and share my moments, good and bad with them.'

Kelly put her drink down on the table. 'Listen, Rose. You have everything you want except the one thing you truly desire. I'm not trying to be cruel but maybe you need to look at it from a different perspective. You went to London to find Max and instead you found your family again. Do I think you and Max belong together? Yes, but you can't fight free will. If Max decides to be in mourning for the rest of his life, then so be it. You have to get up and start putting it out there. Start dating. Who knows? Maybe Max was just to remind you that you still have it and you are ready to love.'

Rose felt the tears fall down her cheeks. 'I've spent so long trying to hide how I felt from myself, working and pushing myself so I didn't have time to feel. Now all I do is bloody well cry.' She laughed through the tears and Kelly laughed with her.

'I know, babe, but the universe has a funny sense of humour.

293

No matter how much you or Alice from beyond the grave push Max, if he doesn't want to hear it then he won't. Don't spend anymore time waiting, start searching.'

Rose smiled. 'When I'm ready.'

'Okay, but it's time to start dating again and we have to get you date ready.'

'Why?' asked Rose.

'If you're going back into the market, you need to be fabulous in every way. I recommend a full regime at a day spa and then a session with one of my favourite stylists who will shop for you and reevaluate your wardrobe and rework your look. I tell you, you will feel like a new person.'

'What's wrong with the way I dress?' asked Rose defensively, touching her Matthew Williamson green silk blouse.

'Nothing at all, babe, but if you want to reinvigorate your life, the outside is a good place to start. Then we can work on the inside as you go along. What the hell, Rose, enjoy it. You know I love a makeover, I've been doing them on you since we were fourteen years old.'

The young, well-groomed girl met Rose at the door. 'Welcome to the Cornelia Day Spa, Miss Nightingale.'

'Call me Rose, please,' she said.

Day spas were not an uncommon occurrence in Rose's life but she was nervous all of a sudden, feeling like Dorothy entering the Land of Oz.

'Kelly has called ahead and requested specific therapies she believes you would benefit from most. I hope you find them to your liking today. I'm sure you will,' said the girl assuredly.

Rose did find it all perfect. Massages, skin treatments, a manicure, pedicure, all while listening to a complimentary iPod filled with a vast selection of music. Rose was in heaven. For five hours she didn't think about Max or the boys or anything, in fact. It was exactly what she needed to give her mind a rest and release the tension from her body.

By the time she left at three that afternoon, Rose was in a blissed out state and wandering back to the Four Seasons when her phone rang.

'Hey, Tosser. How did you go?'

'I am in a Zen-like state and I do not wish to be pulled out of it. I've got skin like a twenty-one year old, my body has been kneaded into submission and all traces of stress are gone,' said Rose down the phone.

Kelly laughed. 'Well, good for you. I've organized Sophie to be at the Four Seasons at ten o'clock. You're still free for the day?'

'Yeah, not filming till Thursday,' Rose said, as she walked along East 57th Street towards the hotel. 'I hope you asked her to be kind to me.'

'Of course, she's just gilding the lily. Have no fears, she is the best stylist I know.'

Rose entered the hotel and took the elevator to her suite. 'I only have my travel clothes with me. She won't get a real idea of what I've got in my wardrobe.'

'Stop stressing, girl. I think you will enjoy it. Relax, stay Zen,' said Kelly as she hung up.

Rose walked into her suite and went straight to her dressing room. It was filled with clothes. Some of them were okay, she thought. It wasn't as if she didn't know how to dress herself but she could do with a few more looks, she conceded.

Spending the evening alone in her room, she ate a light chicken salad for dinner, with a mineral water, scared she might bloat for the stylist. Stop being paranoid, she thought, and opened a packet of chocolate biscuits from the mini bar and had some with a cup of milk tea. She munched them defiantly in bed as she watched *Inside Edition*.

When Paul's face flashed across the screen with the headline 'Has he lost it?' she sat forward in bed. Since he had walked out on her when she needed him most and their confrontation during the signing of the divorce papers, she had avoided Paul wherever possible. They had attended a few of the same awards events over the years but they had circled each other at a distance. Rose took little interest in following anyone's career, let alone her ex-husband's, so the story about his erratic behaviour and recent box office failings took Rose by surprise.

She watched as the reporter spoke of Paul's behaviour on a recent talk show. When the host asked him about his recent relationship break-up with a French actress, Paul broke down crying live on air and started to speak in riddles about love and secrets and honour. Rose watched in shock as they spoke of Paul being fired from his most recent film and replaced by a younger star, whom Rose had not heard of before.

The photos of Paul outside Nobu attacking a photographer who had tried to photograph him and his South American surgeon leaving the restaurant were terrible, thought Rose, as she turned up the television to hear more from the judgemental reporter.

'Paul Ross was once the biggest movie star in the world. His string of recent box office failures has resulted in Paul feeling the pressure from every angle. It was only ten years ago that he was married to the English actress Rose Nightingale. They were Hollywood's most successful marriage till she had an affair with her co-star and broke Paul's heart.'

Rose threw a biscuit at the television, which showed a picture

296

of her and Paul in supposedly happier times. 'Oh my God!' she said angrily.

The reporter continued. 'Whether Paul can come back from his most recent public breakdown remains to be seen, but you know we will be first to let you know, here on *Inside Edition*.'

Rose sat in shock. Paul was always so careful with his image. An old-school Hollywood idol, he was friendly with the paparazzi, always gave them their shot and gave great and funny interviews. He only showed his ugly side to Rose, she had thought, till now. Rose turned off the TV and sat in her bed surrounded by biscuit crumbs. Paul was no longer her problem, she thought, and she turned out the light and went to sleep.

The phone ringing in her hotel room woke her up; Sophie Thomas was waiting to see her. Rose asked reception to send her up and put on the plush white robe from the bathroom. She looked at her skin in the mirror as she slipped on the robe. It looked good; the woman at the day spa was a miracle worker, she thought, as the doorbell rang quietly, informing her of Sophie's arrival.

'Hello, I am Sophie Thomas,' said the stylish French woman at the door.

Dressed in tight black jeans, a long sequined silver singlet, with a black turtleneck underneath, she had on high grey suede ankle boots, a dark blue leather motorcycle jacket and silver chain earrings which hung down to her shoulders. Her hair was cropped short and was jet black. She looked like the most glamorous rock chick Rose had ever seen.

'Hello, I'm Rose, and I'm wearing a bathrobe and I'm terribly embarrassed,' said Rose, looking shamefully down at herself.

'Don't be, it is good you are relaxed,' said Sophie, walking inside and taking off her jacket and laying it next to her large, heavy black leather satchel. 'You went to the day spa yesterday, non?'

'Yes, I did, I'm afraid I slept in,' said Rose with a wry face.

'Good, then you will be refreshed. We have work to do,' said the French style icon simply. 'Shall we order coffee and have a chat?'

Rose ordered coffee and fruit for them both and as an afterthought asked for some pastries. If Sophie didn't eat them then she could have them after she left, thought Rose greedily.

Sophie looked out the window at the view of Central Park. 'Lovely view,' she said politely.

'Yes, it is but I suppose the view of my dressing room would be better for you,' said Rose cheekily.

'No, I want to talk first, I want to find out who you are, what you want, what you do,' said Sophie, turning to her and sitting down on the sofa.

Rose sat down. 'I don't know, I suppose I'm in a bit of a rut. I've had a rough time lately and Kelly thinks I need to start dating and "get out there", wherever "there" is,' she said tiredly.

'I see, easy,' said Sophie, opening her satchel. 'I've gone through some of your press clippings to see what your style has been over the past few years.'

Rose cringed. 'Oh no, how awful.'

'No, no, you have some nice looks. The only thing I would say is that they are a bit too similar. They all look the same.'

'Yes, I know what you mean. If I find a shape that works for me, then I wear it. I tend to buy one thing in lots of colours.'

'Oh no, that should never happen,' said Sophie, frowning.

'I know, but I never get time to shop and people send me things, so I try them on and if I like them I wear them.

I've got lots of clothes but not all of them work together, I think.'

'It is a common problem with all women. You need to look at the piece and if you can't wear it with the other things in your wardrobe then you should not have it. We can easily be tempted by the way it feels, even though it's not right for us.'

Ain't that the truth, thought Rose, thinking of Max. He felt lovely but he didn't go with anything else in her life. Now she understood why Kelly had set this up for her. Warming to Sophie's confidence she continued, 'I'm nearly forty and I don't want to look like an old woman but I also don't want to look like a try-hard Hollywood actor. It's a slippery slope, and I could easily find myself wearing things which are too young for me and end up on Mr Blackwell's worst dressed list if I'm not careful.'

'That is not true. You have not made any wrong choices here,' said Sophie as she spread the images of Rose at various events out in front of her. 'You just need more variety, to have fun with fashion more, you are a little too safe.'

Rose smiled. This could be fun, she decided, and answered the door for the room service to come in and set up. Rose poured them coffee and offered the fruit to Sophie. '*Non merci,* may I have a pastry, please?'

Rose smiled; this was an excellent start.

Sophie spent the day with Rose. First, she assessed all her clothes, making Rose try on all the items she had brought with her in the morning. 'You have a wonderful figure, Rose, it is the figure of a woman. I want you to look like a woman, *oui*? It's hard to dress women who are too thin, always alterations and fussing. You are a pleasure to dress.'

Rose preened.

'I've made some appointments at some of the designers

who will be good for you. We will see some today and some tomorrow morning and then we will do shoes, bags and accessories.'

Rose let herself be guided. Sophie took her to Carolina Herrera, Michael Kors, Oscar De La Renta, Jason Wu and the next morning Chanel and Tracey Reese for a few fun pieces.

Sophie had talked to the designers about what they were after and Rose allowed herself to be the house model while the staff fussed around her in the private fittings rooms of the designers' offices. There was not a single piece of clothing Rose did not love. And the way Sophie worked them all together was inspiring. 'You are an artist,' said Rose as she had an amethyst toile silk gown fitted at Carolina Herrera.

'Actually, I am an artist as well as stylist. When I put things together, I think about the emotion, the form, the line,' Sophie replied without a trace of arrogance. 'Fashion is art. Once you see it like that then you will be more aware and careful about what you hang on your body.'

Rose understood, her studies of art at university had been restricted to what was in galleries or hung on walls; she had never considered what she hung in her wardrobe also fitted into that category. She was inspired and started to speak up about what she liked, what felt good on her body, what worked with her lifestyle. They talked about clothes and fashion and image all day. It was the best fun Rose had had since Italy. They finally relaxed at Barneys after hours, which allowed Rose and Sophie to peruse the accessories and shoes department at their leisure, with staff on hand to help them with their needs.

'You need to come to LA to look over what I have there as well,' Rose said as she and Sophie headed back to the Four Seasons, tired but victorious.

300

'Of course, I will be there next week actually as I am filming a TV pilot,' said Sophie.

'Of course you are. You deserve a TV show. What you do and what you know is very accessible and smart, Sophie. You are a stylist of a new generation, working with a woman's body, not making her feel bad about eating pastries,' Rose laughed.

'Oh no, there is always time for pastries. Life is too short for just fruit salad,' said Sophie. She kissed Rose on both cheeks. 'I've arranged for some of the designers' next-season samples to come to you soon. If you like anything then we can discuss, *oui*?'

'Of course, I'm not going to take a step out of my wardrobe without approval from the French Minister for Fashion,' said Rose gravely.

'You have all the right clothes, the perfect body, and you seem a lovely person, Rose. You just have to have the courage to show it now. Tell the world you are ready for whatever is coming next,' said Sophie philosophically.

'Thank you, Sophie. I enjoyed myself. I will call you in LA, okay?'

'Okay, make sure you go out and show off your art. That's an order. Bye.'

'*Adieu*,' said Rose, smiling. It was time to step into the world again, not as a character but as herself. It had been a long time coming.

CHAPTER THIRTY

Calypso sat on the wooden bench under the frangipani tree in her garden. TG was due to arrive any minute. It had been a hell of a day. TG had not gone sailing along the Amalfi Coast as he and Calypso had planned; instead he had come back to LA the day after she had, he said on the phone.

It was late afternoon and Calypso was tired but she knew there were things to say to TG and if she waited she would lose the courage that had accompanied her for the past few days.

She picked up a perfect frangipani flower from the ground at her feet and put it behind her ear. The five petals of the frangipani, she had once read, were said to represent the five states of psychological perfection – sincerity, faith, aspiration, devotion and surrender. Feeling a long way from all of these enlightened states, she got up and walked inside the house. She had changed after meeting with the FBI and the black-mailer. She wanted TG to listen to her, not look at her, so she dressed carefully in black pants, a white silk t-shirt and her favourite red flats. No make-up, and no accessories apart from the flower behind her ear.

She heard a car in the driveway of her house and saw it was TG pulling up in his black Porsche. Feeling nervous, she opened the front door and waited.

'Hi,' he said as he walked towards her.

Calypso felt her stomach flip. Shit, she thought.

'Hi,' she said. 'Come in. Thanks for seeing me.'

'Of course, I was pleased you rang me. I was getting worried.' He kissed her on the cheek. She turned her head at the last minute and his kiss landed on the flower. 'Cute flower,' he said.

'Oh, I forgot about that,' she said and pulled it out.

'Leave it, it looks pretty,' he said, looking at her intently.

'Listen, I'm sorry about the way I left Italy. Something happened and I needed to take care of it.'

'Are you okay now? Did you work it out?' he asked, concern all over his face.

'Yes, I did. It's been a tough time but I managed it okay,' she said carefully.

'Want to talk about it?' he asked.

'No,' she said emphatically.

'All right then. So what about us?' he asked, cutting to the chase.

'I don't know, TG. I'm scared. What you did for me in Italy was wonderful but I need to start to take care of myself. My whole life someone has taken care of me and I need to grow up. I feel like I've had this enormous weight lifted off my shoulders. I'm a grown-up, there's no mother, no boyfriend, no rescue mission out there with my name on it. If I want to live a life that means anything, then I need to do what I want, not what others want from me.' Calypso plucked at the frangipani flower in her hand, sounding braver than she felt.

'I don't want anything from you. I just want to be with you.'

'I don't want you to be my saviour. I can't do that. I need to do stuff for myself. In Italy you were amazing and I'm so grateful for the care you gave me but I cannot rely on that all the time.'

'I'm not planning on being your saviour, Calypso, I just want to be with you,' he said, angry at her logic.

'Every significant relationship I've ever had has been because someone wanted something from me, or for me to do something, or be someone for them. I don't know how to make decisions for myself, for what I want for me.'

'Are you angry about what happened with Raphael?' asked TG.

'No, I understand now. Trust me, I do,' she said wryly. 'I need to get a life, TG. I need to find out what I want. Not what my agent, management or mother wants.'

TG stood up and walked around the room, bewildered. 'So the life you want, I'm assuming it doesn't include me? Jesus, Calypso, I love you. Don't you get it? I love you.'

Calypso started to cry. 'You think you love me because I'm a little girl in your mind. I'm helpless and silly and you need to come on your white horse and make it better. If I'm with you, I don't think I'll be able to find out who I am and what I want.'

'That's total bullshit!' he yelled at her. 'I love you because you are the funniest person I know. Because you are smart as hell. Who else knows that the cassowary is the world's most dangerous bird? No one, only you! I love that you have stayed true to yourself in this fucked up city. Your work ethic is unbelievable, and you went back on set and did your job very fucking well, I might add.'

TG was still pacing the room, wound up to the point where he was almost shouting.

'I love you because of the crazy shit you wear that always makes you look amazing, and you make whoever you are speaking to feel like they are the most important person in the room. I know your life has been shit, I know it's been a struggle from the minute you started to walk. But don't throw us away because you think being alone is the best place for

304

finding out what you want in your life. No one really knows what they want. I don't know shit except that I want you.'

Calypso was sobbing. 'I'm afraid of everything. I'm afraid of you and what I feel for you. I'm afraid you'll take over my life, I'm afraid of what we could have. I'm afraid of being happy.' She looked down at the frangipani in her hand. One petal left. Surrender, she thought.

TG sat down and pulled her into his arms. 'What you went through in Italy was horrific. I get what you are saying and I know Italy seemed like a dream, good and bad, but this is the real world now. We can make this happen. I know it. I've never, ever fought for anything in my life. My life has been charmed in some ways, in ways your life hasn't, but this is the first time I've ever fought for anything. Give us a chance, Calypso. Please.'

Calypso lifted her face to him and he kissed the tears away on her cheeks and then put his mouth gently on hers. Tasting her salty tears, she kissed him back, softly.

'I do love you, I do. I'm sorry. Just stick with me till I work myself out, okay?' she cried.

'Of course, but working yourself out can take a long time,' he said, holding her close.

'Then you might be stuck with me for a while then,' she laughed through her tears.

'Fine with me. I just want you to do one thing for me, okay?' he said into her ear.

She nodded. 'Okay, what?'

'Call me Tim.'

Calypso laughed.

'I want to take it slow, okay?' she said, finally coming out of his arms.

'Sure.'

'I want to be dated and wooed. Did you know I never went

305

on a real date as a teenager? I didn't go to school. Any dates I had were set up by my agent or my mother.'

'Really?' said TG, incredulous.

'Really,' she answered. 'I never went to a prom, I never did football games or roller-skating, shared a milkshake or anything like that.'

'I don't think people really date like that. I think you've read too many *Archie* comics,' he said, laughing.

She stood up. 'You may laugh, Midwest boy, but I am a dating virgin. The only guys I've gone out with are ones I met on set. Sad but true.'

'Okay, I get it, date we shall do,' said TG. 'Can we make out?'

'We'll see. Hand under the sweater seems a long way off for me just yet,' she said primly.

'It seems odd you don't want to be treated like a child but you want to date like a teenager,' said TG, smiling kindly at her.

'I know, but I want to experience myself outside of work. I've told my manager and agent I'm taking a break for a while to plan what I'm going to do with my career and my life. It may not make any sense to you, but I want to live a little. Have fun.'

TG laughed. 'All right, then I've got my work cut out for me.'

Calypso heard her intercom buzz. 'Who is it?' she said into the speaker.

'Hi, Calypso, it's the FBI,' came over the crackly speaker.

'FBI?' asked TG. 'Why are they here?' Concern flooded his handsome face.

Calypso looked away. 'Okay, short story and no judgements from you, okay? If we're going to do this then you need to know the truth.'

TG sat down.

'The phone call I got in Italy was my agent saying I was being blackmailed. He had received a tape and unless I paid two million dollars they would release it to the world on the internet. I set the blackmailer up this morning at the Chateau Marmont and the FBI arrested him after I recorded us speaking. All very tawdry and awful, as you can imagine.'

TG felt his heart in his mouth. 'Can I ask if the tape was of you?'

'Would it matter if it were?' she asked warily.

'No, not at all, I just want to know you're okay. I don't care if you're nude with the seven dwarfs. Actually, I would watch that, not a great example. Calypso, I don't give a shit about anything but our future.'

Calypso laughed and buzzed in the FBI.

'Actually, it was of my mother. Giving sexual favours to a director I worked with a long time ago. Her and I are no longer speaking. It's a complete mess.' She looked sadly at TG. 'Do you think I'm a joke now? I've got my career because my mother blew directors and did God knows what else to them over the years.'

TG smiled at her. 'Well, I cast you and your momma was nowhere near me, so there's one gig you know you got on your own.'

Calypso smiled at him. 'Thanks.'

The female FBI agent and a younger male agent came into the room.

'Hi,' said Calypso, 'This is my boyfriend, Tim.'

'We just started to go steady,' said TG, winking at Calypso.

The female agent looked at them both, a little confused. 'That's nice for you.'

'Ignore him, please,' Calypso said, relieved at feeling something other than stress.

'We've interviewed Jason. He is quite an unwell man actually, and we have requested a psychiatric assessment. I don't think it will go to court. I'm pretty sure it won't. He may be hospitalized for some time.'

Calypso sat. 'He seemed so lost and sad somehow. Deluded about celebrities and the fact he thinks they have perfect lives.'

'He had some items in his house which indicates he was a danger to the community and on this evidence we will be looking for long term care for him, in an institution equipped for his issues. We came today because I wanted you to know what you did was extraordinarily brave and you were great. I know I said it before, but you helped a lot of people today and most of all you helped him, sad as it seems.'

TG looked at Calypso. Whatever she had been through was tough but she had done it and he was proud of her.

'We'll keep you updated with any progress on the case, and you have our word the tape will not be accessible to anyone not connected to the case.'

'Thanks,' said Calypso.

'Have you told your mother yet?' asked the female agent as she left Calypso's house.

'No, we're no longer speaking,' said Calypso.

'Okay, well, do you want us to talk to her for you?'

'No. It's fine,' said Calypso and shut the door after them.

TG sat on the couch. 'What the fuck happened? Agent Scully seemed to think you were the ant's pants. Did you get all Dirty Harry on that guy's ass today?'

'No,' she said, punching him. 'I just did what I needed to do to get the job done.'

'Well, look at you, all cool and stuff in the crisis. So, what

308

about your mom, when are you going to tell her?' he said, crossing his legs.

'I'm not. We no longer speak as far as I'm concerned.'

'Okay, well, I get you're pissed with her for this situation but surely you can work it out,' he said nonchalantly.

'No way, Tim. She gave head jobs to make sure I got roles. I wasn't an actor, I was a pawn and she was my pimp. Once I saw her do this to a director, years ago. I had a shitty audition, I was sick with the flu and the director told me to fuck off because I might make him sick. My mother said she was going to tell him off. Oh, she did all right, she gave him a mouthful. I ran back to the car and pretended I never saw it, told myself I was sick from the flu and hallucinating, but deep down I knew. Now I look back on every role I did as a child that has led me to this moment in my career and I'm suspicious. I don't deserve it. I didn't earn it. Leeza did it for me and I never asked her to do any of it.'

'Well, sometimes you gotta do what you gotta do to get the job done, as you said. I'm not condoning your mother but she wanted this for you so badly, she was prepared to give up a part of herself to get it. Do you think she liked doing it? I doubt it but if she did it, then you never had to. Maybe it was her fucked up way of protecting you.'

Calypso listened. 'I don't know what to say to her. Our whole relationship has been about work. I don't think the mother–daughter thing exists between us. I don't know if I can forgive her or trust her.'

'Maybe you'll never have the relationship you want with her but it's worth talking to her once. If she doesn't get you, then eighty-six her. Who knows, stranger things have happened,' he said, kissing the top of her head.

'Maybe,' said Calypso.

Then reaching up, she pulled him onto the sofa. 'Let's make out. I'll let you get to second base if you're nice,' she said coyly.

TG left late that night at Calypso's insistence. 'Come on. We can sleep and not do anything,' he said as she pushed him towards the door.

'Nope,' she laughed. 'I told you. Slow.'

TG stood at his car. 'Calypso Gable, you are my girl.'

She smiled back at him, tousled and happy from her evening with him.

Next on the checklist of challenges she had to face was Leeza. This one was going to be harder to face than all the others, she realized, and she lay awake all night wondering if the relationship was worth saving.

CHAPTER THIRTY-ONE

The air was cold, thought Sapphira as she woke up. Trying to move her arms, she found they were tied behind her back. She was taped to a chair on the roof of Jack's palazzo. Shaking off the grogginess, she tried to focus in the darkness. She could make out a shape a few feet away from her. 'Wakey wakey, cunt,' said a voice in the darkness.

Sapphira was alert. She had gone into her room, she remembered, and the light didn't work and then she felt arms on her and smelt something unusual as a cloth was put over her face.

'Who are you?' she asked forcefully, trying to cover the fear she felt.

'It's me, Sapphira. You dumped me right before you killed our child. Remember?'

'What?' She was confused. What ex-boyfriend? She frantically racked her brains trying to think.

'It's me, Ethan.' And he stepped into the light that came from the building next door.

Ethan. Jesus Christ!

'Good to see you,' she said, trying not to let him see her fear.

'You too, although I see you all the time, you just never see me,' he said as he lit a cigarette.

He smoked for a while then walked over and stubbed it out on her shoulder blade. She screamed in pain as the ash burned

311

through her skin. 'That's what it must have felt like for our baby.'

'Jesus, Ethan, I told you I was pregnant. I never heard from you,' she said, crying from the pain in her shoulder.

'You told me nothing. You ripped out our little girl and killed her,' he screamed, his spit landing on her face.

'I did, I sent you a message on your answering machine. I remember,' she said, crying.

'I was in hospital, my parents put me away because I was too powerful. I was becoming too strong and they said I needed help. They said it was all the drugs. But I know they just wanted to be rid of me, like you wanted to rid yourself of our baby.'

'I don't know anything about that,' said Sapphira, weeping. 'I'm sorry.'

'You should be sorry. I was away until I went to see you but you were at the hospital, having a fucking abortion. You slut.' He was calmer now.

Sapphira tried to think of what to say. 'I wanted you to help me. Our baby was sick, she was really sick, Ethan. She wouldn't have survived if I'd had her. You have to know that is the truth, please believe me,' she pleaded.

'I sent things to your house. I signed it as your boyfriend and you never said thank you,' he said sadly.

'I get lots of things sent to me, I don't get to see them all. If I had known they were from you then I would have called.' Sapphira was trying to subtly undo the tape he had used on her arms.

'I loved you, Sapphira. We were good together.'

'We spent a few nights together, Ethan. Then I never heard from you again.'

'I went away then. You didn't wait for me.' He started to cry.

312

Fuck, thought Sapphira, he was insane. 'You have to let me go. There's someone else staying here, they might hear us. Just let me go and I will never say anything to anyone, I promise,' she begged.

'I don't think so. Alex is tucked up safely in bed with the drugs I slipped into the drink he fixed himself tonight and took up to his room. I saw you kiss him on the boat, before you threw up like a pig. Drunk, I think you were. You're disgusting.' He spat at her.

How long had he been in Venice, she wondered. 'You came to my house in Perugia, didn't you?' she demanded.

'I've been in all your houses, Sapphira, all your hotel rooms. I am everywhere, you can never get away from me now. I am the constant reminder of what you did to our child.' He spoke calmly and was matter-of-fact. 'Wherever you go, I will be by your side. We will have to work together to make up for this, to atone for what you did to the baby. We will have children together and show the world and God we are prepared to give each other a second chance.'

Sapphira felt sick from fear. What should she do? Agree? Fight back?

Ethan went over to the outdoor table and lit a candle. He took something out of a black bag and hummed to himself while he worked. What the hell was he going to do? Torture her? Make her beg forgiveness from him? She felt as though she was in a dream and tried to shake her head to wake herself.

Ethan walked over with something hidden behind his back. 'I commend your valiant efforts to get off the gear lately. Well done, can't have been easy.'

'How do you know that?' she asked, worried.

'Darling, I know everything. If we are going to be together, and I think you will see we are meant to, then we must do everything together.'

He pulled out a syringe from behind his back. 'I'll go first, then I'll do you. Just like the first time, huh?'

Sapphira wanted to close her eyes and wish herself away but as she stared at the syringe, her body begged for the contents to be poured into her veins.

'No, Ethan, I don't take it anymore. You can if you want, but I don't,' she said firmly, repeating the line her therapists had taught her should she find herself being offered drugs again.

'Once a drug whore, always a drug whore,' he said hatefully.

'No, Ethan, no. I don't want it.'

'Yes, you do, you know you want it. I can see it in your eyes. Your body craves it. One hit and we'll be back where we started and then we can share everything.'

He rolled up his sleeve and plunged the needle into his vein. She watched as he took in the hit. His eyes rolled back and he smiled at her sleepily. 'Nothing like it, huh, babe?'

He sat for a while on the ground at Sapphira's taped feet. Then he got up, walked back to his kit and started mixing up a batch for Sapphira, using the same needle he had used on himself. 'Not the same needle,' she cried.

'You know the rules, Sapphira, we share everything now,' he said seriously.

She started to weep and then scream for help. 'Help, help! I'm on the roof.' She tried to bang her feet on the ground. 'Help me,' she screamed into the night.

Ethan looked at her. 'Don't cry, it will be better soon, I promise,' he said strangely.

She saw him draw a huge amount of the liquid from the

314

spoon into the syringe. 'That's too much, Ethan. I've been clean for weeks. I'll die,' she cried.

'Maybe. If you do, then say hello to our child for me.' He walked towards her, holding the syringe up in the air. 'How can we be together if you kill me?' cried Sapphira desperately.

'I will die also and then we will all be together again, like a family.' He smiled at her.

Sapphira cried and tried to fight back as he pulled the tape, freeing one of her arms. Flailing at him, he swiftly punched her in the jaw, knocking her over in the chair.

'Come on, now. Be nice to me, please. This is not how I think we should behave,' he said, as though he was admonishing a child.

'Fuck off, you fucking crazy asshole,' she hissed at him.

'Fuck you, cunt.' He kicked her on the side of her arm.

As he leaned down to pull her to an upright position, she saw him sprawl across the ground. On the ground, with only one arm free, Sapphira tried to turn herself to see what had sent Ethan across the ground with such force. Shifting inch by inch, she turned the chair to face where Ethan lay. Alex was standing over him. He lifted Ethan to his feet.

'Careful, he has a syringe,' Sapphira heard herself scream.

Ethan was on his feet, trying to kick Alex and stab him with the syringe. Alex stepped back as Ethan lunged at him again. Alex grabbed his hands; the men were pushing against each other.

Sapphira struggled to undo the tape with her one free hand. It was hopeless, it seemed, as she scratched and picked at her other taped arm. Now Ethan punched Alex and he fell to the ground near the edge of the roof. Sapphira watched as he jumped to his feet, his mouth bleeding. Ethan and he faced

315

off against each other, Alex's eyes blazing in the dim light on the roof. Ethan stood, a frightening look on his face. 'You can't rescue the whore, she's mine,' he screamed at him as he turned towards Sapphira.

Alex said nothing, instead roaring at him while he ran towards him. He pushed Ethan with such force, he fell on his front, his arms underneath him. Pulling himself up near the edge of the roof, he looked at them both and Sapphira saw the needle sticking out of his neck. He moaned and then fell backwards off the roof, as Sapphira screamed.

Alex ran to the edge and looked over, watching as the man's body fell into the water below.

'Oh my God, oh my God,' Sapphira repeated helplessly.

Alex ran back to her and swiftly undid the tape and released her from its bindings. She curled into a foetal position, weeping loudly. Kneeling on the ground, he held her, wrapping himself around her. 'Shh, shh, it's all over now. It's all finished, he's gone.'

Finally Sapphira gulped through her tears of fear and pain. 'He was going to overdose me. He was going to kill me,' she sobbed.

'I know, I know. He didn't though, you're here with me, safe,' he murmured as he rocked her like a child in his strong arms. 'Come on, we'll go inside, he's gone.' Picking Sapphira up effortlessly in his arms, he carried her off the roof and down the stairs to his bedroom. Laying her on the bed, he covered her with the mohair rug on the chair. Taking a glass of water, he sat her up and helped her to drink.

She lay down again, clearly in shock, shaking. 'I am so cold.'

He fetched a cashmere jumper from his wardrobe and dressed her in it, tucking the rug around her. 'I'll get something for the burn on your shoulder. Did he do that to you?' he asked gently.

316

She nodded. Alex ran downstairs to Jack's bathroom and rifled through the cupboards till he found some cotton balls and antiseptic, burn cream and a bandage. The man had everything, literally, thought Alex as he took the stairs three at a time to get back to Sapphira.

She hadn't moved and was still shaking in his bed. He knelt on the bed and stretched the jumper down to reveal the nasty burn. As he applied the salves, she didn't flinch. Then he smoothed on the bandage and kissed the top of it. 'All better,' he said.

Sapphira lay still, the events of the evening flashing over and over in her mind.

'Do you want me to call a doctor, the police? You tell me what you want,' he coaxed gently.

'Nothing. Just don't leave me alone,' she said, her voice shaking.

'Not a chance.' He lay next to her and held her hand until exhaustion took over and she slept.

When she awoke, Alex was still lying next to her, his arms protectively over her body. She moved slightly and he woke with a start. 'Hey,' he said quietly.

'Hey,' she answered him.

'What can I get you?' he asked, his face close to hers.

'Umm . . . nothing, I think,' she answered, sore and her shoulder aching.

'I need a piss, a coffee and a cigarette, in that order,' he said.

Sapphira laughed a little. 'Charming.'

'Then I better ring Jack, I think,' he said.

'Yes,' she said slowly. There was so much to take in and her mind seemed like it was spinning.

Alex got up slowly and stretched. Sapphira sat on the edge of the bed. 'You okay?' he asked.

'I'm okay,' she replied and stood. Her head spun and she sat down again. 'A little dizzy, actually.'

'Okay, well, you stay here and I will bring you coffee and a cigarette.'

Alex walked towards the bathroom. As he closed the door, Sapphira shut her eyes and saw Ethan's face screaming at her. She felt the tears coming again and tried to stop them flowing but the emotion was too strong and she cried loudly.

Alex rushed out of the bathroom. 'Oh, honey,' he said and sat down on the edge of the bed next to her.

'I'm sorry,' she repeated.

'Sorry for what?' asked Alex, incredulous.

'Sorry for you having to see that, for you being dragged into my bullshit life. I'm a mess, Alex, a fucking mess and what you saw last night was horrifying. You could have died.' She buried her face into the pillow.

'Well, I didn't die. We're here now. I'm not saying what you went through was not terrifying but you have to believe it's over. This moment doesn't define your past or your future.' He pleaded with her to understand.

Sapphira pulled herself together on the bed. It was over, she thought. The heroin abuse, Ethan and the baby. It was finished. It was time to start again.

'I need a coffee,' she said.

'Come on then.' Alex held out his hand.

In the kitchen, Alex and Sapphira lit cigarettes and sat quietly. He knew not to push her. She was still in shock, he thought.

'I want to tell you what happened to me,' she said eventually.

'You don't have to tell me anything if you don't want,' he said in a gentle tone.

'I want to,' she said, stubbing out the cigarette and lighting another. 'I'm a heroin addict. Jack brought me here to get me clean and he's done a great job so far. He has been the most significant relationship I've ever had. His friendship and belief in me is not like anything I've experienced before. Ethan was the father of a child I aborted long ago. The baby was sick, not expected to survive. I tried to tell him but I found out last night he had been put away by his parents, probably as a result of drug psychosis, I imagine. Although I'll never know for sure now,' she said ruefully.

'He has stalked me for years, although I never knew it was him and the police have never been able to track him down. He was canny and smart enough to not get caught. I even hired private detectives. He became obsessed, obviously with me, and the baby, which he found out about after he left the hospital or rehab or wherever he was. I wanted the baby, I did, even stopped heroin when I found out I was pregnant, but after I had the termination I fell back into it. He sent me a coffin with a baby doll inside it covered in blood the day I got home from hospital.'

As Alex tried to cover his shock and disgust, Sapphira continued, unburdening herself of the secrets she had hidden for years. 'My father died of a heroin overdose, I found him dead when I was twelve. We were never close, but when I shot up, I saw his face again. It brought me closer to him in some fucked up way.' She shook her head at her own screwed-up logic. 'Last night when Ethan was going to inject me again, I realized how much I still wanted heroin. I was happy in some crazy way that I could have it again, even under those circumstances. I've a long way to go to be healed, I guess, and I need to do whatever it takes to not fall back into that life again. Heroin took me away from reality. Now I need to create my own reality, one without the pain and trauma of the last few years and one that actually means something.'

Alex was silent. Finally he spoke. 'It's a hell of a movie of the week, huh?'

'A horror movie,' laughed Sapphira, actually apprehending the craziness of her story.

'Maybe, but at least this one has ended. Now you need to write your sequel.'

'I want to thank you a thousand times for coming to the roof. How did you know? Ethan said he had spiked your drink.' She shuddered at the memory of last night.

'I didn't drink it. It smelt odd. I thought the Scotch had gone off, so I left out the bottle to speak to the housekeeper and went to bed. I was sleeping when I heard screaming. I went to check on you and saw your room was empty, the light bulbs removed and the bedside table knocked over. I searched the house for you then went up to the roof. That's when I saw him.'

The knowledge that he had heard her brought Sapphira to tears again. 'You could have died. Fuck, you could have died.'

'So could have you,' he said wryly. 'The world is filled with crazy people. You got the craziest though, I must admit. Makes my stalkers look like girl guides.'

'I've had enough for a while. I need to get away from here but I can't go back to LA yet. It's too much,' she pondered as she put out the cigarette.

'What about the charity you wanted to start? Why not head to that country that was in the documentary you mentioned to me?'

Sapphira considered his idea. Heading to somewhere remote seemed like the best idea she had heard in a long time. 'Do you think I could?' she asked, doubting herself.

'Sure, you can do anything you want. You wanted to give back, why not this? Doesn't have to be forever, but it may give you the chance to think about other people's problems for a while. Perspective is a powerful healer,' he said, standing to take their cups to the sink. 'Giulia will be here in a few hours, it's nearly 7.00 am. We can talk to her then.'

Sapphira stood up. 'Okay, I will think about it.'

'All right, off to bed to try and sleep for a while,' he insisted.

'I don't think I can sleep.'

'You'd be surprised at what your body needs.'

They stood at the bottom of the stairs. 'Can you lie with me?' she asked. 'I don't want to be alone.'

'Of course, come on.' He led her to his bedroom. Putting her under the covers, he slipped in next to her. She curled into his arms and he kissed her hair. 'Time to start again,' he whispered and she felt herself fall asleep in his arms.

Ethan's body was found floating in the canal the next morning, with a syringe sticking out of his neck. Just another junkie, the Italian police said. His body lay unclaimed in the morgue till he was buried in an unmarked grave a month later on Isola di San Michele – Venice's Island of the Dead.

CHAPTER THIRTY-TWO

New York was Rose's new love affair. Having spent time in the city on and off over the years, she was once terrified of its energy and frenetic pace. Now the city had mellowed since 9/11 and Rose's energy had been kick-started by her experience with Sophie, the wonderful French stylist. Changing her cell phone number, she decided to forget about the medium and live her life right now, instead of yearning for a future that insisted on evading her. After finishing the film, she stayed on at the Four Seasons. Catching up with friends, attending Broadway classics and off-Broadway small shows, Rose was inspired again by the art of the stage.

Leaving the theatre one night, she rang Randy, her agent, knowing he would still be in the office with the three hours' time difference between LA and New York.

'Hello, lovely Randy,' she enthused down the phone.

'Hello, Miss Rose. How is the fair city treating you?' he asked.

'Oh Randy, I feel alive again. I really do. I want to do something in the theatre. Can you have a snoop around and tell me if there's anything exciting I might be suitable for?' she asked as she got into her town car and was driven back to the hotel. 'I'm going to spend some more time here and look for a place to stay for a while.'

'Really? Well, Broadway would be happy to have you. I'm

not sure what's happening but I will ask Karen, who does the stage in our office, to look into it for you. Musicals? Classics? New plays? Any ideas?'

'Not musicals, you've not heard me sing. You might fire me,' she laughed. 'But I'm up for anything else.'

'Okay, leave it with me. Where are you looking to stay?' he asked.

'I have no idea, I suppose I'll get Lauren to call a few realtors for me.'

'How is she?' asked Randy who knew the barest details of the Jerry Hyman case.

'She's great, doing well actually. She's working again three days week for me, which is a blessing.'

'Good for her. Jerry's going to go to jail for a long time, I think.'

'Let's hope so,' said Rose as her car pulled up at the front of the Four Seasons.

'Listen,' said Randy. 'I've got a client who's moving to LA for a while, a TV series, might be a year or more. They have an apartment in New York they may want to rent out. Fully furnished, I would imagine. Want me to speak to his assistant?'

'That would be fantastic, Randy. Thanks,' she said as she walked through the lobby.

Cutting a glamorous figure in skinny black pants, a thin black silk turtleneck, white cashmere short coat with three quarter caped sleeves, and high suede black boots, Rose was the epitome of chic and she felt fabulous. Moving to New York was the best idea she had had in years. Going back to the theatre, getting over Max, it was all coming together.

'Before you go, I've had a phone call from an agent in London.'

'Yes,' said Rose cautiously.

'Your co-star in Italy, Max Craydon, is trying to get in touch with you.'

Rose took the phone away from her ear and thought. Max wanted to speak to her, but she didn't want to speak to him. She was creating a new life for herself and she was over the drama he created in her life. He was damaged and so was she. Never a good combination, she decided.

'Rose? Rose, are you still there?' she heard Randy's voice down the phone.

'Tell them to send through any requests to you and Lauren. I've too much to do here,' she said finally.

'Okay, then. Done,' said Randy, and Rose hung up.

She was adamant about her decision, she thought. Max had led her to her own family again and made her realize she wanted more to her life than just shooting films. She wanted to engage in something and work at it night after night till she perfected it. She wanted to go out with men again and start to live a fuller life.

Undressing, she stood under the hot jets in the shower and thought about her future. She was excited for the first time in years. Life is filled with possibilities, she thought as she hopped into bed and rang her mother.

Randy's client who was moving to LA to film his new series was only too happy to let his apartment to Rose. He called her direct, getting the number from Randy.

'Hey, it's a great spot, Third Avenue, you can walk anywhere and you will love the terrace I have. Gorgeous when the sun is out. I also have a screening room which always goes well at parties.'

'I don't think I'll be having any parties,' laughed Rose.

'It's fine if you do. Enjoy it, my wife and I are very happy here,' he said. 'I will get the keys and alarm code sent over to your hotel. I'd stay to meet you but I've got to get to LA. My wife is looking at schools. She's English, that stuff is important to her. I have to fly out tonight.'

'That's fine. I promise to look after it. Thank you,' said Rose, hanging up and then laughing at his comment about Englishwomen and education.

Rose spent the afternoon trying to pack up her things in the hotel. The clothes she had bought with Sophie did not fit into her bags she had brought with her to New York. She rang the concierge. 'I'm having trouble getting my things packed,' she said, embarrassed.

The concierge was not fazed, used to the problems of the rich and famous. 'Please leave your things, Ms Nightingale. Our butler service can pack and send your things to wherever you would like.'

'Thanks, that's terrific,' Rose said, leaving him with the address of her new apartment. 'Also, a package has just arrived for you, I will send it up straightaway,' the concierge added.

Rose clapped her hands. The keys to her apartment, well, the TV star's apartment, but now hers for a year! Answering the door with her coat and bag in hand, she took the lift down to the lobby and asked for her driver to take her straight to her new home. Opening the envelope in the back of the car, she read the instructions and held the keys in her hand. On the key ring hung a little silver angel. She held it and smiled. Perhaps Alice was sending a message that New York was where she was meant to be. Perhaps this was where she was supposed to be all along, she thought as the car pulled up to the apartment.

The owner had undersold it to her. It was a stunning

residence, not just any apartment. An old limestone house, she thought, as she touched the wall and climbed the ten steps to the ornate iron security door. Opening the door with the key, she pulled out the paper and punched in the alarm code.

It was exactly as Rose had hoped. Warm yet elegant. It was painted a soft cream throughout. On the walls hung prints of horses and dogs, botanical drawings. The foyer was old marble, worn from over the years. As she stood looking at the wear of two hundred years, Rose was so happy the owners had not repolished it. Walking into the living room, she saw the pale cream carpet had a faint *fleur de lys* pattern through it, giving the large room warmth. In it stood an old dark wood grand piano with a Tiffany lamp on top. The couches were grey with bright cushions in pale greens and whites, and there were plants and flowers in the vase on the mantelpiece with a huge modern silver mirror hanging over it. There was a large lacquer antique coffee table, filled high with books and magazines, some of them more trashier titles, thought Rose happily. And in the middle of the table was a wooden carved bowl filled with sea glass and shells.

It was the home of a family, thought Rose, touching the keys of the piano as she passed it.

Walking upstairs to the bedrooms, she found the master suite with a cleared out dressing room for Rose's clothes. The king-sized bed was covered in white linen, with a blue and white toile padded headboard. The carpet was white and there was an open fireplace and an old chaise longue at the foot of the bed. It was entirely to Rose's taste, she thought, thanking the gods or angels that had sent her this sanctuary in New York.

Exploring the rest of the house, she found a room belonging to a little girl, Clara, and a room belonging to a boy, Spencer.

She closed the doors, smiling at the things they had left behind. The terrace looked lovely, she thought, staring at the snow as it fell on the plants growing outside, the table and chairs set up in case there was a spontaneous barbeque.

Rose's favorite room though, was the bathroom in the master suite. A huge, free-standing clawed foot bath stood in the centre; the floors were polished dark hardwood boards. The vanity was an old Victorian chest that had a marble sink in the centre of it, with an old framed mahogany mirror placed above the sink. On the other wall, there was a large Victorian dresser with a small chair, covered in eggshell blue silk. The marble mantel on the facing wall held a small series of silver figurines of women bathing.

Rose walked around the house; she felt like she was in another country, part England, part New York. She looked in the kitchen and found a folder filled with takeaway menus. Why did they have a kitchen if they never cooked, she thought to herself.

Calling the Four Seasons, she requested her things be sent over as soon as possible and settled her bill over the phone. Walking back into the living room, she sat down at the piano. She'd had lessons as a child and the keys felt familiar as she touched them. Starting to play what little she could remember, she found she was rustier than she had thought. Standing up, she lifted the piano stool lid. Just as she had thought, it was filled with music, from beginners' to experienced levels. The mother must play and the children are getting lessons, she thought as she pulled out *Piano for Beginners*. That's what she would do while she was here: start playing the piano again. She had forgotten how much she loved it. She had forgotten a lot of things she had loved once, before her marriage to Paul. Working her way through the piano book,

Rose stopped and stretched her arms and fingers. They were sore from the workout but it had felt so good not to think about anything but the music in front of her, almost like a meditation, she thought.

Hearing the doorbell ring, Rose jumped up and ran to the door; her things had arrived from the hotel. She instructed the Four Seasons driver to take them up to her room and then tipped him $200 dollars.

'Thank you, Ms Nightingale,' he said warmly. 'You staying in New York for a while then?'

'I might stay here forever,' said Rose, smiling, feeling like she was about to burst from happiness.

'Well, we would be glad to have you,' he said in his Bronx accent and left Rose alone.

Rose rang Lauren. 'Hello, darling, I'm in. I feel like I did when I went to university, ridiculous really.'

'No, I get it, freedom, all that stuff,' Lauren said down the phone from LA. 'What do you need me to send over to you from here?' she asked.

'Nothing, really, I've got everything I need. Just let people know where I am if they ask. Also, I'm available for social events in New York, if invitations come my way. I might as well get out and live a little while I'm here.'

'Absolutely,' said Lauren. 'I have a few already, hang on, and let me get them.'

Lauren put down the phone and Rose walked upstairs to her bedroom. Looking at the large number of boxes and cases on the floor and the bed, she felt overwhelmed.

Lauren came back on the line. 'Okay, so there is a cocktail party at the Whitney. A dinner with some historical art society at the Frick and an opening night party, VIP at the MOMA.

328

Also some opera invites and theatre you're already going to. Any of those appeal?'

Rose was unzipping a dress bag with a navy Chanel silk evening gown with a white camellia at the waist inside. She hadn't worn it yet; it was only bought at the insistence of Sophie. 'Yes, they all appeal. Schedule them in and RSVP yes to all, as long as there are no clashes.'

'Really? Wow. I don't mean to be rude, but I'm surprised. You never went out in LA.'

'That's because I was hiding in LA, Lauren. No more hiding, time to get a life, as they say.'

'I've got some messages I will email over, nothing important, a few I've taken care of myself for you.'

'Thanks, you are a doll,' said Rose gratefully.

'A man called Max Craydon has rung a few times also, the guy from the picture. He said he really needs to talk to you but your cell phone isn't working. I didn't tell him you changed the number. He sounded nice though, not crazy.'

'I can't talk to him, not yet anyway,' said Rose, sighing. 'I just want to get settled in New York, and then I will deal with that. Tell him I'll contact him at a later date. Actually, tell him nothing. Just say I'm not available to speak to at this time,' said Rose harshly.

'Sure,' said Lauren, knowing not to pry into her boss's life but thinking that Max did sound lovely on the phone; they'd spoken for quite a while, about nothing really, but it was one of those easy conversations which flowed.

Lauren hung up from Rose and sat thinking. She knew Rose and Max had had an affair in Italy; her sources on set had told her. They also said he was very nice, and that Rose was smitten with him and the boys when they visited the set.

329

Lauren wondered what had happened, why they had split so quickly. One minute Rose was flying to London, now she was moving to New York. Running away is more like it, thought Lauren.

Picking up the phone, she dialled London. 'Max? It's Lauren Grasser, Rose Nightingale's PA. How are you?'

CHAPTER THIRTY-THREE

TG pulled up to Calypso's house in a red convertible Corvette with a surfboard in the back seat and sounded the horn. She ran outside. 'Where's your Porsche?' she asked, looking at the car.

'This is my other car,' he said. 'You ready?'

'Oooh, my other car,' she teased and ran back inside and collected her favourite straw bag and hat and locked up the house.

Climbing into the seat next to TG, she kissed him lovingly. 'Hello, you.'

'Hello, mermaid,' he said and started the engine.

As they roared off down the road, she yelled to make herself heard over the engine. 'Where are we going?'

'Surprise,' answered TG and turned up the Beach Boys CD on the car stereo.

Calypso laughed. All TG had told her was she had to bring her bikini and a book, which she had. The rest was to be discovered as the day went on. Driving out of LA, they headed along the picturesque coastline. It was a glorious LA day and Calypso could not have thought of a better place to be than with TG in the car, singing 'Help Me Rhonda' at the top of their lungs.

'How do you know this song?' asked TG as they drove along. He turned down the stereo slightly.

'My dad loves the Beach Boys, we always used to sing to them when I was a kid.'

Calypso smiled at the memory. Leeza and her father were always on her mind. This was the longest they had not spoken and while she enjoyed the peace at some level, she missed the contact with her mother and father. She had not yet approached her mother, or answered her father. She had instead taken some much-needed time away from them to think things through. For the last two weeks, she and TG had spent most days together. He had kept his promise to date her and they had been to the movies, out to dinner at casual places, and had seen Kelly and Chris, who were excited about their baby's arrival in a few months.

Calypso was enjoying the downtime and had been reading, surfing the net and moving furniture around in her house, one of her favourite pastimes. She and TG had still not slept together since Italy; not that they didn't want to, but Calypso was enjoying the waiting. TG didn't stay, much to his chagrin, but he took it well, prepared to wait for the girl of his dreams, he told her.

As they rounded the coast in the red car, TG pulled off onto an unmade road and drove down a bit further. 'Where are we?' asked Calypso, not recognizing her surroundings.

'We're at my beach, baby,' said TG as he stopped the car and jumped out. Pulling the surfboard out of the back, he opened the trunk of the car and pulled out a cooler, towels, a beach umbrella and two fold-out chairs. 'You grab the umbrella and the towels and I'll get the rest,' he said.

He picked up the items and walked into the scrub. Calypso hurriedly picked up the umbrella, threw the towels into her bag and followed him, afraid of being left behind and lost.

They walked through the scrub and came to the top of a cliff. They stopped and Calypso looked over; the drop down was terrifying but the water in the distance sparkled and the beach below was practically deserted.

'Only locals come here,' explained TG as they carefully navigated their way down the path in the cliff. 'It's where I surf when I get the chance.'

Calypso walked behind him, minding her footing until they were on the sand.

'We can set up anywhere you like. I've brought food and drinks and you can chill while you watch your boyfriend catch some pipes,' he said, adopting a surfer accent.

Calypso laughed. 'This is really funny, you know that don't you?'

'You said you wanted to date like they did in high school, so this is what we're doing. You watch your man surf and tan up to look pretty for me. You know, if you really loved me, you would cut out the letters of my name and stick them to your stomach so when you tanned it would say "Tim" across your belly and then the entire world would know you were my girl. Or you could wax my board for me?' he said suggestively.

'Never gonna happen, my man, but nice try,' said Calypso, laughing hysterically. 'Do girls really do that?' she asked as she wrestled with her fold-up chair.

TG took it off her and set it up easily. 'I don't know, I saw it in a surf movie years ago. Made me laugh then and still does.'

'I can see that. All right, surfer man, get into those waves so I can be impressed,' she said and took off her denim cut-off shorts and perched under the umbrella, rubbing lotion into herself.

'No, I'll help you first, I think,' he said, eyeing her toned legs.

'I'm fine, thanks anyway,' she said primly.

'You're doing my head in, Calypso. I think about you every night and every morning. When can I get into bed with you again?' he asked as he took off his t-shirt.

As he stood with his back towards her, looking at the surf, she saw the mermaid tattoo on his back. 'Don't pressure a girl,' she said, laughing.

He turned around quickly and knelt down to her height on the chair. 'I'm sorry, babe. I don't want to pressure you. You take as long as you like,' he said, worried he was pushing her, remembering Raphael in Italy.

She smiled at him. 'It's fine, just give me some time. I'm enjoying getting to know you, Tim. I think things moved too fast in Italy for us. I was lonely and scared. Now I want to hang out with you, learn you. You know?'

He kissed her nose. 'I get it, I do. I just miss being in you,' he said.

He grabbed his board and ran for the water. Calypso watched her namesake on his back and thought about TG, her parents, the blackmailer and her career. Whatever Leeza had planned for her life did not include the last few months, she thought to herself as she watched TG in the surf. Rifling through her bag, she pulled out the booklet she had brought with her and started to read.

An hour later TG emerged from the surf happy. 'Did you see me catch that big one at the end?' he asked breathlessly.

'Yes, I did, it was very good. Well done,' said Calypso, as though speaking to a child.

'Fuck off,' he said good-naturedly, flicking her with his towel. 'Lunch?' he asked as he opened the cooler. 'I'm starving.'

He pulled out containers from the cooler.

'What is there?' Calypso asked, hungry.

TG was opening lids and spreading them out on the towel. 'I've no idea. I asked the deli round the corner from my house to pack it. Vegetarian items included also,' he said, shaking a container of salad at her.

'What ya been reading?' he asked with his mouth full, pointing at the booklet on the towel next to Calypso.

She turned it over and held it to her chest. 'Okay, so here's the thing. I've been thinking about my life and where the hell I'm going. I want to do something different for a while.'

As she spoke, the nerves came into her voice.

TG looked at her closely. 'It's okay, tell me what's on your mind. I'm cool with whatever you want to do.'

Calypso took a breath. 'I want to go to college.'

'That's great,' said TG, tabbouleh flying from his mouth.

Calypso laughed. 'I have to sit some exams to graduate high school but then I want to go to UCLA and study. I'm not sure what, I've narrowed it down to production and some literature studies. I don't know which but that's part of the fun, the not knowing. What do you think?' she asked, pushing her tortoiseshell vintage Cutler and Gross sunglasses back on her head.

'I think it's fucking great,' he enthused. 'I've always wanted to go out with a college girl.'

'No, be serious. Do you think I'm kidding myself?' she said, touching his arm.

'I think it's great, I really do. You want to learn about the world and experience real life, then why not start where so many others have started their adult life? College is a blast and I think you'll soak it all up. Enjoy it, baby, you've earned it.'

Calypso felt relieved. 'I don't know why I was so nervous about telling you. Maybe that you wouldn't want to be with me if I wasn't acting.'

'What you do doesn't matter to me, you should know that.'

'I guess I've been defined by my job for a long time.'

'Eat up, girly, then I am gonna teach you how to surf,' TG said. 'If things at college don't work out then maybe you can join the pro surfing comp and travel the world.'

Calypso and TG spent the afternoon lying in the sun and swimming, and TG attempting to teach her how to surf, unsuccessfully. Back at Calypso's house, she ran into the bathroom. 'I've gotta have a shower, I have half the sand of the Pacific Ocean in my hair from being dumped so many times.'

TG started to unpack the cooler and put the dirty items in the dishwasher. She stood, looking at him, so domesticated and kind. Whoever said a man packing a dishwasher was foreplay was right, she thought. 'You coming?' she said playfully, standing in the kitchen doorway.

'You sure?' he asked, holding a container of olives.

'Hurry up before I change my mind,' she said as she walked down the hallway, stripping off her clothes seductively.

Calypso turned on the water in the large shower and TG stepped under. They soaped each other all over and TG washed her hair of all the sand. TG was hard as soon as he had got into the shower, but Calypso pretended not to notice. As they washed the soap off their bodies, she held his face. 'Make love to me,' she said simply.

TG took her from the shower, dried her gently and then led her to the bedroom, where he lay her on the bed and explored

336

every part of her body. Calypso let herself be loved, instead of fucked. She let him kiss her in every crevice of her body, to be touched and stroked. When finally TG entered her, their eyes locked as they met the rhythm of each other's bodies and they came together quickly, the past few weeks of denial catching up with them. TG rolled off Calypso. 'Sorry that was a bit fast,' he laughed.

'It was perfect,' she answered lazily. 'I missed you being inside me also.'

He kissed her nose again and held her tight.

'Do you know what I want to do?' she said from the crook of his arm.

'What?' he answered.

'I want pizza, Antiques Roadshow and then for us to spend the night in the same bed. Sleep or no sleep, you decide.'

'Done,' he answered.

And that's what they did, with a little sleep but not much.

In the morning Calypso was calm. She knew she had to face her mother at some stage; she had just wanted to know exactly where she was in her own life before she let Leeza barrel her way back in and start to try to take over again.

Calypso put a new coffee filter in the machine and turned to TG. 'I'm going to see my mother today.'

'That's good, isn't it?' he asked carefully.

'We'll see. I deserve an apology and an explanation. Leeza isn't so great at owning her shit though, so I have no expectations. I want to see Dad though.' She poured milk into two mugs with Disneyland characters on them.

'Then go in with an open mind and an open heart, babe. Just listen and then decide later.'

Calypso handed him the mug with Goofy on the front. 'Is

337

there something you're trying to tell me?' he asked, turning it to face him.

'Never!' she laughed in mock indignation.

They sat in the morning sun, TG happier than he had ever been and Calypso just wanting to get the meeting over with Leeza.

CHAPTER THIRTY-FOUR

Jack rushed back as soon as Alex rang him to tell him what had happened. 'I should have been here,' he said, draining a glass of Scotch in the lounge.

'It's okay, Jacky, I was here,' said Alex without any ego.

Sapphira smiled at him and took his hand in hers. Alex left it there and Jack glanced at them, noticing their hands. It was obvious when he came home something had happened, not just with the attack from Ethan but also between Alex and Sapphira. There was a bond, a connection Jack could not quite place. It wasn't sexual; Sapphira seemed mellow and relaxed. It was more than that, loving almost.

'Have the police made any inquiries?' asked Jack.

'Nothing as of yet,' said Alex.

Giulia entered the room. 'Sapphira, there's a call for you in my office. I think you may want to take it.'

Sapphira left the room and Jack looked at Alex intently. 'What else happened between you two?' he asked.

'Nothing, Jacky. I promise. Just hand-holding and lots of hugs. She's in no condition to do anything apart from try to process what the fuck happened on the roof,' said Alex.

'Well, I don't know how much she's told you but she was a little fragile before this, so take it easy on her. She's not the usual starlet from Hollywood you're used to,' said Jack, more than a little protectively.

'Hey listen, she's told me everything as far as I know – the baby, Ethan, the heroin. Her father. There are no secrets. I would never presume that her imparting this information to me makes me any more special than you or requires me to give her a mercy fuck to make us all feel better. She deserves better than that and if the only thing she wants from me is friendship, then so be it,' Alex said, standing to face Jack.

'Bullshit, you want her. I've seen how much you've wanted her from the minute you set eyes on her. That's why you haven't gone home yet. There's no more media on you and Heidi. Go home and get started on your own life,' Jack said angrily.

'Jesus, Jack, you sound pissed. Why? Because you can't fuck her? You like her being here because you are so fucking lonely from living this lie. You love her like I do, the only thing is that I'm not gay and you are,' said Alex in his face. 'Or are you pissed because I saved her and not you?'

Sapphira stood in the doorway, listening and watching. 'You both saved me. Jack, you saved me from myself, and Alex, you saved me from Ethan. I am more grateful to you both than you will ever know. Jack, I love you with my heart and soul but you're gay and I'm not even going to say what we know in our hearts. This will never change, not even for me. The love you have given me has been like none other I've ever experienced. I know we will be friends for life.'

Tears started to flow down her cheeks and both Jack and Alex started to go to her but she held up her hand to stop them from coming closer.

'Alex, your bravery and kindness are incredible. I know I would have died on that roof if you hadn't come up. The past twenty-four hours you have been there for me every step of the way through this nightmare and I'm blessed to have you in my life. I know you are attracted to me, I know I'm attracted to you, but I can't have any sort of a relationship with you besides friendship until I am better and stronger, emotionally and physically. If you cannot wait for this, then I understand. I may never want this, I don't know. Does this make sense to you both?'

Jack and Alex nodded their heads. She walked towards them. 'I won't come between such wonderful friends. If this happens, then I will leave both your lives.'

Jack pulled her to him and hugged her. 'I love you, Amelia. You are the bravest woman I know.'

She held him tight. 'I love you too, Jack.'

She turned to Alex. 'Friends first?'

'Of course,' he said.

She hugged him close, it felt good. Then she pulled back in his arms. 'I'm going to Africa in three and half weeks to look at the work I spoke to you about. I would love it if you would like to come with me?'

Alex looked at her for a long time. 'I'd be honoured.'

The next few weeks were a blur of organizing, which was captained by Giulia, the most capable woman in the world, thought Sapphira as she ran them through the flights and visas, and organized the immunizations and itineraries for both her and Alex.

Sapphira insisted she wanted no publicity. Instead, she and Alex would fly on a private plane to Egypt, stay for a night and then get a connecting flight to Ethiopia from Cairo. Jack did what he could to help them both, organizing clothes for Sapphira that were suitable for Cairo and a small video camera for her to document her journey.

'You are a sweetheart,' she said as he lumbered down the stairs, carrying bags for her.

'You have all your medication?' he asked as he placed them by the double back doors.

'Yes, I'm going to get the implant when I come back, so I will be off the Naltrexone tablets. It will be much easier.'

'Have you got your Chinese herbs?' he asked firmly.

'Yes, I have the stinky herbs. Who knows, I might meet a voodoo doctor who has even worse smelling potions for me, although I doubt it,' she laughed.

Alex came down the stairs, with a backpack in his hands. 'I've got everything. You ready?' he asked Sapphira.

'Yep,' she smiled at Jack, tears in her eyes. 'I don't have anything else to say but thank you,' she said, holding him close.

Jack touched her face gently. 'Go and do something great, Sapphira. I know you have it in you.'

He and Alex hugged and then they left. As they sat in the boat and left for the airport, Sapphira noticed a few paparazzi outside the palazzo as she looked back. The relationship between her and Jack had created a feeding frenzy in the media. Imagining if they discovered she and Alex were travelling to Africa together made her shudder.

'You okay?' asked Alex, concerned.

'I'm fine, just wondering what we do if anyone finds out about us going to Africa together.'

'Fuck them. We can't live our life worrying about what the minivan mums think about us when they read their trash mags each week. Jack will be fine. Don't worry, he's the smartest person I know. He'll think of something and he will come out shining as always. I swear that man is touched by an angel.'

Sapphira laughed. 'He is clever, I will give him that. I don't know anyone who is as smart as him in managing his own image. He should be in PR.'

Sapphira and Alex flew to Cairo on a small plane. 'You know I can fly a plane, that's why Jack calls me Amelia, as in Amelia Earhart,' she said as they took off.

'Really? I would love to fly. I ride motorbikes, it's as close as I can get,' he said as he looked out at Venice disappearing below.

'You should do it. It's amazing when you are in control. Incredible feeling, like being a bird.'

She and Alex sat comfortably next to each other in the large recliner seats. The young hostess came and offered them lunch and drinks. Sapphira and Alex took a chicken salad and a mineral water.

'What are you going to do when you get to Ethiopia? What's the first thing on the list?' asked Alex.

Sapphira took out the comprehensive itinerary Giulia had given her. 'We fly to Addis Ababa and then get a car to the centre, which is in the capital. They know we are coming. Giulia has booked us a two-bedroom suite. I hope that's okay, that's all they had,' said Sapphira, not looking at him.'

'Fine by me,' said Alex, looking out the window at the clouds.

They sat in silence till they arrived in Cairo, Sapphira reading the literature Giulia had given her on the foundation while Alex slept. When they arrived in Cairo it was night and they were whisked away in a car to the Four Seasons and taken straight to their suite. Opening the curtains, Sapphira looked out at the bustling city below. How far she had come, she thought, in every way.

Alex came and stood next to her. 'The city that never sleeps, huh?'

Sapphira laughed. 'Well, I'm going to try to sleep. Wish me luck.'

Sapphira walked to the door of her bedroom. 'Night, Alex. Thanks for coming with me.'

Alex turned to look at her, his handsome profile lit from the light outside. 'Night, babe. Sing out if you need me.'

She walked into the bedroom and after unpacking her night things, brushed her teeth and looked at herself in the mirror. She looked the best she had in years, more alive and excited, like something great was about to happen. She looked happy, no longer haunted. Climbing between the clean sheets, she lay for a while and then tossed and turned. Sleep was hard to come by since Ethan but she was loath to take anything to help her. Trying to get her body into a natural rhythm was harder than she thought. She sat up and turned on the light. Walking into the lounge area, she crossed to the bedroom door. She knocked gently.

'Alex? You awake? Can you come and lie with me for a while? I can't sleep. I know it's embarrassing, but could you?'

Alex had been lying awake thinking about Egypt, Sapphira and Africa. He had woken a few times since the incident with Ethan to find her curled up beside him in his bed. Nothing had happened between them; not that he hadn't imagined it, but she seemed so frail and scared. He would wait until she gave him a sign either way of what she wanted.

He wasn't surprised when he heard the knock on his bedroom door. When he opened it he saw Sapphira standing in a white singlet and navy and white polka dotted silk boxer shorts. Alex looked her up and down.

'These are Jack's,' she said, pulling at the shorts. 'I stole them. Don't tell him but he has so many gorgeous things, I couldn't resist. He hadn't even opened them,' she laughed.

'He has so many things in that dressing room of his. No straight man I know has that many pink shirts,' laughed

344

Alex. 'So, what's cooking? The sandman has vacated the building?'

'I know. It's driving me insane. I want to sleep but then I freak myself out. It's weird,' she said, getting into bed and pulling the covers up around her.

Alex got in next to her on top of the covers. 'All right, let me do my magic.'

Sapphira lay down next to him and put her head on his chest. 'Nope, it's weird with you on top of the covers, you have to get in,' she said.

Alex got up and crawled under the covers in his sweat pants and t-shirt. Sapphira snuggled up against him and Alex lay still. He smelt good. He stroked her hair gently. Sapphira felt her leg cramp from sitting on the plane and moved her hand down to rub her thigh muscle. Her hand skimmed over Alex's body and she felt his erection. She left her hand there and he looked down at her.

'Hello,' he said.

'Hello,' she answered back. 'What is this?'

'That's always there when I lie with you. Comes with the territory, I'm afraid,' he said, searching her face.

Sapphira slipped her hand underneath his sweat pants and found he was wearing no underwear. 'I like it,' she said sexily.

'It likes you,' he said and then kissed her passionately.

Sapphira felt her body respond. She pulled off her shorts and singlet and then tugged at Alex's clothes, desperate for him. They sat on the bed, waiting for each other to make the first move. Then Alex lunged at her.

'Christ, I've wanted you for so long,' he said, his hands running on her svelte body. He touched her tattoos and kissed the burn on her shoulder.

Sapphira felt her legs open and she guided him into her

slowly, enjoying the sensation of him entering her. He pushed himself up onto his arms, his muscles flexing as he watched her face and their bodies met in passion. Then he rolled her so she was on top. He held her breasts as she ground herself into him hard. She leaned down, her hair falling about her face and kissed him as she came. Her passion was too much for Alex and he came with her, crying her name into the night. She fell on top of him, her body exhausted, and then she wept. He held her until she lay next to him.

'You okay?'

'That was the first time I've had sex without drugs in a very long time. It was amazing, you're amazing,' she said, turning to face him.

He rolled over and looked at her. 'I'm happy to be a part of this moment. I think you are amazing, we are all amazing,' he cried out, laughing.

Sapphira hit him. 'It's a big deal for me, what just happened.'

He looked at her seriously. 'It's a big deal for me, too.'

And then they slept.

Flying into Ethiopia, Sapphira and Alex went straight to the hospital. It was unlike anything Sapphira had ever seen. Mothers and babies lined up, some as young as eleven years old. The attending doctor took them on a tour.

'Most of the women we can help, some of them need ongoing care and support though. The injuries they receive from long labours, usually when their bodies are not mature enough to cope with childbirth, result in them becoming incontinent – both their bladders and their bowels – and then they are ostracized in their villages. Their husbands take new wives and the women have to fend for themselves with their

346

child. If we get them quickly enough then we can help but many do die during birth.'

Sapphira and Alex met the doctors and nurses, and had photos taken with those who knew them from their films. But many of the women who came from the remote villages did not have any idea who these white people were.

The doctor continued. 'Some of the women come to us in labour. Their families bring them but often it is too late. We can save the baby sometimes but not the mother. Often the family doesn't want the baby, as it is another mouth to feed. So then we have to put the babies into orphanages. It's a terrible situation.'

Sapphira felt her heart break. 'What happens to them then?'

'Nothing. They stay till they are able to look after themselves. Some of them get adopted but Ethiopia's not that popular for adopting couples from overseas, it seems,' said the doctor.

'Can I see the orphanage as well?' asked Sapphira. 'I want to be able to help the women and the children,' she said passionately.

'Of course, it's not far away. I can ring them and let them know you want to visit,' said the doctor.

He walked away, leaving Alex and Sapphira in the hallway with the waiting women and babies. Alex took Sapphira's hand. 'It's pretty full on, huh? I had no idea how bad it was.'

'Who lets their child get married at ten years old?' asked Sapphira, angry at the thought of childhoods lost.

'It's cultural. It will take generations for this to no longer become acceptable. Your role is to help those who are here now.'

'You're right, but I'm devastated for these women and those children left behind. I didn't realize either how much help they need. They need money, material aid and most of all, awareness,' she said, thinking. Taking the video camera out of her bag, she started to film and speak into the microphone. 'We are in Addis Ababa, we are bringing your attention to the women and children who are suffering at the moment.' She turned the camera around so she was filming herself. 'I want to make you aware of a great programme that Alex and I are working with.' She walked over and started to film them together. Alex put his hand up to pause the camera. 'Are you sure you want me in it?'

'I'm sure. If people see us together on this tape showing what we have seen here then we will get more media coverage. It will be news around the world,' she said, facing him.

'It's a hell of a way to announce our relationship,' he said, raising his eyebrows. 'It is a relationship, I'm assuming?'

Sapphira turned the camera back on to them. 'I'm here with Alex, my boyfriend, and we want to tell you about this amazing programme helping women and children in Africa.' Turning it off, she looked at him. 'Happy?' she asked, smiling.

Sapphira and Alex took the short car trip to the orphanage, driven by a translator organized by Giulia. Sapphira was shocked at the state of the orphanage; although the children were fed and clothed, they had little to play with and the living quarters were modest to say the least.

'At least there's a school for them to attend,' said Alex.

Sapphira filmed as they walked around, the children smiling shyly for the camera. The orphanage director took them around the grounds, talking while the translator spoke to Sapphira and Alex.

'He says they have very little money for things. They try to keep the children in the best condition they can but the orphan crisis is of epidemic proportions here at the moment.' They walked to the side of the building. 'This is where we house the children under one year,' said the translator.

Sapphira looked inside and saw rows of cots with babies inside, some asleep, with several young women attending to the children, while others played in the dust with the few meagre toys they had. Sapphira saw old ramshackle prams dotted about the yard, with babies in them.

The translator listened to the orphanage director and then spoke to them. 'Some of the babies go to foster families or sometimes family members come to claim them but many are just left here.' He pointed towards a pram near the fence. 'That baby there was found yesterday, under a tree, she is very sick. They are trying to give her some sunlight and warmth as she cries a lot and disturbs the other babies.'

Sapphira stood and stared at the pram. 'Under a tree?'

The translator spoke to the director again and then said to Sapphira. 'Yes, she was found under a tree out in the plains. Some aid workers who passed her brought her in. She's about two weeks old. It's quite common for female babies to be abandoned like this. She's been crying non-stop, won't accept a bottle. The doctor who looked at her said she is a little malnourished but has nothing significantly wrong with her, as far as he could see.'

Sapphira handed the camera to Alex, who kept filming. She walked towards the pram, her heart beating wildly. Could it be her, she wondered. Leaning over the pram, she peered in. The baby stopped crying and looked at her, tears framing her brown eyes. 'Hello,' said Sapphira.

The baby stopped and listened to her voice. Sapphira lifted her out of the pram and held her close. Holding her and rocking her, she started to sing the song her father sang to her, before his addiction rendered him helpless.

> *'Dodo, L'Enfant do,*
> *L'Enfant dormira bien vite*
> *Dodo, l'enfant do*
> *L'enfant dormira bientôt.'*

Alex watched through the camera, mesmerized by Sapphira and the small baby. The translator watched with the orphanage director and they spoke briefly and then the translator spoke to Alex.

'Maybe she can try her with the bottle? She will not take it from anyone.'

Alex called to Sapphira. 'She needs to be fed. Want to try? She doesn't seem to like the bottle.'

Sapphira nodded her head but kept looking at the baby, singing. The nurse brought out a chair and a pillow for her to rest the baby on and handed her a bottle of formula. Sapphira let the nurse get her in the right position and then spoke to the baby. 'Little one, have your bottle and then you'll feel better. Okay?'

The baby turned her head to the direction of Sapphira's voice; she started to root at Sapphira's arms for food, and Sapphira gently put the teat of the bottle into her mouth. She drank steadily until the nurse told the translator Sapphira had to stop and burp the baby. Sapphira sat her up and rubbed her back like the nurse was showing her and the baby let out a colossal belch. Alex laughed from behind the camera. Sapphira leaned the baby back and kept feeding her, the baby watched Sapphira's face while drinking the entire bottle and then closed her eyes as she drained the contents.

Sapphira put her up on her shoulder and rubbed her back again. She could hear the milk going down into her stomach. The baby burped again and Sapphira placed her gently into the pram, blissful and milk drunk.

She turned to Alex, who was still filming her and the baby. 'That's her, that's my baby. She was born around the time you saved me. She told me in a dream she would come back and that I had to find her. I have. I'm here. She's mine, Alex, and I am hers. I know it in my heart.'

CHAPTER THIRTY-FIVE

CHAPTER THIRTY-FIVE

Rose had taken New York by storm, attending every event Lauren sent her way. Gallery openings, parties, museum fund-raisers. She was profiled in American *Vogue* as the new style icon, photographed in many of the outfits she and Sophie had chosen. With a new shorter haircut and make-up expertly applied by the make-up artist Kelly had recommended, Rose was having the time of her life. Randy and Karen, back in LA had suggested she audition for a new play by a young London writer whose previous works had been shown at the Donmar Warehouse. Rose had not auditioned since she was first married and was nervous, tearing apart her wardrobe looking for the right outfit. She rang Sophie in despair.

'I've got nothing to wear. Everything is too formal,' she moaned.

Sophie, who was in LA, listened. 'Rose, you have many clothes, all of which are fine. This is not really about the clothes, is it?'

'I suppose not. I'm afraid they will think I'm just some silly Hollywood actress who has a hankering to tread the boards.'

'Then don't let the clothes speak for you. You need to be comfortable and wear what the character represents to you.'

'That's the trouble, I haven't read the script. It's just a conver-sation and if the director likes me, then he will use me.'

'Okay, then you need to be yourself. I want you to choose

something that when you wear it you feel like your most fabulous self.'

Rose stood in her dressing room and looked at the hangers and the colours hanging off them. Finally she found what she was looking for. 'The grey silk Issa dress?' she asked.

'Perfect,' said Sophie. 'Wear it with your black Prada heels and those tights I sent you, the two-tone ones from Chanel. *Oui?*'

'*Oui. Merci*, Sophie,' said Rose.

She hung up the phone. As she slipped on the dress, the silk floated down around her and she tried to stay calm. Auditioning was good for her, she reminded herself. Keeps you fresh, on your toes.

As she was leaving, Max crossed her mind but then she pushed the memory of him away. She no longer received messages from Lauren or Randy about him, so she figured he had got over her. I hope he's kept the house clean, she thought as she ran to the car waiting for her.

The audition was at the director's home in the West Village. Rose had Lauren send over his bio and press clippings. He was the wunderkind of Broadway; everything he touched turned to gold. Rose hoped he would at least consider her, as he was notorious for ending meetings after five minutes.

As the car pulled up, Rose checked her sheer lipstick in the silver mirror in her handbag. 'That's as good as it gets,' she said to herself as she alighted from the car and walked up the steps to the brownstone.

Ringing the bell, a man came to open it. 'Nick?' she asked smiling. 'No, I'm Jake, his boyfriend. Come in.'

He led Rose through the hallway down to the lounge at the end of the house. Books were piled everywhere. They lined the hallway as though a well-read hoarder was in residence.

Rose tried not to trip on a pile of what looked to be photography and art books as she made her way down the tight space. Walking into the kitchen, she found the director, Nick, feeding a little Chinese toddler in a high chair. 'Hello, I'm Nick and this is Ava. I would shake your hand but it's covered in pineapple juice,' said the balding, thin man, wearing horn-rimmed glasses and a smile.

'Hello, I'm Rose. Hi, Ava,' said Rose, bending down to the divine child in front of her.

The child held out her sticky hands to be picked up by Rose.

'No, honey, the lady is wearing a nice dress. She doesn't want juice all over it.'

'It's fine, nothing a bit of dry cleaning can't fix,' Rose said.

She unbuckled the child and picked her up. The child leant her head against Rose's shoulder and played with the silver hoop earrings Rose had put on at the last minute.

Nick laughed. 'Well, good for you. You must have kids then?' he said as he cleaned up in the kitchen.

'No,' she said, untangling the child's fingers from her hair. 'I don't, I would have liked to but I'm afraid that ship has sailed.'

'Never say never. Who knew Jake and I would be fathers but we are and it's the best thing we ever did,' Nick said as he walked over to Rose and Ava. 'I will get Jake to take her so we can talk.'

He tried to extract Ava from Rose's arms, but Ava would have none of it. Instead she let out a giant roar and buried her head into Rose's neck.

'Oh, dear. I swear I haven't touched any child attraction spray,' laughed Rose.

'Then I guess Ava will come to the meeting. Would you like

that, Ava? You stay with Rose and come and talk to Daddy in his study?'

Nick walked down the hallway and Rose carried Ava behind. 'Excuse all the books. We've bought the place next door and are renovating, building a library, so they stay here till it's finished.'

'Oh, that explains it. I thought you had a supremely educated squatter living here,' she said.

Nick laughed uproariously. 'Touché! Rose is funny, Ava.'

Ava hung onto Rose and settled in her lap when they sat in the front room, looking over the street.

'I'm happy to meet you today. I read a lot about your work and the playwright's work, it seems fascinating.'

Nick looked her in the eye. 'Why the theatre, Rose? There's no money in it, eight shows a week, crappy dressing room and at best, a Tony award which nobody gives a shit about in LA. So why?'

Rose took a breath and with the comfort of Ava's little body on her lap, she spoke from the heart. 'I've spent a long time running away from living, if that makes sense. I've immersed myself in working in film after film so I didn't have to feel anything or pursue anything. Theatre does not allow that kind of indulgence. I want to feel again, to be nervous, like now, to not know what's going to happen next. I want to hone my craft and work with brilliant people who understand what it is to work to get something right. Theatre is alive, it breathes and has moods and good nights and bad nights, it is without vanity and it exists to entertain. I want to experience that again.'

Nick looked at her for a long time and then spoke. 'You're not right for this play I'm about to stage.'

Rose felt forlorn. Rejected by Max, rejected by theatre, she had not made an impact on anyone but Ava so it seemed. 'Well, thank you for seeing me anyway. It was nice to meet you and Ava,' she said, looking down.

'Just because you're not right for this one doesn't mean you're not right for other plays,' he said as he rifled through some papers on the desk behind him.

Please, not the 'buck up' speech from the director, it's too shameful, she thought to herself as she tried to stand, but Ava sat like stone on her lap.

Nick turned around. 'Where are you going?' he asked, puzzled.

'Well, I should go, if I'm not right,' she said, trying not to let herself sound sulky.

'No, you're not right for this one, but I'm also directing a revival of *Private Lives* by Noël Coward and I think you would make the perfect Amanda. I've cast the other roles but have been on the hunt for an Amanda. When I got the call from your agent saying you were looking for work in New York, I thought I would see you. Interested?'

Rose sat down again.

She was elated as she left Nick's house. They had spent several hours discussing Coward and his work, among other things, and she felt like she had just received her first ever paid acting job. As her car headed home, Rose rang her mother with the good news. Since she had flown to London and had reconnected with her parents again, she had spoken to her mother almost every day, connecting and talking about their lives. Her mother was so proud of her.

'I loved seeing you in the plays at school,' her mother said.

'Does that mean you'll come and see me on Broadway?'

asked Rose, expecting the usual excuses as she walked towards home.

'You know, we just might,' said Wendy.

Rose laughed with joy and hung up.

Rounding the corner to her house, she was surprised to see some small boys sitting on her steps.

'Rose,' they cried and ran towards her.

'Oh my goodness,' said Rose, surprised, looking around for Max.

He stepped out from the side of the steps. 'Hello, Rose,' he said, waiting to see her reaction.

'Hello, Max,' she said, her breath taken away by the sight of him.

She turned her attention back to the boys. 'Come in, come in,' she said, and opened the door and switched off the alarm.

The boys crowded her with questions and news as she tried to put down her things.

Max calmed them. 'Let Rose into her own home, please.'

'All right then, who wants something to eat?' she asked, knowing the answer.

'Me, please. We were waiting for you for hours,' said Milo. 'My bottom has gone to sleep.'

Rose pinched it. 'Is it awake now?' she asked, and Milo ran away, screaming with delight.

Walking into the kitchen, Rose opened her fridge. Except for a lemon and a jar of cocktail onions, courtesy of the home's owners, she had nothing suitable for the children to eat. 'Okay, I have nothing, it's very much Mother Hubbard's Cupboard,' she said, peering into the fridge. 'But I do know the best place in the world for cupcakes.'

The boys cheered. 'Let me get changed and we will go for a walk, okay?'

Max stood with his hands in his pockets. 'Sure,' he said, smiling at her.

Rose felt her stomach flip and ran upstairs to get changed. While she dressed in jeans and a pale pink cashmere sweater and her beloved Chanel ballet flats, she cursed him for still having that effect on her and then listened as she heard the boys banging on the piano, while Max tried to stop them. Grabbing her warm Prada jacket, she listened for a while at the top of the stairs and then came down to see them sitting in the living room waiting for her.

'My bottom likes this chair better,' said Milo from a feather cushion on top of a wing back chair by the fireplace.

'I'm glad,' said Rose. 'Let's go for a walk and wake your bottom up.'

She grabbed her keys, purse and sunglasses. 'Everybody out,' she cried, and the boys tumbled out onto the street covered in a fresh sheet of snow.

Rose and Max walked behind them silently. Finally he spoke. 'Thank you for being so kind to the boys.'

'I love the boys,' she said simply.

'I know,' he answered.

She stopped, the boys playing on the sidewalk ahead of them. 'Why are you here, Max? What do you want? You made it clear in London you're not over Alice yet. I cannot fight for you with a dead person.' She felt tears forming behind her sunglasses.

Max took his hands out of his pockets and held her arms. 'Rose, I'm sorry. I behaved appallingly. You bloody cleaned my house and then I tell you I can't be with you. It was like an episode of *EastEnders*. It wasn't just Alice keeping me away from you, it was the difference in our lives. You saw how I live. I was ashamed to bring you into that. You deserve better. After you left I thought about you constantly. I was so confused that I finally went and saw a counsellor and talked about you and Alice and the boys.'

Rose held her breath, trying not to cry.

'I was sitting at home, drinking that venom that Lucia gave me, the limoncello. She gave you some too, didn't she?'

Rose nodded.

'Paint stripper but it was as close to Italy and you I could get and it came to me. You're the one I'm supposed to be with. I wanted to find you and speak to you face to face like this. I would go anywhere to talk to you, Rose, you must know that.'

'I don't know that, Max. I don't know anything. I didn't mean to fall for you but I did. I thought it was just sex, but it seems I can't do casual sex very well.'

'Me neither, Rosie,' he said gently.

Rose's face was pale beneath her oversized glasses. She pulled them off and held them in her shaking hand.

'I want to be with you, Rose. I will just have to show you, I guess.'

'Maybe, but I can't promise anything, Max. I have a new life here and I like it. I feel like I'm a part of something. It's good. Even if some of my dreams didn't come true, I'm not sorry to be here.'

Max stood with his hands in his pockets, looking defeated. Rose didn't feel as bad as she thought she would; she felt powerful and strong. She was sorry he had come all this way to New York but if he thought she would fall into his arms then he was mistaken.

'I have things to do, Max. It's great to see you and the boys again but I have to go,' she said, crossing her arms.

'If you don't want me to contact you again, I won't.'

'I'm not sure, Max. Just give me some time to think.'

'Okay,' said Max, stopping the boys running ahead. 'Boys, come back.'

'I thought we were getting cake,' complained Milo.

'Another day,' said Max.

'Daddy's doing a play here,' Jasper said to Rose. 'We're going to see it.'

'Great. That's great, Max. Well done,' Rose said genuinely.

'Yeah, the film has opened up some doors for me and shut some others it seems,' he said, trying to keep the bitterness from his voice.

Rose let the comment slide.

'Bye, Rose,' said Milo sadly, and he reached out to her to be picked up.

Rose held him close and kissed his soft cheek. Hugging the other boys, she waved them off and watched as they walked down the avenue. There was a time when Rose desperately wanted to walk with them. Why had she refused Max's offer to have that moment, she wondered.

Rose spent the next ten days avoiding Max's calls. He sent her flowers each day, till she texted him to stop. The house was looking like a funeral parlour, she thought. He then sent her books he thought she might like, tickets to *La Bohème* at the Met and a gift basket of Jo Malone Orange Blossom products. She texted him thank you messages on her phone but gave him no indication of her decision.

Instead, she used the time to learn her lines for *Private Lives* and explore New York. The city revived her and the walking

360

gave her time to think. A walking meditation, her trainer called it, back in LA. She had stopped training in New York; instead she walked and even ran, feeling more energetic than she had in years.

Max had written her letters and hand delivered them to the house. She saw him on the security video, his handsome face trying to peer through the frosted glass by the door. But she didn't answer, still unsure of what she should do. To go back to Max and have him push her away again, away from him and the boys, seemed like the cruellest punishment and she wondered if she could endure it again. Perhaps it was better to be alone than to love. Love is a risk and she was through taking chances, she thought as she watched Max walk down the front steps of her house and onto the street.

Rehearsals started on the following Monday for *Private Lives* and Rose headed to the theatre filled with excitement. It was good to be a part of something and although dreams of Max filled her nights, she hoped the days of rehearsal would tire her out and fill her sleep with Noël Coward instead of Max.

As she pushed open the door to the studio space, she saw Nick, the director, who waved at her. 'First one here, Rose. Gold star to you.'

Rose hugged him. 'Hi, thanks so much. It's so great to be here,' she said warmly.

Sitting down at the trestle table, she pulled out her script and her pencils and Nick brought her a coffee. 'The other actors are on their way. I'm thrilled to have you all on board.'

'Who are the other actors, actually? Randy, my agent, said he didn't know,' Rose said, sipping the bitter coffee.

Nick was about to answer when his assistant handed him a phone and Nick gestured he would have to take the call.

Rose sat waiting for the other actors, feeling like it was the first day of school.

The door opened and an actor walked in who Rose recognized from his work on some art house films and who she knew had recently done a play in the West End. He walked over to her. 'Hi, I'm Marcus. I'm a big fan.'

'I'm a big phoney, haven't done a play in about twenty-five years,' said Rose conspiratorially, 'so any help would be greatly appreciated.'

Marcus laughed and Rose stood to lean over the table to shake his hand and spilt her coffee all over the table. 'Oh, shit!' she exclaimed loudly and looked up and saw Max standing in the doorway.

He took one look at her and turned and walked out of the room.

Rose saw the look in his eye and realized he thought she was swearing about him. Pushing back her chair, she ran out of the room and into the corridor of the theatre. He was taking long strides down towards the entrance and Rose ran after him. 'Max! Max!' she called but he didn't stop.

As he pushed open the doors and walked into the street, he walked towards the kerb to hail a cab. Rose caught up to him and tugged the sleeve of his jacket. He spun around. 'It's okay, Rose. I didn't know you were in the play, that's how Nick likes to work. He needs an ensemble and your reaction was enough to tell me you can't and don't want anything to do with me.' Tears were in his eyes.

Rose cupped his face in her hands. 'No, you fucking idiot. I spilt a cup of the world's worst coffee on my suede skirt. I was swearing at that. I didn't even see you come in.'

362

Max wasn't listening. 'I've tried, Rose. I've tried over the last two weeks. Maybe I need to work harder and longer to try to convince you that I love you, that I want to spend the rest of my days with you, but I don't think I can go through you pushing me away like you did when I came to your house. Maybe you did it to me because that's what I did to you in London and I'm sorry. You deserve more, Rose.'

'I know. I do deserve more than that, I had to realize that also.'

'I'll leave the play, Rose, don't worry. I'll disappear from your life, you just have to say the word. Tell me now and give us both some peace and I'll be able to move on.'

Rose took her hands away from his face. 'I do love you, Max. I'm just afraid of us hurting each other, of it not being forever. I want it but I'm afraid of it.'

'Nothing is forever, Rose. But we can have a bloody good time while it lasts. We come into the world alone and we leave alone. But with the time we have left, let's make it the best we can.'

A cab pulled up next to them. 'You want me to go?'

Rose looked at him and silently asked the universe what she should do. She looked to the sky. There was a jet flying overhead, leaving a vapour trail in the cold sky. As the wind blew across the man-made clouds they spread out like angel wings. Somewhere Alice was smiling, she was sure of it. Rose laughed and turned her face to Max and smiled. 'Stay,' she said and Max pulled her into his arms.

Rose and Max wasted no time coming together again. The boys and Max moved into the house and Rose and Max looked for schools, found a nanny for the boys and helped them settle into the city.

The rehearsals were fantastic. Rose and Max were in perfect sync in every way and Nick could not have been happier with their performances. 'It's amazing, you two live together and then spend all day together and every night. Don't you get sick of each other?' he asked one day during a break.

Rose and Max laughed. 'We were just talking about this last night. I've spent my whole life waiting for him, so I take whatever time I can with him now,' said Rose, looking lovingly at Max.

Max smiled and winked at her. Rose forgot how much fun it was to be in a theatre again, watching the other actors run their scenes. The bustle and the waiting that goes with theatre. Rose would sit with Max in the seats up the back and marvel at her own luck to be with him now, to go home to the boys.

On the eve of opening night, Rose was terrified. 'I can't do it, I can't, I don't know what I was thinking,' she said, sitting on the chaise longue in the bedroom, clutching her knees to her chest.

'Yes, you can, Rose, you can do anything. You're talented, so funny on stage I have to stop myself laughing. You are going to blow everyone away. People will barely remember me. I will be that man who acted opposite Rose Nightingale,' he said, sitting down next to her.

Rose leaned her head on his shoulder. 'That's not true. You're a much better actor than I am. Coward rolls off your tongue. I would love to hear you read Shakespeare.'

Rose and Max sat on the chaise longue together then she jumped up. 'What are the boys doing?'

'Watching the hundred and nine channels on your TV, some of them four at a time with the new split screen feature they've discovered. A show for each of them and one left over,' said Max, shaking his head.

'Good,' said Rose, sliding out of her bathrobe.

Max raised his eyebrows at her. 'Whatever are you doing, Ms Nightingale?'

'Feel like working off my nerves. Want to help?' she said, standing in front of him naked.

'What an excellent idea,' he said, and picked her up and tossed her on the bed.

Opening night was a huge success, made all the better with Rose's parents and Kelly and Chris in the audience.

Rose and Max danced at the after-party to old show tunes played by the band. Rose was delirious with success and happiness; Max content to have her in his arms again.

'You'd be so easy to love, so easy to idolize, all others above,' sang Rose in his ear.

'Extraordinary how potent cheap music is,' he quoted Noël Coward in her ear.

She laughed. 'All you do is quote Noël Coward,' she said. 'Have you not had enough of him yet?'

'Not yet,' he said, and they swayed together, both a little tipsy from the champagne.

'Time to go,' said Max, seeing Rose's eyes begin to close.

'Yes, please. I'm stuffed,' she moaned.

And saying their goodbyes, they went into the New York night.

'The boys loved it,' said Rose in the back of the car, her head leaning on Max.

'Yes,' he said. 'Dominic tried to convince me he should come to the after-party, so he was very disappointed when the nanny said it was time to go home.'

Rose laughed. 'Dominic wants to be a grown-up. Bless him, he can go to an after-party when he stops sleeping with a teddy.'

Arriving home, they looked in on the boys, all asleep in their beds. 'So sweet,' whispered Rose, looking at Jasper, his arms stretched above his head.

'All children are sweet when they're asleep,' hissed Max.

Rose stifled a laugh. Kicking off her shoes in the hallway, she padded into the bedroom and lay on the bed. 'I'm rooted.'

Max walked into the dressing room and took off his suit and slipped on his robe. 'Well done, Ms Nightingale. You were sensational,' he said, sitting at the end of the bed and rubbing her feet.

'You weren't too bad yourself, Mr Craydon,' said Rose with her eyes closed.

Max left the room while Rose undressed and put on her pyjamas. He returned with two glasses.

'What's this?' she asked.

'Lucia's poison,' he said, handing her a glass of the limoncello. 'It reminds me of us.'

They raised their glasses and sipped.

'Happy?' he asked.

'Ecstatic,' she answered.

'I love you, Rose,' he said. 'You are the bravest, most together person I know. Thank you for giving me another chance.'

Rose sat up. 'Listen, Max, I'm not as sorted as I might look. It's taken almost up until you arrived in New York to get my life together. There's more to me than you know.'

'You don't hold any mystery for me, darling. You don't. There isn't a particle of you I don't know, remember, and want,' said Max, quoting her line to him from the play.

'I'm serious. I want to tell you something. Something few people know. I figure if we are going to try to be together then you need to know this about me.'

Max nodded, listening.

'A long time ago I was married, married to a man who was very unhappy with his life. His unhappiness wore down my sanity to the point where I didn't know if I existed or not. I was in pain, heartbroken and I had a breakdown. A full breakdown. I tried to kill myself, Max. I went to hospital for a few weeks and then when I was released I flew to Poland, made a film and came back and divorced him.'

Max shook his head, stunned at her revelation. 'Jesus, Rosie. I'm so sorry you went through that. I knew you were married to that film star but I didn't know it was so awful for you. He must have been an idiot to lose you.'

'He wasn't an idiot, we were just not meant to be. We made each other very unhappy.'

There was silence in the room.

'Are you afraid to have me around your kids now that you know I was once an unhinged mental patient?' asked Rose fearfully.

'Are you afraid to have me around because of my shocking housekeeping skills?' he asked in return.

'Well, as long as we accept each other's absurdities, then we will be fine,' she laughed.

Max took her hands. 'Rose, we all have our brand marks of pain in life. Some of them have burnt our souls deeper than we would have liked but we are stronger for it. Whatever pain you felt in your marriage only makes you more certain about what you want now, I'm sure.'

They held hands, smiling.

'Rose?'

'Hmm,' she said as she lay back on the bed.

'I'm glad you didn't kill yourself.'

'I'm glad too,' she laughed.

Max took a sip of the drink. 'Rose?' he asked.

'Yes?' she answered sleepily.

'Will you marry me?' Max asked.

The next morning, in Perugia, Lucia picked lemons from her tree. Lemons were the final ingredient in her spell for Rose and Max. Lemons were all about marriage. Lucia always knew it would work, lemons hadn't failed her yet.

CHAPTER THIRTY-SIX

Leeza was waiting for her in the street when Calypso drove into the cul de sac. Calypso was calm and in control, prepared for Leeza's dramatics and accusations. Stepping out of the car, she parked in the driveway and saw Leeza waiting by the door. She was wearing no make-up, her hair scraped back into a ponytail. She wore pink sweats and no shoes.

'Hi, Leeza,' said Calypso.

'Hi, baby. Come in, your dad really wants to see you,' said Leeza, nervously.

Walking inside the house, Calypso felt tired. She sat on the white leather lounge in the living room and looked around. Framed photos of her sat on every surface and hung on the walls. As she looked at her life in photos from babyhood to now, she realized every photo Leeza had displayed was on a set or was for a promotional purpose. There were no photos of Calypso playing outside, or riding her bike for the first time, no friends and her laughing, no joy.

The realization that happiness had not been her companion during these years came to Calypso and she spoke harshly to Leeza. 'I just wanted you to know I worked with the FBI and we have handled the issue with the blackmail. I hope this will be the end of it.'

Leeza sat on the chair, her hands clasped in her lap. 'I am so sorry, Calypso. I am so sorry.' And she started to cry.

Calypso was unmoved. 'Leeza, are you sorry you did it or sorry for the inconvenience you have caused?'

Leeza wiped her eyes with the pink sleeves of her zip-up top. 'I'm sorry for everything,' she said softly.

'That's great, Leeza,' said Calypso sarcastically. 'It doesn't change the fact you did everything in your power to manipulate outcomes for me in my career that I may not have necessarily wanted. I hate to think what else you did or are capable of.'

Leeza was silent.

'Well, what do you want to say?' asked Calypso, frustrated at Leeza's silence.

'I can't say anything. I know what I did was wrong. I knew it the minute I walked out of the door. I wanted so much for you to succeed, baby. I wanted you to be a star and look at you now,' Leeza said, smiling at her wanly through fresh tears.

'I don't remember ever being asked what I wanted, Leeza. Never, in fact. You ran my life as though I was you. There were no boundaries, you were the one who wanted to be in these pictures.' Calypso gestured at the side table covered in frames. 'Look at these, I am a product to you.' She held up a pink china frame with 'birthday girl' written on it and a picture of Calypso blowing out candles on a birthday cake. 'It wasn't even my real birthday, it was on the fucking show,' she screamed.

'But you look so pretty,' cried Leeza.

'Oh Leeza, you have no idea, do you? I have no life. I've worked for you for years. I was your little slave.'

'Well, you've done okay, haven't you,' yelled back Leeza, angry. 'You're famous, you have money, what else did you want, for God's sake?'

'I wanted a childhood, Mom,' said Calypso, sitting down again, feeling defeated. Coming to see Leeza was a mistake,

370

she thought, she would never understand what Calypso was trying to express.

'I did the best I could. I did what I thought was right. Your father and I were never going to get anywhere. I wanted more and when we had you, and you were so beautiful, I knew we had a ticket out of being ordinary,' she said, her eyes on Calypso's face but her mind back years before.

'Mom, we are ordinary. We are all ordinary, that's the kicker in this. I am ordinary. I am so ordinary you felt you had to blow directors to get me the work.' Calypso laughed harshly at her own logic.

'You were never ordinary,' said Leeza, shocked at Calypso's argument. 'You could have been anything,' she said, her eyes widening.

'Then why didn't you let me be anything else? Why did you choose this life for me?' she yelled, throwing the frame down on the carpet at Leeza's feet.

'I didn't know anything else, Calypso, goddammit! I was eighteen when I got pregnant with you. I never thought this would last, but to your father's credit he stayed around. We were poor, baby, real poor. I never had enough schooling and your father left to start work as soon as he found out I was pregnant. The only thing I knew was the movies and the TV. It seemed like the best life for someone who didn't know anything about nothing. I could never have done it; it was easier to put you out there. Then you started to get work and I don't know, I guess I forgot to be your mother and I became your manager. I don't know how to make this better. I can't go back in time and fix it, Calypso. I wish I could, but I can't.' Leeza picked up the frame at her feet and looked at the picture of Calypso. 'Your life was prettier in these photos than in real life, I guess I wanted to believe that's how it really was.'

'Leeza, you're out of your mind,' said Calypso, standing up. 'I didn't come here today to tell you anything other than the news the blackmailer is in custody.' Walking towards the door, she turned at the last minute. 'Oh yes, and that I'm leaving show business for a while. I'm going to go to college. Tell Dad I said hi, and tell him I'll call him as soon as I can.'

The look of shock on Leeza's face was priceless.

Calypso drove home and laughed till she pulled into her driveway. Walking inside she found the UCLA booklets she had read on the beach with TG. She found the number and dialled it. 'Hello, I would like some information on admissions, please.'

TG was supportive of her choice to go to college. He was spending most of his time either with Calypso or in the editing suite on *The Italian Dream*. 'It's really good, it's fantastic, actually,' he said as he watched Calypso sand down a new outdoor bench she had found on a sidewalk rubbish dump. 'Look at you go. Geez, if you don't want to be an actor anymore then you can always become a set decorator. You work those tools better than I could,' he said admiringly.

'It relaxes me. I love to transform things,' she said, wiping the perspiration from her forehead, a stray curl sticking to her temple. 'I'm glad the film is good. It's a great script with a great director.'

'Thanks, babe, but everyone is good in it. You are so gorgeous. I forgot I knew you and watched some of your scenes last night. I was totally absorbed by you,' he said, smiling at her lovingly.

'That's because you're sleeping with me,' said Calypso, laughing at his enthusiasm.

'No, I swear, you are good, Calypso. I know you think acting is not where you want to be right now but don't let it go completely, you are wonderful in this, trust me.'

'I'll take your word on it,' Calypso said as she knelt down to sand the legs of the bench.

'Have you decided on what courses you're going to take?' asked TG as he played with a piece of used sandpaper.

'I have, actually. I've enrolled in film and television producing and also dramatic literature,' she said casually.

'That's great, babe. I'm proud of you. A producer, huh? Look out! Now I can hit you for funding.' He jumped up and pulled her into his arms.

'Maybe. Let me start it first. I just thought I would like to produce someday. Make my own projects, be in charge of my own destiny for a change.' She put her hands into the pockets of his jeans and they held each other close.

'You know when you said before that I'm just sleeping with you . . . you know it's more to me than that?' he said, searching her eyes.

Calypso met his gaze. 'I know.'

'I love you, Calypso.'

'I love you too, Tim,' she said, and they kissed slowly and gently. 'I've got something to ask you.'

'Yes,' he said as he kissed the top of her head.

'Do you want to move in? I understand if you don't, but you're here all the time and I figured we might as well. I know I said we should take it slow and we have but . . .' Calypso's voice trailed off and she was nervous.

TG pulled away and looked at her. 'You can't be serious?' he said, his face puzzled.

'I'm sorry. Too fast?' she asked, disappointment flooding her face.

'No, but where the hell would I put all my crap? You and I

are like packrats. Yes, I think we should live together but we need to find a bigger place, babe, and one with a workroom outside for your stuff,' he said, pointing at her half-sanded bench. 'And with a study for you and a games room. I would like to get a dog, too. Is that too much for you? Do you like dogs? I always had dogs when I was a kid.'

TG was so excited, Calypso started to laugh at him. 'Calm down, oh my God, you're crazy.'

'Crazy for you, my Calypso,' said TG.

The house hunting was another matter. Between Calypso selling her beloved property and starting college, as well as looking at houses whenever they could, Calypso and TG found their schedules clashed. She threw her hands up one night.

'I can't do all of this. It's driving me insane. You find the house. You know what I want, what I like. You tell me when you find it and I will move in.'

And that is what TG did. He found a beautiful Spanish villa from the 1920s with a full work shed for Calypso's projects, a pool with mosaic tiles around the edge and palm trees and a frangipani tree. There was a study, a huge rumpus room for TG's toys, an office for him, four bedrooms and a balcony that looked out over LA.

He rang Calypso who was packing up her precious items. 'I found it. It's unoccupied. Settlement terms are ours to choose. It's fucking perfect, babe,' he yelled down the phone from his car. 'We can move in next week if you want.'

Calypso who was knee deep in bubble wrap and boxes looked around at the chaos. She had refused to let anyone come and pack; she was still fearful of her experience with the blackmailer. 'Do it. I trust you. Sign the papers,' she said as she opened a roll of bubble wrap.

'You sure?' he asked.

'I'm sure and can you get someone to help me pack this shit? I don't care if my underwear is on the front cover of the *National Enquirer*, this is doing my head in,' she said angrily down the phone.

TG laughed. 'Leave it with me, babe.'

One week later, TG and Calypso were following the moving van from his place to their new home. 'I can't believe I still haven't seen it except in the pictures you took,' said Calypso as they rounded the street and parked behind the van in the driveway.

'I know,' said TG. 'Your stuff is coming this afternoon and then we get to play house.'

Calypso stood in the driveway in her denim shorts and TG's t-shirt tied in a knot showing off her brown flat stomach. TG looked at her and his heart lurched. She was everything he had hoped for and the fact they would now be living together made him happier than he could have imagined. She calmed him down, made him laugh at himself. Helped him to think outside of just the world of film. She was his Calypso and he was never going to let her go as long as he could help it.

They walked together from the car, holding hands. TG opened the front door and swept Calypso into his arms. 'I have to carry you over the threshold.'

'Don't be a dick. That's only if you're married,' she laughed.

TG set her down inside the house. The moving men were still undoing the doors to the truck and setting up the ramps to bring the furniture inside. They stood in the empty house and looked at each other and Calypso giggled. 'All right then, show me around.'

TG led her into the living room, which looked out over the pool and the stone deck. It was gorgeous. 'I love it!' squealed Calypso.

Then they walked through the kitchen and into the study that was on the other side, also looking over the back garden. It was perfect, with built-in bookshelves and lovely light.

'It's perfect,' said Calypso, clapping her hands.

Then he walked her upstairs to their bedroom. The room was empty except for a semi-circle box frame on the wall. 'The owners have left something here,' said Calypso, walking into the room, squinting her eyes in the half-light. TG opened the shutters and Calypso's hands flew to her mouth. Tears fell from her eyes. A huge vintage poster of a mermaid in a martini glass was framed on the wall. The girl in the poster had a remarkable likeness to Calypso and she stood entranced by the image.

'I saw it and bought it even though we weren't together. I hoped one day you would see it,' said TG.

'I love it and I love you,' she said, spinning to look at him.

'Then marry me,' he said softly into her ear.

She pulled back and looked at him strangely. 'Did you just say what I thought you said?'

'Yes,' he said sheepishly.

'Are you sure? You know I'm a handful, I'm emotional and moody and you will have a shocking mother-in-law,' she tested him.

'I can handle Leeza,' he said.

'But can you handle me?' she asked seriously. 'For the first time ever, I've no idea where my life is heading and who knows where I'll end up.'

'Well, I'm hoping it will be with me,' he said, looking at her intently.

'Then okay,' she said simply.

'Okay? Okay? Is that your answer? Like I asked you whether

you wanted Mexican food for dinner?' He grabbed her around the waist and lifted her into his arms.

'Get over yourself, you're nowhere near as good as Mexican food but you'll do.'

She laughed as he spun her around the room till they fell over, dizzy and hysterical. They were home.

18 months later
Los Angeles

The Italian Dream US premiere brought everyone together again. The women walked the red carpet together, holding hands. Their genuine joy at seeing each other again was caught by the international media and the images of Sapphira, head thrown back laughing at Calypso dancing on the red carpet with Rose, made newspapers across the world the next day.

Sapphira in an emerald snakeskin print, silk strapless Lanvin dress and an antique silver Ethiopian Coptic cross around her neck, looked for Alex, who stayed at the back of the carpet. He nodded at her, smiling and giving her a wink. She loved him and had finally allowed someone to take care of her occasionally. Alex and Sapphira's union was strong and she had learned over time to let go of controlling her life and make room for Alex and Melesse.

When they had first brought Melesse back to the US, she had been sick and Sapphira didn't know how she would have survived the long nights in hospital without Alex beside her, taking over when she needed to sleep on the uncomfortable cot in the tiny room. Now Melesse called for her daddy and mummy and when she did, Sapphira thought her heart would burst.

Calypso in a pale yellow Vera Wang chiffon 1920s style dress, with a diamond butterfly brooch on one shoulder, glowed. Partly from the tan she had got in Mexico the week before after her wedding to TG and also from being happy with where she was in her life. 'College is great,' she told one reporter. 'I just finished my first year. Lots of work, but everyone has been really kind to me on campus and Tim lets me study with no interruption. We're both really busy.'

'You two got married recently, I heard. How was the wedding?' said the female reporter.

Calypso gushed with the joy of a new bride. 'It was last week, actually. Tim and I have to travel the world soon for the film's release and so we thought we should do it while I'm on a break from my studies and we can see each other while we're on the road.'

'Tell us all, what did you wear? Where was it? Who were the guests?' said the single female reporter, swept away by the idea of a wedding.

'Um, it was on the beach in Mexico, we had a big party, Mexican food, which I love and just close family and friends. I wore a vintage tulle prom dress actually, with bare feet and frangipanis in my hair,' said Calypso, smiling at the memory and looking for TG on the red carpet.

'I hear your mother has just released a budget clothing line for JC Penny? How's that going?'

'Great, really great. She's always wanted to be in fashion and since she's no longer my manager she has found other opportunities, which is making her happy. She's here tonight with my dad somewhere.' Calypso waved inside at the people milling in the theatre.

'Your parents were in Mexico with you for your wedding?' asked the reporter innocently.

'Of course,' said Calypso.

The truth was it had taken a long time and some serious family therapy to reunite Calypso and her mother. It was a caveat of TG's that she tried to work things out with Leeza before they married. Calypso did it for him, not for her mother, but slowly, over time, they reconnected again. It was better and different this time. Leeza had been offered the chance to collaborate on the clothing line with other mothers of famous children and she relished the opportunity. It gave her and Calypso something to talk about other than Calypso's career and TG. Leeza thought she was the next Donna Karan and her clothes were actually wearable and flattering, if not a little loud with the prints and the colours.

Calypso and TG spent time with them, and Leeza relished having a young handsome son-in-law in show business and Calypso's father enjoyed having another man around. TG liked having a family in LA.

'And you have been at college for the last year? How is that?' asked the reporter, ignoring the calls from the other reporters for her to let Calypso go.

'It's great. I love it. Everyone is really nice and smart. I've had my work cut out for me,' laughed Calypso.

'And what's next for you and TG? Babies on the cards?'

'Noooo! We do have a new baby in our home though. Our new puppy, Luna. She's all we can handle right now,' laughed Calypso.

Rose and Max walked the carpet, stopping for an English reporter whose accent they recognized. 'Hello, we have Rose Nightingale and Max Craydon. You look lovely, Rose, who are you wearing?'

'Alexander McQueen,' said Rose, touching the delicate beading on the silver bodice.

The reporter continued. 'People are declaring you the next

Burton and Taylor, Olivier and Leigh. Film, Broadway, marriage and now six-month-old twin daughters, what else is there for you both?' asked the reporter.

'None of those couples had happy endings,' laughed Rose, hanging onto Max's arm. 'I hope we do better than them.'

'And I can't afford the jewellery Richard gave Liz, so the comparison is out, I'm afraid,' said Max drolly.

Rose interrupted. 'Can we say hello to the boys, who I know are watching with my parents who are babysitting back here for us tonight?' Looking into the camera, she waved. 'Hello, Dom, Jasper, Milo. Fifteen more minutes and then bedtime, okay? And don't wake Hero and Viola. Love you.'

The reporter laughed at Rose. 'You certainly have the right tone. How is it being a mother to five children within twelve months?'

'Happily chaotic,' answered Rose honestly.

'She is brilliant,' said Max, leaning in to the microphone. 'She's always doing something with them, taking them somewhere, with a baby on each hip and loading a plastic bow and arrow for one of the boys. She's an amazing multitasker, my wife.'

Rose looked at him, smiling and blushing.

The reporter spoke to Max directly. 'Now, you're filming on your new hit TV show, which is huge in the UK and the US. Any chance Rose will make a guest appearance?'

'I'm just enjoying being a wife and mother right now,' said Rose. 'I don't know when I will work again. Not for a while, although I'm directing the kinder Christmas concert, if that counts. And then next year we will take the play *Private Lives*, which we did on Broadway, to London which will be wonderful.'

Married in London, Rose had worn a blush silk Carolina Hererra dress and Max a proud smile, with the boys as his groomsmen, and the whole family went straight into domestic bliss. Rose was happy at home with the children. The boys were a handful, Dominic and Jasper testing her early on when she and Max first married, but they settled once they realized Rose was there to stay. Rose noticed her Jo Malone Orange Blossom perfume had found its way onto Milo's bedside table and sat next to Alice's half-empty bottle of Diorissimo. She left it there and bought herself a new one. It made her happy, sharing the table with Alice.

The twins were a surprise. Rose and Max agreed to let the universe decide whether they would have children. Twelve months later, on their first wedding anniversary, Hero Alice and Viola Elisabeth arrived at 11.01 am at the Hospital of St John and St Elizabeth in St John's Wood.

Rose took to mothering with the zest of a woman ten years younger than herself. Max was right, she was a born multitasker, and in between parenting, she worked on a script idea with Calypso, to whom she had become very close since filming in Italy. They sold Rose's apartment in London and Max's house and bought a larger house in Belgravia. It was large enough to accommodate all the children and with a much-needed garden for Rose's sanity. She kept her home in LA, finally able to fill it with the family she yearned for. She was at peace in both houses but loved it more when her parents came to babysit her children when she and Max went out in London.

The reporter looked at Rose again. 'How did you react when Paul Ross recently announced his retirement from films and moved to South America? Is there any truth to the rumours that he's planning to come out as a gay man?'

Rose looked at the reporter with a steely gaze. 'I thought it was wonderful for Paul to move and start a new life. I speak to him occasionally and he sent us a lovely gift when Max and

I had the twins. As for his sexuality, that's none of my business and certainly none of yours either. Are you gay?' she asked the reporter who everyone knew was, but who insisted on claiming his heterosexuality to anyone who would listen.

The reporter bowed his head, embarrassed to be reprimanded on live TV.

That was the sound bite that went across the world, taking the heat off Paul and putting it on the reporter instead.

TG was being interviewed by an Italian reporter, who quizzed him about Raphael's departure from *The Italian Dream*. 'You know, he says he never took the heroin. Do you think he will work in the US now with this against his name?'

TG scratched the side of his blond head. 'I'm not sure. It's a very sad situation and I hope he gets the help he needs.' Looking into the camera, TG smiled and said, 'Get better, buddy. We are all praying for you.'

The reporter continued, 'You replaced him with Dante Sanzrio who has become a big star in America now. Did you know he would be so good?' said the reporter, preening at the thought of his countryman being so famous in the US.

TG smiled. 'Yes, I did know. He was great on set. Everyone loved him. In fact, I'm about to shoot a new film with him, Jack Reynolds and Alex Wright soon, a heist movie, which should be a blast. Shot all over Italy and France.'

Across the carpet, Sapphira rested her head on Alex's shoulder while Jack stood beside them, his arm around Alex, smiling. They were almost blinded by the flashes of the cameras going off in their direction.

The tabloids made much about Alex splitting up Jack and Sapphira. However, media savvy as ever, Alex and Sapphira returned to Venice with their baby, Melesse, and made several well-timed public outings with the three of them and the baby. Jack's blessing was everything to the media and he gave it willingly.

Staying in Venice, they married quietly at Jack's palazzo with only close friends and family present. Sapphira wore a simple white strapless silk Dolce and Gabbana dress, with beaded Ethiopian bangles and earrings and held the sleeping Melesse during the vows. She and Alex made vows to each other and to the tiny Melesse. Calypso and TG attended, Rose was heavily pregnant and was forbidden to fly but she made a sizeable donation to Sapphira's foundation.

During Alex's speech he showed the video of him and Sapphira in Africa and the first time they saw Melesse. He explained it meant 'eternal' in Ethiopian and that Sapphira always knew she would come into her life. There was not a dry eye in the house. Jack cried the most, of course.

Settling down in Monaco, to stay out of the crazy life in LA and to be close to Jack, with the only real family Sapphira had ever known, was suiting her. The climate, the people and the proximity to the rest of Europe didn't cause Sapphira to feel claustrophobic – and Alex was happy to be wherever she and Melesse were.

Now she was the face of Kelly's successful make-up line called Blessings. This was a job that suited her as she got to work from home with Melesse and Alex, with part of Kelly's profits being donated to Sapphira's foundation. The first season of make-up had sold out and Sapphira had just signed on to do another season. Shot by Alex at their home, with Kelly doing the make-up and Sophie styling Sapphira, the photos were beautiful and fun and showed Sapphira and Melesse playing together in their garden and inside the house. Alex's favourite was of Sapphira asleep between takes, on the day bed outside on the terrace, with a sleeping Melesse on her chest, her chubby hand clutching at Sapphira's pink silk singlet, her new tattoo of an eternity symbol for Melesse on her upper arm, covering where she had been burned by Ethan in Italy. This photo became the hero shot for the campaign and Alex had it as his wallpaper on his phone.

Walking inside for the screening, the reporters yelled out to Sapphira. 'Would you say Italy changed your life?'

She turned her head and looked over her elegant shoulder. 'In every way,' she called back and walked inside the theatre.

The following year *The Italian Dream* cleaned up at all the major awards. Sapphira won the Oscar for Best Actress. Although she tried not to show her emotion, she was overcome when thanking Jack and Alex and dedicating it to Melesse.

TG was nominated for an Oscar for best direction, which he was thrilled about and the film won for best script. *The Italian Dream* also won for Best Ensemble cast at the SAG awards, which brought them all together again. Rose hosted a lunch the day after at her house in LA, with all the children, and Calypso brought Luna the dog.

And yes, Kelly had a little boy called Otis.

Read on for an exclusive interview with Kate Forster and a guide to the Perfect Locations in Italy.

IN CONVERSATION WITH KATE FORSTER

1. If you were stranded on a desert island, which book would you take with you?

Can I take two please? 'Boat making for Dummies' and a blank book in which I would journal, write down ideas and hopefully keep me inspired and sane.

2. Where does your inspiration come from?

Inspiration comes from being a pop culture vulture. I am an avid reader of everything on which I can feast my eyes; online, magazines, books, blogs, the public notices in the newspaper are perfect little stories in themselves sometimes. Inspiration may come from a small piece of information about someone fabulous in an interview, an insight into their life that makes me take notice and try to read between the lines. Once I get that, the story just flows.

3. Have you always wanted to become a writer?

No. I have had many jobs before this, jazz singer, actor, radio host, producer and a general manager in advertising. It is as though all these moments brought me here. I could not have been a writer before now as I would have had nothing to write about. Now when I look back at my life, I see that all the roads I took and the jobs I did along the way were leading to this.

4. What's the strangest job you've ever had?

When I was acting, I played a woman who received a bionic ear implant in a national television commercial. It was a huge advertisement which featured the man who invented this amazing, life changing technology. After the ad aired, strangers came to me in supermarkets and in the street, holding my hands and a few with tears, congratulating me on new found hearing. I tried to explain I was an actor playing the role but they didn't want to hear it (excuse the pun). I ended up just going with it as people were so pleased for me.

5. When you're not writing, what are your favourite things to do?

Reading books, having massages, cooking, looking at things online, watching television and films, talking to my dogs, seeing my girlfriends, hanging with my family.

6. What is a typical working day like for you? Have you ever had writer's block? If so, how did you cope with it?

I am very set in my writing ways. I start with coffee, made by yours truly. I have perfected this as I am superstitious that if I have a bad coffee the story will evade me. I read all my blogs, then I write my blog for the day. The blog writing is a nice way to ease into my writing day.

I write from 10am till 2pm then I am very tired. Then I play a silly iphone game that stills my mind or I sleep for half an hour. I have since discovered that sleeping is a big part of a writer's life. I get tired and I write fast and furiously, between five and eight thousand words a day sometimes.

I don't get writer's block as much as I get stuck with the direction of a story. There are so many choices for the character and I want to make sure I make the right one. If I get stuck I do some exercise. The act of moving shifts the thoughts and often I will have a solution in the middle of a dance class.

As soon as I finish one book I start another. I don't want to lose momentum and there are so many wonderful stories to be told.

7. Do you have any secret ambitions?
To see one of my books become a film one day.

8. What can't you live without?
My laptop. It is my lifeline, my connection to the world and where I can bring my thoughts to life.

9. When you were a child, what did you want to be when you grew up?
An model/actor/travel agent who secretly worked as secret agent, travelling the world being fabulous and solving crime.

10. Which five people, living or dead, would you invite to a dinner party?
Tina Fey, Elizabeth Taylor, Sandra Bullock, Coco Chanel and my best friend. Girls' nights are the best.

The Perfect Italian Locations

Hotel Brufani – The oldest hotel in Perugia and arguably the most elegant. On a hill with the best views of the historic city, it is the place where celebrities stay when in town. Guests have included Charlie Chaplin, Bruce Springsteen and the Queen Mother. Perfectly situated, it is a wonderful place to stay during the Umbria Jazz Festival.

Sandri Pasticceria – The home of chocolates and desserts in Italy. One of the best features is the gorgeous windows where they display their tempting wares. It's impossible to diet when faced with such treats. Try the hot chocolate and admire the original Art Nouveau interiors.

Umbria Jazz Festival – Usually held in July, this is one of the most important Jazz festivals in the world. The city is alive till all hours of the morning as people descend upon it to soak in some of the wonderful music. Some artists who have performed are B.B. King, Sarah Vaughan, Herbie Hancock and my favourite pianist, Oscar Peterson.

Galerie Nationale – The national gallery in Perugia has one of the best collections of art from the region dating from the 13th to the 19th century. All the art mentioned in *The Perfect Location* is actually in the gallery. An incredible collection organised by chronological history.

Flea Market at Todi – Held the second Sunday of each month. Bring your cash and your bargaining skills and work out how to get your treasure home.

Al Covo – A sentimental favourite with Americans Venice and deservedly so. Always lovely food, ambiance and spectacular service. When in Venice, do as the tourists do and visit Al Covo.

www.ingramcontent.com/pod-product-compliance
Ingram Content Group UK Ltd.
Pitfield, Milton Keynes, MK11 3LW, UK
UKHW022326250325
456726UK00004B/152